THE KINGS OF HELL

DONOVAN

I0662260

By Alexis Maree

THE KINGS OF HELL
DONOVAN

ALEXIS MAREE

THE KINGS OF HELL
DONOVAN

CONTENT WARNING

This book contains scenes of dark natures which may trigger some readers - eg; torture, coarse language, vivid scenes of sexual activity. Not all possible triggers have been mentioned.

By reading further, you, as the reader, are continuing with the understanding that this book has darker overtones and that not all possible triggers may have been mentioned. The author and any who contributed to this work cannot and will not be held accountable for a reader's state of mind or actions they may take due to the contents in this book

OTHER BOOKS BY ME

ALEXIS MAREE

THE KINGS OF HELL SERIES:

The Kings of Hell — Cole
The Kings of Hell — Adrik
The Kings of Hell — Malik
The Kings of Hell — Harkyn
The Kings of Hell — Tamas
The Kings of Hell — Before The First

THE NEPHILIM SERIES:

Outcast
Wayward

T. MAREE

THE LEAH REYNOLDS SERIES:

Sins in the Silence
Sins of a Daughter
Sins of the Past
Sins of the Enemy
Sins of the Forbidden
Sins of the Blood

STANDALONES

Falling for the Mountain Man
Colorful

LUNA MAREE

L'Amour Island
Her Sir & Sire
Theirs
Together
Rent Me: Flynn

THE KINGS OF HELL
DONOVAN

DEDICATION

To my friends and family,

Without you, these books would not be possible.

ACKNOWLEDGEMENTS

Thank you as always to my family for your ongoing support and encouragement.

Thank you, Quell, for fitting me into our crazily hectic schedule and providing much-needed feedback and advice. You were my saving grace for this story.

As always, a huge thank you to my ARC team!

And last but never least, thank you to my readers. Your support and kind messages of encouragement and excitement push me to write, and I couldn't be more grateful for your love of my characters and the world they live in.

READING ORDER

Mostly, the order is pretty straightforward, but with the Nephilim books now coming into play, things are a little different.
The reading order thus far is as follows to get the most out of the series:

The Kings of Hell – Cole

The Kings of Hell – Adrik

The Kings of Hell – Malik

The Kings of Hell – Harkyn

Outcast – The 1st Nephilim Book

The Kings of Hell – Tamas

Wayward – Nephilim Book 1.5

Before The First – A Kings of Hell Prequel Novella

The Kings of Hell – Donovan

THE KINGS OF HELL
DONOVAN

PROLOGUE

DONOVAN

By now, you have the gist of what's going on between Heaven, Hell, and everyone stuck in between; so I won't take much of your time going over it again.

But here are the highlights.

Angels and Rogue Demons = bad.

Demon Kings = good.

I know, it's a little confusing for those who believe in the traditional idea that Heaven is the place you want to go and Hell is the place you want to avoid. For regular humans, neither is a place you want to be, but at least if your soul goes to Hell, it'll deserve the pain it's going to suffer.

Hell is on lockdown. After leaving it for too long to eradicate the hordes of Rogue Demons on the surface, we'd been forced to drag every single Demon back to the depths of Hell for retraining, and we'd locked the gates behind them. Now, those who had turned against us were being used as a training tool, a reminder to the others of the pain they'll suffer for their betrayal. Those who were on the fence were also being retrained, ironing out any final thoughts on joining the Rogue Demons. And for those who had remained loyal? They were just getting extra training and rewarded by doing the torturing. Until we could find a way to make sure every Demon who left Hell was loyal, no one would leave.

In the meantime, my brothers and I were hunting down the

Rogue leaders responsible for turning so many of our kind. From our estimations, there were a few hundred of the bastards still roaming topside. These fuckers had gone so long without coming back to Hell, that their connection to it was basically non-existent, and they had been able to withstand our call.

It was no matter, though. My brothers and I were making use of the down time to hunt them down and make sure not a single one remained before letting the rest of our Demons out.

Well, most of us. Corvin, it seemed, had put himself in a permanent time-out. Devlin said he wasn't sure if he'd ever come out, and for now, it was probably safest he stayed there.

And me? I was looking for Trinity, my unruly and slippery mate who managed to constantly evade me.

She knew she was mine; she knew we belonged together. We had a history I hadn't filled Mika or Cole in on—a more intimate connection I had refrained from telling the others about because Trinity had asked me not to. I needed to find her—now more than ever. The danger for Witches on their own was bad enough, but Trinity was constantly putting herself in situations where she was a target, and I was losing my goddamn mind thinking of her being captured… again.

Something was brewing out there, something bad, and while Demons and Angels were always on the brink of war, it felt more perilous than ever.

I was getting close to Trinity—I could feel it. I just hoped I found her before it was too late.

CHAPTER ONE

TRINITY

Six(ish) years ago...

Something was coming. I felt it crawling under my skin, stirring in the shadows just beyond sight.

The darkness had been stalking me for days, and now, it was here. I could taste it in the air, powerful and alluring.

But I wasn't afraid. I had been preparing for this moment.

Sure, I could hide out in the Oasis in between missions, but this was where I stayed current on what was happening in the world. It was important I didn't isolate myself too much, but the danger was that Demons and the like could often track me down.

My go-bag hung heavily over my shoulder, packed with everything I'd need to disappear. The wards around my temporary house shimmered faintly, humming with quiet power. Several traps lay in wait—silent, deadly, crafted from both old and new magic.

I could run. I could vanish, slip away into the night before it found me, but that wasn't an option this time. If I fled, it would follow, and whatever it was would change course and keep hunting me.

No.

I needed this thing to come here, to step into my carefully woven snare and remain trapped. Only then could I bind it or, if it proved too strong, escape while it writhed helplessly in my traps.

So, I waited.

The silence pressed in around me, thick, suffocating, almost deafening in the stillness. I didn't dare move, not even to breathe. The creature knew I was here, and it was patiently waiting.

Calculating.

It was probably aware of the traps inside, but if it wanted me, it would have to break through to get to me because I wasn't going anywhere.

I could wait.

I closed my eyes and took a slow, deep breath. Reaching out with my mind, I felt for its presence, locating it like a faint pulse through the dark. Frustration simmered in its emotions, sharp and hot. A flicker of irritation. And, against all reason, something like amusement.

My lips pressed into a thin line. Amused? The creature found my traps *funny*? We'd see how comical it felt when it was stuck in my traps, helpless and unable to move.

Come on, I have things to do, places to be. Make your move already!

I exhaled slowly, willing patience into my limbs. But every nerve was pulled tight, strung and ready to snap at the slightest touch. This wasn't my first time turning the tables on a creature hunting me, and it wouldn't be the last.

I was good at this, at setting traps, at seeing what lay in the dark. The traps I'd crafted were intricate and layered with ancient wards and sigils, complicated enough to slow down even the cleverest foe. At least, they had been so far. If I'd done it right, the creature wouldn't leave here unless I let it… or unless the trap no longer had a life force to detect.

Minutes slipped past, then more. My neck ached and my back was stiff from not moving. I shifted restlessly, fighting the exhaustion waiting caused.

Hours passed and still no movement.

Damn it.

I was usually patient, but even I had my limits. I wondered if the other creatures I'd waited out had simply been too impulsive, too eager to strike, because this thing waiting for me had no intention of making a mistake.

Almost too quiet and too quick to register, there was a whisper of wind—soft, eerie—a shriek spearing toward me like a warning bell.

My eyes snapped open just as the front door exploded inward, shards of wood raining to the floor around me. I staggered back, heart pounding and breath catching in my lungs.

The creature tore through my wards as if they were nothing, snapping them with a careless wave of its hand. For a moment, pure fear crashed through me—the raw, terrifying power it wielded was staggering. It moved faster than I could track, dismantling my traps in seconds, two of them gone instantly and the third resisting longer but faltering.

Adrenaline flooded my veins, and any stiffness vanished as I scrambled upright, hands weaving magic in frantic preparation. Was it a Demon? The creature—whatever it was—was male. He *felt* like a Demon, but... no. There was something else, something more. I raised my hands, power crackling and ready to strike, but then it stopped.

He was frozen.

My breath hitched, and my heart pounded in my ears as I stared, waiting for an attack that never came. Intelligent blue eyes locked onto mine—sharp with frustration and impatience.

I swallowed hard and scanned him, feeling the sheer power that radiated from him. He was trapped like a fly in a web, feet barely touching the ground, and his arms were raised as if reaching for me.

A cold shiver ran down my spine, equal parts fear and something else—something like unease and curiosity.

"Wait," he called as I took a step back.

My breath caught. That voice... I *knew* that voice.

Something inside me flared—bright, hot, painful—like recognition buried deep as the sound of it crashed through my head, invoking emotions it had no right to bring forward. Tears pricked at the edges of my vision, and I was overwhelmed with a sudden urge to collapse, to sob, to throw myself into his arms. What the *hell* was that?

Alarm ripped through me, and I planted my feet. It had to be a trick, some cruel manipulation, maybe a magic designed to shatter my defenses. Maybe he could twist emotions, make me think we were old friends and coax me to lower my guard.

I forced myself to look at him again, this time keeping myself detached.

And ... *those eyes.*

They pulled me in, familiar and warm and terrifyingly inviting. Forcing myself a few steps back, I tried to create space between us and whatever strange pull I felt. I was scaring myself.

"Wait, please. Trinity, you need to listen to me."

Distrust leeched into my bones. How did he know my name?

"Stay away from me," I whispered, backing away.

He frowned, muscles tensing, eyes assessing as if searching for a way out. He was powerful, dangerous... and somehow, he knew my name. I'd made some noise rescuing witches, but nothing that should have drawn this kind of attention.

"Your sister sent me."

If he thought that would calm me, he was sorely mistaken. I

narrowed my eyes and suspicion burned through me.

Last I checked, Tomika was oblivious to her true nature and was buried in her own investigations. I kept my distance from her for good reason. It wasn't safe.

"You're a liar," I hissed, pushing more magic into the trap to strengthen it.

His jaw clenched, blue eyes blazed with raw insistence.

"What are you?" I demanded.

Something about him changed, softened, waves of assurance coming off him as if he hoped I wouldn't feel his subtle *push*.

"Let me go, and I'll tell you."

I shook my head. "Nice try."

He shrugged, a crooked smile tugging at his lips. "Couldn't hurt to try."

I said nothing, just watched, sensing the weight of power pulsing off him in waves. I'd felt him stalking me for some time, he was impossible to ignore when something that dark and potent roamed nearby. No matter where I moved, my magical alarms whispered warnings so I could stay informed about who—or what—was in my town.

I'd learned long ago that preparation for the worst paid off, and this creature had set off every one of my alarms.

I felt the darkness in him, like a cloak woven from shadow itself, but the usual marks of evil were... missing.

Forcing myself to keep calm, I wore a mask of indifference. He was dark, powerful, but not evil.

How could that be?

"Looked your fill?" he asked, eyes gleaming with mischief.

I blinked, refocusing on his face instead of the band of tanned flesh I saw peeking out from beneath his shirt. My eyes were drawn to the way his muscles narrowed between his hips, creating a kind of V that disappeared beneath his jeans. And was that the tail end of a tattoo visible above the waistband?

He smirked, the corner of his lips curling into a knowing grin that sent an unexpected flutter through my belly.

Oh, hell no.

I could not find this monster attractive—that was so wrong on every level. And yet now that it was pointed out, I found myself stealing glances, heat creeping into my cheeks.

I've missed you.

The feeling struck me like a lightning bolt—raw, confusing, unrelenting. There was something about him, something that left me feeling adrift, as if I were yearning for something deeper than life itself.

How? What was happening?

He spoke, but I tuned it out to the best of my abilities, disturbed by the way his voice made my throat tighten and my heart ache. His voice was like velvet—soft, alluring, captivating.

And worse, I didn't think he was doing anything to try and manipulate me. It was just… him. Everything about him felt like a trap made specifically for me, and me alone. My soul felt torn, aching, desperate to run to him, to never let go.

I stumbled back another step, fear of my reaction clawing at me. I needed to get away.

"I mean it, Trinity," he called as I spun and fled.

His voice, the way he said my name, sent a shiver racing through me. It wasn't fear this time, but not dread either. It was something else entirely.

"You can't run forever. There are things you need to know. It's not safe out there," he called, voice strained.

I shook my head, refusing to look back even as he cursed under his breath and struggled against my trap.

Throwing a hand over my shoulder, I poured one last surge of power into the trap, sealing it tighter. Then I slipped out the back door, disappearing like shadows in the night.

~

A few months later...

The Demon King had found me again.

I closed my eyes, bracing my hands against the cool porcelain countertop, its hard-edge biting into my palms as I drew in a long, steadying breath. My pulse was a drumbeat in my ears, an old, familiar rhythm of fight-or-flight.

Since our first encounter, I'd buried myself in research, combing through every obscure grimoire and piece of folklore I could find—anything that might tell me what he was and how I could defend myself. The conclusion I'd reached was grim: there wasn't much I *could* do. He was the Demon equivalent of an Archangel; a force of Hell wrapped in tattooed flesh.

And he knew my name.

My stomach tightened. Because no, not just my name that he knew. I'd found him looking into my entire life history—he was hunting me. Not other Witches, not relics, not power. *Me.*

Why?

In my digging, I'd learned enough about the Kings of Hell to realize just how improbable my escape had been the last time we met. The trap I'd used then had worked only because it had caught him off guard. I had been lucky, that was all.

But I was ready this time.

I knew his name now, too—Donovan, Sixth King of Hell. Even

thinking his name was dangerous. It sent a shiver through me, and had heat pooling in places I had no business feeling warmth for a creature like him. Months had passed since our encounter, and still, his memory was a slow-burning ember in my blood. I'd considered asking my Seer friend for information, but I was scared of what she'd say, what she'd see.

In all my research, I'd found nothing that explained why I reacted to him the way I did. The Kings couldn't create feelings out of nothing, but they could fan an existing spark until it became a blaze. With my protections in place, I should have sensed any attempt at manipulation, but I hadn't. Which meant this feeling—whatever this was—might be my own doing. That was perhaps the most disturbing thing of all.

I lifted my head and studied my reflection in the small bathroom mirror. I looked tired, drawn. The dim light deepened my blue eyes until they were almost black, framed by pale skin and unruly black hair. With a sigh, I raked my fingers through it, twisting it into a rough ponytail just to get it off my neck. If I had to fight tonight, I needed it out of my way.

I'd always been a nomad, and now, with both Angels and Demons back to hunting witches, moving constantly wasn't just instinct; it was survival. A moving target was harder to hit, after all.

Still, I hadn't stopped helping others get to safety when I could. There were so few of us left, and too many had already sold themselves to the Angels for the illusion of safety. The rest needed someone willing to risk everything to keep them free. Leaning over the sink, I splashed cold water on my face, feeling the droplets trail down my neck before I snatched up a towel and dried off. One last deep breath, one last look in the mirror, and I turned away, squaring myself for the confrontation ahead.

His presence pressed at the edges of my awareness—thick, impossible to ignore. My bag was already stashed at the Oasis, so all I had to do was trap him again. Could I kill him? The thought flickered in my mind, but my gut clenched violently at the idea. It wasn't just distaste for ending a life—it was visceral, wrong on some primal level.

Shaking it off, I left the bathroom and stepped into the sparse living room. I never invested in much furniture, not when I might leave at a moment's notice. Tonight, the only piece left was a single armchair.

An alarm flared closer to the house, and my muscles coiled tighter. I hated how a thread of anticipation wove itself into the tension, how part of me was almost eager to see him again.

I checked each trap in the room, feeding more power into their glyphs until they hummed faintly against my senses. My mental wards were bolted tight, so nothing would get into my head tonight.

I had barely sunk into the chair when the front door exploded inward, a dramatic flourish on his part. Still, the crash echoed like thunder in the small space and a gasp tore from me as smoke and dust curled into the room, framing a tall, dark silhouette. It was him.

"Honey, you're home," I greeted lightly, crossing one leg over the other, keeping my voice even despite the spike in my pulse. That smirk—lazy, confident—was exactly as I remembered, and I silently cursed the way my stomach flipped.

Could you train your body to crave the sight of one person? Because if so, I was halfway there without meaning to be.

"I see you've redecorated," he drawled, his voice a velvet brush against my nerves, causing goosebumps to rise along my arms. His gaze swept the room, taking in the empty space and, I was sure, the traps I'd laid out in plain view.

I gave a small shrug, looking around as if seeing the place for the first time. "I was going for 'lethal chic.'"

His mouth curved again. He stepped forward, but I clicked my tongue in warning.

"One wrong step and you'll regret it."

Instead of stopping, his smirk softened into something almost pitying.

"Sweetheart, you are powerful, and clever. But you cannot hold one as powerful as me."

"I did last time," I reminded him.

"You caught me off guard," he corrected with a careless shrug. "This time, I'm prepared."

"Oh, how embarrassing this will be for you."

He shot me an unimpressed look. "I highly doubt you're ready for me, Witch."

I smiled faintly. "Then please... step on in."

He heard the dare in my voice, and he paused a moment to consider his next move. I met his gaze steadily, chin propped in my hand, elbow braced on the chair's arm as if I didn't have a single care in the world.

"You've been running for months. Surely, you're tired," he said, his voice dropping lower and velvet-like.

I rolled my eyes. "If you're trying to seduce me with your voice, you'll have to try harder."

A low chuckle slid through the air like smoke. "Baby, you have no idea what I could do to you with just my voice."

My heart betrayed me, tripping over itself in my chest, but I refused to look away. "Then by all means, Demon King... come in and show me."

He watched me a moment longer before turning his attention to the first trap. It wasn't all that intricate, but that was the point.

"As I was saying," he said, stepping forward carefully. "You've been running from me for months. Aren't you curious why I'm chasing you?"

I scoffed. "You're a Demon King. Isn't chasing with the threat of abduction and torture considered foreplay for you?"

"Abduction? More like retrieve and rescue," he countered.

I tilted my head to the side. "Is that what you say to all your prey before you eat them?"

His smile was... wolfish—there was no other way to put it.

"You look like a tasty morsel, and I could definitely devour you."

Heat flooded my cheeks despite my best efforts to hide it. I swallowed hard, forcing myself to regain composure. Something flickered in his eyes as they dropped to my lips. Hunger, yes, but something alarmingly close to longing too.

"As your intended prey, should I be threatened by that comment?"

He tipped his head to the side. "You say prey, but that doesn't describe you well at all. You have too much bite to be prey."

Something inside me warmed at the way he saw me. I wasn't something to hunt and eat, I was a challenge. For whatever reason, knowing he didn't see me as an easy catch made me feel better.

"I don't bite Demons," I answered, trying to sound casual. "You all taste awful."

He grinned. "Careful, sweetheart. I might just take that as an invitation to prove you wrong. Demon Kings aren't like other Demons."

I snickered. "I bet you say that to all the girls."

"Only the ones I want to take me up on the invitation."

An image flashed across my mind—quick, barely a second—but it was filled with so much longing, a deep ache I felt to my core.

It was me, pressed against a wall, Donovan holding me there, his mouth on mine, my skin so hot it felt like it was burning.

I let out a shaky breath, eyes flying back to his face. Did he do that? How? My mental guards were impenetrable, I knew that for certain.

The air between us thickened with tension and something unnamable. It wasn't until Donovan looked away that I felt I could breathe again. His blue eyes appraised the trap, and he raised an eyebrow.

"You think this will stop me?"

I shrugged. "It might slow you down, and I'll have another chance to escape."

He nodded. "Maybe. But if you really wanted to escape, I wonder why you are here waiting for me, sitting in my shadows."

"*Your* shadows?" I repeated. He nodded, and so I reached into my inner jacket pocket, pulling out a box of matches and shaking them at him. "I can fix that."

Donovan's eyes searched my face again—intent, penetrating, filled with a kind of recognition neither of us should have at our second meeting. Yet it was a feeling reflected in myself. Somehow, I knew him.

"Well then, little Witch... light the match," he dared, voice dropping low. "Let's see which of us burns first."

Before I could respond, he stepped forward, setting off the first trap. A pulse of light flooded the room, a glyph previously unseen on the wall burning bright as fire leapt around him, winding and confining, before vanishing in a puff of smoke. The Demon King wasn't even singed.

He raised an unimpressed eyebrow. "Fire? Really? I expected more."

I grinned and shrugged as he stepped forward. "That was just a warmup."

"I see," he murmured, eyes flicking to the next trap.

I tensed as he stepped into it. Razor-wire crackled like a whip, attempting to wrap itself around his neck, magic pulsing with bright white light. It took a second longer than the fire, but almost as quickly, Donovan caught the wire, wrapping it around his arm before it extinguished, disappearing as if it had never been.

"That was cute," he taunted.

"An appetizer, dear Demon King."

Amusement flared in his eyes. I knew he was enjoying this, and not so deep down, so was I, but I couldn't let myself get caught up. I was coiled tight inside, waiting for the perfect moment to move.

He stepped to the side, triggering the third trap. Several blades shot out of nowhere, flying straight at him. He dodged them all except one—catching it bare-handed, flipping it so he held it by the handle. A simple blade in his hand looked downright lethal.

"Witch," he began, feigning surprise. "Are you flirting with me?"

"No, Demon King. Trust me, you'll know if I'm flirting with you," I returned, holding out my hand for the blade. He stepped toward me — exactly as I'd planned — and a sigil flared beneath his feet. The binding spell snapped shut with an audible hiss and pop. From the knees down, he was stuck. His deep blue eyes glittered back at me.

"Clever Witch," Donovan whispered.

I bowed slightly, waving my fingers and making the blade in his hand disappear. "I feel like I should take a photo and frame this moment. What's this, two to me and zero for you?"

Frustration rolled off him, but so did admiration. "If we're going to keep score, be prepared, Witch. Next time, I won't play nice."

Something about his tone sent prickles up my arms. I pushed up from the chair, tugging my jacket closer. "I guess I'll take my leave now, then, and enjoy my win."

"Wait," he called. It was one word but felt raw, strained, pulled from somewhere deep inside him.

My breath caught, and I swallowed hard and took a step back, all earlier levity gone. "No."

"Trinity, we have things to discuss. You need to hear me out."

"There's nothing I need to talk about with a Demon King. Nothing you say can be trusted."

"Witches are being hunted, taken—"

"I know," I cut in, glaring. "You and your kind helped nearly wipe out our entire species hundreds of years ago, and it appears the hunt has started again."

"No, not us," he said, pained. "Angels are taking Witches, and they're never seen again."

I sighed and nodded. "I know."

"If you know, then you have to admit you could use my help," he offered.

I shook my head. "And what? Be your prisoner instead of theirs? No. I am a Witch. At our core, we're not meant to choose sides. Someone gets hurt, and we heal them, end of story. We were never meant to be bound to one side. It's because of your kind and the Angels that the balance went so far off in the first place. I will not be a part of that."

"You won't be a prisoner. Please, listen, this is different."

He tried to move, but the spell held him and he nearly fell. Blue eyes burned with frustration and warning, and I backed up another step.

"The spell won't last forever; a few hours, a day at most. You won't see me again. Do yourself a favor and stop looking for me. I will never willingly choose a side. And if you make me, you'll regret it."

He said nothing after that. I took one last look at his rugged face and those familiar blue eyes before shaking my head at myself, before I spun on my heel and left out the back door, refusing to look back.

CHAPTER TWO

DONOVAN

Five(ish) years ago...

"Do yourself a favor and stop looking for me."

She'd said that almost a year ago, but, well, that was never going to happen. Despite how much Trinity had seemed to mean it at the time, she also appeared to love that I kept looking for her. Over the next several weeks, she carefully laid a paper trail that I followed without second thought, which led me into yet another of her traps. I knew she had the power to really hurt me if she wanted to, maybe to even kill me, and yet none of her traps did more than keep me immobile for a set amount of time. Just long enough for her to get away.

I closed my eyes and immediately she was there—her smile, her eyes, the way her dark hair shone in the moonlight. I was addicted to the sound of her voice, to the way she rose to my every taunt and threw attitude at me with fire and cutting words. She was wary of my power, but she wasn't afraid of me, and I was glad for that.

The last thing I wanted was for her to fear me.

I wasn't sure whether it was the fact that I already knew of our impending bond, or if it was just how she was, but already she'd gotten under my skin. My feelings for her were growing with every passing day, as was my desire to be with her at long last. Lately, she'd started leaving me smart-ass notes and letters, little taunts that told me she was loving this game of cat and mouse as much as I was. Was I desperate to get to her and keep her safe?

Absolutely. Did I want to take her and ensure my oath to Tabitha was finally fulfilled? More than almost anything. It was burned into my very bones to find my mate, mark her, and protect her. But chasing Trinity across the country was by far the most fun I'd had in a long time. And as long as she was being safe, I was enjoying myself too much to try harder to catch her. I smirked as I thought about our communications over the last few months. The first letter had been unexpected but had left me grinning for days. The message was short and to the point.

Having trouble keeping up, Demon King?
—T.

I admit, her words fueled me on, and I put more effort into my hunt after that, determined to live up to my rank.
But she was flighty, intelligent, and moved between places with an ease I did not expect of a Witch. Before I knew it, I made it to a new house I thought she'd be in, but was greeted with several traps that exploded at once, leaving me stuck once again. Out of nowhere, a piece of paper burst into existence before me, floating gently to the ground at my feet. The words made me laugh.

Hell King,
Your pursuits are becoming predictable. Are you losing interest? Or have you found another Witch to relentlessly hunt and never capture?
—T.

She was feisty, no doubt, and her power seemed to grow stronger every week. Lately, the only way I'd been able to track her was through the trail of bodies left in her wake. Rogues and Angels alike were falling like flies. At first, I couldn't find any pattern in the killings, but the taste of her magic lingered everywhere, and I knew it was Trinity.

Then, at a few of the battle scenes, I sensed something else—a faint strand of another's magic. Suddenly, it clicked. She wasn't just hunting; she was rescuing Witches, those being captured by Angels or hunted by Rogues.

She was protecting them as fiercely as I was hunting her.

I thought about telling her more—about the Prophecy, our shared fate, my gut feeling that she was the lost love of my life reborn—but all that felt like a conversation better left face-to-face.

She was already elusive enough.

Nothing like telling the woman you're falling for who is already running from you that she's your universe-approved soulmate to scare her off completely.

Thankfully, however, I'd managed to leave her a few messages of my own. Over the last few months, we'd started having strange and strained conversations. Sure, they were mostly insults and snarky retorts, but information was slowly seeping into them and I felt like she was slowly, and begrudgingly, getting to know me. And her one request? Don't tell Mika. It was difficult to keep our conversations to ourselves. She said she had her reasons, but she needed to know she could trust me with this one thing. And so, I'd kept our secret.

Now, I just needed her to stay still long enough to really talk to me, to listen...

I blinked, and looking around at my surroundings told me two things.

One: I'd fallen asleep again thinking about Trinity and our expeditions.

Two: This was a psychic realm.

Drawing in a deep breath, the scent of her was everywhere, her magic interwoven into every fiber of this realm.

I was in some kind of meadow by a riverbank. The grass was long and yellow, swaying in the gentle breeze, and the sky was blue. Several trees lined the riverbank I was on, and the sound of the gently flowing water and the rustle of leaves in the tree was peaceful.

"What are you doing here?"

I turned at the sound of Trinity's voice, and seeing her standing there made every cell in my body stand up and pay attention. It was sunny here, and there was something sweet perfuming the air. I could almost taste it.

"You tell me," I returned, dragging my gaze over her. She was barefoot, her long dark hair bound in a loose braid. She wore a long skirt that dragged along the ground and a blouse that left a strip of skin visible around her stomach. Around her shoulders she was bare, the material hugging her upper arms instead, and the front was laced up with a string. My mouth went dry at the idea of tugging on that cord and watching the material fall open. I made a valiant attempt to lift my gaze to hers, but the look on her face told me she knew exactly what I'd been thinking.

"Why would I know why you're in my dream?" she asked, hands on her hips.

I cocked an eyebrow. "Because this isn't a dream, it's a psychic realm. And usually, they happen because someone intended to do it, or someone desperately needed to see the other and pulled them in during sleep."

Trinity's eyes widened slightly as she recognized the truth, but she didn't allow it to shake her for long.

"So," I began, taking a slow step forward. "Which is it? Because either way, you *want* me here."

She scoffed. "Dream on."

"I don't need to," I reminded, stepping closer again. "You brought me here, Trinity. Whatever you wanted me for, I'm here now."

She swallowed hard at the inuendo buried in my words, and the flare of heat between us was almost too much.

"I don't want you here," she protested, but her words were weak, breathy.

"Are you sure?" I asked, taking another step so that she had to tilt her head back to look at me. "This is a psychic realm. Things here might *feel* real, but it's not *really* real," I said softly, tempting her.

The pink of her cheeks deepened and fuck it all if I didn't want to take her here and now, hard and fast. That look made something inside me turn feral.

"I know how these realms work," she said, but her voice was soft, a whisper.

I didn't say anything to that, I just slowly raised my hand to touch her skin. Even here, the way it felt to touch her was all-consuming, and I almost groaned. The connection between us crackled with power and she gasped, eyes wide and confused, but bleeding into something else, something hotter.

Her eyes caught the sunlight in a way that made my chest tighten, and I had to remind myself to breathe.

We didn't speak for a while. Words felt unnecessary. The silence seemed to say enough all on its own.

I edged closer so that the heat of our bodies collided and the chemistry between us was palpable. Without any prompting, Trinity moved her hand to brush mine, tentative at first, and I took it, curling my fingers over hers.

The touch was electric, sending a thrill up my arm.

Consciously or not, she'd called me here because she wanted

me, and as her mate—whether she knew it or not—I could do no other than see to her needs. For too long we'd been dancing around one another, taunting each other, tempting each other. The pressure had built until we'd come to this moment and she'd pulled me here.

I leaned in, testing the waters, and began lowering my head to hers. The blue of her eyes was bright in the sun, her long lashes lowering slowly as our breath mingled, and finally, after years of wanting her, I pressed my lips to hers. It was gentle, soft, a tentative beginning to make sure we were on the same page. She responded immediately, the subtle arch of her body toward me snipping at the chords of restraint I'd previously held. Her lips were warm, soft, and insistent, and the sensation stole my breath.

My hands moved to her waist, drawing her closer, feeling the curve of her body pressed against mine. It was euphoria in the physical form. She was here in my arms, her body against mine as it always should have been. The kiss deepened, growing more urgent, more demanding. Trinity's hands found the back of my neck, tangling in my hair as if holding on to the moment itself. I was lost to her. She could have asked me for control over my legions in Hell, and I'd have handed over the reins with a smile on my face. She was it for me, she was mine and I was hers. Completely.

Every touch, every brush of fingertips, every shared breath heightened the ache between us until it was almost too much to bear. She tugged me closer still, her body moving restlessly against mine, and I responded in kind.

I needed more, *we* needed more. Slowly, I began backing her up, our steps slow and small so that it almost felt like we were dancing. Her back hit the trunk of a tree, and I braced my hands on either side of her, leaning in until everything else ceased to exist. My lips trailed down her neck, tasting the curve of her shoulder, and a soft gasp escaped her lips.

I felt that to the depths of my soul.

She trembled slightly beneath my touch, the tension coiling and uncoiling with every press of my body against hers. Her hands slid over my chest, exploring, claiming, and I responded instinctively, mapping her with my fingers as though memorizing every inch.

The beast in my chest roared for release, to mark her, to take her. She was here, in our arms, but I knew it was impossible in this realm. Brushing my mind against hers, she was open, but a block still remained, keeping me distant. Some part of her didn't trust me, and I knew I still had work to do to earn it.

She tilted her head back, eyes half-closed, lips parted, and I kissed her again—slowly, deliberately, tasting, teasing, learning. Her breath hitched against me, and the warmth of her body seared against my own, igniting a fire that continued to build and build.

"Donovan," she gasped as I nipped at the cord in her neck and my body became painfully hard. Everything about her already kept me half ready to go just by looking at her, but my body was in overload right now.

Her hands slid down my back, nails grazing skin, drawing low, muffled sounds from deep in her throat. I groaned softly into her mouth, letting my lips, my hands, my whole body learn the language of hers. Her fingers gripped the hem of my shirt, and I helped her yank it over my head. Those beautiful blue eyes of hers grew dark, the pupils almost eclipsing the blue as her body flooded with need. Her hands gently traced my heated skin, tracing the patterns of my tattoos, her touch like a brand.

Mine.

The word rang loudly in my head once again, and I gripped her waist harder, pulling her tighter, my mouth lowering to take hers again, harder this time, claiming. I wanted her. I needed her.

I let my hands roam up to her shirt, and I slowly tugged at the string binding her shirt. The moment it fell loose, I tugged her shirt down and open. The gasp she released engraved itself into my head. Pulling back, I moved my gaze from her dark eyes and lower to the way her breasts spilled out. Lowering my head, I pressed kisses down her chest before kneeling before her. Sapphire eyes glittered down at me. Her lips were swollen and cheeks pink. Slowly, I leaned in to press kisses across her breasts before drawing a hardened nipple into my mouth. Her whimper nearly undid me, and I used my other hand to tease her nipple. Her hips moved slightly, seeking relief, and I continued to torment her, wanting her as desperate for me as I had been for her from our first meeting.

Her fingers held my head, cradled it as I laved attention on her breasts, and I found myself hard enough to break stone. Fuck, she smelled amazing, her skin was hypnotizing, and the sounds she made were like music to me. I never wanted her to stop. Slowly, I began kissing my way down her stomach, taking a moment to flick her belly ring with my tongue. I hadn't noticed it before, but it sent me a little crazy seeing it. All the while, I tugged at the waistband of her skirt, slowly slipping it down the long length of her toned legs.

I groaned, my dick weeping.

She was bare beneath her skirt. Her feminine scent called to me, and I continued my perusal down her body.

"Donovan, I—"

I lifted one of her legs and placed her knee over my shoulder before I pressed a kiss to her core. She gasped, and I dragged my tongue along her drenched slit, the taste of her now an addiction for me. Everything about my mate was made to draw me in— from her personality, her image, her scent, her taste, even the sound of her voice. It made sense to me that this moment would be like finding my own version of a drug.

She arched her back as I used my tongue to flick at her clit, and my fingers slipped inside her. I pressed her against the tree to hold her still while I took my time teasing and tasting her. After several long moments I was still focused on my task, but she was pleading with me, her voice strung high and desperate.

"*Moya lyubov'*, do you need more?" I whispered, kissing the inside of her thighs.

"Please, Donovan, don't make me wait anymore."

Glancing up at her from my knees, I was struck by the most beautiful sight I'd ever seen. Fuck, she was gorgeous.

I carefully slid her knee from my shoulder and stood up. She kept her gaze locked with mine, and I dropped my hands to my jeans and began loosening them. Her breath stuttered and her eyes dropped to my hands as I pushed the material away. When I was free of all clothes, I watched her blue eyes grow wide and dark. I gripped my cock, stroking the length, shuddering slightly. I was so ready to go it was almost painful.

"Donovan…"

"Now, *lyubov'*, come here," I whispered, my voice rougher than it normally was. Trinity raised her gaze to mine again, a flicker of uncertainty, but I pulled her against me and lowered my mouth to hers, catching her small gasp as our bodies pressed against one another.

Heat pooled low in my stomach, coiling, pressing, demanding, and I felt her match me, her need of me, giving herself to me in ways she rarely allowed. The moment I held her close, she melted against me, her hands sliding up my arms to press against the back of my neck. Her tongue brushed mine, our lips devoured one another's, and the moment she began to rock against me, I almost lost it.

Sliding my hands down her waist to her backside, I stroked and caressed her for a moment, noticing how well she fit into my hands.

"Up," I whispered against her mouth and used my hold to lift her. She went with me, wrapping her legs around my waist and the movement forced my cock to slide against her wet entrance. We both groaned and I shuddered, needing her like I'd never needed anyone before.

I didn't wait anymore, I didn't ask, I didn't test or tease. I adjusted us so that the head of my cock lined up with her and she rocked her hips forward. Swearing under my breath, I felt myself slide inside her and groaned.

Trinity whimpered, her head falling back as I surged forward, burying myself inside her hot body. Colors burst behind my eyes and from one moment to the next, I lost all sense of control. Holding her tightly, I began fucking her, driving myself inside her. Her cries of pleasure and whimpers for more only fueled my desire. I kissed her harder, teeth nipping and tongue tasting. My hands slid over her breasts and her hair, holding her close, driving us closer and closer to the edge that was *just* out of reach. She pressed herself harder against me, and I felt the tremor of her anticipation, her surrender to the moment.

Time slipped away, and there was just her and I. The sounds of her pleasure rang in my ear, driving my need higher, my desire to please her far deeper. I needed her, I needed to give her this, to take what was mine.

"Trinity," I whispered, gasped, my throat aching and body strung tight like a pleasurable pain.

The first ripples started deep inside her, her body winding tighter, her inner muscles clenching around me harder. I gritted my teeth as I continued thrusting into her, watching her eyes close as pleasure became too much.

"Almost there, baby. I can feel you," I grunted, about to lose control myself.

Her eyes flew open at my words and almost at the same time her mouth fell open as she cried out. Watching pleasure take her over was my undoing and I threw my head back and groaned as I came hard and fast, feeling her body clench around mine, milking me for everything I was, everything I had. For a moment, I was sure I'd gone temporarily blind and deaf. Static seemed to ring in my ears and my eyes felt blinded.

I don't know how much later Trinity began running her hands over my shoulders and chest, but it wasn't until then that I finally came back to us in this realm, my body still buried within her.

She used her hands to bring my face down to hers so she could kiss me. It started slow, gentle, and turned into something deeper but still leisurely. I fed from her as she did me, the moment drawing on for what almost felt like forever.

When we finally broke, it was only just enough to breathe as something deep and raw settled between us. I rested my forehead against hers, our breaths mingling, hearts hammering in tandem. Her eyes were half-lidded, lips swollen, and there was a softness there that made my chest ache.

"Where are you, Trinity? Why will you not come to me?" I asked gently.

She closed her eyes for a moment, strands of dark hair sticking to her face with sweat. "I can't."

"That's not an answer," I argued.

"This isn't normal, Donovan," she whispered, still struggling to regain her breath. "What we feel, this chemistry between us… it's unnatural and shouldn't be happening."

I watched a moment longer before I leaned in to kiss her gently. "I'd argue it feels like the most natural thing in the world. It does for you too, but that scares you. Admit it."

She swallowed hard, eyes darting between mine before she nodded. "You're right."

I wanted to tell her everything right then and there, to explain the prophecy and our bond, but something told me it still wasn't the right time. If I told her now, she'd run, and I'd never find her again.

Instead, I grinned. "You'll find I often am right."

She rolled her eyes. "If you're going to be smug anytime I admit that, I'll never say it again."

My grin deepened. "Wanna bet? I reckon I can make you come again."

She raised an eyebrow. "I don't doubt you can."

"Right now," I said, slowly rocking my hips against her. She gasped, her muscles rippling around me. I was still hard, desperate for her all over again.

"You're quite arrogant, aren't you?" she asked, her words shaky. I shrugged. "Hard not to be when I'm right all the time."

She leaned in and kissed me again, slow and deep before pulling back with a wicked grin. "Prove it."

And I did.

Twice.

CHAPTER THREE

DONOVAN

Now...

She grinned at me, sun filtering through the treetop canopy, her long dark hair loose for once and cascading down her back. It was a rare afternoon where nothing needed doing, and I could sit with my two favorite people and just enjoy the day.

Tabitha spoke, her words unclear, but she was laughing at someone to my right. No matter how hard I tried, though, I couldn't turn my head to look at them. It didn't matter. The feeling of contentment pulsing from within me was more than enough to lull me into complacency. I didn't need to know who she was talking to. All was well. I was with the woman I loved— the two people I loved most, actually.

Tabitha's gaze met mine again, that spark of laughter filling me with joy, and the overwhelming flood of warmth and love coming from her was all that mattered.

Love.

Yes, the sixth King of Hell had fallen in love, and I couldn't find it in me to give a single fuck. I denied it to my brothers, knowing full-well they would try to talk me out of spending time with her, reminding me that it was doomed and couldn't go anywhere. But I didn't care, I didn't want to give their potential words any weight by allowing them to be spoken aloud.

Tabitha loved me too. I could see it, feel it.

Neither of us spoke the words, though. Our feelings seemed too fragile. I felt that if we said the words, set them free into the universe, they would become a target for the forces around us telling us we belonged on opposite sides of a never-ending war, and I despised the feeling. So, instead of setting those feelings and words free, I held them close, protected them from the harm the outside world could do.

Just like I did for Trinity.

No, Tabitha.

Wait...

I frowned as confusion blurred my thoughts and the smell of burning wood began to permeate the air. It felt close, too close. I should have felt alarm, but the sense of contentment I felt being here was too tempting to let myself get distracted by whatever was going on around us. Tabitha's eyes met mine again, and they flickered, changed slightly. Still blue, still beautiful, but the shape altered, became wider, darker. I blinked and they were normal again, all Tabitha.

"Donovan?" she asked, but her voice wasn't... hers. Not the way I remembered it. It still sounded pleasant, musical, beautiful enough to ease whatever worries tried to drown me daily, but it wasn't hers.

I knew it though. I knew that voice, the gentle lilt, the breathy edge.

The scent of smoke grew stronger, and the urge to look at the person on my right increased, but I just couldn't do it—my head wouldn't turn. Unease wound its way inside me, pulling tighter so that I was beginning to panic.

I needed to turn my head, I needed to see, I *had* to get to whoever it was and protect them. I loved them too, desperately. I would die for them. But I just couldn't—

"Donovan!" Tabitha's voice was urgent, demanding, and when I looked at her, those blue eyes were filled with desperate tears, fear shining brightly back at me.

"Tabitha... what's going on?"

"Please... save us."

Her fear nearly drowned me and I got to my feet, ready to face whatever threat was against her. Whatever was coming didn't stand a chance. I'd die before I let anyone hurt her and... I snarled when I couldn't remember their name, their face, nothing. Who was this person? How did I know them? Why did I love them so much and yet not know who they were?

Trinity's cry wrenched my attention back to her—wait, Trinity? Where was Tabitha? I staggered when I saw that Angels had her, their grips harsh and bruising as they dragged her away from me. We were no longer in the forest enjoying the afternoon. We were standing in front of Tabitha's home as it burned, and the Angels were dragging my mate away toward the house.

"No!" Denial ripped through me as I lunged toward them, determined to save her, but I found myself powerless, weak. Something was draining me of my strength; I couldn't even summon enough to shake off the hands holding me still. I'd already lost Tabitha like this, I was *not* going to lose Trinity too.

"Donovan!" The voice was in my head now, pleading, sobbing, and the sound tore at me. I couldn't tell whose it was— Tabitha's or Trinity's. Confusion twisted at me. How were both women here at once? They existed hundreds of years apart, and yet they were one.

They were the same.

A small whimper drew my attention down, but again, I couldn't see who it was, only that I wanted to burn the world down for taking her from me. Someone held my hand, and over Trinity's pleas for help I glanced down, expecting to see Tabitha's hand. But the size was all wrong. This hand was smaller, softer, almost childlike—

"Donovan!"

"*Malishka!*"

The word tore from my lips as I shot up, breath ragged and painful as a wrenching took place in my chest. Too many emotions flooded me at once, the smell of smoke still in my nostrils. I rolled onto my hands and knees, fingers digging into the grass beneath me as I tried to ground myself.

Too much—it was too much. The memories, the confusion, the emotion, all of it felt too heavy and was dragging me under an ocean of water I couldn't hope to swim out of.

Closing my eyes, I forced myself to count my breaths in an attempt to calm my racing heart and help my burning lungs to relax once again. I frowned as the word I'd said upon waking sank in.

Malishka.

In my dream, I'd said it to… well, I think it was Trinity, or Tabitha. The word was an endearment that meant *baby girl*. I'd loved Tabitha, but I couldn't remember ever calling her that, and the endearment was better suited to a child. I had always called her *moya lyubov'*, which translated to *my love*.

I shook my head. I must have, at some point, called her that. And if not, it was a Russian word just like when I called her *my love*. Maybe the wires in my brain got crossed. In any case, it was a dream. No, it had been a memory, but it had morphed into a dream. Trinity hadn't been there all those years ago, yet I saw her there, I heard her voice.

Somewhere deep inside, I knew what that meant, but it made losing Tabitha all the more heart-wrenching.

Groaning, I forced myself to take another deep breath and frowned. Smoke…

I'd smelled smoke in my dream, but that made sense because Tabitha's house had been on fire. And yet it lingered…

The familiar sound of a popping fire finally sank in and I shot up and looked around. The grove of trees I'd been sleeping in were on fire.

"Fuck," I hissed, waving my arms to draw the fire back to me. The blackened grass and trees around me smoked and smoldered, but at least the fire was out. Coughing, I brushed the grass off my legs and looked around. The damage wasn't too bad, and the fire hadn't spread far.

Great, I was starting fires in my sleep now.

Groaning, I rubbed the back of my neck as tension seeped in, and I let out a long, tired exhale.

I'd been hunting my mate for far too long, and it was beginning to weigh on me. Not just the search or the constant disappointments, but the fear I felt at her being out there alone when the world was turning on Witches, and Angels were planning something epically fucked up. No, we didn't have a proper grasp of what this something was… yet. But it was only a matter of time before we found out.

It just made me more determined to see Trinity. Another memory tugged at me; this was far more recent but increasingly painful.

"Why do you run?" I'd asked, desperate for answers.

"To keep you safe."

To keep me safe. *Me.* That wasn't how this was meant to go, damn it! *I* was the King of Hell. *I* was the immortal one with immense power and eight brothers who, together, could do some serious damage. And yet my mate was out there, alone, doing fuck knows what, and her reason for not being with me was so that she could keep *me* safe.

I hated it. I didn't care if it made me sound misogynistic or like a throw-back to the dark ages. My woman was out there alone, fighting, scared, hunted, and *she* was doing the protecting. Nope, I hated everything about it and was determined to find her and bind her. It was the only way to truly keep her safe.

Thanks to my brothers who'd already found their mates, we knew now that if a mate died after being marked, she could come back, it just took time for her soul to find its way back from the in-between. At the moment, if Trinity died, I'd have to wait fuck knows how long for her soul to be reborn and for me to find her again, holding up three other brothers binding their mates in this lifetime. That was even if she managed to be reborn. Death seemed to have a vendetta against Witches and was apparently hoarding their souls, not allowing the cycle to continue for their rebirth.

I personally thought he was affronted at having souls not go through the process of judgement before being sent to Heaven or Hell. I wasn't sure how Witches came into existence—no one really seemed to know—but I was going to assume it wasn't God, and we knew it wasn't Lucifer.

Giving the grove around me one last look to make sure the fire was truly out; I wrapped myself in shadow and transported myself to a small suburban town. I looked around wistfully, taking the time to remember how this had once looked.

Small mountains had once surrounded the area, but over time, as humans grew in number and their inventions became more efficient, they'd levelled everything and put down their roads and their houses. I looked at a cluster of small independently owned shops, but I wasn't looking *at* them, not really. I was seeing the group of smaller homes that had clustered together to form the farm Tabitha had once lived on. Where I now stood was the exact place I'd knelt as Tabitha and her family had burned in that fire, where Angels had held me still and forced me to watch and listen to her scream.

I closed my eyes as visions of that day came to me, their edges frayed and fragile. It always bothered me that details of that time were so... torn. It made no sense. I could remember moments from centuries before Tabitha with perfect clarity, but *these* moments were fuzzy in my head. Maybe it was because I'd loved her so much and the moment had been so traumatic, but that explanation didn't sit right with me either.

Something about my memories of then had been bugging me for a long time, but had only really started pressing on me a few years ago when Mika first came to us. I'd known twins ran in her family, and when she admitted to having that star birthmark, I knew she was one of two. Once we understood the prophecy, I'd felt it deep in my bones that her sister was my mate, and I had been relentless in my pursuit of her ever since, knowing I was chasing my future. But the more I looked back on my past with Tabitha, the more I realized something was wrong, like my mind had purposefully hidden details or entire sections of time from me. No matter how hard I tried, I couldn't bring them forward.

I played with the idea of asking my brothers' mates—my sisters—for help in retrieving the memories, but I wasn't sure how much they'd see if they did. And if what they saw was really so bad that I'd hidden it from myself, then I didn't want them to witness it either. While I knew my brothers would understand my need for clarity, I also knew they wouldn't appreciate their mates being potentially traumatized.

I smiled softly when I thought about how my brothers had all changed over the years as they found their mates.

Cole had always been a bit of a dick, but in a way we all found funny. It was good to see him care about someone other than us and himself, and how fiercely he protected Mika. Territorial was another word for the way he acted, but it all stemmed from a place of love.

Adrik had been excited to find his mate from the beginning, eager to accept what he saw as a gift from the universe, and I understood how he viewed it this way. We were Kings of Hell, and so the only romantic entanglements we could have were with other Demons who shared our longevity but who died easier, or humans, and their lifespans were short. There was no way in hell any of us were taking up with an Angel.

We couldn't allow ourselves to truly lay claim to anyone or love them, or our existence would be one of constant loss. So, Adrik had taken having a Witch mate who could claim immortality once they were marked as a gift and hadn't looked back. And now he was going to be a father. My head still spun thinking about it, but I had to admit I was eager to meet our niece. None of us had thought we could have children, even when the books said we could, until Cali became pregnant. He was going to be a great dad. Overbearing and smothering, but still good.

Seeing Malik fall in love had been the funniest. He'd been arrogant as all fuck about getting a mate. He'd been adamant that the moment he found his mate, he'd mark her and be done with it and deal with her emotional fallout later. My brother had been so sure he could do it and not feel an ounce of guilt. Watching him fall for Sawyer and learn to put another's needs above his own was refreshing and kind of vindicating.

To learn that Harkyn had completed a bond with Dimitria four years prior had been a shocking revelation, and watching him suffer in order to keep space between himself and his young mate had been painful. Thankfully, we'd been able to find a way around his Word and save him, and he'd made no attempt to hide how much he loved and wanted Dimitria.

Then came Tamas...

Tamas used to be a happy-go-lucky jokester. He was arrogant, but not overly so, and he loved to sleep around as much as the rest of us. He was quick with a smile or a joke, and he loved to prank. After getting wounded protecting Dimitria, a group of Witches had placed a curse on him. It slowly turned him from the fun-loving brother we all cared about, to an asshole of massive proportions who pushed away anyone and everyone who loved him. He'd been cruel and thoughtless, and I'd truly worried we had lost the brother we loved forever.

But then he found Raven.

Of course, he'd royally fucked up with her at first, almost losing her in several horrific ways before finally claiming her properly again. Bit by bit, he was coming back to us, and it was good watching him be himself more and more. Seeing the way he loved his mate beyond anything else always created an ache in my chest because I wanted mine. I had looked for her for so long, but she was always out of reach, purposefully running all because she was trying to keep me safe.

I snarled under my breath. Safe from what? That was what pissed me off the most. I had no answers as to *what* she meant and what the danger was. If she would only tell me, I could find a way to help her get rid of the threat, but she seemed insistent that me knowing would somehow place me in further danger.

I sighed and rubbed my head.

I had to get back to Hell, if only for a little while. I needed to check on my realm now that Hell was on lockdown for the foreseeable future, and I felt a need to be around my family. It had been weeks since I'd last seen them, and I wanted to check in and make sure everything was going smoothly.

Since Hell had gone on lockdown, it had helped my brothers and I to start hunting the problematic Rogues. The ones left on the surface had been too long without a connection to Hell, and so they had apparently been able to withstand our call for all of them to come back. That meant that they were unusually powerful for their kind.

They were also the ones who usually commanded armies of the Rogues, and we were determined to use this time to wipe the fuckers out once and for all. We'd left the Rogue Demon issue get out of hand, too complacent that we were stronger. They'd almost taken us over, and we'd never let things get that bad ever again.

Taking one last look at where Tabitha's house once stood, I wrapped myself in shadow and thought of home.

CHAPTER FOUR

TRINITY

I'd never thought violence could be beautiful before, but the grace with which he moved—each swing of his sword—was art in motion. Every arc painted a picture of deadly elegance.

The Rogue Demons surrounding Donovan outnumbered him ten to one, yet he never faltered, never hesitated. No fear marked his face, no sign of pain despite the agony I could feel radiating through our connection. Every strike was precise, deliberate, a brutal dance only he knew the steps to.

My breath caught when, for one heart-stopping moment, I thought he was lost to me. A sword, wielded by a creature of his own creation, came slicing toward his neck, the moonlight glinting off its edge. The moment seemed both fast and impossibly slow, too swift to stop, yet so stretched that every detail carved itself into my mind.

Somehow, against every odd, he twisted out of death's path, spinning with lethal grace, his own blade cutting clean through his attacker. Blood sprayed in an arc around him, but his focus never wavered.

The number of enemies shrank with each heartbeat, but my lungs stayed locked, my heart lodged in my throat. I could do nothing but watch.

His pain washed over me in waves, each one heavier than the last. His strength was bleeding away, but he never let it show. His strikes still landed with power, his face set in unshakable determination. If not for the tether between us allowing me to feel the wounds as if they were my own, I'd never have guessed how close he was to collapse.

These Rogues were different than others of their kind. They were older, stronger, more disciplined than the usual chaos-driven ones I was used to seeing. But even they could not match the Demon King.

The shadows around me shifted, rippling unnaturally, as if something within them strained to break free, pressing against a sticky, suffocating membrane. My mouth formed a warning, but my voice didn't exist here.

I watched, powerless, as more Rogues emerged, closing in. The King of Hell saw them too. With nothing more than a tightening of his jaw and a lethal calm in his eyes, he accepted the truth of his fate and fought on, his movements as relentless as ever.

We both knew this was his end. Alone, injured, and cut off from his brothers and surrounded by his enemy. The poison on their blades was eating through him with every second, and there was no escape—not without slowing, not without dying sooner.

Then the world sharpened to crystal clarity. The Rogue before him crumpled in a heap, and Donovan's eyes found mine. Impossible, but they did—bluer than I had ever seen them, shadowed by the truth that we would never reach each other. Behind him, the Rogues closed in, blades raised, their monstrous faces twisted in triumph.

"I'm sorry, *moya lyubov'*," he murmured.

I tried to scream, to beg him not to give up, but it was too late. Sound came back in a rush as if it had previously been lowered, and my attention swung back to Donovan who stared at me with sad, accepting eyes as the Rogue Demon behind him swung his sword, his aim perfect and heading straight for Donovan's neck.

I wanted to scream. I tried to, but the lump in my throat swelled until it silenced me completely—

I fell back into myself, rocking hard on the grassy hill as my lungs fought for air and terror tore through me.

Gasping, I dug my fingers deep into the cool earth, clinging to it as though I could drag myself back from the edge of what I'd just seen. The grass was damp beneath my palms, the scent of soil sharp in my nose. My cheeks were wet with tears, my body trembling beneath the weight of a loss I hadn't truly suffered, yet it clawed at my soul as if it had already happened.

It hadn't. I told myself that over and over, but I couldn't erase the memory of his eyes—bleak with acceptance, shadowed by regret.

I am sorry, moya lyubov'.

My stomach twisted, the threat of nausea rising. I closed my eyes and forced my breathing to slow, tilting my head back until my hair slid over my shoulders. The afternoon air was cool against my damp face, and a prayer to Aradia slipped out in a whisper.

"You see now, Trinity," a voice rasped from across from me, cutting into my thoughts. "You must go to him. It is time."

I swallowed hard and lifted my gaze to Dinah. The Seer sat cross-legged in the grass, her long braid of thick white hair draped over her shoulder. The pale blue of her eyes was so faded they were almost white, yet they locked on me with unsettling precision despite being blind. Deep lines etched her face, each one telling of years lived and burdens carried for the continuation of our people.

Go to him.

The words settled heavily in my chest. For years I'd avoided Donovan, kept my distance when all I wanted was to be near him. After escaping Heaven, I had wanted nothing more than to throw myself into his arms, but that was impossible. Dangerous. Months ago when the fifth King of Hell, Tamas, had been badly injured, I'd stayed long enough to try and heal him despite knowing Donovan would show up at any moment. Seeing him then—seeing Mika who begged me to stay—had nearly broken me. I'd run when all I wanted was to stay, and now Dinah was telling me I no longer had to. The idea was as tempting as it was terrifying.

"I can't go to him."

"You must," the Seer countered.

"Dinah… are you sure?" My voice was raw, as if scraped by the vision. It was as if she were offering me this gift, but I wanted her words to be real so badly that it had to be a trap. She had to be wrong.

Dinah tilted her head in that uncanny way she had, seeing far more than her blindness should allow her to. The gift of her Witch heritage let her glimpse the future, but her truer skill was far rarer—looking directly into a soul and finding what it most wanted to hide.

"You fear your feelings for him," she said softly. "You fear his feelings for you. They are intense, all-consuming. You worry he will overtake you, smother your identity."

I fought not to squirm under her gaze.

"A union with the Demon King is *meant* to consume," she went on. "He will eclipse you, as you will eclipse him. But it will not erase you; he will complete you. Alone, you are only half."

Her words lodged deep in my chest, but were tangled in both dread and something dangerously close to hope.

"You will understand when you stop fearing what was always meant to be," she added. "Refusing him again will have far worse consequences than before."

"I've never refused him," I said, frowning. "Not really."

Her smile was slight, knowing.

I sighed. "You won't explain what you mean, will you?"

She shook her head. "Go to him, or all will be lost. The future of the Brothers' Nine hangs on a precipice, and with it, the fate of the world."

The vision she'd shared with me flickered in my mind, sharp enough to make my stomach lurch.

I'd stayed away from Donovan because I knew that if we were alone together, I wouldn't be able to leave. I had craved him since the first time I saw him. Our instant connection had been alarming. I didn't know him from Adam, and out of nowhere, this Demon King arrived, telling me that my sister needed me, that she was safe, but that Angels were hunting me. I had laughed—actually laughed—in his face. I'd placed a spell on Mika years ago that would help hide her abilities so Angels and Demons would not be able to scan and find her. It was the only thing I'd been able to do to keep her safe. Then this Demon King showed up to tell me she was living with his brother and wanted to see me?

Yeah, it sounded ludicrous.

But then I went looking for Mika, and she was nowhere to be found. I feared she was in Heaven, but the Demon King's words had echoed in my head, and I knew then that she was gone. For months I'd researched his kind, their abilities and the lore surrounding them. I was surprised at what I found. More than anything, I was surprised about the information I found on the sixth King of Hell specifically.

While I'd found ample information on Hell, its Kings and other Demons, the information on Donovan was more than any of theirs. He had once been a friend to the Witches, specifically, my ancestor, Tabitha. Tabitha had been the one to come up with the Oasis and she and the rest of my family from centuries ago had created it.

The Oasis, a place for Witches to live undisturbed by the goings on of Angels and Demons alike. We could live here without fear of being taken or being forced to choose a side. It wasn't just the Wardwell Witches welcome here, of course. We brought anyone who wanted to stay, but some didn't like being so disconnected.

In our records, there was an entire book dedicated to Donovan and his relationship with my ancestors, but particularly Tabitha. They had been friends once, *close* friends. While the texts didn't specify exactly what they were to one another, I read between the lines and felt like there had been more between them.

More than that, I *felt* the words. It was as if I'd read the events of the book a long time ago and was re-reading them, parts of it all feeling familiar. I found this strange, as I'd never read the words before.

It was then I started watching him, staying one step ahead. Our interactions had been brief, very cat-and-mouse, and many times I left him notes and letters to antagonize him. Was it smart? Probably not, but he seemed bent on hunting me down no matter what, so I saw no harm in leaving sarcastic quips for the Demon King to read. It had given our game an element of levity. Then I'd been taken.

I closed the door on the memories that tried to rush forth and breathed deeply. It was in Heaven that the prophecy had been revealed which, according to Heaven's Seer, involved me and Donovan. So, of course, Heaven just had to throw a wrench in the fate's plans, completely messing up any chance there was for me and Donovan to fulfil our destiny.

It was why I ran now, why I kept him at arm's length despite my feelings for him.

"What if I don't go to him?" I asked Dinah, my voice low.

"You saw what will happen."

I shook my head, frustrated. "So, my options are to let him die which will start a war that will surely end the world as we know it, or I go to him and have a slightly *smaller* chance of ending the world?"

Dinah's pale eyes stayed fixed on me.

"You are stronger than you believe, Trinity. If you trust him enough, he will come through for you. I think you already know this."

I grimaced and looked away. I didn't *know* it. I just... felt it. Since escaping Heaven, I'd been tracking him from a distance. Not stalking—watching, learning. He could be ruthless, even merciless, but when it came to his brothers and the women in his family, there was no compromise in him. That thought both thrilled and terrified me.

"Trust him, Trinity. Trust yourself."

I knew Dinah was right. But there were lines I couldn't cross, truths I couldn't risk him discovering. I couldn't give in to the part of me that wanted to run straight to him. Yet if I didn't go, the vision would become reality.

Standing, I gave the Seer a slight bow of respect. Dinah was an elder of the Witches in the Oasis, and she was the reason I was safe and protected as a teenager. Without her, I don't know how long I would have made it on my own. Turning on my heel, I started to walk away when she called me back.

"Yes?"

She hesitated, eyes flicking back and forth as she seemed to be working something out.

"When you go to Donovan, take Leviah with you. His fate is

now tied to yours, and it will serve you both best if you see the Demon King together."

I was already shaking my head. Hell no. Leviah was an Archangel, and Donovan would kill him.

"Trust me, my dear."

I wanted to deny her and tell her she was crazy. The idea of my friend meeting Donovan alongside me made me want to throw up. I couldn't risk him, but Dinah looked so damn certain. Neither agreeing nor disagreeing, I sighed before waving goodbye and walking away. Dinah's words looped in my head like a stubborn chant.

The grassy hill sloped gently into a dirt path ahead, one of many worn smooth by centuries of Witch's footsteps.

The Oasis seemed to breathe with age-old magic. It was woven into every blade of grass, threaded through every tree. It clung to my skin and curled in my lungs before my mind returned to Dinah's warning.

Refusing him a second time will, I fear, have consequences far worse than last time.

The words rippled down my spine. I had never *refused* Donovan—only told him our time hadn't come, that we'd be together when it was safe. That wasn't refusal, was it? And if there'd been no consequences I could recall from the first time, why did something deep inside me—bone-deep, soul-deep—shiver in agreement with Dinah's warning?

But I couldn't go to him, not until I was certain it was safe. I'd given up so much in the past to keep Mika safe, I'd gone through so much in my attempt to rescue and protect Witches from Angels and Demons alike. I'd sacrificed a lot to keep Donovan and his brother's safe… I couldn't let it all be for nothing.

No, until I knew for certain that it was safe, there was no way I could go to Donovan; not when I knew what was at risk if I was wrong. The Seer in Heaven and her little friend had done something to me up there. They'd ensured the destruction of Hell and its Kings if Donovan marked me. I could tell Donovan, sure, but he would throw himself into finding a way out of it and get himself killed. So, until I could find another way to undo what was done, this was how it had to be. And I wasn't wasting my time; I had a purpose. I was rescuing those who would otherwise be dead or enslaved. That was a worthy cause, and a perfect use of my time.

"Trinity!"

Speaking of good causes...

I turned with a grin to find Wren striding toward me, her wavy, reddish-brown hair bound and twisted back. I don't think I'd ever seen her with it out, but then again, she was always on the move with one mission or another.

I did good work, I knew that. The things I did, the people I saved, they were all important. But Wren? She was on a whole other level. For years, she had infiltrated the Angel's inner circle and had been working with us to bring them down. She was one badass double-agent. I didn't envy her the job she'd chosen for herself. That level of concentration, of danger, was not what I was made for. I knew I took more risks than most, but Wren looked death's most lethal warriors in the face and called them *cute.*

"Hey, Wren," I greeted as she stepped closer.

"Did you just come back from seeing Dinah?"

At my sigh, Wren gave me a sympathetic smile. She'd been at the mercy of Dinah's visions before, and knew the frustrations that came with it. While Dinah believed in telling us some things, other things she said were not to be known right away. I got it, I really did, there was a time and a place for everything, and knowing too much too early could change the course of those things.

But... come on!

"So, have you got another mission to head out for, or was this personal?" Wren asked as we kept walking.

"Both," I answered. "Before she showed me the something personal, she showed me a young Witch in need of saving in two days. She'll be trapped with Rogue's hunting her," I answered. When it came to Dinah's visions, I had no way of knowing where the girl would be until she was in that alleyway, so finding her before was pointless. Whenever Dinah shared these with me, I *felt* everything. I could taste the air, smell the smoke and the blood, feel the pain the object of the vision felt. It was all-encompassing, so I felt the girls fear and determination to fight until the end.

"Poor girl," Wren sympathized. My mind rolled back over the vision and once again, I felt that same draw to the girl I'd had when I first saw it, a pull I could not explain. She was young, and I have never seen her before in my life. She looked scared but defiant. But there was just *something* about her that felt like I'd met her before, that I somehow knew her.

"And the personal?" Wren asked, raising an eyebrow.

I sighed and shook my head. "She says it's time for me to take action on something I have been steadfastly refusing to do for years. But I don't agree. It's not time, there's too much at risk." No one but Leviah and Dinah knew about the prophecy of the Brother's Nine, and that was the way I wanted it to be. I wasn't sure what the others would think if they knew I was one of the few prophesied to be with a King of Hell.

"Are you going to listen to her?" Wren asked as we neared the village center where most of the buildings were.

We had a Hall where meetings and group meals were held, a

healing wing for the badly wounded, and a few other buildings used for storage and making things. A lot of people mingled here throughout the day when they weren't tending to the community gardens or their own homes.

I sighed. "I don't know. She seems certain, and the vision I saw was..." I trailed off, words failing me. Wren seemed to understand what I meant.

"But I *know* what will happen if she's wrong, and a *lot* of people will die a *lot*. Isn't it worth erring on the side of caution?"

Wren was silent for a moment as she thought and slowly shook her head. "I mean... I have never heard of one of Dinah's visions being wrong. And if the potential risk of being wrong is really that bad, do you think Dinah would tell you to do something if she wasn't absolutely certain it was the right thing?"

I glowered at the ground. Damn Wren and her logic. Instead of answering her, I muttered under my breath and she laughed.

"Maybe the reason you don't want to do as Dinah says is because you fear something else other than the potential risk to others?"

Again, I wanted to argue and tell her she was wrong... but was she? I'd put off going to Donovan for so long, always reminding myself of the risk if he bound us, but was that truly the only reason I'd stayed away? Was I honestly afraid of letting him consume me? My thoughts, my actions, my world? I mean... yeah, a little. But wasn't that kind of love also something most women strived for? Because as Dinah said, he would overshadow my whole world, but I would do the same to his. It was balanced, with each of us caring more about the other than ourselves, and in that way, we would both be happy and cared for.

"I don't know," I finally answered, my mind a mess.

Wren squeezed my forearm in sympathy before we drew to a

stop. "Whatever the case, I know you'll do the right thing. You always do."

I shrugged, not entirely sure she was right. "Are you heading off now? Do the Angels need you back?"

She shook her head. "Not yet, but I can feel something is happening. They'll probably want me back in a few days, and I never like leaving them for too long in case they start to think I'm loyal elsewhere."

I stared at her, amazed. "I don't know how you do it, how you balance both worlds and live in such danger all the time."

Her smile was small and tight. "It's all I know," she answered. I felt the weight of her words, the heavy story that lay behind them, but I also knew now was not the time to ask for more information, assuming she'd give me any of it anyway. With another smile, Wren tipped her head at me in goodbye before she turned away, continuing toward the village.

I whispered a small prayer to Aradia that she would protect Wren as she strived to save so many. Before I'd been taken by the Angels, Wren and I had spoken only a handful of times. She tended to keep her distance from those here because she knew her job was so dangerous. Creating bonds with people meant she had vulnerabilities, but also if anything happened to her, she would leave people hurting. She'd looked for me when I'd been taken, after Dinah and a few Elders had called on her to tell her what happened, but she had to be careful. While she'd earned the trust of many of the Angels in Heaven, she was still a Witch, and if she showed too much interest in a captured Witch, they'd start looking at her more closely, and she couldn't risk her hard-earned position just to know more about my situation. It was a hard decision, and some might even call her cold or callous because of it, but I knew what she risked daily to maintain the position she'd gained. I would have hated to be the reason she lost it if she'd tried to get me out. She did too much good.

"So, more good news, then?"

I turned around to find Leviah striding toward me, sunlight catching the perfect symmetry of his features. Angels always had that porcelain, otherworldly beauty that made people soften, trust... until you saw the truth beneath.

Most were stone-cold under that glow—unforgiving. Cruel.

Leviah was a rare exception.

"I assume you went to see Dinah?"

I sighed. "Yeah. We have a new lead to track down."

"And?"

"And she said it's... time."

His brows lifted. "Time?" Then his eyes widened. "As in—"

"Yeah. It's time to let Donovan find me."

Leviah had known about Donovan since he got me out of Heaven. He'd heard the Seer recite the prophecy, and he knew that certain Witches were destined to be with certain Kings. Heaven's Seer knew I was meant for Donovan and after thinking I knew more about this and torturing me for weeks to get information, they decided on a better way... on a trap.

But Lev also knew how desperately I wanted to be with Donovan. He'd been the one to take me to him several times, watching me as I watched Donovan from afar, getting to know the Demon King I was to be bound to. He saw my struggle to stay away, to withstand the calling in me to go to him and finally be where I was meant to be.

Leviah raised a dark eyebrow, silver-blue eyes flashing. "And you're not happy because...?"

"I don't know!" My voice rose with frustration. "I've avoided him for years, and now I'm just supposed to waltz in and say, 'Hey, if I stay away any longer, you'll die, so we have to do

this—but also, don't bind us or you'll start the apocalypse.'"
Leviah chuckled.

I glared. "It's not funny."

"It kind of is."

His arm came around my shoulders, pulling me into a sideways hug as we walked. "You knew this day was coming. Don't tell me you haven't imagined it."

Of course I had, more times than I could count. If I wasn't reliving my torment in Heaven, I was dreaming of Donovan's arms around me, of finally stopping the endless running. But no fantasy could match reality.

We'd barely shared minutes together in person, and yet—I loved him.

It had happened slowly, through notes and teasing challenges, through watching him protect his brothers, my sister, and countless Witches. Even from afar, I'd seen his ruthlessness toward enemies and his unwavering loyalty to those he loved. I'd seen the way he hunted me with relentless determination, how my traps and taunts only fueled his pursuit.

I'd seen how single-minded he could become when hunting me because he thought he could protect me, because my sister wanted me safe. My heart tugged every time I thought about the journey he'd been on these few years looking for me and the way he never gave up.

Then there were his letters and signs letting me know he was still searching, still thinking of me. Some gestures were subtle, others... not so much. Like the time my cruel foster father died in a manner both mysterious and brutal. Donovan had been there. I hadn't needed proof of who rid the world of that monster, and knowing he'd done it because of what I'd suffered in that home showed how much he cared.

Every time Donovan came close, every time I felt him near, it nearly broke me to keep moving. My soul wanted his—wanted to bind to him. But there were things he didn't know, truths that could put everyone at risk. Until now, I'd believed I had time to fix them first. Dinah had made it clear that I didn't.

I was still chewing on that when—

"Trin!"

The familiar voice snapped my attention back and I smiled warmly as Robin came closer, a hand on her rounded belly, her eyes shining with warmth.

"Robin, you look amazing," I greeted, returning her brief hug. She laughed. "I look fat, but I'm okay with that."

Robin had been through hell—imprisoned, violated, almost broken—and still she was here, carrying new life with fierce love. This was why I made the choices I did, why every sacrifice I made felt worth it.

We chatted for a while about the baby and about her sister Raven.

Her sister was bound to Tamas, the fifth King of Hell. I'd been there on a particularly brutal night when Tamas had almost died in his efforts to save Dimitria, his brother's mate. I'd been trying to bring Dimitria to the Oasis, but Tamas had other plans. Trying to help save him had almost cost me my freedom, had almost brought about the death of every King of Hell. The domino effect that would have started that night was too horrific to even consider. But Raven was wonderful, caring, and I was glad when I heard that Tamas and his brothers had been able to break her out of the grasp of Camhael and the other Angels. Even thinking his name sent a shudder through me.

"Anyway," Robin said softly, adjusting the basket of vegetables in her arms. "I had better get these to the kitchen. Are you heading out again soon?"

I shrugged. "Not tonight, but soon enough."

"Just be safe, and if you see Raven…"

I smiled. "I'll let you know everything."

Robin gave Leviah and I another small smile before she stepped past us to the village.

Leviah and I moved on, the path crunching under our feet.

"So, have you worked out what you're going to say to your Demon King yet?" he asked tauntingly.

"Keep it up, and I'll magic duct tape to your mouth," I warned.

"Wouldn't help," he said, making sure his lips were pressed together when he said it.

My gaze dropped to the silver ring on my thumb. The telepathy enchantment had been invaluable for missions with Leviah, but it always felt… not wrong, exactly, but like he was occupying a seat that belonged to someone else.

And I knew exactly who that someone was.

Sighing softly, we pushed on while two parts of me battled over what to do now.

Did I go to my Demon King? Or should I keep running?

CHAPTER FIVE

DONOVAN

"Are you ever in Hell anymore?"

I rolled my eyes at Adrik's dramatics and continued my silent stroll along the beachfront, enjoying the way the deep purples and oranges of the fading sunset were bleeding into the velvet blue above.

"Not if I can help it. Why?"

"Just making a point is all. Anything I can help you with out there?"

I frowned. *"Not really. Why, are you looking for an escape route? Going stir-crazy being on lock-down with your mate?"*

Since his mate had become pregnant, Adrik had been even more strict with Calixta than he normally was. Her visits to the healer's tents where she often was during the week had been limited to once a week, and only when Donovan was absolutely certain it was safe for her to be up there. Because he was refusing to allow her on the surface any other time, she had laid the same restraints upon him, reminding him that any pain he felt, she'd feel, and that couldn't be good for the baby. Not to mention if he got himself killed, that kind of loss and stress on her would certainly affect their baby's health. Unable to argue with her, he'd agreed to stay back and enjoy the last few months of their time alone before a baby took over their lives.

It sounded nice… and claustrophobic. I knew my brother, and he loved his mate, but to not be allowed to go anywhere or do anything was driving him insane. At least he got the distraction of handling his Demons in Hell.

Poor Calixta had one night a week to do the things she loved before she was brought back to her realm.

"You know you can't be out here," I reminded him, stopping to admire the view.

I could feel his frustration through our connection. *"I could just come to you for a few minutes. You know, if you desperately needed it. Calixta would understand."*

I laughed out loud and shook my head. No, she wouldn't, not when I had seven other brothers I could go to for help if I really needed it.

"Are you asking me to get into a life-threatening situation and call on you so that you have a reason to get out of the house for a time?"

"If you're a real brother, you will," he threatened.

I grinned. *"Not a chance I'm risking Cali's wrath falling upon me. That woman can be merciless."*

Adrik groaned. *"Malik would,"* he taunted.

I scoffed. *"Go ask him then, if that's the case."*

He was silent for a moment before I heard him swearing. *"When did all my brother's become such pussies?"*

"About the time they all became mated to powerful Witches who won't hesitate to use their combined magic on each of us in retaliation."

Adrik growled. *"Again, I say… pussies."*

I shook my head. *"If you believe that, I'll just pass this information onto Cali then? I'm sure she won't hold a grudge against you for trying to find a loophole in your agreement. And her being pregnant won't amplify her already fiery nature one bit."*

"Go fuck yourself, Nova," Adrik snapped, and I laughed out loud again.

"Good luck with that, brother. Now, I'm going to continue my leisurely stroll on the beach. I might go for a hunt later. I'll just see where the night takes me."

"Again, brother. Go fuck yourself."

I laughed as Adrik broke the connection. I gave him endless shit about the position he'd put himself in, but honestly… I was envious that he had someone at home waiting for him, that loved him so much, that cared about his safety enough to get mad whenever he put himself in jeopardy. I knew Trinity was out there and she cared for me, but until she was here, until she was *mine,* I was left feeling incomplete.

"Help!"

The scream jolted me out of my thoughts and I whirled around at the sound, eyes peeled for the danger.

"Please, someone, help me!" a woman screamed again, her voice nearby. I moved quickly over the small sand dune before she came into view. She was injured, bloodied and bruised, and sparks of magic shot out from her fingers.

Witch.

I watched as her magic hit a dark figure chasing her, but it was weak and didn't slow it down. White wings burst from the creatures back and my gaze narrowed on the Angel closing in on her.

Fucker.

Gritting my teeth, I ran forward, drawing a Demon Blade from my boot. I took aim and threw it. The blade whistled through the air to lodge itself in the Angel's head up to the hilt. The Angel rocked back forcefully, toppling lifeless to the ground by the time I reached the Witch.

She stared at me with wide eyes as she panted, dark hair loose and wild. She backed up several steps, holding out a shaking hand as if to ward me off. I kept my distance from her as I moved to the Angel to remove my blade, keeping a wary eye on her.

"Stay back," she whispered, clearly frightened.

"I'm not going to hurt you," I assured, looking her over carefully. She was in her mid-thirties, maybe, and hurt. But something about her looked familiar to me. How? Had I somehow seen her before?

"Have we met?" I asked.

She screwed up her face and shook her head. "What is that, some kind of pick-up line?"

I shook my head, lips twitching. "No, I was genuinely asking."

She swallowed hard and shook her head. "No, we haven't met. I... I know your mind though, Demon King. I don't want anything to do with your kind."

"Nor his, I imagine," I said, tipping my head to the dead Angel on the sand.

She swallowed hard and shook her head. "No."

"Do you have somewhere safe you can go? Friends? Family?"

She didn't answer for a long moment. "I have sisters, but we were separated a long time ago. I don't know where they are now."

I nodded slowly. "I have friends who can help with that—other Witches. They can locate your sisters for you, if you'll come with me."

She frowned at me, backing up another step. I held out my hands, palms up. "I'm not trying to trick you."

She glared and I grinned again. "I know you can't trust that, but I swear I'm not. I just want to help."

"That's what the last guy said," she whispered softly.

I frowned. "The last guy?"

She swallowed hard and looked around. "I... The Angels took me, they held me in Heaven for... months. They tortured me, they kept asking me questions I had no answers for."

A chill worked its way up my spine. "What kind of questions?"

She crossed her arms over her stomach. "Uh…" She hesitated, swallowing hard, eyes glistening with tears. "Something about a place, some kind of place for Witches. I don't know, I've never heard of it. They just kept going on about a place Witches had created to hide from Angels and Demons. They want the location."

"And you don't know where this place is?"

She shook her head and glared at me. "No! No such place exists; at least, not that I've ever heard of."

I held up my hands again, a silent apology for upsetting her. "You mentioned someone else? Someone who lied to you."

She hesitated and swallowed convulsively, a shimmer of pain in her eyes. "He said he was there to help me, to save me. He… he got me out of my cell and told me he was going to keep me safe, that he couldn't stand by and let them torture me anymore. He said there was a right and a wrong, and that… that what the Angels were doing was wrong."

I felt like I already knew where this was going. "This someone… who was it?"

She sniffled loudly. "He… he was an Angel. I thought… I thought he was my friend. I know, it's stupid, right? Angels aren't our friends, but… he seemed so genuine."

I tried not to draw parallels between her story and Trinity's. Because of Trinity's letters, I knew she had been held in Heaven, I knew she had been rescued by an Angel, but I didn't know details. Just because the same thing had happened to this Witch didn't mean Trinity's friend was conning her… did it?

"Where is this Angel now?" I asked, turning to look at the Witch again.

Her eyes went wide. "I don't know. When we got out and it became obvious that I really didn't know where this place was, he told me I was useless and a waste of the Angels he'd been forced to kill to sell his story to me. He was going to take me back to Heaven. I managed to get away, but they've been chasing me ever since."

Fuck!

Had Trinity already taken her Angel to her sanctuary? If he was the same Angel, had he already passed along its location to the others? If not, how long did they have before they were overrun? I looked at the Witch again and swore.

"What's your name? I'm Donovan."

Something on her face shifted, and she hesitated. "Nera," she answered.

"Nera, I know it's a lot to ask considering the betrayal you just went through, but I need you to come with me. I know someone who can protect you, who can get you to a safe place, but I need to warn some friends that they might be in danger. I don't want to leave you out here alone and unprotected."

She shook her head and backed up. "First, I don't know you. Second... nowhere is truly safe for any of us, not from Angels and not from your kind."

I sighed. "I know it feels that way, but I promise... there is somewhere you can go. But I need you to come with me now. I need you to talk to some people so they can hear exactly what you told me."

Again, she hesitated, and I wanted to ignore her wants and needs and just take her. I could. She didn't appear to be at full strength and she wasn't as fast as me. I could do it, but I wanted her to trust me.

"How do I know you won't betray me too?"

I shook my head. "You can't, not really. But I'm asking you to trust me anyway. Out here, the Angels will find you again sooner or later. At least with me you have a fighting chance of

71

staying away from them."

Her silence was long, but I could wait... a while, anyway. The news she'd shared with me whirled around in my head over and over, and all I could think about was getting to Trinity before it was too late. What if what happened to this Witch had also happened to my mate?

I stepped toward the Witch, hoping to convince her somehow, to invite her to feel my emotions and know that I was telling the truth when I said I wanted to protect her. But before I took more than a step, an overwhelming feeling of power washed over me, one I was all too familiar with. Not because it frightened me, but because it belonged to one kind of creature, and I wanted nothing more than to blast it into the netherworld. Turning on my heel, I spun in time to see an Archangel appear before me.

But not just any Archangel...

Uriel.

Flashes of memory came back to me, scratching against my brain and burning in my soul. Tabitha and her family being herded into her house, the way he laughed as their screams echoed across the valley. His taunts reverberated through my head as the memories of him hurting Tabitha played over and over, and I could barely breathe through the haze of red coating my vision.

"Donovan... it's been a while," he greeted, his grin cocky and self-assured.

"Fuckface, ready to die?" I snarled, curling my hands into fists.

He laughed, the sound full of condescension. "You poor, deluded Demon King. You really think you have a chance of defeating me?"

"Only one way to find out," I returned hotly, backing up to Nera again. "Stay behind me."

Six more Angels appeared behind Uriel, swords drawn and eyes filled with hatred.

"If you think you can win, then let's see," he taunted, raising his own blade.

I drew my sword, and just as I was adjusting my grip, something hit me in the back, something powerful and painful that stole my breath and sent me flying forward to slam into the sand below. I grunted as my entire body locked tight and my lungs refused to take in another breath.

Uriel's laugh was genuine this time, full of smug superiority.

"Poor, deluded Demon King. Always trying to save the Witch in distress," he murmured, moving into my line of sight as my body refused to move. I watched with growing rage as Nera stepped up beside him, her face full of glee.

"He's right; it's a fatal flaw of yours," she taunted.

Fucking bitch.

She was working with the Angels; I should have known. Anger burned hot in my veins, and I started working quickly on a plan to get out of this mess.

"So, you mentioned about a safe place for Witches. We're going to need to know where this is," Nera continued.

"Go fuck yourself, Angel-loving whore," I spat. She looked properly affronted and Uriel placed a hand on her shoulder. The shot of power she lashed at me was expected, but it stole my breath nonetheless.

"If you don't know how to get there yourself, then you need to tell me who does so that I might properly question them about it," Uriel continued as if there hadn't been an interruption.

"Eat a dick," I snapped.

Uriel gave a dramatic sigh, but the gleam in his eye told me this was exactly the response he'd been hoping for.

"I think we'll need to take this conversation elsewhere," he said before jerking his head to the other Angels. Three of them sheathed their swords and started towards me, pulling iron cuffs from who the fuck knows where.

I wanted to struggle and fight back, but my body was still paralyzed. The spell was wearing off, but not fast enough.

It looked like Adrik was going to get the call for help he had begged me for earlier. I was just reaching for my brothers when the air suddenly changed around us. It was charged, heavy, a sort of weight that accompanied a vicious storm. The wind picked up and the sound of thunder booming ominously overhead was loud, the kind of sound that you could feel in your bones. I managed to tilt my head—progress—in time to see a dark figure appear, massive wings spread wide and dark.

Amazarak.

My relief at seeing the Nephilim leader was unexpected, but I chose to ignore it as the Angels turned to look at the powerful creature. Uriel swore and looked between me and Zarak before shimmering away.

"Fuck," I snarled, focusing on my limbs, desperate for them to move. If I could get my hands on the Witch, I could find a way to get the information from her on where Uriel liked to frequent these days. That fucker's days were numbered, and I intended for them to be in the single digits now.

"Good evening," Amazarak greeted, his voice oddly formal, but it carried across us all with a weight that made the hairs on my arms stand on end.

"Be gone, Nephilim scum, this doesn't involve you," one of the braver—or more stupid—Angel's warned. Zarak's dark eyes landed on the Angel and he looked unimpressed.

"I'm going to give you all this one chance to leave with your lives. Ignore it, and your blood will soak the ground where you stand. Your choice."

"Any Angel who leaves here will be branded a traitor," Nera warned loudly.

I grunted as I pulled my legs up beneath me, my arms shaky but holding my weight.

"What does that make Uriel, then?" I asked. "Coward," I answered for her.

Her eyes glinted, and for the first time I began to wonder if she was all there.

"Nice try, Nephilim. We're not afraid of you," another Angel piped up, and I didn't need to be a Witch to hear the lie in his voice. Amazarak looked bored as he took in the Angels around him, his gaze hesitating over the Witch before landing on me. "Want to help?" he asked.

I groaned. "Save me a few. I just need a minute."

Amazarak's lips twitched before his eyes turned flat and cold and his attention moved back to the Angels. "Well, what are you waiting for?"

With a battle-cry I felt was more to hold onto his courage than to prove his ferociousness, an Angel charged at the Nephilim. The others followed suit quickly, and I managed to stagger to my feet, legs shaky and threatening to collapse beneath me at any moment.

Come on, fucking hell. I swore to myself, taking a stumbling step toward the Witch, Hellfire forming in my hand only to flicker out.

She turned to look at me, and I saw the wheels turning behind her eyes as the Angels continued their fight. With a hiss of frustration, she pressed a pendant around her neck and an Angel appeared beside her.

"I'll be seeing you," Nera warned before she and the Angel shimmered out.

Fuck.

I steadied myself as I turned to watch Amazarak slice through one Angel before spinning to decapitate the last one, his head rolling down a small slope before coming to stop near the water's edge.

"I thought I asked you to save me some," I called as the Nephilim's gaze came to rest on me.

"I left the Witch, but she was too much for you it seems," he answered calmly, sheathing his sword.

I sighed. "They almost trapped me."

"They *did* trap you," Zarak corrected. "It just didn't hold."

I glared. "Thanks for the clarification. Why are you here, anyway?"

He looked me over carefully before shrugging. "I felt the presence of an Archangel nearby, accompanied by a Witch and several other Angels. When I felt a Demon King amongst them, I thought I'd see if you wanted any assistance."

I grimaced. "Yeah, well… thanks."

I sounded less than grateful, but it was a stab to the pride that I'd been taken down so easily.

"Do not feel bad, Demon King. Using a Witch as a lure is how they have managed to capture many of my kind."

I raised an eyebrow. This was news to me. "Really?"

The deadly look in his eyes answered for him. "Yes."

I nodded slowly and looked around the beach again, frustrated. "Any answers yet as to *why* they have been taking your kind rather than just killing them?"

If I hadn't been watching so closely, I would have missed the small movement in his eyes that told me he knew something. I waited, and Amazarak finally sighed and stepped closer.

"We debated whether or not to tell you and your brothers, but I think we know each other well enough now to trust each other. At least, to know we're not going to attempt to harm one another," Zarak began.

Unease pricked at me and I nodded. "We have no reason to harm any of yours."

Amazarak paused, eyes narrowed again.

I raised an eyebrow. "Do we?"

He shook his head. "Not for anything we are doing, but I do not know how you will react to the news that our existence puts yours and your brothers at risk."

Again, I looked at him with confusion. "Explain."

After another moment of sizing me up, Amazarak crossed his arms over his chest and watched me carefully.

"It has come to our attention that Angels are taking my kind because our blood—when twisted with specific spells—is toxic to yours."

My eyes widened and I stared in shock. "How? I've never heard of Nephilim blood being used against us. The only thing Angels have ever managed to do differently in recent years... is..." I trailed off, mouth falling open as I stared at him.

Zarak grimaced. "The poison they have been coating their Angel blades with... yes. It's Nephilim blood."

Fucking *what?!*

"But... how?"

He shrugged. "That, we do not know the specifics of. Just that they use Witches to spell the blood before they embed it within their blades. It stops you from reaching out to your brothers telepathically, and after some time it weakens your ability to shadow and use Hellfire. Aarin told us when they had him that they constantly drained his blood, almost to the point of death. It is why they have resorted to capturing my kind rather than outright killing us."

Motherfuckers!

"I trust this news does not prompt you or your brothers to hunt my kind down in an attempt to eliminate the threat to you or to attempt to use our blood in retaliation against the Angels."

I shot him a look and shook my head. "Even if we were so inclined, do you really think our mates would allow it?"

He shrugged. "I cannot base the safety of my people on what I truly hope. I need assurances in this instance."

I nodded slowly. "I promise, Amazarak. I speak for all my brothers when I say none of us will be interested in hunting you or yours for your blood. Besides, even if we did try and use your blood against the Angels, I doubt it would work. You're part Angel."

He raised an eyebrow and looked at me as if I was missing something.

"What?"

Zarak sighed as if he were dealing with a difficult child. "I realize what I am about to say may not have occurred to you due to your complete and valid hatred of all things Angelic, but you and your brothers are also part Angel. Or did you forget that Lucifer was an Archangel?"

His words felt like he's slapped me and stripped me of my hellfire all in one swift motion. "Fucking take it back!"

Zarak seemed to find my utter revulsion humorous and simply smiled. "The truth can hurt, I understand that."

I grimaced and shook my head. I felt like I needed a shower. "So..." I trailed off, pushing past what he said, not wanting to think about that right now. "What you're saying is, with how potent your blood is to us, it would be worse against the Angels with an altered spell?"

He shrugged. "I do not know, nor do I care to find out. But..."

that would be a theory I can imagine you or your brothers bringing to light one day."

"And you thought to bring it up first because...?"

He stared at me, black eyes flat, thunder booming. The ocean waves slammed into the beach, the tide rising far too fast to be natural. Lightning arced impressively across the sky and the smell of ozone was strong as the wind whipped around me.

"I tell you so you know I am aware of the theory, and I wanted to remind you all that deciding to test it would be unwise."

Not a lot scared me in this world, I was a powerful Demon King and knew what I could handle. But even we had been smart enough to avoid Nephilim where we could. Not because we were afraid, but because we had no quarrel with them. But I knew to even consider using their blood for our own purposes would tear a rift between our kinds that would never heal, and start a war on a second front that we did not need.

Unease rippled through me at the clear warning and I nodded slowly. "Understood, but none of us would be interested in requiring one species to suffer so that ours could thrive. Angels are the dick bags, not us."

Amazarak studied me carefully a moment longer before he nodded, and everything around us began to ease back. It still freaked me out that he had any sway over the elements at all, another thing we had no explanation for.

"Now that we have that out of the way," Amazarak began, sighing. "I have another warning for you."

I groaned but listened. If the Nephilim leader was coming to a King of Hell with a warning, it was worth listening to.

"We have reason to believe that Angels are now intentionally creating Nephilim."

I blinked several times, my mind blank. Of all the things he could have said, I had not been expecting that.

"After centuries of trying to eradicate you all? Why?"

He shrugged his massive shoulders. "I assume it's because it takes too long and too much power to capture and subdue a full-grown Nephilim, so they are resorting to creating their own and killing their mothers once their use is over."

I jerked back in shock. Angels were assholes of the first order, we already knew that. But this? This was a whole other level…

I sighed. Really, I shouldn't be surprised at the levels they'd stoop to.

"I assume this is another way for them to have Nephilim blood on tap?"

Zarak nodded. "That, or they finally admit that we are a superior species to them and intend to train some Nephilim from childhood. They've decided we're too powerful to continue to have as an enemy and want to create their own Nephilim soldiers, brainwashing them to be on their side. It's the only way to even the fight between us and them."

"Motherfuckers," I whispered. The potential for the fallout of that was… I shook my head, not sure what to do with that information.

"How did you get to this conclusion?" I asked, frowning.

He watched me carefully a moment longer and seemed to debate telling me something.

"Look, I don't care. If you guys want to keep your secrets, fine. You've warned us of a threat and I'm thankful. I'll let my brothers know so they're aware but—hey, why didn't you go to Cali with this?" I asked, breaking off mid-sentence as the thought occurred to me.

Calixta was his friend more than any of us, surely he'd have told her.

"Cali is not out much these days. I assume it has something to do with her being with child?"

My eyes narrowed. How did he find out? She hadn't been allowed around anyone else since it became obvious that she was pregnant. We couldn't risk word of a Witch carrying a Demon King's baby getting out and making her more of a target, and she was cloaked whenever she did her weekly healings.

"Did Shaye and Hariel tell you?" I asked, thinking of the only people outside my brothers and their mates who would have contact with the Nephilim leader.

Zarak shook his head. "No, I am perceptive. I felt the child's heartbeat when she helped us to break into Heaven."

Fuck, he'd known before the rest of us.

"Well… yes. Adrik has been keeping her closer these days," I answered, annoyed.

"Good," the Nephilim answered. "Her and the baby's lives are more important than her being out on the surface at the moment."

I kept my smile to myself, knowing Adrik would love to know he had another ally against Cali being on the surface. After another moment, Amazarak stepped closer, scanning around us to make sure we were alone. I did the same, knowing whatever he wanted to say would need to be kept between us.

"Your Witch, Trinity. How is she?"

I stepped back, unsure how he knew about her. My questions must have been all over my face because he raised an eyebrow. "We have crossed paths a few times. Most recently was about a month ago."

My heart skipped a beat. I hadn't seen her in almost five. "You saw her a month ago?"

"Yes," he said, eyes troubled. "Is she healing up okay? The fight she was in left her a little injured, but she promised me she'd be okay."

Fury flooded through me that she'd been hurt. That Amazarak had seen her more recently than me. That she'd been out and in danger and hadn't told me!

"Calm, Demon King," Amazarak said softly.

"Don't fucking tell me to calm down," I snarled.

Again, he waited, patience and interest written across his face.

"Is she okay?" I asked.

He hesitated. "That is why I was asking you. She said she would be okay and left shortly after."

"Well, what was she doing? How did you get involved?"

He paused, eyes searching before a small smile twitched his lips. "She rescued a Nephilim baby."

Shock ripped through me and I stared at him. "Bullshit."

He shook his head, a light in his eyes I'd never seen before. If I didn't know any better, I'd say it was pride and happiness. "No. She found the mother—somehow already aware of the danger— and kept the Archangel and his Witch companion distracted and got the mother and child to me."

I closed my eyes on the words, trying not to be furious for the risks Trinity was taking after I'd already lost her once. An Archangel *and* a Witch. Alone?

Wait...

"Was she alone? Was someone helping her?"

Amazarak searched his memory. "I didn't see the fight. The mother was cursed when she reached us and died shortly after, but she managed to get the child to us. She told me Trinity's name, that she was at her home, and so I went there to make sure she was okay. She was injured but okay in the end. She gave us a few seconds warning before another Angel showed up, this one was apparently her friend. They left pretty quickly."

Fuck.

Was this Angel really her friend? Nera had spun a story similar to Trinity's—too similar—and it could have been to throw me off. But what if it was true? What if Trinity was in danger, was being played, and didn't know it?

"I have a question, I wonder if you can answer for me?" Amazarak said, changing the subject.

Sighing, I ran a hand over my head and nodded. "Sure, why the hell not?"

"I have noted a steep decline in Demon activity. Have you all been keeping them in check more than usual?"

I shook my head. We weren't announcing the news for all to know, but Amazarak and his kind were safe.

"Not quite. For obvious reasons we are not announcing the news, but Hell is on lockdown. There was corruption and mutiny among them. We managed to lock them up and no one is to go free until they have undergone intense re-training. Those who remain out here are Rogues who have been gone from Hell too long so that they no longer feel as strong a connection with it. They are harder for us to control."

The Nephilim looked intrigued, but didn't bother to ask any further questions.

I sighed, exhausted. "Any more announcements you want to make?"

His lips tilted in a half-smile and he shook his head. "No, that is all for now, but I thought it was time you all knew. Maybe knowing what is in the Angel Blade poison, your Witches can begin to find a way to counteract it."

I nodded, grateful for the knowledge. Nothing felt worse than being disconnected from my brothers.

With another look, Amazarak stepped back and launched into the air, his wings powerful and impressive.

Well... fuck.

Sighing, I knew I had to deliver this news to my brothers. They needed to know, and then hopefully we could find a way to get around how fucking devious the Angels were.

Then... I needed to get to my mate and make sure she was safe.

CHAPTER SIX

DONOVAN

Present Day...

A wall in Hell was... broken.

Power bled from the crack in Hell's walls, curling through the air like smoke I couldn't see but felt against my skin. It was ancient in a way that made my bones ache, and there was something... final about it, as though an end to this story had already been decided before we even knew what it was. Standing before it, letting that pressure roll over me, was like bracing against an unseen tide that was building to something powerful. The worst part was the not knowing.

None of us—me, my brothers, their mates—had any real idea what was leaking through. Was it just the raw magic of Hell itself, trapped for eons in these black marble walls until Tamas' fury had fractured them? And if so, how much could seep out before it changed something we couldn't undo? Or was there something else, something with a mind behind that pressure? Tamas' rage had cracked the floor, his fists slamming down in helpless fury while his mate was being assaulted.

The force had traveled up the wall like a shockwave, splintering the marble. During Cole and Mika's wedding, Raven discovered a steady bleed of whatever lay beyond. Since then, the women had been working at the edges, chipping carefully to learn more. It wasn't recklessly done. If anything felt wrong, they would stop. Calixta had been crafting contingencies, ways to seal the breach if what was in there needed to stay buried. So far, no revelations had been made—only more of the same oppressive hum that made the skin along my arms tighten. Still, the crack was wider now, its edges flaked and raw from days of work.

I stepped closer, leaning in until the cold from the stone seeped into my face. Something inside caught my attention—a shadowed shape, half-hidden, like an object swallowed by the marble and still struggling to break free. My frown deepened. Maybe it was nothing. Maybe it was just the stone playing tricks in the dim light.

But as I stared, I could have sworn it pulsed.

"The guys are taking bets on it if you want in," Tomika said as she stepped up beside me, her gaze fixed on the wall.

I smiled down at my brother's mate—a woman I'd long since considered a sister—and shook my head.

"What are the guesses so far?" I asked, folding my arms and letting my eyes slide back to the thin fracture in the stone.

She exhaled and shook her head. "Cole thinks it's some kind of monster God made before Lucifer was cast into Hell, and that it fossilized in the wall. Adrik believes the power we're feeling is just Hell's own essence and we're accomplishing nothing except ruining it."

I inclined my head slightly. Adrik might be right—it could simply be the raw energy of our home—but the faint, insistent itch in the back of my mind wouldn't let me dismiss it so easily. "What do the others think?"

She grinned, rolling her eyes. "Malik says it's Elvis."

I snorted. "Of course he does."

"Harkyn says it's tied to the power of Hell, and Tamas reckons it's the wrath of your mother for damaging her precious walls."

That earned a laugh from me. Our mother would have been livid if she knew we'd cracked what everyone thought was an impervious wall.

"And the rest?"

Mika shrugged. "Devlin and Corvin haven't been around much. Cassius hasn't given a guess, but he's definitely interested—he's been combing through the old records in the basement to see if there's anything about the construction of The Great Hall or the circles of Hell."

I nodded, the thought pulling me in. I'd never considered how the Nine Circles were actually made—they'd always just existed. But someone had to have built them. Maybe God Himself. Either way, understanding their creation might tell us what's inside them now.

"Do you ladies have any guesses?" I asked, turning toward her.

Mika tipped her head, her blue eyes thoughtful. "No, but we all feel... pulled to it. There's something in there, a rhythm almost alive. If it's the core of Hell's power, we'll cover it back up and pretend we never found it. But if it's something else in these walls—don't you want to know? What if it's dangerous? What if it was placed there by the Angels?"

A frown drew my brows together and my gaze slid back to the crack. Could the Angels have hidden something here—a weapon? A way to watch us? Influence us? The thought made my stomach turn, and I had to resist the urge to step away from the wall entirely.

"You're being careful though, right? Not pushing yourselves too far?" I asked.

"We're careful. Thanks, big brother," Tomika teased.

Her smile caught me off guard—not because I was secretly in love with her, though when she'd first come to Hell I'd noticed her beauty, her spark, her wit. But she'd quickly become my sister in every way that mattered. Still, when she smiled like that, I saw Trinity.

Her twin.

No, they weren't identical, but the resemblance was strong. Mika had begged me to find her years ago, and although I'd failed for far too long, I could feel it in my bones—I was closing in. Soon, I'd have Trinity somewhere safe and out of the constant danger she seemed drawn to.

Trinity risked herself to protect others, finding Witches who were lost or hunted and taking them somewhere even Demons and Angels couldn't track. She'd saved Dimitria before fate bound her to Harkyn, and she'd rescued Raven from a Demon camp moments before she'd been sacrificed.

She was saving my sisters and other innocents, but the thought of her facing those dangers alone every day made my gut knot.

Soon, I'd be there for her. I wouldn't cage her, but I'd stand beside her every step of the way. As for my family, we had other battles to face.

After speaking to Amazarak the other night about the poison on Angel Blades and what it really was, I'd called a meeting to inform my brothers. Obviously, they'd been outraged, and even though I'd already spoken for the Kings of Hell, I reminded them all of Amazarak's not so subtle threat of retaliation if we thought to use the blood of his kind for our own purposes. As I'd predicted, everyone was horrified at the thought.

The news that there was a Nephilim baby was a surprise, and immediately Cali was demanding details, but I told her she'd have to reach out to Zarak herself because I didn't know anything else. Now, we had a crack in Hell's wall, Hell's gates were closed until further notice, and we needed to find an antidote to the poison Angel's used on their blades. On top of all that, four of us still had to get our mates and keep them safe. Sighing, I stepped back from the wall.

Mika's eyes shadowed as she studied me. "You're heading out again."

I nodded. I'd been home very little lately, and wouldn't stay until Trinity was safe. Some fools believed killing the Kings would spark a stronger age for Demons. I suspected it would collapse Hell entirely. A few months ago, we'd been trapped here, nearly overwhelmed with the force of rebelling Demons, and the only way to keep the hordes from overrunning us was to lock the gates.

At least with Hell on lockdown, it gave me the chance to search for my mate. I'd spent weeks ensuring my Knights were loyal, punishing the truly treacherous and brutally retraining the rest. Demons didn't learn through gentle words—they learned through pain and fear. For now, my orders were clear: Cassius would oversee things when I wasn't around.

"Any closer to finding Trinity?" Tomika asked, a flicker of hope in her voice she tried to conceal.

"I think so," I admitted. "But I don't want to get your hopes up. She's smart—too smart to be caught easily. She's got help, though, so that's something."

Even if that help was an Angel. Besides her being in near-constant danger, it was my least favorite thing about the whole situation.

Mika's shoulders sagged, worry in her eyes.

"I'll find her, Mika, and I'll bring her back to you," I promised. Those words were beginning to feel empty to me, and I hoped they weren't meaningless to her. I'd been saying the same thing for over four years now, and while I was closer to accomplishing it, I still had no real way to bring Trinity home.

Mika's eyes shone, and I pulled her into a quick hug. I'd

promised Tabitha—Mika and Trinity's ancestor—that I would protect their bloodline. I'd failed for too long, so this was my chance to make it right.

"Would you get your damned hands *off* my mate?"

I turned with a grin as Cole strode up, his glower only half in jest. Instead of letting go, I tightened my hold on Mika. "I'm allowed to hug my sister."

"Can't. Breathe," she wheezed.

I released her and Cole swept her into his arms, black eyes glittering dangerously.

"I'm glad we caught you before you left," a new voice called. Adrik and Cali approached, and my eyes immediately went to Calixta's rounded belly. Pregnant women really did seem to glow, and the sight stirred every protective instinct in me.

"Got a theory on what's in the wall?" Adrik asked.

I shook my head. "I'm with you—it's probably just Hell's essence."

Cali studied me. "You're not completely convinced."

Bloody Witches and their extra abilities.

"No," I admitted. "I thought I saw something."

Mika leaned forward to look, and I pointed out the faint curve within the crack that kind of looked like an object buried behind the wall.

"I didn't see that before," Cali murmured.

"Me either," Mika said.

"What do you think it is?" Cole asked.

"Could be nothing—just uneven stone," I said, but something deep down nagged at me, and I knew whatever it was, it wasn't just wall.

"So, you're heading off again?" Adrik asked.

"Yeah. She's close, I can feel her. Something is coming, and I need to be there to protect her."

Before the conversation could dig deeper, more of our group arrived.

"Brother, are you joining us on the next Rogue hunt?" Malik asked, smiling warmly at his mate, Sawyer, who stepped into his embrace.

"No, I'm going after Trinity. I don't think I'll be back for a while."

Malik shrugged. "More Rogues for me, then."

"Pretty sure I've got you beat on the Rogue headcount," Tamas gloated, and Malik looked incensed.

"The fuck you do."

"Wanna bet?" Tamas offered, his grin wicked.

"You're on," Malik said, and the two shook hands.

I grinned, a part of me wishing I could go along just to watch the two of them battle it out. Tamas was slowly becoming himself again, and in moments like this, his old self shone through brightly. I knew what he'd gone through with that curse, but I was beginning to believe it was possible his old self was still there, waiting to break through.

"If you need me, though, reach out," I said, glancing around at my brothers to emphasize my willingness to be there if they needed me. "Don't wait until the problem is too big if you need my help."

We'd all felt what it was like when Malik died a while ago, and *none* of us were willing to go through that again. That echoing cavern where our brother had once occupied space in our head was as unnatural as it got for us.

Harkyn waved me off. "No, brother. You focus on your mate. Get her safe, that's what matters."

I nodded, appreciating their understanding. "But call me if you need me."

Mika hugged me again. "Be safe, Nova. Bring my sister home."
"That's the plan," I assured. Something told me that this time
things would be different.

With a final look at them all, I shadowed out of Hell, senses
wide, reaching for the one person I couldn't stop chasing.

CHAPTER SEVEN

TRINITY

Heaven: Two years ago...

The cell door opened with that same soft, final click that had started every nightmare for the past however long I'd been a prisoner in here.

I didn't look up, there was no point. Knowing who it was wouldn't make a difference in the pain I'd endure. Whether it was Camhael or one of his obedient lapdogs, I already knew the routine—drag me out, ask the same questions, demand the same answers I would never give, then make sure I screamed enough to remind me I was powerless against them.

The air shifted. The footsteps were lighter than Camhael's, but still measured. I dragged my gaze upward, preparing for whatever new torture awaited me.

The Angel in the doorway wasn't a stranger exactly—I'd seen him before, passing in the endless blinding halls, always silent, always watching. His thick black hair barely brushed his shoulders, framing a face carved in sharp, clean lines. His eyes were a strange silvery-blue, cool and steady where most angels' gazes burned and glowered.

"Get up," he said, voice low and even.

I pushed myself up on raw, trembling arms, keeping him in my sights, my back to the corner. "I'm not in the mood for company."

"I'm not here to hurt you."

That was a new line, and my laugh came out hoarse, my voice weak from screaming.

He stepped inside, the door shutting behind him with a whisper and I pressed myself against the wall, hoping to keep distance between us. "I'm going to get you out of here. Now. But you have to move."

I blinked at him, trying to read the trap in his words. "Right... and you're doing this out of the goodness of your heart?"

He didn't answer that, just crossed the space of the narrow cell in three long strides. The moment his hand closed around my arm, heat flared—not the scalding burn I'd learned to dread, but something steadier, almost grounding.

"Do you want to stay?" he asked. It wasn't a threat; he wasn't mocking me. It was a simple, flat question.

My heart stuttered. I didn't want to trust him. I couldn't, and yet...

I swallowed hard. "Fine. I'll go with you, but if this is some angelic test—"

"It's not," he assured and eased me toward the door, his movements careful but urgent.

"Wait," I whispered, tugging back.

The Angel looked at me, confused, impatient.

I swallowed hard. I needed something from him, anything he could give me to trust him, but what could he do in five seconds that would suffice?

"Umm... what's... what's your name?" I asked, shakily. It wasn't enough to trust him, but it was something.

His slashing eyes scanned my face briefly, his expression unreadable. "Leviah."

I whispered his name back to him, feeling it, getting a sense for him.

"Ready?" he asked. I shook my head, but shifted beside him to look out the cell door anyway.

The corridor was the same impossible white that made every hallway in Heaven feel like it bled into the next. The air was too clean, the light too sharp. My companion's wings were nowhere to be seen—retracted in that strange way angels could make them vanish with a subtle roll of their shoulders. My bare feet made no sound on the polished floor, but my heartbeat felt loud enough to echo, and terror gripped me at the idea of being caught. I could only imagine the pain they'd put me through for attempting to escape.

We moved as quickly as I was able to, and whenever he stopped, I stopped. When he darted forward, I followed, my body shaking from more than just exhaustion. I didn't know who he was, or why he'd risk punishment for getting me out, but for the first time in months—no, longer than months, maybe—I was outside my cell.

Somewhere out there, Donovan had to be wondering where I'd gone or if I was even alive. We'd been in contact, trading barbs, small notes, cleverly hidden traps meant to annoy the other. I knew he'd be looking for me, and I hated the idea that he was left wondering what happened to me. After sharing a highly erotic psychic realm dream one night, I'd reluctantly put a shield up in my head, preventing myself from calling him like that and from him dragging me into one as well. As much as I wanted to be with him again, I knew it was wrong. Or at least, at the time I'd thought it was wrong. Knowing now about the prophecy, I was kicking myself. I'd tried to remove the wall in my head since being here, but I was too weak, too burned out. What if I could have somehow reached Donovan in here? At the very least, I could have kept talking to him so he wasn't hurting so much. At most, he might have been able to find a way to get me out.

But now was not the time for what if's and if only's.

Leviah and I kept to the shadowed edges of the corridor—not that there were many. Apparently, Heaven didn't believe in shadows. Everything gleamed: the smooth white walls, the marble floors, even the air, which seemed to glow faintly with its own light. My eyes ached from it, the unrelenting brightness stabbing into my skull like a needle. This was a place that offered no dark corners to hide in, no relief.

Leviah moved like water: smooth, deliberate, soundless. He didn't look back at me often, but when he did, his silvery-blue gaze was sharp, assessing whether I could keep up. I could feel his restraint, the way he didn't dare move too quickly or too slowly, as though either might draw attention.

Every time we approached an intersection, his hand came up in a silent command to wait. He would listen, head tilted slightly, muscles tight as bowstrings. More than once he caught my wrist and drew me into the narrow frame of a doorway or a shallow recess, his body angled just enough to shield mine from view. I could feel the residual heat from him, the faint brush of his arm against mine.

I held my breath each time an Angel passed, terrified of the moment their gaze might flick toward me and we would be found. I could already hear the shout, the slam of boots on the marble, and then the crushing grip of Camhael's hands on my arms, hauling me back.

Camhael.

Even thinking his name made my stomach twist. His voice was the one I'd heard the most during my captivity, cold and measured when he questioned me, venomous when I defied him. He'd taken pleasure in breaking my body, in burning through my reserves of magic until I thought the well inside me might be dried up forever. I could still smell the sharp, metallic tang of my own blood in that cell, still feel the raw burn in my throat from screaming until no sound came out.

I was walking on scraps of strength now. My magic still flickered somewhere inside me, but it was faint, unreliable. Every spell I'd tried recently had left me dizzy and shaking, as though I were trying to lift an unfamiliar weight.

After a few more turns, Leviah stopped in front of what looked like a storage alcove and motioned for me to step inside. "Wait here," he murmured. "Don't move until I come back."

Before I could ask where he was going, he was gone, his footsteps fading in the endless brightness.

I held my breath as fear tried to overwhelm me. I didn't know him, I couldn't trust him, and yet his presence the last few minutes had been a safety net, some kind of assurance that I would be protected if the other Angels found me. He was gone now, and I was terrified someone would find me and drag me back to the cells, and I'd be punished.

I leaned against the wall, my body trembling now that I wasn't forcing it forward. My mind was screaming at me to keep moving, to not stand still for even a second—but I didn't know the way. If I left this spot, I'd be walking straight back into the jaws of the trap.

The silence pressed in around me, and my thoughts slid back to the reason I'd been brought here in the first place.

I'd learned about the prophecy two weeks into my captivity. Not from Camhael, of course—he liked to hint and tease, to make me think I knew less than I did—but from a Seer. She'd been brought into my cell, where Camhael had been working to make me talk. She told him everything in a soft, dreamlike voice: that I was destined to be a mate to the Kings of Hell. It was the first time I saw the Angels look at me like a tool instead of a threat. That was why they kept me alive. It was why Camhael hadn't finished me, no matter how many times I refused to talk. He wanted a way to get to them, and when he looked at me, he saw a way to get it.

I didn't know if I believed in fate, but I knew this: if they believed it, then I was in more danger than I'd ever been before. I'd told them nothing; my will was still mine, unbroken. But each time Camhael came to me, I wondered if it would be the day that changed and my mind would finally crack under the weight of it all.

A shiver ran through me, and I pulled my arms tighter around myself. I didn't even know how long I'd been gone. Days? Weeks? Months? I imagined Donovan searching, setting traps, wondering why I hadn't come. Was he angry? Worried? Had he given up?

The thought of him thinking I'd abandoned him cut deeper than anything Camhael had done to me. And if Leviah failed, if we were caught, I'd never get the chance to explain.

The moment I heard the faint shift of air behind me, my body reacted before my mind did. I jerked back, hands half-raising in the clumsy beginnings of a defensive spell I wasn't sure I could cast.

"It's me."

Leviah stepped into the narrow alcove, the white light spilling across his sharp features. His black hair brushed his shoulders as he leaned close, his voice barely above a whisper. "The way ahead is clear. For now."

Even whispering, his tone had weight—steady, controlled, the kind of voice that sounded like it had commanded legions. I didn't know how many Archangels roamed these halls, but something told me there weren't many like him.

We moved again, his stride long but measured so I could keep pace. The marble floors reflected the faint gleam of his boots; the air was unnervingly still, carrying only the distant hum of Heaven's wards—magic so dense and pure it was almost suffocating. Every few steps I could feel it brushing over my skin, prickling against what little magic I had left, reminding me that I didn't belong here.

Leviah slowed near another intersection, head tilting, eyes narrowing as he listened. I forced myself to match his stillness, to ignore the way my lungs wanted to gulp air after too much shallow breathing.

Then, somewhere far off, there was a shout. The sound seemed to reverberate through the walls, followed by the rising clang of bells. The air shifted, charged with movement.

An alarm.

I didn't need Leviah to tell me it was for me.

"Run," he ordered, and then he was moving, his hand clamping around my wrist and dragging me into a sprint.

The corridors blurred past—white, endless, blinding. My bare feet slapped against marble, every step sending a fresh lance of pain up my legs. Behind us, the shouts grew louder, sharper, the sound of pursuit causing adrenaline to flood my exhausted body. Leviah didn't look back. His grip on my wrist was unyielding but never crushing, his strides eating up the ground that I struggled to mirror.

A flash of movement drew my attention ahead. Two Angels stepping into the hall from a side passage, blades drawn.

Leviah released me just long enough to roll his shoulders, and his wings unfurled in a single fluid motion. One moment they were gone, hidden; the next, they were out—massive, white-feathered arcs that filled the corridor with their span. The sight hit me in the chest; it was both terrifying and beautiful at once. He moved faster than I could follow. His blade was a long, silver-edged weapon I hadn't even seen him draw, and it caught the first Angel's sword mid-swing, twisting it away in a shower of sparks. The second barely had time to react before Leviah drove an elbow into his ribs, sending him sprawling.

"Go!" His voice cracked like a whip, pulling me forward.

Pain wracked my body, both mine and the feeling of theirs. My mental shield was down, and I was struggling to protect myself from their agony. Gritting my teeth, I ran, heart hammering, the scent of hot metal and blood in my nose. Every instinct screamed at me to look over my shoulder, but I forced myself to keep my eyes ahead.

When Leviah caught up, he fell into place at my side, blade still in hand. His breathing was steady, his movements as precise as before, but I could feel the urgency radiating from him now.

We turned another corner—and skidded to a halt.

Four more Angels blocked the hall.

I felt the weak flicker of my magic, the way it wanted to answer my call but couldn't quite. My chest tightened—if Leviah fell here, I'd be dragged back to that cell. Back to *him*.

Camhael's face flashed in my mind. Those cold eyes, the slow curl of a smile that told me everyone broke eventually.

Not me. Not yet.

I forced my magic forward, attempting to shape it into a barrier, but the effort felt like trying to catch smoke in my hands. The taste of copper on my tongue became prominent, but I ignored it, shoving the weak shield outward—a weak but tangible shield that bought Leviah the space he needed.

He was everywhere at once, his wings sweeping, blade flashing, movements so fluid they told of centuries of use.

The corridor rang with steel on steel, the clash echoing through the marble halls. One Angel went down hard; another staggered back with a wing torn and bleeding.

The last two faltered, glancing at each other, and Leviah pressed the advantage, his blade a blur. When it was over, he turned to me, eyes sharp, chest rising and falling faster now. "Move."

We ran again, my muscles screaming, my lungs burning. Somewhere ahead, the hall opened into a wide chamber. Through it, I could see the faint shimmer of the outer wards and what I assumed was the last barrier before freedom.

And standing in front of it, blade in hand, was an Archangel. I didn't know him, but the flash of regret I felt from Leviah told me that he did. We slowed, Leviah's hand tightening on my arm, and when he spoke, his voice was low and carrying a dangerous edge. "Hariel. Step aside, don't force my hand. Too much blood has already been spilled tonight, don't make me add yours to it."

Hariel's gaze flicked to me, and something shifted in his expression. His jaw clenched; his wings twitched, just once, before settling again. It was obvious that his conscience was at war with his orders.

For a long moment, no one moved.

Then Hariel exhaled slowly, his shoulders sinking. "I hope you retain your freedom," he said to me, voice quiet but clear. His eyes shifted back to Leviah. "Make it hard. Make it quick."

Leviah gave the smallest nod—then struck out, the hilt of his blade connecting sharply with the side of Hariel's head. The Angel crumpled to the marble floor, unconscious, not dead. There was no pause, no time to look back as Leviah pulled me forward through the shimmering wards, the air snapping cold around us as we crossed.

The world beyond Heaven hit me like a gasp—darker, heavier,

real. My knees buckled, and Leviah caught me before I could hit the ground.

"You're safe," he assured as darkness clouded my vision, and I gave in to it.

~

I woke to the smell of smoke and pine.

The surface beneath me was uneven, rocky, and warm from the fire nearby. My first instinct was to flinch, to brace for the burn of chains on my wrists, but it never came. When I tried to sit up, every muscle in my body screamed, but before I could push through the pain, a shadow moved across my vision.

Leviah crouched beside me, his silvery-blue eyes scanning my face with the kind of precision that made me nervous. His black hair hung forward in loose strands, brushing his jaw.

"You'll live," he said simply, as if the statement itself were an anchor. "But you need rest."

Rest.

The word felt foreign. I'd forgotten what it meant to sleep without fear of waking up to Camhael's voice, his questions and cruel patience.

The fire crackled softly as Leviah moved around the space, and somewhere in the depths of the forest, a bird called in the night. The air was cool on my skin, but thick with the scent of earth, not the sterile stillness of Heaven's halls.

I was free... and yet it didn't erase the ache in my chest.

Donovan.

I didn't even know if he was alive. For all I knew, Heaven had gone after him the moment they heard of the prophecy and my connection to him. The thought made my stomach twist. I wanted to see his face, to hear his voice, to reassure myself he was still out there. I needed to let him know that I hadn't given up or run away from him. If I could've sparked enough magic to contact him, I would have reached out to him right then, but my magic felt scorched down to embers. The constant suppression wards in Heaven, the draining cuffs, the endless white nothingness... it had all eaten away at my strength.

The memory of how I'd ended up there pressed forward, unwelcome but relentless.

And then I'd seen *her*.

The Seer's face was pale, almost luminous, and her voice was calm, without an ounce of remorse, as she told the Angels the prophecy of the Brothers' Nine, information that would forever change my life.

Camhael's mission had changed then. He wanted to make sure I understood that destiny could be rewritten, and that they were going to use me to do it. I'd survived him—his questions, his hands, the chains, the slow, methodical pain—but I didn't know how much longer I could have held out if not for Leviah.

Leviah was tending the fire, contemplative eyes flicking to me as he worked. He didn't speak much, at least not that I had experienced. But there was something about his silence that wasn't cold, it was like he was giving me space.

"Did you know?" I rasped.

The Archangel glanced at me and waited for me to elaborate.

"Did you know the others had taken me? What they were doing to me?"

He looked away again, eyes drawn to the fire. He was silent for so long that I didn't think he'd bother to answer.

"Not right away," he answered softly. "When I did find out, I

went to see you—the Witch they captured—and I did not agree
with what they were doing."

"But you didn't stop them," I interrupted, chest burning with an
invisible pain.

He shook his head but met my eyes. "I did not. I have not
questioned the rule of Heaven in my entire existence, and I have
lived far longer than you can imagine. I have always believed that
we were on the side of right."

I frowned, struggling to understand. "Then why rescue me
tonight? Why risk everything?"

More silence, but I was beginning to realize this wasn't an
attempt to dodge my question, but rather to answer in an
adequate fashion, like he was organizing his thoughts.

"Lately, it has become obvious to me that not all is right in
Heaven. Something is afoot. God is no longer giving the orders,
and I did not swear my fealty to another, only our Father.
Allowing them to torture you for no good reason was not
something I could abide. I could not look myself in the mirror
and be proud of who was looking back."

"And the prophecy that was revealed had nothing to do with
your actions?"

He didn't bother to deny it. "No, the prophecy was most
certainly one of the reasons."

"And the other?"

"There is a right and a wrong in the world," he answered simply.

I blinked in surprise. "So, saving me was about soothing your
own conscience?"

Dark eyes met mine, a glint of warning in them. "No. It was
about doing the right thing."

I didn't say anything to that and instead allowed silence to
envelope us once again. Leviah moved to my side and handed me

a canteen filled with water, his expression unreadable.

"Got anything stronger?" I joked, taking the canteen gratefully. His expression didn't change, which only made my lips twitch. "Sorry, are my constant questions getting in the way of your tall, dark, and broody persona? Wouldn't want to ruin that devastatingly handsome warrior class thing you have going on." The faintest glint lit his eyes—there and gone in a blink, but it was enough. Okay, he had a sense of humor. I could work with that.

I stared at him for a long moment, taking in the quiet power in his stance, the memory of what he'd done to get me here, the Angels he'd cut down, and the rules he'd shattered. I fully took in the sacrifice he'd made, the life he'd just burned behind him, because there was no way Heaven wasn't hunting him now. Whatever his motivations were in getting me out, he'd painted a giant target on his back and saved me from a fate worse than death.

"Thank you," I whispered before my throat tightened and emotion tried to overwhelm me.

He held my gaze, and I knew he understood what I meant. This wasn't just gratitude for pulling me out of my cell, although that was definitely part of it. It was for losing everything he'd ever known, for stepping away from his entire world to give me a chance at my own.

He didn't reply—he just inclined his head slightly. Words, it seemed, were too inefficient for acknowledging our new reality.

CHAPTER EIGHT

TRINITY

Present Day...

The sun was just beginning to bleed out over the horizon, streaking the Oasis skies in copper and violet. I sat cross-legged at a low table, pushing a map toward Lev while he sharpened one of his endless supply of blades. He always did that when we planned—some old soldier habit, I guessed.

"We could take the alleyway entrance to the north," I suggested, tracing a finger along the jagged ink lines.

He gave a slow shake of his head. "Too visible. And according to Dinah's vision, it'll be crawling with—"

"Rogue Demons," I finished for him, rolling my eyes. "Yes, I know. I feel like you say that about every plan we put together."

"Because it's true about all plans we make. The Rogues are damn near constant at this point." His lips twitched, eyes flashing with amusement. Although, lately I had to admit that while there weren't as many Rogues about, the ones who were here seemed somehow... stronger, faster, more lethal. I wasn't sure what I preferred—a few that were harder to kill, or a group that weren't as strong.

"Just once," I said, leaning back on my palms, "I'd like to go somewhere that isn't filled with celestial soldiers or Rogue

Demons. How nice would it be to save a Witch from, I don't know, a raging river or an almost hit-and-run?"

Lev snickered. "Dream big, Witch."

We traded easy barbs more and more over the years, the kind of teasing that was born of months—years now—of fighting side by side and hard-earned trust. Lev wasn't just my rescuer anymore; he hadn't been that for a long time. He was my constant, my best friend.

When I considered how Leviah and I had started up, it was amazing we'd come this far and remained this close. He was an Archangel, one of Heaven's deadliest warriors, and he'd spent countless years serving Heaven and its armies. Now he worked against them, side by side with a Witch destined to be the mate of a Demon King. If Leviah didn't have to pass through the protective shields of the Oasis every time we came and went, a part of me would think he was playing a long con and trying to earn my trust in order to betray us. But the shielding that protected this place was ancient and incredibly powerful. It kept out anyone who had any ill intent toward Witches or those who resided here.

We were working on a plan to save the girl from Dinah's vision, the one I'd find in the alley. No matter what, I still felt that same pull toward her. Something about her felt… familiar. I knew I hadn't met her before or seen her. I knew she was a complete stranger, and yet… I *knew* her. It was ridiculous and impossible, but my gut told me that she and I were meant to find one another.

"What is it about her that has you so on edge?"

I jerked my head up to see Leviah studying me across the table, those handsome features sharp but at ease around me. It only seemed to be me that he let his guard down for, even after living here for two years.

I shook my head. "I'm on edge with all the Witches that need saving. Their safety is always important to me."

Leviah gave me a knowing look. "Something about her is different for you. Is it because we lost the last one?"

My breath stuttered at the reminder, and I dropped his gaze. We hadn't lost a Witch on my last rescue mission but a human woman. She'd given birth to a Nephilim baby and had no idea what was so different about her child, only that it was. I admit, I was impressed with the lengths she'd gone in order to protect her child even though she'd had no idea what she would need to protect it from. Some kind of maternal instinct must have warned her, and I applauded her for not ignoring that instinct. In the end, it was what saved her baby.

While fighting the Archangel that had been there to collect his daughter, a Witch on their side threw a curse I was too slow to block. It attached itself to the woman, and I knew it was too late for her. Sending her to Amazarak had been my last effort to save the child, and my heart broke knowing I'd been too late for the mother.

Thankfully, Amazarak had been there for her and took the child in as his own. It saddened me that the mother was gone, but I was forever grateful the child hadn't been taken by the Angels.

"No," I finally answered, sighing. "It's not that. It's just... I don't know." I shrugged and leaned forward again, looking at our map. "Something about her feels so familiar."

"And you don't know why?" Lev pressed.

I shook my head. "Not a clue."

Silence fell between us as he considered my words, and I continued to look for ways we could get to the girl and get her out with the least amount of fighting and potential risk. I tapped the map again. "The south entry. But we'll have to skirt the buildings here, which means we'll need—"

My words died in my throat and something in me tightened, squeezing my lungs. A wrongness settled over me, sudden and sharp, coiling deep in my chest like a hot wire threading through my lungs.

Lev's eyes snapped up. "Trin?"

I swallowed hard. "Something's wrong."

My gaze moved as if pulled to the open doorway of my cabin, and I found Dinah standing on the opposite side of the path, her pale eyes on me as if she could see me.

It was time.

"Trin?" Lev had gone very still as he watched me cautiously. "What's wrong?"

I didn't want to say it out loud, because saying it would make it real, but the answer came anyway. "Donovan."

Lev set the blade down so fast it clattered against the table. "Then we go. Now."

"Wait!" The word came out sharper than I intended as I shot to my feet, but it froze him mid-step. I appreciated his immediate move for action, he knew what Donovan meant to me, and his lack of hesitation to help me save my mate—a creature that had been his sworn enemy since the dawn of time—only further proved his loyalty to me.

"I love that you're willing to help me get to him even though the two of you are likely to hate each other, but you can't come with me. Wait for me at the clearing instead," I said, referring to one of the safe places Leviah and I had hidden before bringing him to the Oasis the first time.

"The hell I can't," he shot back. "Dinah even said I should be there with you from the start."

I shook my head and forced my voice to steady. "He's in a battle, he'll be in a blood-lust. If you show up, the only thing he'll see is an Archangel. He'll attack before he asks questions."

Leviah stared at me for a long moment, jaw tight. "So, you're asking me to watch you walk into whatever this is *alone?*"

"I'm not asking you to like it, Lev. I'm asking you to trust me. I don't want to risk you getting hurt."

Lev stared at me with those intense eyes of his, an inner war waging within him. I knew this was hard for him to accept. Leviah was a warrior, sitting by while others took the risks was not the norm for him, and since being exiled from Heaven, I was the person he considered most important in his life. Letting me go off without him as backup was not something he'd easily accept.

And he didn't.

"No," he answered, jaw tight. "I won't go near the Demon King, but I will stick by you and protect you. If he tries to attack me, I'll shimmer out and let you handle him and come back when you have had a chance to explain. I'm not letting you go into a battle without me."

"We don't even know if it will be a battle," I said weakly, knowing it was a lie.

"The vision Dinah showed you was clearly a battle, Trin. If you feel him in danger now, then that's what is happening and I will not let you go alone. So, are we going to waste time, or are we going to go save your mate?"

My mate.

Hearing Leviah say it out loud somehow made all this more real in a way it hadn't been before, and for one moment, I actually felt scared. Not of Donovan, not of being bound to him. Acknowledging what he was out loud while making moves to bring him into my life suddenly made what we were to one another blindingly clear, the idea of accepting him and then losing him was almost too much.

Lev stepped forward and gripped my upper arms, silver-blue eyes filled with understanding. "I know you're scared, Trin, but it's time."

I forced myself to take a steadying breath and nodded, letting the decision settle on me. Anticipation fluttered in my belly, and I gave Lev a nervous smile. "Okay, let's do this. But promise me you'll keep your distance from him, at least until I've had a chance to introduce you."

Lev's smile was small and he nodded. "Of course."

He reached down for his blade and we did a quick check of our weapons before Lev held out a hand for me. Thanks to Dinah's vision, I knew where Donovan would be when he needed me. I took Lev's hand and drew in a deep breath, preparing for whatever awaited us on the other side.

We shimmered in a hum and a rush of cold light, and the world dropped out from under me

—and slammed back into focus amid a living nightmare.

We had dropped right into the battlefield, charred earth stretched in every direction. While I'd been able to *feel* where to find Donovan, I had no idea what country or part of the world we were in, but there didn't seem to be any form of civilization nearby, and that was enough for now. The air reeked of sulfur and copper, thick with the taste of blood. And in the center of it all…

Donovan.

He was a dark but formidable figure in the chaos, every movement precise, deadly. Ten against one, and still he carved through them with the same controlled brutality I'd seen in Dinah's vision. His sword moved like an extension of his will— sweeping arcs that split Demon's in half, brutal thrusts that impaled others.

But these weren't the mindless Demons I often dealt with. They were faster, more coordinated. They moved with power and intelligence—countering and anticipating moves made against them. They were here to *end* him.

And they were getting damn close.

Leviah swung into action beside me. He was everywhere, slashing, stabbing, removing the danger to me as I tried to decide what I should do first. Should I run straight to Donovan and help him? Or should I stay here and simply lessen the threat of numbers that would soon overwhelm him?

Donovan was hurt, I could see it in the smallest of tells: the subtle hitch in his step, the brief tremor in his grip, the unnatural pallor beneath the blood streaking his face. The Angel blades they used were the ones embedded with poison, and it was eating him alive.

Seeing them with these blades made me furious all over again, because it only proved that the Angels were working with these creatures, betraying everything they were meant to stand for.

Panic swelled up my throat as I watched Donovan fight. I needed to get to him, but to do so, I'd have to cut through a wall of steel and teeth. And I'd have to kill to do it.

I'd killed Demons before, of course, but it hurt. My inner guards were pulled high to dull the pain already running rampant over the battlefield, and I put aside my inclination to heal and forced myself into the mindset of fighting.

And then I saw him stagger.

It was small, almost nothing, but I saw it. My heart lurched— and that was when I saw the Demon behind him raise its blade high... just like in the vision.

"*No!*" The warning ripped from me before I could stop it.

Donovan's head snapped toward me, dark blue eyes locked with mine across the chaos. Recognition flared—then something deeper, heavier. Sorrow. I saw the words shaping in his mouth I'd seen in the vision.

"I'm sorry, moya lyubov'."

I didn't let him say them.

Power burst from me in an arc, a sphere of white fire skimming just over Donovan's shoulder, slamming into the Demon behind him. It went down screaming, the stench of scorched flesh curling in the air. Before the shock could fade from his face, I launched another blast into the chest of one trying to flank him. It was enough. Donovan pivoted, his sword catching the next attacker mid-swing, and I was moving into the fray, into the storm of steel and blood.

I wasn't sure what had happened here, how this small war started, but I didn't care. Despite the lower number of Rogue Demons I'd seen lately, there had to be at least twenty of them still fighting, trying to overwhelm their King.

The first Demon came at me with a jagged spear, but I ducked low, slashing upward to slice through the sinew of its arm. I ignored the instant recoil in my gut as it roared, black blood spraying as I smashed a vial of corrosive poison against its chest. The stuff hissed, eating through his armor-like skin, and the Demon collapsed, convulsing with ear-piercing screams. Revulsion tried to pull me under, but I fought back, determined not to pay it any attention. There was no time to breathe, much less regret the need for such violence. Another lunged, the impact driving me back several steps. I twisted, but not fast enough, and pain flared hot as its blade grazed my ribs.

I swallowed the hiss of pain and countered another strike. Already the battlefield was a sea of agony pressing against my mind, every gash and broken bone of others screamed in a chorus I had to block it out so it wouldn't drown me.

And the whole time, despite the danger to myself, the corner of my mind was locked on Donovan.

"Are you okay? Do you need me?" Lev's voice in my head was a mere brush, and I could tell he was being careful so as not to distract me.

"I will be when Donovan is safe," I returned as I drove my sword through a Demon's chest before blasting another in the face with raw power.

The fight blurred into instinct. Block. Strike. Blast. Move. My arms ached, my legs burned, and every nerve felt pulled tight and raw. I'd fought Rogues and Angels alike before, but never this many at once, and never for such a long period of time.

Somewhere, Donovan took a heavy hit. We weren't even bonded yet, and still I felt it—a hot, crushing spike of pain in my chest that wasn't mine. My head jerked toward him in time to see him stagger, then surge forward with a vicious snarl, splitting his attacker clean in two.

The poison was still working through him, slowing him down, but his face never betrayed it. To anyone else, he was still the unstoppable Demon King.

Just as I thought we had a handle on this, that we could come out on top, a wave of power washed over the field of dead bodies and I shivered. I knew what that kind of power meant, and unfortunately for us, it was *not* good. I blasted another Rogue in time to see an Archangel appear several yards behind Donovan.

Donovan split a Rogue Demon in two and turned to see the Archangel. I was too far away to hear their words, but the wave of raw fury flowing from Donovan told me this was someone known to him.

The Archangel looked superior, smug, and Donovan brandished his sword, ready for the fight.

"Leviah?"

"I see him," Lev responded with a harsh grunt. *"Uriel."*

I licked my lips, throwing another wave of power at a Demon staggering his way over to me.

"Why do I get the sense that these two have a history?" I asked, casting a glance at my friend to see him rip his sword from a Demon, kicking him down a hill at the same time. His eyes met mine, hard and unforgiving.

"Because they do. The two have a feud going back hundreds of years. Donovan has been hunting him while Uriel hides behind the gates of Heaven."

I wanted to know why, what had happened, but now was not the time to get answers.

"I have to help him," I said, carefully making my way closer.

"Don't!" Leviah's warning was sharp enough to draw me up short. *"You risk distracting Donovan. I will go. Trust me, he will not be his best if you are anywhere near Uriel—it'll be to his detriment."*

I frowned. What the hell did that mean?

Before I could say anything else, Leviah's wings unfurled with a shrug of his massive shoulders and he was across the battlefield in seconds. Uriel caught sight of him, and the look of disgust on his face left me no doubt as to what he thought of my friend.

Before either Uriel or Donovan could do anything, Leviah flew right into Uriel with a tackle before shimmering, taking them both out of the battle.

"No," I breathed, my lungs burning with fear. I gasped, dread for my friend stabbed sharp and painful.

What the hell did he just do? He was exiled from Heaven, as much an enemy now as the Kings themselves were.

They would kill him. Did Uriel shimmer them out? Or had it been Leviah?

"Lev—" I started to reach out when I was suddenly gripped from

behind, sharp claws digging into either side of my waist. I cried out and immediately reached back, power in my hands. The moment I touched the Demon's face I let it loose, blasting the Rogue several feet back. My side burned and throbbed, but I had no time to see how bad the damage was.

The battle had started again. Donovan fought while I struggled to keep the enemy in my line of sight, blasting them away when I could and forced to use my sword when they got too close. Little by little, the tide shifted. The roars of the enemy grew fewer, their lines thinner. But my body was shaking from the effort of keeping my sword raised, and my magic was running low. The burn that seared and bubbled up my arm hurt most, but I had to force away the pain and focus on the fight.

Thankfully, no Demons were standing near me, and Donovan seemed to have a handle on the last two he was facing off.

"Leviah, where are you? Tell me you're okay," I called, needing an answer.

There was nothing for a moment and my panic began to rise.

"I am here, Trin."

I leaned down to grab my sword still impaled in the chest of a Rogue before turning in a circle, my body exhausted and emotions strained.

And then there he was. Leviah started toward me from the bottom of a small hill, sword in hand, face streaked with blood and grime. Relief flooded through me at the sight of my friend and my eyes stung with burning tears.

"That was reckless, stupid, and I am so mad at you right now I don't even have the words!"

Silver eyes flashed at me, but I couldn't tell whether he was angry or amused at my outburst, and I didn't care. I just cared that he was alive.

I turned to make sure Donovan was okay and watched his gaze lock on Leviah's approaching form with a terrifying rage. He was moving before understanding sank through my foggy brain, and my reaction a second too slow.

"Donovan, *don't!*"

His sword was already in motion, whistling toward Leviah as my friend turned, blade raised to block the inevitable strike he had to know was coming. Unprepared, his block was weak and Donovan's strike knocked Lev's blade out of his hand.

"Stop!" I tried again, running toward the two. I don't know if my cry was too quiet for them to hear or if they were too focused on the fight at hand, but Donovan was raising his blade again, and Lev was defenseless.

I wasn't going to make it.

Summoning my magic, I threw it toward my mate, desperate to protect both males from pain or death. Donovan's sword flew out of his hand and both he and Lev stumbled back from one another from the force of my power.

Silence fell, and I staggered, gasping, my chest tight, the taste of copper thick in my mouth.

Donovan jerked his attention to me, eyes wide with surprise, confusion written across his features.

"He's—he's my friend," I managed to say, breathless, chest heaving.

Donovan's body was a map of wounds and blood and his breathing was heavy, deliberate, like every inhale took effort. But his eyes...

His eyes locked on me, burning as if I was the only thing that existed in the world. With one look, every fear, every reckless step, every act of violence I'd just committed to reach him felt justified.

The battlefield was still ringing in my ears, the lingering echoes of metal on metal and the hiss of dying hellfire.

But it was Donovan's eyes that drew me like a magnet through the carnage and wreckage around us.

I hadn't even had a chance to properly catch my breath when he started toward me, purpose in every stride.

His eyes locked on me like there was no one else in existence, and for a heartbeat, my instinct screamed to run. Years of habit, of sprinting ahead and leaving him nothing but traps and taunts, all of it was forced to come to a jarring halt because I was done with that.

I was *finally* done running, and anticipation to know what it was like to be in his arms grew quickly.

Donovan didn't slow, he didn't speak. His stormy eyes were on me, locked so he'd see the tiniest hint of any intention I had to run. I knew what was coming. I knew it, but still it was beyond anything I could have properly prepared for.

Instead of speaking, he reached for me, one arm hard around my waist, the other cupping my jaw—and then his mouth was on mine with a longing and passion matched only by my own emotions.

And all I could think was… *finally*.

We didn't need words; we didn't need to explain anything to one another. This was a moment that had been put off for years, and it was finally here. His lips were hard and demanding, not asking but taking. I didn't give a single damn—he could take all he wanted, everything I had was for him. Giving in after waiting so long was like being caught in a storm and we were the lightning rod. Years of chasing and running, every near-miss, every note, every glance that had lingered a beat too long—it all crashed into us at once.

I kissed him back because I *needed* to, because I'd dreamed of this.

He was okay, he was safe, he was here.

The feel of his soft lips against mine was everything I'd ever dreamed. He kissed like he fought—hot and passionate, all in and with purpose and need. I was lost to it, drowning, and I'd never been happier to sink beneath the waves.

When we broke apart, I didn't step back and neither did he. His forehead rested against mine, our breaths tangled and ragged.

"You kept running," he murmured.

"I had to," I replied, my voice raspy.

"Not anymore." It was a declaration, an order. "You're mine now."

My heart twisted—not from fear of him, but because I couldn't tell him what made me lethal to him and everyone he loved. I wanted to say yes. Gods, I wanted to let him bind our souls, to stop pretending I didn't feel the way I did.

But if I let him, I'd doom him.

And his brothers.

My sister.

And the world.

I forced a smile—something wry and familiar, a shield between us. "Careful, Demon King. I might take you seriously. And love between a Demon King and a Witch can be hazardous to your health."

He looked at me like regret was the furthest thing from his mind. "You're worth any risk."

My chest ached with the need to tell him. I *should* tell him. But if I did, he'd throw himself at the problem like it was just another battle... and it would get him killed. This was something I had to figure out for myself.

I couldn't lose him now.

So, I kissed him again instead, deep enough to distract him, if only for a little while.

CHAPTER NINE

DONOVAN

Mine.

The word detonated in my head the instant my gaze found her, a raw, possessive truth that seared through my chest and roared in my blood and felt branded on my palm. For a moment, I couldn't move—hell, I couldn't breathe. She was *here*. After years of chasing shadows, Trinity stood within reach.

Her long black hair was pulled back, but a few rebellious strands clung to her cheek, damp with sweat. A faint streak of dirt marred the smooth line of her jaw, and she looked battle-worn and unbreakable all at once.

Fuck, she was beautiful.

My body ached, poison burning through me, injuries shouting to be acknowledged, but the sight of her standing there after all this time was enough to dull it all, if only for a short time.

The space between us felt fragile, like if I took one wrong step or let my gaze shift, she'd disappear on me again.

The Archangel's presence still burned in my periphery, and every instinct told me to kill him, to rid of the threat he posed to my mate.

"He's my friend."

Trinity's words echoed in my head, and I despised them. I knew she had the help of an Angel, that she'd stayed close to one these last few years, but damn it, did it have to be a fucking *Archangel*? The desire to end his life here and now was held back by her words and her words alone.

"He's my friend."

Fuck. I couldn't exactly take the fluffy fucker's head and still expect her to stay still long enough for me to bind her to me and be happy about it. I ground my teeth through the need to kill the Angel. Trinity was a powerful Witch, and she had sharp instincts. If she'd been friends with this Angel this long, then I had to believe he was an anomaly like Hariel and that he was actually on her side.

So why then had he protected Uriel?

Even thinking the assholes name filled my vision with a murderous haze, and I struggled to hold onto my control.

Trinity staggered, those impossibly blue eyes locking on mine. Everything I'd been holding in—months of frustration, years of longing—it all hit me in a wave so strong it nearly doubled me over.

She wore dusty, form-fitted jeans that hugged every line of her body, a belt slung low around her hips holding small vials, intricate devices, and blades that flashed in the muted light. Her torn green shirt offered sinful glimpses of pale skin, teasing and taunting without even trying. I had memorized her form, but reality was sharper, more vivid.

I recalled the moment she arrived and her magic cut through the air, ripping past my head to annihilate the Rogue Demon that had been poised to take my life. I hadn't even registered the bastard in my blind spot. One moment I was knee-deep in gore, the next, the world was lit with her power.

If she hadn't come, I would be dead.

The realization hit slow, like a cold knife slipping between my ribs. Trinity had saved me, she had stepped into danger for me and evened what would have been impossible odds.

For me.

Everything else—the remnants of battle, my injuries, they all fell away. The second I saw her fighting, my world narrowed to her and her alone.

And she didn't run.

I was moving before I knew I'd decided to, leaving the Archangel behind and crossing the battlefield in long, hungry strides. My body ached and protested, but I paid it no heed, not when she was so close, not when she wasn't running or hiding. When I reached her, I didn't give her the chance to disappear. My arms enveloped her, eyes glued to hers so she could in no way misinterpret my intentions. Pausing for a second, I lowered my head and crushed my mouth to hers in a kiss that was years overdue, every ounce of pent-up desire, rage and longing pouring into it.

She tasted like fire and defiance, like something older than magic, something carved into my very bones by fate herself. The satisfaction of finally touching her was intoxicating, but it came tangled with a hunger so sharp it bordered on pain. I wanted her like I wanted nothing else, and to finally hold her in my arms was a feeling I couldn't even describe.

When the kiss broke, I kept my hands on her like she might slip away if I didn't hold her there. Experience had taught me it was a very real possibility, and I wasn't taking any chances this time.

"You kept running," I said, my voice rough, raw.

"I had to," she answered softly, though steel edged her words.

"Not anymore. You're mine."

Her magic hummed against my skin, fading from the fight but alive where we touched, like it knew as well as I did that this was where she belonged. The urge to bind her, to seal our souls together so she could never leave again, struck me with such force I almost acted on it. My palm itched and burned, a reminder that I had the power to end the chase here for good. But then she smiled—slow, almost wicked. "Careful, Demon King. This kind of attraction between a Demon King and a Witch can be hazardous to your health."

"You're worth any risk," I told her, and meant every syllable. There were reservations in her eyes, and I knew it had nothing to do with kissing me and everything to do with whatever the hell she was hiding.

Her next kiss was fiercer, hungrier, but it wasn't surrender or acceptance of what I wanted. Not yet. There was something behind her eyes, something unspoken still holding her back. Whatever stood between us, I'd tear it down soon enough. I wasn't losing her again.

My soul burned for her—deep, relentless. She whimpered softly against my mouth, her fingers tangling in my hair, and the sound drove a low growl from my throat. She parted for me, and for a perfect, dizzying heartbeat, the rest of the world didn't exist. For this one moment, we were both exactly where we were meant to be.

She pulled back first, breathing shaky and hands trembling, and I had to force back a smug smile that I had something to do with that. The playful warning in her eyes told me I hadn't shoved aside the emotion well enough, and my lips twitched.

A million questions assailed me, and I tried to figure out which I should ask first. There was so much I needed to know, so much that didn't make sense, but I had no idea where to start.

Trinity must have sensed it because she gently pulled back and nodded at me. "We need to get out of here, then we can talk."

I kept my hand on her lower back, unable to let her go. I felt the Archangel approach and again, and it took far too much control not to lash out and kill the thing. It was bred into me—into all my brothers—that all Angels sucked, but Archangels were the worst. It wasn't just that they hated us and wanted us dead. It stemmed from every shitty thing they'd done or allowed to happen to our father and mother.

Every Archangel in existence had been around in the days when Lucifer had still been an Angel. He'd been cast down alone, with no one by his side. So, when we looked at these fuckers, it wasn't *just* for the shit they'd pulled since we'd existed, but for standing by and allowing their brother to be cast aside.

And now Trinity was friends with one of them.

"Donovan, this is Leviah, my friend. He is the one who got me out of Heaven," Trinity explained, pulling back to gesture at the nearing Angel.

Tearing my gaze from her had never felt more wrong, but I did it in order to take in the potential threat. Leviah was tall, broad, and built like a warrior. He wore his hair a little longer and shaggier than I knew most Angels to. He was still stupidly symmetric in that way all Angels were, no imperfections beyond the blood and grime that coated his face after battle. His eyes were an odd silver-blue, and they flashed in the light, unique and guarded.

He was about as comfortable with me as I was with him, it seemed.

Neither of us moved to get any closer or speak, and I jerked my chin in acknowledgement. He looked me over carefully before tipping his head once in return.

Trinity muttered something under her breath I couldn't catch, but judging from the frustration rolling off her, I had to assume it was an insult of some sort at the two of us.

"We need to get out of here and go somewhere safer. I was thinking the meadow?" Trinity said, her words directed at Leviah.

He nodded once and moved to her side. I stiffened, hating him so close, and I hated it more when Trinity took his hand. Grinding my teeth, I pulled her closer to me and tried to ignore the way another male was touching her.

Before I could explode from possessiveness, the world around us suddenly vanished.

I was used to the sensation whenever I shadowed, but this was different. We weren't falling, there was no wind or feeling of flying. We remained as we were, but as if my body was left behind and only my soul was being transported. Just as suddenly, it all stopped and the sensation of my body catching up and slamming into me was overwhelming.

I staggered away from Trinity and heaved, my stomach twisting and protesting the sudden shift.

"What the fuck?" I hissed, hating every moment of that.

"It's not comfortable, but I thought it would be like shadowing," Trinity said, her hand pressing gently to my shoulder. I felt a small flow of energy from her, and at once my head stopped spinning and my stomach settled.

"That's nothing like shadowing. That felt as far from natural as I can get."

"I gather shadowing would feel much the same to me," Leviah said evenly, but I could detect the small note of gloating in his voice as he watched me struggle.

Trinity, obviously catching the note too, shot him a look of reprimand, and I liked that she came to my defense.

"Fuck doing that again," I grumbled, pushing myself upright. Trinty's hand slid from my back, but I caught it before she could get too far. I didn't want to ever stop touching her. Her warm eyes met mine, and her breath caught. I didn't bother to hide my thoughts from her, my wants and needs, and it made every craving inside me burn hotter when I could see those needs reflected in her.

Leviah sighed heavily and Trinity blinked, the moment breaking. Again, I refrained from lashing out at the Angel as he stepped closer. Their gazes locked in some unspoken communication and every territorial part of me slashed at me, refusing to acknowledge their bond. I knew they weren't speaking telepathically, that was impossible, but this was somehow worse because it meant their unspoken words were born of years of depending on one another.

"I'm going to go scouting; I'll be a while. Make sure to ward the surroundings?"

Trinity nodded and the smile she gave him was one of affection and appreciation. "Want me to heal you first?"

Leviah shook his head. "I'll go see Dinah and come back. Just... be careful." he said, and his eyes held Trinity's with some unspoken meaning.

She nodded, a flash of frustration rippling across her face. Without looking at me again, Leviah marched away before shimmering, his form disappearing from sight. Trinity gently tugged her hand from mine and I reluctantly let her go, watching as she whispered words under her breath and provided a ward around the clearing, protecting us from being found.

I watched her work, tasted her magic in the air, and simply soaked it in. Watching her was an addiction in itself, and I found myself appreciating every one of her assets.

"Are you done?" she asked.

I blinked, having not realized she was watching me check her out.

"I haven't even started," I replied honestly.

She smiled bashfully, and fuck it all if that look didn't do something to me. Hunger stirred, grew, and I threw caution to the wind.

"Fuck it," I hissed, stalking toward her.

Wide blue eyes settled on me, but she didn't back away as I pulled her into my arms again and kissed her like my life depended on it. I poured everything I felt into that kiss, every want, every frustration, every ounce of love I had for her. I wanted her to know what she did to me, how much I needed her, wanted her.

"Donovan," she whispered against my lips, fingers stroking my cheeks.

"No more, Trinity. You're done running. This is it. I can't do this anymore."

"I know. I'm here. No more running."

Her words burned me like nothing else could and I jerked back to look at her, sure I'd just imagined the words. Her eyes were glassy with unshed tears, and she stroked my cheeks, her smile shaky. She meant it, I could see that, but she was scared.

Every protective instinct I had roared to life, demanding to know the threat so I could vanquish it, but it wasn't as simple as that.

"You mean it?" I asked, running my hands from her wrists to her shoulders and down her side.

She nodded. "I'm done running, Donovan."

Joy lit up bright and hot inside me and I kissed her again, slower, gentler, but still as intense. Her lips were soft and pliant, and the taste of her was a drug I'd never experienced before, and I knew there would never be anything like it out there for me again.

I was holding my future in my arms, my reason for being, my purpose to exist in this world, and knowing it was overwhelming and so right. Nothing felt better than this.

"Wait," Trinity whispered, pulling back again. I sighed and she smiled softly at my displeasure.

"I'm not running, but you can't take me to Hell with you, and you can't bring Tomika to me yet."

I frowned. "Why?"

She hesitated. "It's just… it's not safe yet, okay? I don't want to risk her getting hurt."

I shook my head and pulled back. "Enough of this, Trinity. I need you to start telling me the truth, and I need it to be now. I need answers. You can't expect me to follow requests like that without an explanation."

She looked torn as she paced away from me.

"Trinity."

"I know," she said sharply, turning to face me, her eyes troubled. "I want to tell you, and you're right, you deserve to know. It's not fair of me to keep asking you to wait, to hold off and to not do things without answers, but…"

"You said no more running; I mean that both emotionally *and* physically. Whatever you're afraid of, I can protect you if you'll let me. Whatever the danger is, we can handle it together or with the help of my brothers—"

"No," she cut in again, tone sharp and final.

I raised an eyebrow. She swore and ran a hand over her head, her eyes grazing over me again, burning with confusion.

"I…"

"Explain it," I snapped, taking three long strides toward her. She tipped her head back to look at me, eyes bright and filled with a multitude of emotions. I could feel her when she was this close, the emotions tangled and snarled as she tried to detangle one from the other.

"What is going on, Trinity? I want to know, now. No more running, no more hiding facts. Damn it, where the hell have you been? What happened to you when you were in Heaven? Why were you there? Why did they keep you? What did they want?" I shot each question out as it popped into my head and continued before she could interrupt.

"For fuck's sake, you have no idea the hell I was in while you were gone and I couldn't find you. I was already lying to Mika about the fact that we've been in communication over the years because you didn't want her to know but wouldn't explain why. Then I had to lie to her again when you disappeared and tell her you had just gotten better at hiding. I knew who had you, but I had no way to get to you or stop whatever the fuck they were doing to you. Then you got out and you tell me it was an Angel who saved you. Now you're telling me not to bring your sister here, that is not safe, but you won't tell me why. I deserve a goddamn answer."

"You do—"

"Then tell me! You stopped reaching out to me months ago, and it's been driving me insane. The last time we spoke in Hariel's house, you told me we couldn't be together because you were trying to keep me safe. Safe from what? Explain that to me."

"I will, just—"

"No more excuses—"

"Will you shut up for a minute?" she snapped.

I glared down at her as she glared right back up at me, both of us flushed with frustration.

"I will answer your questions, but can you please let me heal you first? You don't realize it, but I can feel every one of your injuries and they are *painful*. You aren't doing too well; you've turned gray and the poison from the Angel Blades is doing too much damage. Let me heal you, and we'll talk."

I huffed out a frustrated breath at her, but now that she'd mentioned it, sensation from every one of my injuries came screaming back and I staggered, feeling suddenly weak. I'd been running on adrenaline, denial, and fury, all emotions masking the physical condition of my body.

Forcing myself to take a deep breath, I slowly moved to a tree and leaned against the thick trunk, hating that she was right. If she hadn't pointed it out, I likely would have ignored my injuries and argued until I fell over dead.

Trinity knelt in front of me, and I noticed the blood on her shirt and shook my head when she reached for me. "No. You're hurt, heal yourself first."

Her lips twitched, but her eyes stayed fierce. "I'm already healing. Witch, remember? Besides, my wounds are superficial, yours are life-threatening.

I caught her wrist and turned her arm, needing proof. I was relieved to see that the burn I'd seen earlier was knitting closed even now.

"It's my duty to look after you, to see to your health before mine," I said, my voice low, the marking urge rising like a tide at the thought of claiming her forever.

She scoffed. "I *am* healing. And if you're going to keep protecting me, then I need you alive. You won't be unless we treat the poison because it's killing you. So, let me do what I do best."

Her defiance made something hot and unsteady twist in me. She was right, of course. Without her, I was already half gone.

Forcing back a sigh, I let her work, but I couldn't stop watching her.

She was here.

The thought kept circling. Every time my eyes traced the line of her face, the pull to mark her sharpened.

I caught a flash of silver on her fingers and reached for it. She paused and slowly pulled the ring from her middle finger and stuffed it in her jeans pocket.

"What was that?" I asked, raising an eyebrow at the strange action.

She smiled tensely. "It's a telepathy ring. I made one for me and Leviah so when we're rescuing Witches or in a fight, we can still talk."

Something in my gut soured at the idea of another man talking to her in such an intimate way, especially since I hadn't yet been given that same benefit.

"And you're taking it off now because?"

Her gaze rose to meet mine beneath thick lashes. "Because I'm with you."

Well... *fuck*. Alright, that went a long way to soothing any sour thoughts I had about her telepathy ring with another male. I studied her for a moment, trying not to show my glee at her decision. Her lips twitched, feeling my enjoyment before she glanced away.

"Where have you been, Trinity? Why were you running all this time? Why did you come for me now?"

Her blade flashed, slicing away what was left of my shirt. She didn't look directly at me, but her gaze lingered for a fraction longer than necessary on parts of me that were *not* injured, and despite everything, I got some satisfaction from that.

"I've been saving vulnerable Witches, and I have been running because they need me. It's not safe for us to be together yet, but I came for you because... of course I would."

Her words landed like a blow. Heat seared my side at the same moment, her healing setting nerve endings alight. I forced the sound in my throat down.

"Why isn't it safe?" I asked, scanning for potential threats.

She smiled faintly. "Relax, I wouldn't still be here if the danger followed us here."

"So, it's gone for good?"

Her expression shuttered. "No. It's not gone," she murmured, moving to another wound. The poison burned, then dissipated, her power sweeping through me like cool water dousing fire. She worked at on sections at a time, ridding the poison before healing the injured part.

"What's going on?" My voice hardened. "Tell me, and maybe we can face it together. I won't let you go again, Trinity. I can't. Where you go, I go. Your enemies and fears are mine now." I caught her hands, felt the tremor in them, and the instinct to mark her surged so hard I almost did it without thought. Her blue eyes lifted, cutting me deep, and she brushed her fingers along the scruff of my cheek, soft and assuring.

"I promise, Donovan. I'm not leaving you again."

She'd said it more than once already, but hearing it again still flooded me with relief. I'd felt the pull to bind her from the start, but now it was near-feral, a need that sat in my bones, urging me to act.

But then she drew back, lips twitching before her gaze lowered.

"But I can't tell you exactly what the danger is. Not yet."

My growl was automatic. "Why not?"

"Because you'll try to fix it and get yourself killed."

"You don't know that."

"I do," she said firmly. "A Seer told me. The danger isn't something you can solve by killing a powerful Angel. It's more complicated than that."

"Then explain it," I pressed, leaning forward. She pushed me back, her palms hot against my bare chest. The need to bind her jolted through me at the contact, sharp enough to make my breath stutter.

"Do you remember a year ago when you found me? You could

have taken me then, marked me. I wasn't prepared, and I was weak. You could have ended the chase there and taken me, but you didn't."

I remembered, and my decision had weighed on me ever since. For a long time, I regretted my inaction because she never let me that close again. She'd seemed fragile, vulnerable, and marking her when she was in such a state felt wrong, like I was taking advantage of her situation. It would have been wrong, and something in my core told me not to, not yet. I'd lain awake many nights wondering if I made the right choice.

"Yes, I remember," I finally said.

She hesitated. "I need you to find that strength again."

"You said you were done running," I snapped, my hand closing around her arm, pulling her to me. She landed on my lap, warm and solid, her scent wrapping around me.

"I am," she soothed, panic flickering in her gaze. "I'm not leaving you—so long as you give me time."

My heart hammered, the thought of letting her go again making my vision narrow. "Time?"

She nodded. "Time. I can't tell you why yet, but I need you to trust me. I want to be bound to you completely... but not now. Not until it's safe."

Her words were chains pulling back on my every instinct. Every second we remained unbound was a second she could be taken. "Explain more."

Her expression was tortured. "I can't."

"Trinity, you have no idea what you're asking of me. This need—it's burning through me."

"I know," she said, but she didn't. So, I showed her. I let the raw, pounding urgency roll from me to her, the way my soul reached for hers like it would tear itself apart if it couldn't latch on.

Her breath caught, eyes widening as it hit her.

"Every second will feel like this," I said, my voice low, rough. "I won't have peace until it's done, and you want me to live like this without a reason?"

Her expression wavered, torn between desperation and resolve. "Donovan... please. You can't..."

I pressed my forehead to hers, dragging in air, fighting the instinct that clawed at me to bind her *now*. She had my heart already, and she could have my body. I wanted her to have my soul.

But did she have my trust?

CHAPTER TEN

TRINITY

"You have to tell me something," Donovan whispered, his voice raw with restraint. "Give me a reason, you owe me that."

I inwardly groaned and tried to think of how to explain things in a way that would satisfy him and not give away everything. It wasn't just him I was protecting here. Swallowing hard, I stared at the pulse in his neck and let out a long breath.

"Heaven has a Seer—a couple of them, actually—but one in particular is strong. She saw that I was destined to be bound to the sixth King of Hell," I began, unable to stop my hands from trailing down the hot planes of his tattooed chest. Something stirred in my lower abdomen, a fluttering that forced me to take a shaky breath.

A low rumble in his chest drew my eyes to his face, and Donovan's burning blue eyes were watching me. "Don't get distracted."

I smiled softly and considered playing some more, because I knew he was just as likely to get distracted as I was.

But I needed to tell him because how else would I convince him not to mark me? I knew at the end of the day I had no say over that, no power. We were here together now, and if he wanted to, he could mark me whether I wanted him to or not.

"The Seer told me about the prophecy," I continued. Donovan stiffened beneath me. "You eluded to it enough, but I wasn't sure. You know everything, then?"

I nodded. "Yeah, the Seer recited the whole thing. Apparently, she was able to see that I was the next Witch to be marked, and so the Angels took me."

Donovan frowned, and I reached up to smooth the crease between his brows. "What did they think you could do for them? What was the point in taking you?"

I sighed. "At first, they wanted to make sure I didn't know anything. They wanted to know more about you, our future, and your brothers. I knew nothing, obviously, only what I'd gleaned from our months of cat and mouse. And honestly, that wasn't much, so I didn't tell them anything. Despite their best efforts..."

Donovan's fingers tightened on my hips, and I pushed on before he could ask more questions.

"It's not worth rehashing, honestly. Their questioning sucked, and after a while, I don't think they were even expecting answers, they just wanted to break me and see if they could use me in another way. I lost track of time; it's kind of hard to tell day from night up there. I later found out it was about three months, and that's when Leviah came for me."

"After three months?" Donovan bit out, tension radiating from every line of his body.

I shot him a hard glance. "He has his reasons, and I accept them." He ground his teeth, that muscle in his jaw flexing, his dark eyes furious.

Sighing, I continued. "At first, I didn't trust him, and he didn't ask me to. But he said he needed to get me out of there, and that he couldn't watch this continue."

"How big of him," Donovan muttered.

"Do you want me to tell you what happened or not?" I snapped. He glared but jerked his head once in answer, the gesture reminding me somewhat of a petulant child.

"Anyway," I said, sighing. "He got me out. It took some time to get out of Heaven, and we almost didn't. He was forced to kill many of his kind to manage it. Hariel—the ex-Angel you know—was our last barrier. Leviah asked him to step aside, to not make him kill him, to not force his hand in this. Hariel allowed us to pass, and because of that we got away. I was too weak when we got out, I could barely stand much less conjure any magic, so Lev kept us moving every few hours. Without him, I wouldn't have made it, Donovan. I owe him my life."

He didn't say anything, he just watched me, but I could feel the barrage of insults he wanted to throw at Leviah for leaving me in the cell that long.

"When I finally had some magic, I cloaked us both so we wouldn't have to move so often, but for months we had to keep moving to make sure we stayed safe. It took me a long while to have enough strength to stand on my own, and when I could, Leviah offered to leave me alone. Afterall, the Angels were after him more than me at this point, he felt that he drew unnecessary danger, but we protected each other."

"And that's when you reached out to me," Donovan added, thinking back to that night. I'd needed to see him, it had been desperate, honestly. I'd sent him a note using a magical raven I conjured. It could find him anywhere. I had to see him for myself, hear his voice, let him know that I was okay. I'll never forget the look on his face the first time he laid eyes on me.

"So, for the past two years since you got out of Heaven, you've been on the run?"

I shook my head. "No, I have a base in the Oasis."

He raised an eyebrow in question and I smiled. "The Oasis is the place Tabitha and her family created; a safe place for Witches where we don't have to fear being hunted."

At the mention of Tabitha's name, I felt the wrench in Donovan's chest and surprise flicker across his face.

I smiled gently. "I see you remember her."

He swallowed hard, and his emotions became tangled, heavy, complicated. "Yes."

I nodded slowly. "I read about you, you know?"

He frowned and I shrugged. "We have extensive records in the Oasis, and due to your personal relationship with Tabitha and your hand in helping the Wardwell family all those years ago, your name pops up a few times in the history books."

Donovan's heart thudded hard beneath my fingers, and he looked torn.

"You loved her, didn't you?"

A breath rushed out of him, and I felt his awkwardness beneath the layers of remorse, pain, and longing.

"It's okay," I said with a small smile. "You've been alive for thousands of years. If there wasn't at least one woman who meant more to you than all the rest, I might have begun to wonder at your ability to love at all."

Donovan shook his head and reached up to tuck my hair behind my ear, his eyes dark and considering.

"Tabitha was... a chapter of my life that still hurts. I can tell you all about her one day, but for now, I feel like there are more pressing details we need to discuss."

I frowned and considered urging him to talk, but the heaviness of his heart urged me not to push the subject tonight.

Closing my eyes, I pressed my hands to the heated skin of his chest and pushed more healing magic into him. The poison was pretty much gone, and I helped his naturally quick-healing body to heal faster, ensuring there were no infections and not a single drop of poison left.

"Trinity?"

I opened my eyes and my breath caught at the sheer beauty of his velvety blue eyes. Gods, the man was sinfully sexy. His eyes sparkled and a smirk curled his lips, causing my lower abdomen to clench and flutter.

"You explained some of what happened, but nothing yet to tell me *why* you want me to hold off marking you. You said you understand the prophecy, do you know everything it entails?"

I nodded slowly. "Four bonds: heart, mind, body, soul."

"Does that scare you? Is that why?"

I shook my head and smiled. "It should. I remember when I first saw you and the instant connection I felt to you was... not normal. You spoke and I just... I felt like I'd heard your voice a long time ago, or in a dream I had once. It was so weird, but I could swear I knew you. My heart..."

He watched me, eyes warm. "What?"

I hesitated in answering. "You spoke that first time, and I felt I knew you. My heart just... broke. It was like you had been dead. My heart knew you were dead, and when I heard you again, I wanted to cry and throw myself at you. I had never seen you before in my life and I knew you were powerful and dark, and I wanted to go *to you*?" I stared at him, incredulous. "*That* scared me."

He didn't say anything else as he waited for me to answer.

"I couldn't get you out of my head. I dreamed of you. I heard your voice when I slept. I couldn't shake the feeling that I knew you on a level that was impossible. When I found out about the prophecy, I felt... relieved. It finally answered the insane feelings I'd been having, the need to see you, the sensation that I knew you on some deeper level. Learning about it helped."

He nodded, thumbs brushing back and forth over the exposed skin of my waist. "So... why the hesitation?"

I groaned and considered what to say. If I told him, he'd want to fix it. He'd get himself killed or hurt. I had a solution for the problem, but it wasn't one I was willing to consider yet, so I was looking for another.

"Trinity," Donovan prompted. "I need an answer here. I don't want to do anything against your will, but I need to know why it's so important we wait. Everything in me is screaming to mark you, to keep you safe. If I can't, then you have to tell me why."

I studied him, thinking. "And if you don't agree once I explain?"

He didn't answer right away. "Then I guess we talk until one of us agrees."

"You need to tell him, Trinity."

I gasped at the new voice and before I could really comprehend what happened, Donovan stood with me in his arms and placed me behind him. His whole body radiated power and protectiveness, and a little part of me swooned at his immediate response to protect me.

Peeking around the Demon King, I frowned at Leviah and Dinah at the edge of the clearing.

"Dinah?" I asked, stepping around Donovan. He took my hand, holding me half behind him as if he didn't know what to think of the situation.

"You need to tell him why, because you are right, he cannot complete this binding."

"Who are you?" Donovan demanded, and the power in his voice made me shiver. I'd never heard him use that tone before, and it reminded me how easily he could overpower me if he wanted to, and how often he hid that fact.

"This is Dinah," I introduced. "She's a Seer and lives in the Oasis."

My gaze flicked to Leviah, who shrugged.

"She found me the moment I returned and wanted me to bring

her to you. She said it was urgent. And…"

"And what?" I asked, frowning when he looked less than pleased. Dinah stepped aside and someone else stepped forward someone I was *not* happy to see.

"What the hell is she doing here?" I snapped, stomping forward, power surging in my hands. Donovan pulled me back to him as the second Seer stood staring at me as if I were the scum beneath her shoe.

"Who the fuck is she?" Donovan demanded, his voice thicker now.

I forced myself to breathe, knowing my anger was only fueling Donovan's. "She is one of Heaven's Seers. She was there when they tortured me, and she did *nothing* to stop them. What the hell are you doing here? Dinah, why did you bring her?"

Seers were Witches with the added ability of foresight. She had betrayed her own kind to align herself with the Angels. She was a traitor.

Dinah held up a hand, her entire being serene when all I wanted to do was scream at her.

"Irena and I do not see eye to eye on many things, and while I do not agree with the path she has chosen for herself, she reached out to me because there is one thing we both agree on."

"That is?" Donovan asked through clenched teeth.

"That you cannot mark Trinity."

"Why? Damn it, someone tell me!" Donovan snarled.

"Trinity is cursed," Irena blurted, her voice soft but carrying. I glared at her, not wanting Donovan to know yet, but it appeared the choice was taken from me.

"Cursed?" Donovan asked, confused.

"Yes. In Heaven, the idea was to trap you and the Kings using her. The curse she possesses will act as a virus, infecting you the moment you mark her and then your brothers, should any of them reach out to you telepathically. The moment they do that, they'll be infected and then so will their mates. It will weaken the Kings, the structure of Hell, your command of your armies and eventually, Hell will fall."

I glared at her, wishing I could hurt her somehow. She might not have been the one to curse me, but she hadn't stopped it, either.

"Trinity?" Donovan asked, looking at me.

"She's telling the truth," I admitted, turning back to him. "This is why I put it off. It's not just you I risk, but your brothers, my sister, their mates. Hell will fall into chaos, Angels will fight, humans and Witches will suffer, and with you and your brothers out of the picture, Heaven will win."

He didn't say anything for a moment, and I knew it would take him some time to digest it all. I knew Demons weren't the big bad most people believed them to be. They served a purpose, and since barely anyone knew what really happened in the afterlife, they didn't know that going to Heaven wasn't the reward they were told it was. I wondered if people knew, if they would try so hard to be good.

Donovan pulled back and strode away, running a hand over his hair, swearing under his breath.

"Donovan?"

"Is this real?" he asked, pained eyes meeting mine. "Can we trust her?" He gestured to Dinah.

"She saved me as a child. She got me to safety," I told him.

He shook his head. "That doesn't answer my question. Can she be *trusted*?"

I understood his worry, that Dinah had been playing the long game, but I trusted her. I felt her genuine need to protect and save people. "Yes," I answered simply.

Pain lanced through his eyes before he turned away and let out a long breath. We all waited in silence as he processed this, and my heart ached for him. Donovan turned back to the Seers, blue eyes blazing. "I can't keep this up much longer. Even now, knowing what is at stake, I struggle to hold back."

Dinah nodded slowly. "I see that, but you must remain strong."

"Why do you care?" I asked, jerking my head at Irena.

She looked at me with distain, like she'd prefer not to talk to me ever again. "Because as much as I despise you and them, as much as I'd prefer to see you both dead, Heaven acted too rashly. This is not what the world needs. It will be its end."

"But Heaven would be in power, isn't that what you want?" Leviah asked.

"Isn't it what *you* wanted?" the Seer shot back at Lev.

"Once," he answered. "In the beginning... but I see that's wrong now."

I turned back to Donovan and his tortured eyes met mine.

"I don't know if I can do this," Donovan admitted. "I am trying, but I have been fighting this urge for too long already. And now you want me to wait until... when? How do we break this curse?"

"We can't," I interrupted quickly.

"Kill the Witch who cast the curse," the other Seer said at the same time.

Donovan looked at me and then her, then back again, an eyebrow raised in question. "Which is it?"

"Both," the Seer answered with a smirk. "To end the curse she must die, but you'll never get close enough to her to do it."

I bit my tongue to stop myself saying something I'd regret and waited as Donovan took in this news.

"There are many different futures right now, Demon King," Dinah began, pale eyes on my mate.

Donovan watched the elder Witch with focus.

"All of them stem back to your decision going forward regarding this bond. Only two I see will work out well for the fate of the world."

"And those would be?" Leviah asked when no one else did.

The Seer sighed. "Either you kill the Witch who gave the curse, then you will be free to mark your mate. Or you do as your brother did, and make it impossible to be near her without dying."

I frowned. "What?"

Donovan glowered. "Harkyn. He met Dimitria when she was too young, but he was struggling not to take her anyway. Despite what others think, we have rules, morals. He gave her his Word, a promise not to go near her ever again or attempt to make contact with her. It was a blood bond, and if he broke his word, he'd die."

I sucked in a sharp breath and shook my head. "You can't do that."

"What other choice is there?" he shot back. "I can make different terms to my Word than Harkyn did, but it would keep the world safe if I stayed away."

I was already shaking my head. "But I just got you. I finally got you." I whirled to look at Dinah. "You said it was time, you said I needed to go to him."

She nodded. "I did, but certain facts have since altered the future I saw and are making it impossible."

"There has to be another way," I whispered.

"There is," he admitted slowly, reluctantly. "I can hold on for as long as possible and see where the road takes us."

"But…" I hesitated, stepping closer. "I can already feel how much you struggle. Will you be able to hold out?"

He raised a hand to stroke my cheek, eyes warming, softening as he looked at me. "I'll do whatever I have to if it means I don't have to leave you again."

My heart warmed at his words and I leaned into his touch, wishing we didn't have to keep this distance.

"Well, I don't need to be here for this," Irena said with a disgusted looked.

"Why did you come? Why did you both come tonight?" I asked, turning to look at them.

The Seers looked at one another and then back to me. "Because we knew if you saw Seers from both sides of the war telling you the same thing, you would take it seriously. This is not a minor issue; it's world-ending," Dinah explained.

"I'm out of here," Irena grunted. "If anyone asks, we never talked, I was never here."

I rolled my eyes and watched her stalk away from us, muttering under her breath about Demon Kings and the Witches who fucked them. Well, she was wrong there. I hadn't yet had that delicious honor.

"So, what do we do now?" Donovan asked.

I looked back at Dinah, my question clear and she shook her head. "He can't come to the Oasis yet. I have to put it by the other elders and the other residents. No Demon, much less a Demon King, has entered the Oasis before."

"But this is Donovan," I reminded. "He was a friend to the original creators."

Dinah nodded. "I know, and I understand. I believe that knowledge will go a long way to easing a lot of their worries, as would knowing his connection to you."

I swallowed hard, having known somewhere deep down that it would get out one day. Sighing, I nodded. "Tell them. Donovan is not their enemy, nor is he a threat."

Dinah nodded and smiled gently before turning to Leviah. "I would like to go home now, and I believe these two need some time alone. You can come back for them tomorrow."

Leviah raised an eyebrow at being ordered around and dismissed so easily before the corner of his lips crooked up. "Very well, I'll escort you home," he said, casting a questioning look at me.

"I'll be okay," I assured.

With one more nod, Leviah took Dinah's hand and the two shimmered out, leaving Donovan and I alone once more.

CHAPTER ELEVEN

DONOVAN

The silence that followed their departure was heavy and filled with unspoken words.

So, this was what Trinity been hiding from me all this time.

She'd known this was our fate and had been carrying this burden alone.

"Why didn't you tell me?" I asked quietly.

Trinity turned and began pacing, her face angled away so I couldn't read her expression. It didn't matter; I could feel her in a way I didn't feel others. We hadn't completed a single bond, but I knew her better than she'd like, despite the limited time we'd spent in each others company.

"I was afraid you'd act rashly. That you'd try to set a trap for the Witch and get yourself killed or captured. I was protecting you."

"It's not your job to protect me," I snapped.

"No?" she demanded, turning to face me, eyes furious. "Then what is my job? To be the little woman you have to look after, to protect from the world? Am I to sit by and watch you shield me over and over from all the things that could hurt me but I am not afforded the same right?"

I opened my mouth to tell her that's exactly what it meant, but I stopped myself just in time. She was *my* mate, damn it. *I* was meant to be protecting her.

She raised an eyebrow at me, waiting, daring me to agree.

"You should have told me," I said instead. "We should have been working on this together. At the very least, I would have known what was going on, and maybe your sister and the other women could have helped put together a plan, something that would work. They're incredibly fucking powerful."

She was already shaking her head. "And risk Mika? Risk any of them? I know what Heaven, the Angels, and the Witches who align themselves with them are capable of. The thought of any of them getting their hands on those women, on my sister…"

Her voice broke off into nothing, horror etched into her features, and I was reminded once again that she'd been held captive in Heaven for months and tortured. The reminder tasted like ash in my mouth.

More questions assailed me, things that had been tugging at me for years but for which I had no answers. I paced back and forth, my eyes on her as I considered what to ask first. There was too much unknown, too much she had to answer for. She turned away from me and began gathering wood from nearby to make a fire. The sun was sinking lower and she'd likely start to get cold soon. The moment the wood was piled and Trinity was out of the way, I threw a small fireball at it. The fire latched and lit up the area around us.

She gave me a look—part amusement, part reprimand.

I stopped pacing and just watched her for a moment, my gaze falling to that birthmark on her arm, the same one Mika had. It was in the shape of a star, and a sign of the Wardwell bloodline. "Why didn't you reach out to Mika before now?"

The words were out of my mouth before I could stop them, sharp enough to cut through the silence. She blinked, lifting her eyes to me where I stood a few feet away, the fire between us. I wasn't looking at the flames though—I was watching her face. The fire caught in her eyes, and when she spoke, her voice carried a mix of defense and resignation.

"I was protecting her."

I frowned, the confusion pulling at me. That didn't make sense. "How? I don't understand. You obviously love her, you miss her, and you have no idea how worried she's been about you all these years. Tell me... what happened after you left your foster home and got out on your own? How did you survive and learn? Why didn't you go to your sister?"

I wasn't accusing her, but I needed to know. The questions had been building too long, and this wasn't just idle curiosity—it mattered.

She took a slow breath, eyes fixed on the fire as the embers shifted and spat. "I did find her," she said quietly.

I tilted my head, frowning. "When?"

"When I was still a teenager. Dinah—the Seer—found me earlier and knew what I was, who my family was. She gave me a safe place to live and helped me get a handle on my magic. I had been with her for a few months when I tracked Mika down. I'd finally found my footing at the Oasis, started learning what I was, what my bloodline meant. I wanted to find Mika, to tell her everything."

Her words dug into me, heavy with something she wasn't saying yet.

"She was walking out of a coffee shop," Trinity continued, swallowing against the memory. "She was smiling at an older gentleman as she held the door open for him. Her hair was longer, and she had this... glow, like she was happy. Safe."

I stayed silent, watching her, already sensing the turn this story was about to take.

"I wanted to run to her," she admitted, her voice tight. "I wanted to throw my arms around her, to let her know that I was alive and we could finally be free together. But Dinah stopped me.

She… saw something. She told me Mika and I have a destiny—one she couldn't fully see because it was shrouded, tangled in too many threads to follow. But there was one thing she was certain about: our destinies would not unfold properly until Mika 'saved a life that could end her own.'"

My brow furrowed harder. "That doesn't make sense."

"It didn't to me either," she admitted. "All I knew was that Dinah believed if I interfered before that happened, it could have repercussions that would ripple through centuries and cost thousands of lives, probably more."

I let out a low breath, eyes flickering to the fire. "So, you just… walked away?"

Her throat worked, her voice wavering. "Not without trying to protect her first. I knew Angels were hunting Witches, and Demons wouldn't hesitate to take her if she started using magic without knowing how to shield herself. She didn't even know what she was. So, I begged Dinah to help me put a spell on her—something to hide her magic, at least a little."

My eyes narrowed, not in anger, but as pieces started slotting together. Realization stirred. "That's why…" I trailed off, shaking my head as I remembered. "When Cole explained how he first met Mika, he couldn't figure out what she was initially, not until she started healing him. He could sense something, but it didn't add up."

Trinity nodded. "The spell wasn't perfect. I didn't have anything of hers—no personal item, no strand of hair—so it was weaker than it could've been, but it was enough. She could use her magic in small ways without setting off alarms in every dark corner of the world. She could heal, hunt Demons… and stay hidden."

I leaned back slightly, studying her. "All this time…"

Her gaze met mine. "All this time, I've stayed away because

Dinah told me of the chain reaction that would start after Mika saved a particular life. This chain of events had apparently already been delayed for too long already. If it didn't happen in our lifetime, she feared it never would. And if I'd gone to Mika before then... it might have never happened at all."

For a moment, neither of us spoke. The forest seemed to lean in around us, listening, and the only sound was that of the fire popping before she spoke again. "I pictured what it would be like to walk up to her door and have her remember me. I almost broke a hundred times. But every time I got close, I remembered Dinah's warning. One selfish choice could destroy everything, and now... now I see what Dinah was talking about. If Mika never met Cole, the prophecy never would have been activated and none of what's happening would have happened."

I stared at her for a long moment, holding back the need to go to her, to wrap her up and shelter her, to mark her and ensure she'd never be alone or lonely again. I closed my fingers over my aching palm, knowing I'd make her mine one day, but it wouldn't be yet.

Her shimmering eyes met mine across the flames, and every desire I had for her came roaring back to the surface.

"Come here, *moya lyubov'*," I ordered softly.

Even across the distance, I saw her breath catch and eyes bleed hot and needy. I knew the affect I had on her body, because it was the same one that raged through mine.

"Donovan... we can't," she whispered. "Any bond... it could trigger the curse."

"Come. Here," I ordered again, my tone stern, a command. She hesitated a moment before slowly standing and moving closer, her eyes on me. I was mesmerized by the way she moved, by the sway of her hips and the way her lips were slightly parted.

When she was close enough, I placed a hand on her lower back and pulled her flush against me, my body practically weeping in relief at holding her close again. Sliding my hands down her lower back and over the curve of her ass made her breath stutter and I wanted to groan in response. Fuck, what I wouldn't give to bury myself inside her right now and have her make that sound again.

Gripping her firmly, I lifted her. Her eyes widened in surprise, and I grinned up at her as she hurriedly wrapped her legs around my hips and her arms around my neck. Moving to where we'd been sitting before we were interrupted by the others, I slowly sat down with her in my lap, settling against the trunk of the tree.

"Donovan," she whispered in warning, but I kept her tight against me.

"I need to feel you, mate. We have been apart too long, and this eases the ache somewhat."

After a small hesitation, she slowly dragged her hands from the back of my neck down my still bare chest, and her eyes followed them, drinking in every second.

When she pulled her eyes back to mine and our gazes locked, I felt the weight of everything we'd been through, and everything we'd fought to hold back between us. It was overwhelming, intoxicating, and if I didn't move away soon, it would take over both of us.

Slowly, almost hesitantly, she reached up and slid her fingers into my hair and I desperately needed her to do more. Her breath hitched, lips parting slightly just before she leaned in, brushing her mouth against mine. The kiss started soft— tentative, searching—but it didn't stay that way. It caught fire almost instantly, urgency sparking in my chest until it burned through both of us.

My hands found her waist without thought, fingers digging in as I pulled her closer, needing her nearer, needing all of her. She shifted so there was no space left—only heat, only the maddening press of her body against mine. The sheer force of wanting her like this threatened to undo me.

Fuck.

There was only one other time we'd been as close as this, and that had been in a psychic realm. I relived that dream often, over and over, drunk on the way she made me feel, even in a dream-like realm.

Her hands traced the line of my ribs, leaving streaks of fire in their wake, and I felt the storm building between us, wild and unstoppable. The sound that escaped her—small, desperate— shot through me like lightning. I smiled against her lips, drunk on the taste of her, and tightened my hold, pulling her flush against me. My body rocked beneath hers, unable to keep still, and the way she gasped nearly drove me out of my mind.

Her breath mingled with mine, warm and uneven as we kissed again. Slower this time, deliberate. She melted into me, and I swore I'd never felt anything more perfect in my life.

My hands roamed across her body—possessiveness in every movement, claiming her in the only way I could. One slid up her back, pressing her tighter against my chest, the other framed her jaw, my fingertips trailing lightly across her smooth skin. Even that smallest touch scorched me, branded me in a way that I knew I'd never erase. The way she looked at me with those wide eyes filled with heat and longing was nearly my undoing.

Slowly, I gripped her hips, guiding her, rocking her against me. The sight of her reaction—her breath stuttering, eyes widening as she looked down at me—was enough to nearly break my control. I knew we should stop, that there was danger in how far this was going, but I didn't want to. The way she clung to my shoulders and rocked her hips told me she couldn't let go either. Her fingers tangled in my hair, tugging gently, and the kiss shifted again—fiercer, urgent, desperate. The world narrowed to her and only her. The scrape of my beard against her cheek, the hammer of her heart against my chest, the intoxicating heat of her pressed so tight against me I never wanted to be without it.

"Donovan," she whispered shakily, a warning in her tone as if she was going to tell me to stop.

"Trinity," I pleaded, panted, my voice sounding raw even to my own ears. "Don't stop, *moya lyubov'*," I whispered against her lips. "Let me see you fall apart for me. Give me this."

Her eyes rolled back at my words, and I almost cried out in triumph. My skin was burning, every nerve ending overwhelmed and demanding to be touched. I kissed my way from her lips to the line of her jaw, down the sensitive slope of her neck and she shivered, a gasp tearing from her lips.

I murmured to her in Russian, words I knew she didn't understand. I encouraged her, told her how beautiful she was, how much I wanted to bury myself inside her so we could finally be one. There was no one else in existence in this moment, just her and the way she felt in my arms.

"I…" Words seemed to fail her as I urged her on with my hands on her hips, rocking myself against her to increase the pressure, watching the pleasure build on her face.

"I need to see you, Trinity. I need to hear you," I grunted, my voice thick and attention narrowed solely on her.

"Fuck," I groaned as her nails dug into my chest, sending a jolt of pleasure straight to my straining cock. "Come for me, *moya lyubov'*. You're almost there, I can feel it."

I took my own pleasure from her, in raptures of the way she

moved, the way she sounded, the way she felt against me as she chased her climax. Seeing her like this was a memory that would be forever etched into my mind.

As if my words had acted like a summons, Trinity shouted my name once more before her spine bowed and she threw her head back, crying out as pleasure overwhelmed her. I gritted my teeth against the need to follow her over, determined this be just about her. And fucking hell, was it worth it.

Her hips continued to move against me even as I felt the tension begin to drain from her body. She slowly straightened in my arms, her blue eyes heavy and drowsy with pleasure, and that look fucking did it for me. I speared my fingers into her thick hair and dragged her mouth to mine, drinking from her lips like she was the most exquisite wine and I was addicted.

She gave as good as she got, her body soft and pliant against mine, her lips moving, parting to allow me entry.

Over and over I kissed her, swallowing her moans, whispering dark needs against her lips so that her body continued to spasm and shudder. When she pulled back a few minutes later, her cheeks and chest were flushed, and I felt the quick thud of her heart against my chest.

And her eyes... they burned as they locked onto my face, and I desperately reminded myself not to mark her, not to brand her as mine. There was too much at stake, but *fuck!*

The hard bulge trapped between us hadn't softened any, and she seemed to have noticed too. Without looking away from me, she dragged her hand down my chest to the top button of my jeans, yanking it open.

"Trinity..." I warned, desperate for more while hoping she'd stop. Before I knew it, she had tugged me out of my jeans and ran her soft hand up and down my hard length.

"Fuck," I bit out, clenching my teeth.

No one had touched me in a *very* long time. My breath left in a low hiss as she began to stroke me, and the pleasure on her face as she gave it back to me was nearly the end of me. Almost better than her touch was the look on her face as she did it. To have someone so happy simply to give me pleasure was an aphrodisiac in itself.

Fuck, was I going to be able to hold to my promise? Or would I fuck up and mark her now?

"I... Trinity... I do not know if that is a good idea," I groaned, but I made no move to stop her as my lids grew heavy. Shit... this was too good.

"You need this," she whispered jerkily.

I groaned because she was right, and her lips tilted in a victorious smile. She continued to touch me, to stroke me, her thumb sliding over the flared head of my cock, using the pearly beads that collected on top to lubricate my shaft.

Fuck, fuck, fuck.

She was watching me, listening, paying attention to what set me off and she was figuring me out quickly.

"Fuck, just like that," I grunted as she twisted her wrist as she dragged her hand up.

I'd wanted this for so long, waited for what felt like forever, it was so surreal to be with her here and now, feeling her hands on me and seeing how much pleasure she got out of touching me. She leaned forward to nip at my neck, and I groaned as her hot tongue swept out to ease the small sting. Gnashing my teeth, I tangled my hand in her hair and yanked her head back to crash my mouth to hers as her strokes picked up in speed.

Oh, fuck...

My cock throbbed and pulsed, thickening in her hands as my hips jerked helplessly beneath her and I got closer to that edge. "Let me feel you come, Donovan. Give it to me," she whispered, pulling back just enough to meet my gaze.

I was done.

Groaning loudly, pleasure overwhelmed me and I came hard and fast, my seed spilling out over her hand, my cock jerking as I came in a crashing force. Blindly, I reached for her again, bringing her mouth to mine as she continued to stroke me. Little by little, our kisses became less urgent, and she pulled away, our breaths mingling as we came down from the high we'd experienced.

I could still feel her—the way her hands stroked and squeezed, and need for her began to build again. Something primal stirred within me, an ancient fire that flared to life beneath the surface. I knew what was coming—the raw, fierce urge I had to fight back when everything inside me demanded I take her now and make her mine.

I smothered the need, sliding my hands down her sensitive ribs and she shivered at my touch. The war within me raged on, and I concentrated on the smooth expanse of her ribs, counting each one as a way to distract myself from what I wanted to do.

My fingers moved then to tighten on her waist, and I closed my eyes as I drew in a long, ragged breath.

"Trinity," I breathed, voice low and rough, laced with a hunger and demand. She started to move away from me and I tightened my hold as my eyes flew open, keeping her still.

"*Don't.*"

One word, a command, and she froze. She had to have seen the tension in me, felt the inner conflict that raged within. After several long heartbeats, I let out a pent-up breath and loosened my hold on her but she didn't move. Trinity pressed her palm against my chest, feeling the rapid thud of my heart, and I felt her influence as she tried to steady me.

Gently, I pulled her close once more, pressing my forehead against hers. "I don't know how long I can hold back."

"I know," she said softly.

Slowly, we separated just enough to breathe, hearts still pounding in sync, hands lingering as neither of us was ready to let go.

Without looking at me, Trinity waved her hands in the space between us and I smiled when I found myself clean and redressed, including a shirt. She, too, looked clean and redressed, and I inwardly sighed at knowing I wouldn't get to watch her change clothes.

"Stop looking at me like that," Trinity whispered, trying to sound strong.

I smirked, loving the affect I felt it have on her body. "You first."

Swallowing a smile, she slid off my lap, but I didn't let her get far. I pulled her against me, tucking her to my side with an arm wrapped around her. She didn't fight me, and I smiled as I pressed a kiss to the top of her head, marveling at the fact that she was here in my arms. She was *here*.

There was no more running, no more excuses. We were together now, and I'd do whatever I had to ensure it stayed this way. Now we just needed to get rid of her curse so we could be as we were truly meant to be.

CHAPTER TWELVE

TRINITY

"Why doesn't the idea of being bound to a King of Hell bother you?"

Neither of us had moved for a long time, simply sitting together in silence. It was nice to just sit and *be* with him, a rare moment of contentment. I frowned and pulled away to look up at him. Blue eyes stared back, shadowed and curious.

"I told you."

He shook his head. "No, you explained that you felt relieved to finally understand why we had such a connection, but not how you were so okay with your fate. I am a Demon King, you are a Witch. I know you know things aren't as black and white as good and evil. There are shades of gray everywhere... but I am far from a saint and being bound to me will have limitations on your freedom. Do you understand that?"

Honestly, I hadn't thought too much about how my freedom would be impacted.

"Limited how?"

He thought for a moment. "Your sister, before being bound to Cole, was an independent journalist who wrote predominantly about crime. She would hunt down Demons who worked in league with humans and would help the police find someone to blame for brutal deaths. Since being with Cole, she still helps others, she and Cole still hunt Demons who hunt humans, but she's never left alone to do it. While Cole doesn't keep her chained up, there's not a lot she can do without running it by him."

I raised an eyebrow. "So, she's a prisoner?"

"No," he answered and sighed. "Being mated to us has a lot of draw backs. Rogues and Angels alike will hunt you more than ever because they see you as our weak point, and so you'll never be allowed topside without someone with you as added protection. It's a harsh reality and I can understand how it would upset you, but it's the only way to ensure your safety and that of the rest of us. You know firsthand now how the Angels having even one of us—mates included—can put all of us at risk."

I nodded slowly, understanding what he was saying. It sucked, and I wanted to rebel against it, but he was right. I hadn't considered this side of being his mate, of the restrictions that would be placed on me. They weren't unfair, either, which made it all the harder to hate.

"What else should I know?" I asked.

A smile tugged at his lips, as if something I said was funny.

"What?"

Blue eyes sparkled at me and he shook his head and scratched at the scruff on his face. "Nothing. It's just… I swear I could hear all of my new sisters scream one word into my head just then." Donovan's chuckle was warm and full of affection, and a smile tugged at me.

"Oh? What was it?"

He sighed, his gaze considering me as it swept over my face. "Babies."

My eyes went wide and he chuckled.

"You mean with anyone or…"

He shook his head. "No. We can have children only with our mates. I found this out after Mika and Cole got together, and seeing their faces go pale was hilarious. They'd been going at it like rabbits for weeks, and I can guarantee neither ever thought about using protection."

I laughed a little, but it was weak, shock still rocking me. My heart fluttered again as he reached out to brush my hair back, gaze soft.

"I think you would make a beautiful mother, but there's no rush for us."

I swallowed hard. "So, none of you have children?"

Donovan hesitated before answering. "Not quite. Cali—Adrik's mate—is pregnant with a baby girl, and we're all excited to meet her."

Something warm flooded my chest at the idea of him playing with his little niece. "And you... want children?"

"Yes." The word came out quick, sharp, almost forceful. I blinked at him in surprise, but he looked just as shocked at the forcefulness of his reply. A burning flash of emotion ripped across his chest as he spoke, the complete certainty that this was what he wanted. I pressed my hand to his chest, hoping to ease some of the fierce emotion that seemed to have rocked him as much as me.

"Yes, I want children," Donovan said again, calmer this time, placing a hand over mine on his chest. "Ours will be a Demon-Witch hybrid, and we have no idea what we're in for with that. Before finding out we could have kids, it had never been a consideration for me. But since discovering it's possible... yes. With you, I want kids. Whenever you're ready."

I nodded slowly, taking time to consider what that would look like.

"Do you want kids?" he asked, and try as he might, he'd been unable to keep the spark of hope from his voice.

I smiled gently, my heart melting at the idea of him with *our* baby in his arms. Gods, why was that such a freaking sexy picture?

"Yes. Like you, I hadn't really given it much thought. Life hasn't given me space or time to think about it. But I think I want children, especially if it's with you. Just... maybe not right away."

His smile was content, happy, and something else that raced across his face before I could fully understand it.

"So... anything else I should know?" I asked, brushing my thumb back and forth over his chest.

He considered this my question and I appreciated the genuine thought.

"From what I have seen of my brothers with their mates, and what I have come to understand after finding you those years ago, I will be your greatest protector and also your biggest pain in the ass."

I snorted and grinned, and he smiled back before continuing.

"Your happiness is of the upmost importance to me. What hurts you, hurts me, and seeing you miserable will not be something I can abide. But before even that comes your safety. I expect you to fight me, push back if you think I am being unreasonable, but I also expect you to reflect and take a moment to see things from my point of view. Sometimes it will be necessary for you to sit out of a fight or forego something you love if it ensures you are safe."

Okay, I liked the sound of that a little less. "I guess we'll cross that bridge when we get to it."

He nodded. "That we will."

"Is that all?" I asked, not sure how much of this was supposed to make me hate the idea of being with him.

He shook his head, lips twitching. "Of all the women mated to a

King of Hell, you seem to care the least about this. Almost all of them have tried to find a way out of the binding—I'm half convinced your sister still is just for the sake of having the option... and to torture Cole."

My heart warmed at that, because if she was, I would help her in that endeavor, even though I had no doubt that we would all choose the life and the Demon Kings we had now. It would just be nice to have the choice.

"I get that. But I just... I don't want to run. Everything about you feels like you're meant to be mine. The first time we met I felt that powerful connection, the feeling of knowing you in my soul before I even knew your name. Why would I run from that?"

His puzzled gaze searched mine before he leaned forward to press a kiss to my forehead. My stomach fluttered at the gentle gesture, and all at once I felt like a giddy schoolgirl.

"You were always meant to be mine," he whispered, stroking my cheek.

"I feel like I was once... in another life. Is that crazy?"

Something about his expression shifted—closed off just a fraction.

My brow furrowed. "What do you know?"

He raised an eyebrow. "What do *I* know?"

"Yes. I can see it in you. You know something. Tell me," I pressed, the demand threading through my voice.

Donovan swallowed hard, and I felt a familiar heaviness weigh on him, regret, heartbreak, and sorrow getting heavier and heavier with each passing second. He dropped his head and ran a hand through his hair. I knew this would be hard for him, but I needed all the information I could get my hands on. With how heavy his heart was, I needed to understand.

"Tabitha."

I sucked in a sharp breath at her name. Velvet blue eyes rose to meet mine and something in me settled, a piece of the puzzle that had always been the slightest bit out of alignment.

"You mean…?"

He shrugged. "I don't have confirmation, we'd have to speak to another Witch to know for sure… but yes. The minute I saw you, it felt like… her. A little different, but still her. If I had to guess, I'd say that your soul is hers, her life is threaded somewhere within you and I felt it. A part of you recognized me because of our connection back then. It's why it was so visceral."

I swallowed hard, my head spinning. I knew I was my own ancestor; it's how it always went. Each Witch, when they died, was reincarnated within the same family. Our souls were marked by our bloodline. The only way to truly destroy a Witch bloodline was to kill them all and not allow for their souls to pass back over. So, yes, I knew I was my own ancestor in a way… but I hadn't ever considered that I might share a soul with Tabitha.

Nothing had been confirmed yet, but having an Elder tell me what I already felt was a minor point at this stage.

The moment Donovan said it, I felt the truth resonate within me.

"Will you tell me about her? About… how you two became so close?"

Donovan hesitated before nodding, a small, bittersweet smile touching his lips. "It feels strange talking to you about her when you share the same soul, especially when… when we…" He sighed, and I knew instantly what he meant.

"You loved her."

He hesitated, swallowed hard, and nodded, eyes locking on mine. "I did. But I never told her."

I frowned. "Why?"

He raised a disbelieving eyebrow as if I should know the answer to my question. "Because I'm a Demon King, and she was a powerful Witch."

"So?" I asked. "It's exactly the same thing now."

He shook his head. "Not quite. The Witch hunts had only just started, so your kind were plentiful. She lived on a farm with more than a dozen Wardwell Witches who looked to her for guidance. We were... friends, of a sort."

I smiled softly. "If it was so taboo, I wonder how that happened?"

His eyes grew distant, as if seeing it all again, and I watched the emotions flow across his face. "Slowly, over time. She healed me several times over the years, and one time I saved her in the middle of a fight. We just... clicked. And after some time, we started spending time together outside of healing and warzones. And after her husband died, she leaned on me a little and I was happy to be there for her. She was feisty, opinionated, stubborn, funny, and clever."

I grinned. "Glad to see the apple doesn't fall far from the tree."

He smiled and reached out to take my hand, but I felt the heavy weight of his past settled again on his chest.

"What happened, Donovan? What caused you so much grief?"

He was silent for several long moments and I waited patiently, hoping he'd trust me with this.

"She had been saying for a while that she felt something bad was coming, something that scared her. She said she and her family had a plan in place, but she worried it wouldn't be enough. She asked me to help train the younger Witches—give them someone to practice against, someone who could teach them the enemy mindset."

"And you helped?" I asked, surprised.

He shrugged. "Tabitha could have asked me for the moon, and I would have found a way to get it for her. I think I told her as much once."

My smile was soft, tinged with sadness. "You loved her a lot."

He nodded. "I did. I think some part of me recognized what she was to me, but back then we had no knowledge of the prophecy and letting myself fall in love with a mortal was just asking for pain. I know now that she loved me too, but we were both aware of what we were, where we stood. We each had responsibilities and…" He trailed off, brows creasing.

"What?"

Donovan shook his head and sighed. "There's… for the last few years, I've had the strangest feeling that I've forgotten some of my past with Tabitha. Losing her was painful—worse than anything I've felt before—and it's as if… there's a block in my head. A wall I've put up to stop myself remembering certain facts so I can keep functioning."

I frowned, worried. "What could be so bad you'd need to forget?"

He shook his head. "I don't know, because what I do remember is horrible, and I could barely function for years afterward. I don't know what could be worse than that."

I hesitated. "What happened?"

He closed his eyes and tipped his head back; grief etched in every line of his face. "I… I got them all killed."

I remembered reading something in the Wardwell histories about a fight that got many killed, but nothing that mentioned so many deaths in one battle.

"I promised her I'd protect her, protect her family, that I'd watch over her kin and keep them safe. But the Angels… there were so many, and it was me against them all. They got to her before I could, and she was hurt, weak. I tried to fight, but they had other Witches on their side who made things more difficult. They overpowered me and—" He swallowed hard.

"It's okay," I whispered, reaching out to take his hand.

He shook his head, flipping my hand over to link our fingers. "It's really not. He made me watch—Uriel."

Donovan spat the name, venom in every syllable. "The Angels pushed her family into their house, then dragged her in too. I couldn't stop them; I couldn't do anything. And then they... they set the whole thing on fire."

A cold shiver rippled down my spine at his words. I swear I heard distant screams and felt the fire's heat racing up my arms. Uriel. I remembered what Leviah had said on the battlefield earlier today, that Donovan and he had a feud that had gone on for centuries. This must be what started it.

"I heard them—all of them... the children. I tried, but I wasn't strong enough. She died, Trinity. She died with them, and I failed her. I broke my promise, and they all died."

His words hung heavily in the air and I could barely breathe beneath his guilt and agony. He wasn't healing from this wound. It was festering inside him, an infection in his blood and soul. Something about his story made no sense to me. Was this excluded from the Wardwell books because of its gruesome outcome? Were they not included because no one there had made it out and the rest was filled in by distant relatives? It was possible, but still, it didn't feel right.

I carefully shifted beside him, tilting his head up to meet my eyes. For the first time, his eyes looked their true age—worn and raw with grief. I pressed my forehead to his and closed my eyes, breathing through the pain to reach for his mind.

He resisted at first, a tremor of hesitation rippling through him, but slowly, reluctantly, he let me in. I dove swiftly into the stormy memories he'd spoken of, the jagged fragments of his past unraveling before me. It was chaos—pain tangled with regret, emotions twisted and warped like broken glass. A frown tugged at my lips, confusion blooming inside me. Something was wrong. His mind had been tampered with, altered beyond natural limits.

I slowed, taking in every detail, tracing the edges of the damage, and then I found it—something hidden, blocked, a crude erasure beneath the surface.

"What is it?" Donovan's voice was low, cautious, pulling me back to the moment, but I could feel the tension coiled in his body, the subtle pull of him leaning toward me, desperate for an explanation.

I didn't answer right away. My eyes stayed closed as I searched deeper, piecing together the evidence. Someone powerful had rewritten parts of his memory, obscuring the truth with a heavy hand. Years were missing, whole sections erased or roughly stitched back together, some fragments locked tight behind invisible walls.

"Trinity?" His voice softened, almost a whisper, his breath warm against my skin. The heat between us thickened, and I felt the raw temptation in his nearness, the urge to close the distance, to reach out and erase the space that kept us apart.

I pulled back, opening my eyes to meet his, confusion mirrored in his gaze, but also something fiercer—a yearning, restrained but unmistakable. "Someone has tampered with your memories of that time."

He froze, surprise rippling through him like a shockwave. All this time he'd thought it was his own mind trying to protect him by not letting him remember. "What do you mean?"

I explained everything I'd seen—the gaps, the distortions. His disbelief was immediate and fierce. "That's impossible. No one can get into my head, no one—not unless I allow them."

I shook my head gently, my voice steady but soft, as I tried to soothe the ache in both our chests. "You know I'm not wrong. You said yourself you feel like things have been changed or blocked. They have. Someone has altered what really happened."

"Can you... can you change them back? Find what's missing?"

His hope was fragile; the question laced with desperation.

I hesitated, the truth forcing me to choose my words carefully.

"I... I'm not confident enough to do it myself. But I might know someone who can, if you truly want to know."

He opened his mouth to answer, but then paused, the weight of the choice sitting between us. "I want to know."

I nodded, a small, reassuring smile softening my lips, though my heart thudded with the ache of what we couldn't yet have. "Then we'll fix it. We'll get to the bottom of it."

He leaned in, capturing my lips with a slow, lingering kiss that spoke of all the things we both longed for but couldn't have... not yet, anyway. I smiled against him, breath catching at how freely he touched me now, how the temptation in his every movement begged for more.

How could a simple touch or kiss from him affect me so quickly, so strongly?

"Tell me again why we can't do more than this?" he murmured against my mouth, voice husky with need.

"World-altering consequences, and not the good kind," I replied with a breathless laugh.

He sighed. "Right... that. And how certain are you that *any* bond we make could trigger it? Because with the way I'm feeling, I'm willing to risk making one or two."

I shook my head and pulled back, stroking the scruff of his chin, feeling a little overwhelmed that he was here and this close for me to touch and kiss.

"We should get some rest. We have a big day tomorrow," I said instead.

"Oh?"

"Yeah." I shifted back to rest against him. "I have a mission to save a young Witch who will find herself in some trouble with Rogue Demons. She's..." I frowned again at the feel of that vision.

"What?" Donovan asked, wrapping an arm around me to hold me closer.

"I almost get the same feeling with her that I got with you. That I know her somehow, somewhere. No matter what, I need to save her, but I just wonder what this feeling means."

Donovan was silent for a moment. "Then I guess tomorrow we save the girl, find one of your Witch Elders and get her to tell you what you don't know. And then we ask if they can recover my memories and answer some questions for us too."

"Yeah," I whispered, blinking slowly. "Like I said... big day." Donovan's lips pressed to the top of my head and I smiled again, for the first time in a long time feeling safe and content.

CHAPTER THIRTEEN

DONOVAN

She slept with one hand curled near her face, lashes dark against her cheeks. I lay beside her, close, but not touching. It had taken me over an hour to slowly slip away from her without waking her. I wanted her to sleep, but I needed to get up, to walk, to burn off some of this feeling.

I was one lucky sonofabitch to find her now, to finally hold her and protect her. She said she was done running from me, and I believed her, but the gnawing pain in my gut was constant now. Until she carried my mark, she was vulnerable—*I* was vulnerable. I needed to mark her to ensure if anything happened, she'd come back to me, that she wouldn't be lost to the other side.

I thought about Cole and Mika, and how distraught my brother had been when he lost her. I considered Adrik, and the pain he'd endured waiting for Calixta to come back to him. Then I remembered Tabitha, and the agony I'd been forced to live through after losing her and her whole family. The grief that drowned me in those early days wasn't something I could live through again.

Thinking of Cole made me heave a small sigh. He needed to know I'd found Trinity. Mika deserved to know, but I couldn't have either of them coming to me and finding her now. Trinity had sacrificed a lot to protect her sister and keep the rest of us safe. Of course Mika would want to come to us now, but like

Trinity said, it wasn't safe. Angels were getting more and more creative with how they hunted Witches and trapped their enemies. I considered Nera, the Witch on the beach who'd managed to fool me. If it hadn't been for Amazarak, I'd be a captive of Heaven right now. But still, my conscience would not let me rest while keeping this secret. And honestly, someone needed to know incase something happened to me.

"Brother," I began reaching out to connect. It took a few moments, but he finally responded.

"New link, who dis?"

I grinned at his smart-ass reply and shook my head, watching the sky above lighten and bleed to a soft gray and the sun slowly came up.

"I have to talk to you about something, but I'm invoking the brother cone of silence. For now, you cannot bring your mate in on this."

Again, there was a long pause, and I had the sense he was making his excuses to get away so we would have privacy. Sure, Mika could still invade his mind from wherever she was, but if he was heading to his circle of Hell, as I presumed he was, she would close herself off so as not to feel any punishments he dealt out. The morning was clean, clear, and crisp. A bird whistled somewhere off in the forest, and I turned again to watch Trinity as she slept. I'd never seen a more beautiful woman in my whole life.

"Talk, we're alone. I assume this has something to do with Trinity. Is she okay?"

At Cole's voice, I glanced back at the sky. *"She is safe. She is... here. With me."*

Silence rang for a moment before the feeling of relief and joy bled through. *"Good! About time! Why did I need to leave Mika out of this, she'll be thrilled."*

I sighed. *"Because you can't tell her... yet. There is a lot going on in*

Trinity's life, levels of deceit and understandings I was not expecting. I want Mika to know, but I do not want to risk anything happening to Trinity and then having to rip that hope away."

Cole's displeasure rang through loud and clear. *"What's there to do? She's there, mark her and ensure her soul is safe. If we cannot come to you because you are in danger, then bring her here. Mika has waited long enough. You can't know the worry that has weighed on her all these years."*

I grimaced. I did know, I'd felt it, but I had not been forced to live it as Cole had. *"I wish I could tell you everything, but it is best you don't know. What I can tell you is that she is safe, healthy, and she is no longer running from me. I am in a position to earn her full trust, and I will do whatever is necessary to earn it and keep it. I won't let her go again."*

Cole was silent for a long time, and I knew he was trying to sort out his thoughts and emotions.

"It's not safe for Mika to see her at all? Even once?"

I ran a hand through my hair, wishing I could give my sister that much. *"It's not that it's unsafe for one meeting. But can you honestly tell me that Mika will allow for a separation between them again after being reunited at last? She won't let any of us tell her to stay away, even if it's for her own good. This is her sister."*

Cole swore and I felt for my brother. *"What is the danger to her? Is it something we can take on together? Something we can help you with?"*

At once, appreciation for my brother washed over me. I knew some part of his offer was for Mika, but I also knew he wanted me to finally claim my mate and have what he and Mika had. He wanted for me to be whole.

Watching Trinity sleep, something tightened in my stomach. *"What we are facing is dangerous, and I'm not sure there's a way to fix it. I'd like to take the time to work on it myself a while before looping you all in. Until Trinity trusts me more, I won't risk any of your mates. You know where Mika goes, so will the rest."*

Again, Cole swore, but he knew I was right. The women had banded together and formed a tight-knit sisterhood. They were the mates of the Kings of Hell. No one would know their lives and struggles more intimately than each other. And when one hurt, they all hurt.

"So, you called just to tell me you have the one thing my mate wants most in the world but that I can't give it to her yet?" Cole asked, a note of annoyance in his tone.

I shook my head and sighed. *"I reached out because I didn't want to keep this secret. And, if whatever we're facing is as dangerous as it appears to be, I wanted someone to know some of what was going on in case things go bad."*

Cole's frustration was loud and understandable. I wished I were coming to him with better news, but at least he would know Trinity was found and safe. It was something, more than we had two days ago.

"Will you tell Mika yet?"

Cole didn't answer right away. *"I won't be able to keep it from her for long, but no, not yet. I'll give you as much time as I can, but I can't guarantee that once she knows you have her, she won't try to work some kind of spell to find you both and bring her sister home. She's worried, Cole. You see how bad it's getting out there.*

I clenched my jaw as my imagination ran rampant with the kind of abuse Trinity had to have suffered in Heaven to have made her as weak as she had been. Yeah, I knew all too well how bad it was out here.

"I appreciate you waiting for as long as possible, Cole. I didn't want to lie, and I wanted you to know... just in case. You know I'll do whatever is necessary to protect her, but I refuse to bring danger to you and your mates as well. I'm walking a fine line here, and I'm not sure yet what

lies ahead."

Cole's frustrations began to fade to be replaced with concern. *"You'll reach out if you need us? Just call out and we'll drop everything."*

A smile tugged at my lips. *"Yeah, I know. Thanks."*

We didn't speak again, and Cole disconnected from our conversation. I breathed slowly and deeply, eyes on the now pale blue sky as the sun finally made its way over the horizon. Trinity would probably be mad at me for spilling the beans, but I would rather one of them know, and if I told anyone but Cole, I'd get my ass kicked. And I'd deserve it. I trusted my brother that he'd wait for as long as possible, but keeping anything from a mate was damn near impossible. We had days at best before Mika started making demands if she didn't outright show up uninvited. I hoped she showed the good sense to think about Trinity's wishes in this scenario, but my hot-headed sister was not always known for thinking first.

I sensed someone nearby, and I was on my feet in an instant, ready to confront whoever it was. But the closer they got, the more I recognized who it was. I wasn't happy, but I couldn't kill him.

I turned back to look at Trinity to see her still sleeping peacefully. If she wanted me to trust Leviah, to have *her* back, then I needed to talk to the Archangel for a moment first. There were questions I needed answers to, and I felt I'd get a better explanation without her there to guard her friend. Steeling myself, I started toward where his lifeforce was coming from, and when I finally spotted him, he didn't look at all surprised to see me. Trinity had put up a ward last night to keep people from entering without her knowledge, but it didn't stop me from leaving undetected.

Leviah stopped several feet from the border of the boundary and I passed through it, watching the Archangel with narrowed eyes. "I figured you might want to talk," he greeted as I stepped closer.

"You figured right," I replied and came to a stop a short distance from him.

Neither of us spoke for a long moment, and I felt he was trying to get a read on me, just as I was trying to do with him. We had nothing in common, nothing but the Witch I loved and who he claimed to care for. For Trinity's sake, I wanted to believe him, but his kind had been my enemy for as long as I'd lived, I didn't know how to trust them. Hariel was an exception, but he was no longer an Angel, and even when he had been, he'd died to save Cali. He'd turned against his own kind because he knew what they were doing was wrong, and he'd put himself between her and his garrison. He'd earned our respect for what he'd done. Trinity claimed Leviah had done the same for her, but I was struggling to accept it.

"You can ask," he said suddenly, moving to sit on a collection of heavy rocks.

"Ask what?"

He shrugged. "Whatever it is that is most bothering you about my presence in Trin's life. Ask and I'll answer honestly. I know you'll be able to tell if I lie."

I raised an eyebrow. "I'm not a Witch, I don't have that ability." Leviah's lips twitched. "No, but you are an ancient Demon King. The best liars in the universe can't get by you, you have a strong sense for deceit. When it comes to your mate, I doubt you'll leave any room for doubt."

I frowned, wanting to hate his response. It was too... good. Too smooth. Then again, maybe he was being honest.

"Explain to me what happened in Heaven. Who took her, how,

why? How did she get out, and why did it take so long?"

I knew the questions were not simple. They'd happened two years ago, and the memories were likely ones he wanted to put behind him. He'd been by Trinity's side since then, and she'd obviously had no reason to doubt him in all that time.

Lev's voice was low and steady as he replied, the words feeling heavy.

"I wasn't in the party that took her, and I wasn't privy to how or why they took her to begin with. I wasn't exactly involved in what happened, but I knew about it," he admitted softly before he let out a slow breath and continued. "But I couldn't just stand by and let them continue hurting her."

"It took you three months," I reminded, trying to force myself to remain calm. "She was tortured for months, and you let it continue."

"I have my reasons," Lev replied sharply.

"Which are?" I ground out.

"If you cease interrupting, I'll get to them."

I wanted to snap at his attitude, but I let it pass. He had a story, and he'd tell it his way, and I'd find out one way or the other if I could take his head here and now.

"I heard the Seer tell Camhael and the other Angels the Prophecy of the Brothers' Nine. The Kings… you're crucial to balance. If the Angels succeed in their plan, if Hell falls, the balance shatters. The world spills into chaos, and the innocent will suffer. I won't be a part of that."

My jaw clenched, but I remained silent as the Archangel continued.

"I might be an Angel, but I believe in balance—between light and dark, order and chaos. Without Hell's order, the Earth would drown under its own weight. Our Father created all of it for a reason, and I refuse to see that destroyed."

I didn't give a shit about his oath to his father or his brothers-in-arms. Every primal instinct was looking for someone to blame for the shadows that lurked in Trinity's eyes, and this fucker was the only one around to latch onto. Still, I forced myself to continue breathing and listened as he spoke.

Lev's gaze hardened as he continued. "I saw an innocent Witch suffering, trapped in a cage with no hope of escape or rescue. So, I made a choice. I couldn't call myself a man, an Angel, or anything else if I let it continue. I knew the decision I was making meant I would lose my home, my people, and that I'd likely be forced to kill my own kind, but I couldn't watch Trinity be hurt any longer."

"You waited for months," I growled again.

"Yes, and I had my reasons," Lev snapped, eyes blazing. "She was nothing to me back then, urgency wasn't a factor. But after knowing what was happening, I couldn't banish it from my mind, and I knew I could not let it continue." He paused a moment to meet my gaze, his silvery eyes hard and unyielding. "You can hate me all you want for that, but I won't apologize for struggling to overcome millennia worth of loyalty to my brethren to rescue a complete stranger, all the while knowing I'd likely have to kill many of them in order to accomplish my goal of helping her escape."

For Trinity's sake, I tried to put myself in his position. I tried to consider what he had to face, what he had to admit and overcome to knowingly turn against his people. It was hard to do, but I managed to... barely.

"After we escaped," Leviah continued flicking a glance at me before speaking again. "After all of it, she became important to me, more than a mission. We protected each other. Trinity is my reason to fight—my only reason now. I'm exiled, hunted by those who once were my brothers. I belong to no one but her, to nothing but our cause, and so I'll keep fighting for her."

Leviah's words hung in the air, heavy and raw. I didn't want to feel the weight of them or the clear, ringing truth.

"I lost everything, Demon King. And I would sacrifice it all again for her. As much as I wished she had not suffered, I would not change how it happened. I needed the time to make sure I was making the right choice, and in the end I got her out. I know it's not ideal, and I know you want another answer, but this is the only truth I have for you."

A heavy silence enveloped us once more as I processed what he had said, and the Archangel seemed happy enough to sit in silence while I let his words rest between us. If what he said was true, then I understood, even though I still blamed him for the suffering my Witch had gone through. Could he not have sorted through his loyalties and figured out right from wrong a little sooner?

"Do you regret it?" I asked.

"Saving Trinity?" Leviah asked, brow furrowed.

"Turning your back on Heaven and your family?"

Leviah sat back slowly and shook his head. "I have not turned my back on Heaven, not the *real* Heaven. It just hasn't been the Heaven I pledged to follow since Lucifer fell and the age of man took over."

I levelled him with a look. "You mean since Lucifer was cast out. Don't go rewriting history."

Leviah's lips twitched and a flash of humor lit his eyes. "So, some of your contention toward me has to do with the way your father was treated."

"And my mother," I amended. "Neither were treated right; both were unfairly punished."

Leviah slowly nodded. "If you'd asked me centuries ago, I'd have disagreed with you. But lately, I can see more and more holes in the fabric of Heaven and the lies we were fed and told to believe. I don't think God has been running things for a while."

I frowned. "So... none of you talk to God? I mean, he's still around, right?"

"Just the inner circle do—maybe five Angels."

"And you all just... believe them?"

Leviah gave me a deadpan look. "We follow orders."

I nodded slowly, not sure what to do with this news. We all thought the Archangels were in contact with God all the time. Unlike Lucifer, he was supposed to still be around.

Silence fell between us again, and despite how uncomfortable I felt, I knew Leviah was telling the truth. I'd watch him carefully over the next few days, but somewhere deep down, I knew this Archangel was on his own, lost, without a garrison and nowhere to call home. Trinity was it for him, his reason to keep moving forward.

Leviah watched me and crossed his arms over his chest. "So, what's it to be, Nephew?"

I blanched. "*Nephew?*"

His lips quirked up in a small grin. "Technically, yes. Lucifer the Archangel was my brother. You are his son. By rights, you are my nephew."

The horror at that revelation made me want to be sick. Of course we all put together the family tree at some point in our lives, but things were different for us. Magic and chaos had been used to create us, it wasn't a matter of blood ties, even though we each carried the blood of Lucifer and Lilith.

"If you think I'm calling you Uncle Lev, you can run me through with a sword here and now," I snapped, feeling like my skin was crawling.

Leviah's smile grew wider. "Don't tempt me with a good time."

I backed up a few steps. "Nope, can't do it. You can fuck off back to Heaven or go solo. I've never felt more violated in my life!"

"Come on, I can be the fun uncle!" he called as I turned away from him.

"More like the weird and creepy uncle," I called over my shoulder, shuddering.

"At least you admit we're family. We gotta stick together," he returned with a smile in his voice. I flipped him the bird as I continued toward the barrier and to where my mate waited for me.

Leviah's laugh annoyed me, but at least I didn't feel like he was going to stab me in the back the second it was turned.

CHAPTER FOURTEEN

TRINITY

I woke alone, and alarm rippled through me.

Looking around wildly, I searched for Donovan, but he was nowhere to be seen. I was about to call out when I heard slightly raised voices somewhere behind me. Rolling onto my hands and knees, I pushed up and saw Donovan turn away from Leviah, flipping him the middle finger over his shoulder as Lev grinned at his retreating figure.

Despite the rude gesture, my heart lifted at the levity I just witnessed between them, and I wondered if we'd actually manage to work together.

"You're awake," Donovan called as he saw me waiting, that smile that melted my heart turning up the corners of his lips.

"I am. What were you two talking about?" I asked, tilting my head in Leviah's direction. Donovan didn't answer, he swept me up in his arms and kissed me. As far as non-answers went, this was by far my favorite. I didn't hesitate to kiss him back, and I knew nothing in life would ever compare to the taste of his kiss. His hands found their way into my hair, tilting my head to deepen the kiss, and before long, my temperature had shot up and I was ready to start yanking off clothes.

"Should I leave again or…?"

I grinned against Donovan's lips at Leviah's words and he slowly pulled back, making sure to kiss me twice more before releasing me.

"Good morning," he greeted, his smile full of satisfaction.

"It is, isn't it?" I returned with a grin.

Leviah muttered under his breath and I turned to look at him with a small glare.

His eyes widened in mock shock. "Oh, she sees me!"

"Good morning to you too, Lev," I greeted, ignoring his smart-ass attitude.

"Are we ready to start planning how to save this Witch today?" he asked, but I could tell he was secretly happy for me. I'd been going on about Donovan for the two years he'd known me, seen me pine for him, worry over him, intervene at times when we both knew it was dangerous—but I couldn't help myself.

"What information have you got?" Donovan asked, taking my hand in his. It was as if he couldn't bear to not touch me, even for a small time. I wasn't complaining.

We went over the plan Lev and I had put together the other day, and Donovan added in his perspective and ideas. I explained my vision several times, making sure he knew each and every angle so we had the best chance of getting her out.

"How old did you say she was again?" Donovan asked.

I analyzed the vision and shook my head, trying not to get sucked into the feeling of familiarity. Where did I know her from?

"Fourteen, maybe fifteen. She's young, scared, but stubborn and ready to fight to the end."

"Did you get the sense that she knew how to use her power?" he asked.

I hesitated and nodded. "Yeah. She's been on her own for a while. I'm not sure how long. To survive nowadays as a Witch on her own, she has to know her capabilities and how to use it to her advantage."

Lev frowned. "So, she's on the run, wary all of things Angelic and Demonic, and we're supposed to earn her trust, how?" Donovan didn't reply, but I could tell he was thinking. I considered Leviah's point. He was right, the girl wasn't likely to trust anyone anytime soon, and definitely not my companions. So that left me to make the approach, but how could I get close enough to her without her freaking out on me? Witches weren't exactly trustworthy lately either.

"Our best shot is that she sees me first. I can get to her, talk to her, and hopefully while you two fight off the enemy, she'll see we're on her side."

"And if she doesn't?" Donovan asked, his eyes steely and expression serious. "If she won't let you close enough to explain? What happens if she attacks you first?"

I shook my head. "I have been a practicing Witch a lot longer than her; I have more than enough tricks up my sleeve to help me. You two focus on drawing the Rogues away and keeping them occupied. Leave the girl to me."

"I don't like this," Donovan grunted.

"I second that," Lev muttered, and the two of them shared a nod of agreement.

I glared, pointing first at Lev and then to Donovan. "No, you two don't get to do this. Lev, you've walked with me into far more dangerous situations and barely voiced a complaint. And Donovan, you get no say in this. I know we're mates, but I am my own person and this is what I do. We're doing this, and that's final."

The guys shared a look and I levelled a dangerous look at them both.

"Uh-uh, no. You two are mortal enemies, you don't get to start teaming up on me when it suits your agenda."

Leviah smirked. "We're not enemies; we're family."

"I will burn you alive if you say that again," Donovan snapped, visibly shuddering.

"See?" Lev said, crossing his arms over his chest and tilting his head in Donovan's direction. "Only family can say that kind of thing to each other and not hurt feelings."

Donovan snapped his fingers, and a ring of hellfire erupted around Leviah who barely even blinked.

His grin deepened, turned teasing. "Isn't he cute?"

"I'll show you cute," Donovan warned, raising his hand, a ball of blue hellfire in his palm, ready to launch.

"Don't even think about it," I shouted and Donovan froze, eyes turning back to me, almost pleading.

"It's just a little singe," he argued.

"No, you cannot set my friend on fire—" I cut myself off and drew in a deep breath. "I can't believe I have to have this conversation with the two of you."

"He'd barely feel it. You'd heal him fast enough anyway," Donovan muttered dropping his hand, the ball of fire and the ring surrounding Leviah extinguishing with a small hiss. The smell of smoke fluttered on the wind and I sighed.

"Are you both done?"

"Sure," Lev answered easily.

I looked at Donovan who hesitated before he sent a small blast of hellfire at Lev, singeing his shirt before my friend managed to put the flames out.

"*Now* I'm done," he said, a grin teasing his lips.

I sighed. "Aradia, give me strength," I muttered and dropped my head into my hands. Shaking my head, I turned away from them and gathered my things so we could leave and save the girl.

Hopefully, the two of them would take their frustrations out on the Rogues and not each other.

I let my senses flare around us to try and get a more accurate read on how many Rogue Demons were in the vicinity. There were at least nine, maybe more. Lately, unless it was for a powerful enemy like a King of Hell, it was unusual to see so many together in one hoard, but they must have decided that they really wanted this girl.

"I will go in first," Leviah said, repeating the plan again. "Once I have them distracted and drawn away from the girl, Donovan can come in and get rid of any Rogues keeping the girl cornered. Once they're gone, then it's up to you to work your magic, Trin."

I nodded, liking this idea. It made Donovan and Lev feel better too as they were effectively drawing the majority of the danger away from me and the girl. Then, all I'd have to do was worry about *her* reaction.

"If the girl doesn't want to come, if she fights too much, leave her," Donovan told me. I opened my mouth to protest, but he held up a hand to forestall my comment before continuing. "If she fights, I'll shadow beside her and grab her before shadowing her to our meeting place. She won't have time to fight me. I know it's important she come with us of her own free will, so it's a last resort."

I didn't agree right away, but finally nodded. "I don't think that will be necessary, though. If Dinah saw this rescue going wrong, she would have warned me. The girl needs to be saved, and we're going to be the ones to do it."

I didn't mention that I refused to accept another outcome. She was special, this girl, important somehow. I was drawn to her in a way I didn't understand, and I knew she needed us, knew she was meant to be with us.

"Are we ready?" Lev asked, and I mentally went over the plan again, checking my supplies and ensuring my magic was at the ready.

"Yeah," Donovan answered, shooting a troubled look my way.

"Oh, wait," Lev said, and I watched him work the silver band off his finger and give it to Donovan. "You should have this."

He raised an eyebrow and looked at Lev before slowly taking it. "Thank you."

Lev shrugged. "If you two can't make any bonds that would otherwise allow you to communicate with one another, then you should at least have the rings. It's better than nothing, and I know you'd prefer to have a way to reach her if you're separated."

Donovan looked uncomfortable and a little speechless, and I hid my smile.

"Thanks."

"Just looking after my nephew," Lev threw in and Donovan gave me an exasperated look that had me chuckling quietly.

"Alright," I said, swallowing my laughter. "Let's do this." I pulled the ring from my pack and put it on.

"If I accidentally set Lev on fire during this rescue, you'd believe me that it wasn't intentional, right?"

Donovan's sudden voice in my head made me catch my breath and I noticed almost immediately that it felt different with Leviah. With Lev, it had always been slightly uncomfortable, unnatural, as if our minds were not meant to communicate in this fashion. But with Donovan? It felt so right I could have spent my entire life talking to him like this. It was as easy as breathing.

"You two are going to have to find a way to get over this relation issue. Whether you like it or not, it's the truth, and he only does it to get a rise

out of you," I replied easily.

Something in his eyes shifted as I spoke, and I realized he was enjoying this form of communication as much as I did.

"I'd rather it be you getting the rise out of me," he returned, his tone thick with inuendo. I shot him a look of reprimand, but it was ruined when my lips tried to curve into a smile.

"Whatever you two are talking about, can it wait until we've completed our mission?" Leviah asked, his tone tired.

"I have no idea what you're talking about," I muttered. I didn't need to bother looking at Lev to feel his disbelief of those words.

"Be safe, moya lyubov'. I cannot guarantee my restraint if you get hurt," Donovan whispered as he stepped closer to me.

"I'll be fine. You be safe. Don't make me have to step in and protect you from the big; bad Demons."

He smiled gently before lowering his head to mine. I kissed him back at once, still in awe at the way the world seemed to shift and rock beneath our feet every time his lips touched mine. Pulling away, he gave me one last searching look before he stepped away. Lev sent me a quick reassuring smile before the two of them disappeared around a corner. Closing my eyes, I whispered a prayer to Aradia that she would protect my guys and give me a way to connect with this girl.

"Alright, we're going in. Be ready."

Opening my eyes, I shifted my position so I could see the edge of the alleyway where I could hear the clatter of Demons and sent myself searching for any nearby enemies once again.

I felt it the moment Lev appeared amongst the crush of Rogue Demons. The flood of bloodlust and fury that burst from the alley hit me even from all the way out here, and I knew my time was coming.

"Now, Trinity," Donovan ordered. I didn't question him, I just ran. If Donovan said he was ready, then I knew he was. No way

would he send me in there when there was danger waiting around a corner.

I hurried forward, my breath feeling strangely hot in my throat as my heart pounded and blood rushed. Running footsteps came closer to me, rushed, stumbling, and I felt her terror like razors against my head. She was so scared.

When she finally rounded the corner, she was looking backward, terrified that the Rogues were following her.

When she finally turned to look where she was running, she saw me and came skidding to a halt, tripping slightly.

"Wait," I called, moving closer. She threw a blast of energy my way as she ran for cover, but I was ready for her and it merely bounced off my barrier. The girl looked around wildly, finding herself backed between a dumpster and a brick wall, just as I had seen in my vision.

"Please, don't be scared," I said, making sure to keep some space between us.

"I'm not scared. Let me pass," she snapped, but her voice trembled. Looking at her in person, she looked even younger than in my vision, and so damn scared. She was dirty, as if she hadn't been able to shower for days, and her clothes were well-worn. Again, I was struck by that fierce feeling that I'd seen her before, that I knew her somehow, or that she was important. "I'm here to help you."

"Help me?" she repeated almost hysterically. "No one is here to help me."

"I am," I assured, gentling my voice. "You can tell. I know you can feel when someone is lying. I promise, I'm only here to help you. A friend of mine is a Seer, and she told me of her vision of you, that you were being chased."

The girl swallowed hard, eyes darting around as if looking for hidden dangers—or a way out.

"My name is Trinity, and I find and protect Witches like you who are on the run and trying to avoid Rogues and Angels. I can help you."

"I don't want it. Go find someone else to save."

My boots crunched on the gravel as I edged closer to the girl as she braced as if waiting for me to attack, her fingers clenched tight around the strap of her backpack. Her eyes, fierce and wide, locked on me like she expected a knife in the back.

"Stay back," she spat when I got too close. I stopped and held up my hands to show I wasn't going to hurt her.

My breath released slowly as I tried to interject some calm between us. "We're not here to hurt you, we're here to save you."

"We?" she asked, voice trembling.

"Incoming!"

I turned to see a Rogue Demon running toward us, lips curled into a snarl. The artfully placed scars across his body were raised and stood out against his darker skin, and his dark eyes were narrowed on me.

"Witch," he snarled.

Raising my hand, I sent a blast of power his way, strong enough that it sent him sailing backward to crash into the rock-strewn ground. He was either unconscious or, if I was lucky, dead. The sharp scrape of claws against stone cut through the air as the fight drew closer and I looked back at the girl, wondering how the hell I was meant to get through to her.

"My name is Trinity, what's yours?"

"What did you mean by *we*?" she asked instead, a look of determination in her eyes.

"Uh—" A flash of silver wings swept past, Leviah's sword flashing light as it cut down a snarling Rogue who had been set on getting to me. Donovan stepped in beside him, his dark aura swallowing shadows whole, eyes burning with a power that made the very air hum and caress my skin. Both of them were in the thick of it, ripping through Demons with terrifying grace.

"Trinity, get down!" Lev called as a ball of fire flew right to my face. I ducked and Donovan was there, roaring his rage at the Rogue who'd tried to attack me.

"Trinity, you need to hurry," Donovan called, his sword clashing with the Demon.

Looking back at the girl, I caught the way her lip curled in disgust. "Seriously? You want me to go with you and *them?*"

"I promise, we're here to help," I tried again.

She gave a bitter laugh, shifting her backpack again, eyes darting and looking for an escape. "Demons, Angels, Witches. What's next? The whole cast of Supernatural showing up to babysit me?"

I laughed gently. "You wouldn't complain if Dean were the one to come save you though, would you?"

She glared at my attempt to bond and I sighed. Kneeling down, I kept my voice low but urgent, needing her to get on board *now*. "I know it's hard to trust. You're not the only Witch who has been hunted and made to feel alone."

"Don't talk to me about being alone," she snapped, standing abruptly, chin raised. "I don't need charity. I don't need pity. I'm not stupid. And I'm not buying whatever you're selling."

I opened my mouth to argue but just then Donovan slammed into the dumpsters beside us and I gasped, feeling the pain slam through him. It was gone almost at once, and I knew he was protecting me.

He groaned and, without looking at the girl, spoke. "Just come with us; we'll keep you safe."

The girl glowered. "Said the man in the van with all the candy.

No!"

I caught the small speck of amusement Donovan felt before he struck out at the Rogue who rushed him again, punching him hard in the face and kicking him into the wall opposite us.

"Kid, listen. We don't have time for this. We can handle taking this lot out, but more are on the way and you can be guaranteed that Angels will follow. If you want to live, you need to listen and get the hell outa here now," he snapped.

"Just let me go. If you really care, you'll let me go," she argued.

"And then they'll track you somewhere else and we might not be there to help," I explained. I was losing my patience and wanted to grab her and teleport her out of there, but I had a feeling it wouldn't be the wisest thing to do. She needed to trust us, to see we cared about her and her freedom. Taking her now would only result in her never trusting us and fighting us every step of the way.

"I can't trust any of you," the girl snapped.

Donovan stepped up beside me then, his gaze assessing as he looked me over before turning to look at the girl. His steps faltered and for a moment he stilled. I swear, he didn't even breathe. A sense of familiarity hit him like a train, and with it a heart-crushing weight that almost took him to his knees.

I frowned, reaching for him before I could think twice about it, and just like that he stepped up beside me, expression closed off. He was breathing again, all emotion gone, and I realized he'd put up some kind of mental shield to keep me from feeling his emotions.

"Listen," Donovan started, darting a look around to make sure there were no enemies nearby. Lev was somewhere further down the alley taking on two Rogue's at once, but no more remained. Donovan's voice was low and controlled, full of that dark authority that made me hold my breath.

"You're standing in front of three incredibly dangerous beings, notorious for being enemies." His gaze was steady as he looked at her. "When was the last time you saw an Archangel, a Demon King and a Witch working side by side?"

The girl didn't reply, but Donovan didn't seem to need an answer. "We are working together for one purpose: to protect you."

"Why?" she asked, suspicious.

Donovan shrugged. "Why not?"

Her eyes narrowed. "So, I'm supposed to feel safe because the biggest nightmare in Hell says so?"

Donovan didn't even blink. "Fair, but what are your other options? You know that even if we let you go and you make it out of here, they'll find you quickly and then what? You'll either be dead in hours with your heart ripped from your chest, or you'll be a prisoner of Heaven where they'll torture you and drain you of your magic for years, all for their own use and amusement."

"And you want me to believe that the three of you want something different for me?" she asked, dark eyes sharp and filled with jaded intelligence. This girl had been hurt before, and she was nobody's fool. She shook her head, lips twisting into a sarcastic smile. "A Demon King, an Archangel, and a Witch. It sounds more like an opening to a dumb joke."

Donovan sighed and shook his head, impatience radiating from every fiber of him, but I knew it was to do with me being in such close proximity to danger. "If you truly don't want our help and are happy to face the painful consequences of your stubborn refusal of help, have at it. We have places to be. For your sake, I hope it's the Rogues who get you. Having your heart ripped from your chest is less painful than what awaits you with the

Angels."

She squared her shoulders, voice sharp. "You don't scare me."

"I'm not here to scare you," he said harshly, eyes glinting. "I'm here to save your ass. I don't really care if it pisses you off in the process."

I watched her, monitoring her emotions as she slowly took in Donovan's words. He didn't pretend to expect her trust, and I could see that was doing more to help us than any attempt I'd made to connect with her.

He must have seen the cracks in her armor too, because he leaned closer, his voice dropped low, edged with dry humor and a hint of challenge.

"Look, I'm not here to win you over in the next two minutes. What I am here for is getting you out of this mess. And if at any point you think I'm about to hurt you, take this." He tossed a blade at her feet—sharp, real, no nonsense. "Use it. Because between fighting off Rogue Demons, putting up with a dipshit Archangel who keeps trying to get me to call him my uncle, and dealing with you, I'm not in the mood to take on any more crap today."

She looked disturbed by his words. "Uncle?"

Donovan almost rolled his eyes and instead gritted his teeth. "Don't get me started. But are you coming or not?"

He'd barely got the words out when there was suddenly an impending feeling of doom in the air, the kind that came with angelic power.

"We need to move!" Leviah called as he yanked his sword from the chest of a dead Rogue. He was injured, but despite the splatter of blood on his face, I could tell they were superficial, the kind of injuries his kind would heal from quickly enough. The girl looked down the alley where the power was coming from, her pale face turning almost translucent, and I think reality was finally sinking in. They were coming whether we were here or not.

"Come on, sweetheart. We want to help you, you have to be able to sense that," I urged, desperately hoping she'd trust her instincts. Mine were screaming at me to take her and run, to allow no further harm to come to her. Leviah jogged over to us, and the girl looked at me, then back at Donovan, her expression unreadable.

"I'm Hazel." Her words were whispered, cracked, the smallest step toward believing us.

"Good to meet you, Hazel, I'm Donovan. That's Leviah, and you've met Trinity. Are we done now? I'd like to leave before more show up."

Leviah snickered. "Afraid you'll have to actually fight tonight, Demon King?"

"I took out more of those bastards than you did," Donovan defended, an edge of mock outrage in his voice I knew was there to further put Hazel at ease.

Leviah scoffed. "Did one of those Rogues hit you in the head? Because it appears you can no longer accurately keep count."

Donovan's tone was mocking . "If I did take out less Rogues than you—and I'm not saying I did—it was to pander to your ego. Trinity asked me to take it easy on you."

"Don't bring me into this," I interjected.

"Afraid to look bad in front of Trinity, Hell King? Or are you really so lacking?

Donovan pushed off from the dumpster. "If that's how you want to play it, fine. Next fight, we keep count and see who is really the better warrior."

"If you insist," Leviah sighed dramatically. "But I'll fight left-handed, so you have a chance of keeping up."

Donovan grinned wickedly. "Ah, so you admit your flaws, nice. I fight just as well with either hand, so maybe I should fight with one arm tied behind my back so you have a chance."

Leviah snorted. "In your dreams, Nephew."

"Fuck off, halo hugger. I'm not your nephew."

Hazel frowned. "Well, actually—"

"Don't you start or I will leave your foot-dragging ass here," Donovan interrupted, turning to include Hazel in the conversation.

Her lips trembled with a repressed smile, and I knew she didn't want to find the situation funny.

"Geez, are they always like this?" Hazel muttered to me.

It was my turn to sigh, and I laid the exasperation on thick. "You have no idea."

"Alright, princess, are you coming with us, or are we wasting our time?" Donovan asked, stepping away as if he was already leaving.

She hesitated a moment before she leaned down to pick up the blade, flexing her fingers around the handle as she tested its grip. Her gaze strayed to the etchings on the blade and to Donovan's symbol on the hilt. Her breath caught, her eyes flying to Donovan and then back to the blade. Her hesitation was only for a moment before she replied. "Fine, but I'm watching your every move."

Donovan grinned, like she just handed him a personal challenge. "Wouldn't want it any other way."

Leviah sheathed his sword, voice calm. "Let's go."

As we moved away from the impending battle, I caught her eyes once more. She was still wary, but something was shifting, and I let myself hope a little. She glanced again at the blade, and I wondered if she had any idea how to use it. We'd have to give her some lessons as soon as we had time.

"Demon King!"

I jerked back around to see an Archangel at the other end of the alley, white wings spread wide, a fierce look of hatred on his face.

Donovan snarled under his breath. "Uriel."

"Give us the girl, Demon filth, and we'll let you live."

Fury rolled off Donovan so thick I felt like I was drowning, but before I could reach him, Lev gripped his shoulder tightly and pulled him back.

"We don't have time for this, leave him."

"He's gotten away so many times before; he has to pay," Donovan ground out as several Angels and Rogues filled in behind the Archangel.

"And he'll get what's coming to him, but not now. Not here. We have other priorities," Lev reminded. *"Donovan,"* I whispered gently when he didn't move. *"Come, we need to leave. Hazel needs to be kept safe."*

He hesitated, but I knew he was going to back down when he heard her name. It was official, whatever I felt about this girl, Donovan felt it too. Now, we just had to figure out what it meant.

"Don't get too comfortable, Uriel. Your last day is fast approaching," Donovan warned, his voice a growling threat.

Uriel swore and took a step toward us before I yanked on Donovan's hand and used my device to teleport us out of the alley.

ALEXIS MAREE

CHAPTER FIFTEEN

DONOVAN

Fuck Uriel and everything about him.

We'd left the alley three hours ago and had been hiking for the better part of it. We were headed for the Oasis, but I hadn't been given the go-ahead to enter. Someone had to go on ahead and ask if I had permission to go in, which is what Lev had decided to go do since Trinity's teleportation device was out of juice and only had one more trip left in it.

We could have sat somewhere and waited, but Trinity and I both agreed that doing nothing was only going to give Hazel a chance to run or have time to rethink her decision. She was scared, she had every right to be, but coming with us now was for the best. So, Trinity chose a meadow that was surrounded by forest and said we had to walk to a meeting point. It was an attempt to keep Hazel busy, but hopefully also give us a chance to know her a little better.

I tried not to think of what would happen if the Elders said I couldn't enter the Oasis. If Trinity was going, then so was I, end of story. As it was, I wasn't too keen on letting the girl out of my sight, either.

I knew leaving the alley when we did was the right choice. I knew it was unwise to attempt to take on Uriel right now, but damn it all! When would I get the joy of taking that dickwad's head from his shoulders?

Hazel swore under her breath as a low branch scratched across her face, and she glared at it as if it had been a personal attack. The Witch had spirit.

Young she may be, but she had been prepared to go down swinging in that alleyway. I'd known it was useless to try and earn her trust in such a short time, and who could blame her for being wary?

Trusting anyone new these days was bound to blow up in your face, but when confronted with an Archangel, a Demon King, and a Witch all together? She was allowed to pause and try to understand what the hell was going on. Unfortunately for her, we didn't have the time for her to deliberate for too long. In the end, I was glad she chose the safety of us rather than the pain and death that awaited her with the Angels or Rogue Demons.

Hazel stumbled for the third time, and I instinctively reached out to steady her, but stayed my hand when she sent me a withering glare. I grinned, loving that she was prickly. I'd dreaded having to calm a hysterical Witch down long enough to get her to listen. Having one throw her attitude about was something I could handle.

"You know her."

Trinity's words whispered softly across my mind, and I shot her a quick glance.

"Never seen her before in my life," I assured.

Trinity gave me a look that said she didn't have patience for half-truths. *"Maybe not, but you recognize her on the same level as I do. There is something about her that is familiar."*

She was right, of course. The second I'd laid eyes on the girl, something about her struck me hard and fast. It was like a swift kick to the guts, and I temporarily lost the ability to speak. I knew for a fact I'd never seen her before. If I had, I likely would have tried to get her off the streets and somewhere safe. And yet, I knew her on some level I didn't understand.

"She is... familiar. But I don't know how or why," I finally answered. *"I feel the same way. I know she is important, special, and I have an overwhelming need to protect her. But she is a stranger to me."*

I pondered that as we walked, not sure what to make of this revelation. For now, I'd put it aside. The only way I saw us getting any kind of answer was to ask Trinity's Seer friend, and she might tell us nothing. Still, it was worth a go.

Hazel staggered again, catching herself on a tree trunk, boots dragging through the undergrowth. I swore, automatically reaching for her and she slapped my hands away.

"I'm fine," she snapped.

"Yeah, you look it—if 'fine' is spelled L-I-A-R."

She rolled her eyes. "Wow, that was lame."

"I am rubber, you are glue," I returned in a sing-song voice, grinning when she snorted and bit back a smile. She had a wicked sense of humor, and enough bite to go with her bark. Teasing and giving her shit right back was probably the best way to keep her going and to stop her from freaking out or overthinking.

Hazel wanted to walk under her own strength. She wanted that choice—needed it—and I could respect that.

So, I let her.

Still, I watched her as carefully as she seemed to be studying me. Whatever she was looking for, I had no idea, but she seemed almost... hesitantly hopeful. I didn't miss the tremble in her legs or the way her breath rasped, or how her eyes, sharp with suspicion, flicked between Trinity and me like she didn't know which of us was the greater threat.

"I'm not some helpless child," she snapped when she caught Trinity watching her with a worried expression.

I tilted my head, watching her. "Could've fooled me. You look one stiff breeze away from face-planting."

Her glare cut to me. "And what, you'd catch me, *Doni*? Don't waste your effort."

Something jagged and burning cut through me with merciless precision. For whatever reason, her using that name for me—sarcastic or not—cut me to the core. I stumbled and reached out to rest my hand on a tree branch, my lungs burning and heart twisting. What the hell was that?

"What's wrong with you?" Hazel asked, and I could have been mistaken, but it looked like a flicker of genuine concern in her eyes.

"Nothing," I lied. "Just giving you an example of how you look right now."

She glared. "I don't need your help."

I smirked. "Oh, don't worry. I won't be offering again."

Hazel's chin lifted, defiant despite the tremor in her legs. "I'd rather crawl than owe a Demon anything."

I met her stare evenly, letting the silence hang just long enough to make her fidget before replying. "Pride is one of the seven deadly sins, you know? But it suits you," I told her before pushing forward again now that the ache in my chest had lessened.

Trinity shot me a look over Hazel's head—half reprimand, half amused disbelief. I only shrugged. The girl didn't need coddling.

Hazel pushed on, boots crunching over dead leaves and twigs. After a few moments of silence, she said tightly, "You think you're so clever, don't you?"

"I don't *think*," I said smoothly. "I know."

Her eyes rolled so hard I thought they might tumble from her head. "More like arrogant."

"Experienced," I countered.

"*Conceited.*"

I grinned. "Confident."

Hazel exhaled sharply through her nose, the sound halfway between irritation and the laugh she was trying not to give me. She shook her head. "I can't decide if I want to kick you or use the blade you gave me to make you shut up for good."

"Always keep your options open—there's more you haven't considered."

She shot me a withering glare, but I could still see that sliver of humor in her eyes. "Don't get comfortable. You and I won't be traveling together for long. I've survived this long without the help of a Demon King—I won't start needing one now."

"Need?" I echoed, feigning surprise. "Who said anything about *need*? You just seem to enjoy my company. Secretly, of course, but you enjoy it all the same."

That earned me a short, disbelieving laugh before she caught herself, lips pressing into a line as if she hadn't meant to let it slip. "You're impossible."

I inclined my head. "That's the nicest thing anyone's said to me all day."

Trinity gave a small shake of her head, though I didn't miss the little smile she tried to hide. Hazel was still bristling, but her steps seemed steadier, her focus sharper than it had been. I knew for some, sarcasm was easier to wear as armor than to wallow in fear.

The forest opened into a clearing not far from a stream. The air was damp, the ground softened by moss, and for the first time since the fight, there was a real sense of quiet.

Hazel's strength gave out at the edge of the clearing. She folded to the ground, not gracefully but with stubborn control, as if she wanted it to be known that she decided to sit right there instead of giving in to exhaustion. Her chin was held high, but her body sagged, and she still tried to look like she wasn't on the verge of collapse. Even beaten, scraped raw, haunted by fuck knew what horrors, she clung to her fire. That kind of strength wasn't taught, it was forged, and respect for the young woman burned bright inside me. I recognized the strength it took for someone to use their traumas and loss and to hone them into a weapon of protection.

Trinity stayed standing, her eyes on Hazel before she glanced around, keeping space between them as she spoke. "We'll rest here. Just for a little while."

Hazel gave the smallest nod and a shrug of indifference, as if she didn't care one way or the other if we stopped or kept walking, but even I saw the way her shoulders sagged in relief.

I leaned against a tree at the clearing's edge, arms folded, mentally scouring the area around us while keeping a part of my attention on the two of them. I considered how today would have gone if I hadn't been here, if Trinity had done it alone as she always had, and I shivered. She sought out Witches like Hazel—the forgotten, the hunted, the broken—and she faced down danger to drag them into safety. She carried that burden willingly, knowing the risks. What if one day she made a mistake? What if she protected the wrong person or made one wrong move, and I wasn't there for her? I shook my head to get rid of those thoughts when Trinity spoke again.

"You should know where we're taking you."

Hazel's eyes snapped up, wary.

"There's a safe place called The Oasis," Trinity started. "It's a sanctuary that has been hidden for hundreds of years from Angels, Demons, and anyone who'd do us harm. Once you're there, nothing can touch you."

Hazel's mouth pressed thin, like she wanted to believe but didn't dare.

Trinity leaned closer, though not enough to crowd her. "It isn't a place people come and go from freely. Once you enter, you can't leave unless it's with me. Only those of my bloodline or who are blessed with a certain spell can come and go as they please. It's for your safety—and for the safety of everyone already there."

Hazel's expression was carefully blank. She didn't argue, but she didn't agree to stay either. She was still hiding information, but I expected as much. It would be crazy for her trust us with everything when she didn't know us.

I finally pushed off from the tree, stepping closer. "And what about me?"

Trinity straightened, turning to face me. There was tension in her shoulders, though her eyes stayed steady.

"You'll be the first Demon King to enter."

I raised a brow. "That's if it'll even let me in."

"The enchantments protect the Oasis," Trinity began. "They'll test you when we arrive, they'll search for ill will toward Witches. If there's any, they won't let you pass. It's that simple."

I gave a single nod, impressed that the Oasis had such a safeguard, but then again, I should have known. Tabitha had never been one to do things by halves, and I could only assume other Witches had poured their power into The Oasis's enchantments over the centuries, ensuring it remained strong. Being tested didn't bother me. I'd never held malice toward Witches, and certainly not my mate or the girl we'd saved tonight.

Behind us, Hazel shifted, hugging her knees tighter to her chest. Her eyes stayed fixed on me, suspicion etched deep. I didn't blame her, I admired her. She was young, still just a girl, and she'd carried herself this far alone.

I could tell just by looking at her that she'd been on her own for a long time. She'd faced Demons, Angels, and who knew what else, and she still had fight left in her.

A flicker of irritation twisted in me as I thought of Leviah away in the Oasis—he'd earned their trust enough to be welcomed alone, to be granted that special spell that allowed him to come and go while I still had to prove myself. Being Trinity's mate should have assured them all I meant none of them harm, but I couldn't blame them for their mistrust. And I couldn't begrudge Leviah the trust he'd earned, not really. The Angel had fought beside Trinity without hesitation, and she trusted him.

Hazel's voice broke through my thoughts, thin and hoarse. "Why would you even go there? You're… you're a Demon."

I raised an eyebrow at her. "Demon *King*."

She stared at me with a deadpan expression, clearly not amused and I smiled and shrugged before crouching down beside her, careful to maintain the space she'd put between us.

"I'm going because it's where Trinity needs to be, and because she asked me to go."

Hazel blinked, caught off guard. She didn't trust the answer, I could see it, but she didn't challenge it either.

Trinity stepped in then, her voice quiet but firm. "You should rest, Hazel. You'll see it soon enough."

She watched us both a moment longer, wariness in her gaze before she leaned back against the tree, her body sagging though she tried to keep her eyes open.

I stayed crouched for a moment longer, watching her, then straightened and looked at Trinity. She stood with her arms folded, gaze sharp on the girl. There was pride burning within me as I stared at my mate, bone-deep and undeniable. She'd made herself into a shield for others, a fire no darkness could ever truly snuff out.

I stepped closer to my mate as Hazel's eyes drifted closed, her chest rising and falling with deep, even breaths. For the first time since we found her, there was no immediate threat pressing against our shoulders. There were no Demons snapping at our heels, just the quiet forest, the soft rustle of leaves, the trickle of the stream not far off.

I flexed my fingers, feeling the familiar burn of the mark on my palm. It throbbed as though it knew what I wanted before I even did. The need to bind my mate—to protect her, claim her—was getting stronger, pulling at me like gravity.

The heat on my palm reminded me that while I was definitely in Trinity's life now, there was still a risk of losing her. It was all too real. She was close—closer than she'd ever been to anyone, and dangerously, achingly close to me.

We moved a few steps away from Hazel, careful not to crowd her. The forest was thick enough to give us some privacy. Trinity's hand brushed mine for just a moment, the move intentional. Her fingers lingered, and I swallowed against the sudden tightness in my chest.

"I've been thinking…" I started, trying to sound casual, though the mark throbbed insistently. "About all of it. About you and about her."

Trinity tilted her head, eyebrow lifting. "Yes?"

"How do you do this?" I asked, letting my thumb brush back and forth over the smooth skin of her hand.

"Without fail, you find them—Witches who need help—and you bring them to the Oasis, and you fight like hell to keep them safe."

Her lips twitched into a small, almost shy smile. "You make it sound heroic."

"It *is* heroic," I said firmly. "But terrifying, too. And you make it look effortless. It scares me, Trinity. It scares me because I know what could happen if——" I didn't need to finish because she understood. She always did.

The forest went quiet around us, the air heavy with something unspoken. I reached for her then, slowly, deliberately, and she didn't pull away. Our hands met, fingers entwining, and the sensation was electric, almost painful. I tilted her chin up, and our breaths mingled, hearts hammering in unison.

The kiss was meant to be brief, but the seconds stretched, and neither of us seemed to be willing to break it.

My hand rested on the small of her back, hers on my chest, and the world shifted and shrank until it was just the two of us again. Somewhere in the back of my mind, I knew Hazel was there, dozing, and Leviah was likely to be on his way back to us. I knew we should break apart, but the pull was stronger than all that knowledge, and neither of us seemed ready to let go.

And then a sound ripped through the night air. A guttural, exaggerated, retching noise.

We froze. My head snapped toward the sound, and there she was: Hazel, eyes wide open, one hand over her mouth, the other gripping the tree beside her for balance.

"Gross!" she cried dramatically. "I don't want to see that!"

I couldn't help the grin that split my face and turned back to look at Trinity who laughed at the girls dramatics.

"You know what, *moya lyubov'*, since having a kid, I find it's getting harder and harder to find a moment of privacy."

Trinity laughed, the sound warm and welcoming. She shook her head, eyes sparkling as Hazel continued to wail in exaggeration.

"I swear, you're impossible," Trinity said, though her hand stayed in mine.

I shrugged, still grinning. "At least with me you'll never be

209

bored."

Hazel huffed at the way we ignored her dramatics, but I caught the fleeting amusement in her glare before she ducked her head, muttering something under her breath.

The moment broke the tension, but not the connection. I looked back at Trinity, my eyes meeting hers with something unspoken and raw.

And just like that, we returned to the reason we were even out here.

Leviah returned then, his presence light but commanding. His constantly searching eyes brushed over each of us, analyzing the situation and probably taking in the air of levity.

"Everything okay?" Trinity asked, and I was grateful when she didn't try to take her hand from mine.

Leviah nodded. "The Elders have informed the others and preparations are being made for the girl. The Elders have requested we go straight to them when we arrive."

"The *girl*?" Hazel asked, her tone thick with attitude. "The *girl* has a name."

Leviah's lips softened, almost a smile, before he spared her a look of contrition. "My apologies, young lady," he said, giving her a sweeping bow. "You are correct. I will address you by your name in the future."

Hazel's eyes were wide as she watched his performance. "*Lady* is going a little far... but okay."

Trinity huffed a small laugh and let go of me to step closer to Hazel. "Hazel, if you're ready..."

She straightened immediately, fatigue momentarily forgotten. Anticipation and fear rolled off her in waves, but she was trying—trying to believe. Trying to hope.

I watched her, heart clenching. The first step was never easy, and she didn't trust us entirely. She didn't know yet if this was another trap, but she'd taken the first step, and now she just needed to take another.

Almost there.

"Let's go," Hazel agreed, adjusting the straps on her bag as if she wasn't frightened, and lifted her chin, expression guarded again, but the fear shining in her eyes was bright. "How do we get there?"

"Click your heels three times and say *there's no place like home*," I answered, smirking.

Hazel rolled her eyes. "How old *are* you, Doni? 'Cause your movie references need updating."

I ignored the way my chest pricked at that nickname and grinned. "Ah, but you understood it, so I'm still good."

"It's simple," Trinity interrupted, holding out her hand. "You just take my hand and take a breath, and I do the rest."

Hazel stared at her hand as if it were a foreign object, and after several long moments, she placed her hand in Trinity's. My mate smiled, the light in her eyes worth every moment of the fight we'd been in, and she turned to look at me.

"Now you."

I grimaced. "This isn't going to be like when we shimmered, is it? Because that fucking sucked."

"Language," Trinity hissed.

"Sorry," I said. "It sucked ass?"

Hazel ducked her head to hide her smile, and Trinity gave me a glare, eyes shining with laughter.

"Let's go," I said taking my mate's hand and pressing a quick kiss to the top of her head.

Then the world fell away.

THE KINGS OF HELL
DONOVAN

CHAPTER SIXTEEN

TRINITY

The device warmed in my hand, runes humming with a familiar pulse that thrummed up my arm as the world folded in on itself. Light—then shadow. The pressure around us increased, the sensation like a summer storm building.

As we reached the wards in place to protect the Oasis, magic crackled and snapped against us, and I tightened my hands on Donovan and Hazel. The magic pressed harder, searching, measuring, weighing. I braced myself, felt Hazel flinch, and I held my breath for Donovan.

Let him in. Please, let him in.

Then the pressure broke.

We landed hard on soft earth, the ground steady beneath our boots. The world snapped back into focus with crystal clarity. The sky and grass, the sharp sweetness of wildflowers filling the air.

Home.

And Donovan was still there next to me.

Relief rushed through me so suddenly that my knees went weak. I released a pent-up breath and closed my eyes for the smallest moment. I'd been almost certain he would make it—the purity of his intent wasn't something I doubted. Donovan had cared for a number of Witches over the century, and I knew his love of Tabitha had only ensured his loyalty to my kind. But a tiny, traitorous part of me had feared the Oasis itself might reject him *because* he was a Demon King, regardless of his feelings and intentions.

Hazel's gasp drew my attention to her, and I turned to watch her as she stared out at the valley before us, her lips parted, eyes wide, shimmering with real hope and relief.

I swallowed hard, my arms aching to pull her close, to tell her she was safe now, but Hazel wouldn't welcome it—not yet. Not from me. The girl still held herself stiff, prepared to cut others rather than to allow herself to be cut again. It was an instinct I could relate to all too well.

Leviah shimmered into full form beside us, his eyes taking in all three of us, and I could have been seeing things, but I could have sworn his shoulders relaxed a fraction at seeing Donovan among us. Was my friend starting to like Donovan's company?

Turning my attention to the valley below, I took it all in with new eyes.

Rolling green stretched out in waves, a sea of hills crowned by sharp-edged mountains in the distance. The sky was impossibly blue, unmarred by the touch of Angels or Demons, endless and pure. The air carried the sweet scent of grass warmed by sun, wildflowers bending in the breeze. Somewhere not far off, the rush of water could be heard from a river winding its way through the valley.

And nestled below us, in the heart of it all, the village. There were homes built of stone and timber, smoke curling gently from a few chimneys. It wasn't large. There were no sprawling cities, skyscrapers, or unnecessary flourishes. Below was just enough for what we needed. A few dozen Witches and their families called this place home, and we all shared what we had. The first time I'd come here, it had been overwhelming. There had been a few less buildings, but still as beautiful as it was now.

The sense of freedom and safety that enveloped me had felt too good to be true, so of course I hadn't trusted it one bit. But day after day when nothing bad happened and no one tried to take my magic for their own, I began to trust that maybe, just *maybe,* there was one place left for Witches like me who needed safety. While I loved the Oasis, I left it over and over again because others needed a chance at feeling this too.

And now Hazel had hers.

I glanced at Donovan to find his attention not on the valley, but on Hazel as the young girl tried valiantly to hide her sheer joy at the sight before her, at what it meant. His expression was unreadable at first, but I caught the softness in his eyes, the way his posture had eased. The Demon King, great enemy of the Archangels, had softened at the sight of one stubborn, wounded girl seeing her first real chance at a life.

And Hazel—though she'd never admit it—was softening back, despite how little she actually knew of Donovan. Something between them resonated, and I realized that for whatever reason, he was the key to saving *this* girl.

I'd watched it happen since the moment we found her, piece by piece. She fought him with sarcasm and bitterness, but he'd given it right back to her. He'd teased, mocked, but he never let his words truly wound her.

He met her fire with fire, and it made her respect him a little. He wasn't trying to get on her good side, he wasn't sucking up to her and telling her what he thought she wanted to hear. Donovan didn't treat her with kid gloves or tell her she couldn't handle her own life. He just laid out the facts, returned her snark with some of his own and he teased her until she couldn't help but smile.

And Aradia above, I loved watching them. I loved the way he coaxed strength from her without stripping away her pride. For whatever reason, Donovan was the one she'd gravitated more toward since meeting, and I was too relieved that she was drawn to one of us that I didn't care who got her here. All that mattered was that she was safe now.

I wasn't sure Donovan even noticed that he was binding himself to her in a way neither would be able to unravel. He felt the same pull to her that I did, the same sense of familiarity and responsibility, and he'd slipped straight into his role as her protector like it was second nature.

Hazel let out a shaky breath beside me. "It's real," she whispered, more to herself than us. "It's... it's really real." Her voice cracked on the last word, and I had to curl my hands into fists to stop myself from reaching for her.

"It's real," I said softly. "And it's yours, if you want it."

The wind carried her silence, and I didn't push the subject any further, remembering all too clearly the way I'd felt the first time I'd come here. She needed to explore it all to really see that it was everything it appeared to be and that she had nothing to fear when here.

"Alright, let's go meet the villagers," Donovan suggested, straightening up.

"The Elders want you to go straight to them," Leviah reminded.

I nodded. "We'll get Hazel settled first and then we'll go."

Without another word, we descended the hill, the sweet scent of grass and wildflowers rising around us. Hazel's pace was cautious, her eyes wide as she drank in the view. Her grip twisted on the strap of her backpack, nervousness rolling off her in waves.

Donovan moved beside me, his presence steady, but there was that familiar smirk in place, like he couldn't resist pressing the first playful jab.

"So," he said quietly, eyes sweeping the nearly empty village below, "I assume the welcome wagon is running late because it needed to load up the complimentary Demon slaying pitchforks and torches?"

Hazel snorted, trying not to laugh. "Oh yes, I believe Trinity was saying that this week there is a discount if you intend to burn a Demon King."

Leviah stepped closer, arching an eyebrow. "I'll make sure they reserve a spot for you in line. Wouldn't want you to miss out on a deal like that."

Hazel's lips quirked and she tilted her head to look at Lev. "Oh, how kind of you. Should I bring marshmallows for the provided bonfire, or will you have that covered?"

I smiled and ducked my head at the banter going on around me and simply let it wash over me.

The village itself was quieter than I expected, and I realized some of the residents must have opted to stay inside or hide entirely while the Elders met with the Demon King. I felt the tension in the air, and Donovan noticed too, though his expression remained composed, unreadable. I knew him well enough to see that he understood the subtle rejection of his presence, but he refused to let it touch him. That careful control of his reactions made me want to smile. It was so very *Donovan*.

We reached the village hall, an old but solid building with ivy crawling up its stone walls. This was where most town meetings were held whenever we needed one, where dinner was held every night so we could gather together and socialize. It was also where the younger Witches or male children of Witches came to do some of their schooling.

Outside waiting on the porch, was a matronly Witch name Yara. She was stout and shorter than me, but she carried warmth and authority. Her hair was silvered, her stance straight, but her eyes flicked to Donovan without flinching. I knew she was assessing him, and he let her. He had nothing to hide.

"Trinity," she greeted as we came to stop in front of the building. Yara nodded stiffly to us, but there was welcome in her tone. "It's good to see you back."

"Likewise," I replied, relieved to be safely back on familiar ground. My eyes darted to Hazel, who now hovered uncertainly beside Donovan.

The older Witch turned her attention to the girl, and her tone softened but remained firm. "And you must be our newest resident—it's good to see you in one piece. We have supplies ready, and a room for you. If you want to come with me, we can get you settled."

Hazel stiffened instantly, every muscle coiling as if preparing to bolt. Instead of moving closer to the building, she backed almost subconsciously toward Donovan. The wave of fear coming from her hurt, and I knew she didn't want to be separated from us yet. She didn't know anyone else, she didn't trust this place yet.

Donovan carefully settled a hand on her shoulder, gentle and reassuring. "You'll be safe here," he said quietly. "They just want to get you settled in."

Hazel's voice was sharp, carrying that stubborn edge. "Where are *you* going?"

Donovan smirked, that air of arrogance thicker than normal. "The Elders want to put me in a time-out while they decide if I can stay."

In a rare moment of vulnerability, I caught the flicker of worry in Hazel's expression as her gaze darted to the others, then back to him. "If they tell you that you can't stay... will you come back and get me?"

The question hit him in a way he refused to let the others see, but his mask of sarcastic indifference slipped to reveal the softer expression beneath.

He was already gone for her and he didn't even see it. Hazel had him wrapped around her pinky finger.

"No one will make you stay anywhere you don't want to," he said, voice low but firm. "But this place is the safest anywhere in the world for you. Try it out first, really think about it. Don't make any decisions until you've given it a chance."

Hazel studied him a moment, weighing the truth of his words before the tiniest exhale of relief escaped her. She nodded, her spine straightening as if accepting both the truth and the promise.

Donovan grinned and winked. "Told you that you'd come to want me around. I'm contagious in that way, like a yawn or a baby's laugh."

Hazel smiled, and for the first time there were no reservations in her eyes. "More like a virus, Doni."

Donovan opened his mouth, no doubt to enter into a competition of insults with the teenager, but Leviah shuffled forward, always conscious of the time we'd already wasted in getting Hazel settled. The Elders wanted us to go to them at once, not when it suited us.

"I'll stay with you while we go to your room, and if you like, I can show you around the village," Lev offered. His tone was calm, easy, not at all demanding, and Hazel nodded slowly, accepting his offer.

Donovan's eyes rose to meet Lev's, serious and unwavering, speaking without words.

Leviah gave him a look of understanding. "I've got her."

With a slow inhale, Donovan took his hand from Hazel's shoulder and nodded. "We'll see you soon."

Hazel took a hesitant step toward Leviah, casting one last look at

Donovan before I saw those walls go up and her carefree mask slip into place. "Alright, Halo, lead the way."

We watched Leviah lead Hazel away, and Donovan wasted no time taking my hand—and I had to admit, I loved that. As we walked toward the council of Elders, I couldn't stop the smile that tugged at my lips. I had dreamed about bringing Donovan here, about us finally being together, and now here we were. It was real, it was happening.

And Hazel.

Knowing we'd gotten to her in time, convinced her to come here where she'd be safe and cared for just soothed something deep inside me. I felt a pull in my chest, the same pull I'd felt when we'd first found her, a sense of inevitability, of destiny. That strange, unexplainable connection that made it clear we were meant to find her, meant to protect her, meant to be part of her life. I couldn't question it; I didn't need to. Fate worked in ways that sometimes made absolutely no sense, but she'd get her way in the end.

I learned that lesson the hard way.

We walked beside each other, hand in hand, neither one of us letting go, and I wondered if he needed my assurance that everything would be okay. He was singled out, a lonely Demon King in an Oasis run by and overrun by Witches who could take him down if they so desired.

"They hide from me, yes?" Donovan asked, his voice a whisper across my mind.

I sighed. *"Never has a Demon been here before, much less a Demon King. They're being cautious, and rightfully so. Everyone here had their lives torn away from them because they were hunted. They want to see what the Elders do before they allow their children to be around you."*

I felt his easy acceptance of my answer, and a wave of affection for him washed over me again. That was part of what I loved about Donovan. He didn't push, he was able to understand a point of view that was not his and he accepted it.

"I don't like these rings as much as I thought I would," he murmured and I frowned.

"You don't like to talk like this?"

"It's not that," he said, stroking his thumb over my hand. *"It feels… unnatural to me, a weak attempt at the way we should be communicating. When I speak to my brothers in my mind, I can feel their emotions, get glimpses of their thoughts and motivations. A lot of layers exist within my kind of telepathy, and I wanted to experience that with you. This way of talking is nice, but it's not the intimacy I had hoped for."*

My heart tugged at his confession, and I leaned into him. *"I'm sorry, Donovan. We'll find a way to get there."*

He nodded, but I felt his worry that it would be too late, that I'd age and die before we ever found a cure to my curse.

Ahead, the clearing appeared where the Elders were waiting. Sunlight shone brightly, turning the long, soft grass into a sea of gold. And there they were—three women, standing in quiet authority, their presence like gravity, pulling us in. Dinah was one of them, and her blind eyes found us with ease.

We stopped a few steps short of them, and I heard the way Donovan's breath caught.

They were old, yes—but old in a way that suggested they had seen far too much in their time.

"These three hold immense power," Donovan whispered in my mind, his tone one of awe.

"There is a reason they are our Elders, and it is not simply due to their age."

The weight of their power pressed down on us, subtle and immense. I could feel it threading through the air, into the earth beneath our shoes, and pressing into Donovan, seeking, searching.

One of them stepped forward. She studied Donovan for a long, measured moment. She wasn't just looking at him—she was peering into him, into the corners of his mind, at the memories he'd hidden even from himself.

"You are... Donovan," she said finally, her voice calm but heavy with power. "The first Demon King ever to walk the Oasis." Her words held no real inflection, so it was hard to decide if she was happy or mad about that fact.

"We have felt your arrival coming for a while," another of the women said, her tone warmer but no less potent.

"The Oasis allows many, but few are chosen. You... are chosen. And she—" She gestured to me, "—is bound to you by fate. That is known to us, and it is accepted."

A flicker of relief passed through me. Trust was not freely given here, and yet, in the eyes of these women, their trust extended to Donovan. They were entrusting in destiny and the universe that such an omnipotent being could not have made such a grand mistake as to pair a Witch with a Demon King.

I watched the Elders note our joined hands, but Donovan did not release me, and I refused to relinquish my hold on him. Something in that simple act felt like an unspoken commitment.

"You are welcome here," the first Elder said. "But understand this: not all who live in the Oasis trust you. You are asked to refrain from wandering alone. Any violence against our kind will not be tolerated. Do you understand?"

Donovan nodded, keeping his grip on my hand steady. "I understand."

His voice carried a calm authority that spoke of experiences even the Elders did not have. I often forgot how powerful Donovan was, and how old. He'd been around for thousands of years, since before cavemen. He'd seen everything there was to see about humanity, and standing beside him now, the weight of his years seemed to press down upon us, speaking of power and understanding I could never hope to achieve.

I brushed my thumb over his knuckles in a gesture of comfort, and he turned to smile warmly at me.

Dinah inclined her head toward him. "Good. Then you may walk with her, learn our ways, but know the boundaries of this land. This is not a place for arrogance or conquest. We trust you will respect that."

I exhaled slowly, letting the tension drain from my shoulders as Donovan simply nodded his acceptance of the terms.

The nearest elder turned to me and smiled softly, the faintest crease at the corners of her eyes lending warmth to her otherwise commanding presence. "You have a favor to ask of us, Trinity, I feel it. What do you need?"

Donovan frowned, shooting a confused glance my way.

"He... needs help retrieving memories," I said, her voice quiet but firm. "Memories that have been hidden or taken from his mind."

"That is not all you wish to know," the Elder pressed.

I sighed. "I... also wish to know my past life. I believe that in a past life I was Tabitha Wardwell."

Saying the words out loud made me dizzy, and also rather arrogant. Tabitha was a legend in the Oasis, the woman who made our safety and lives possible. To claim I was her in a past life felt like I was reaching. And yet, I couldn't shake the way those words made me feel.

The air shifted, and the Elders exchanged glances, subtle but meaningful.

Dinah nodded slowly. "We always noted your soul resonated

strongly with this place. You are of her blood, but until now, it was only speculation that you shared her soul."

I drew a shaky breath and nodded, feeling more confident now in my self-assessment.

"We can help you," the first Elder said. "A past life regression is possible to perform, but it requires time to prepare. At the same time, we can unlock Donovan's memories."

"Whatever you have to do," Donovan said suddenly. "Whatever you need me to do, just tell me. I need to remember.

They all looked at Donovan, their eyes piercing and stern. "Be warned... You may not like what is revealed."

"I don't care," he said, the certainty in his voice strong. "I need to know. Whatever it is... I need it."

Dinah inclined her head in acknowledgment. "Very well," she said. "We will begin tomorrow morning. For now, rest. I can feel each of your exhaustion from here. Feel free to roam the grounds, and you are more than welcome to ensure young Hazel's comfort while she settles."

Donovan looked at me in question and I smiled.

"They know of everyone who steps foot inside the Oasis."

He nodded as if that was explanation enough, and maybe it was. The Elders bid us farewell and we turned away from them, making our way back to the village center. Despite Donovan's anxiousness to discover what was hidden in his mind, his focus was once again on Hazel and making sure she was okay. Smiling to myself, I let him lead us back to the girl we'd saved.

CHAPTER SEVENTEEN

DONOVAN

Trinity and I walked back to the village center with clasped hands, and my mind was focused on what tomorrow could bring. I knew it was possible I'd regret the memories they gave me, but at the same time, I couldn't help the gnawing feeling I got that I needed to know. Something important was missing— *someone.* I remembered again the dream I'd had not too long ago, the one where I was enjoying a nice afternoon with the two people I loved most. Tabitha and... and *who?* Someone else had been there in that memory, but they were hidden from me, and damn it, I needed to know who it was.

I was also interested to find out if my intuition was correct about Trinity. It seemed like too much of a coincidence that the only other person I had ever loved would be her ancestor, and then hundreds of years later discover I was meant to be with Trinity. My soul was destined for hers. That connection I'd felt with Tabitha all those years ago had been a calling to the other half of my soul, but I'd been unable to claim it because the prophecy had not yet been activated.

But now... now it was my time, and I truly believe the two women were one in the same.

I looked around when I felt the eyes of others raking over me, and I noticed there were a lot more people out and about than there had been before. A large group seemed to be congregated around the town hall, and I wondered if they were all there to meet Hazel or if they were waiting to see me. Obviously, now that I'd been given the green light by the Elders, the others were more welcoming to my presence.

I searched the faces for Hazel, wanting to see how she'd settled in. I hated leaving her alone so soon after arriving. The way she'd looked at me, as if I were her lifeline—fuck, the girl knew how to tug at my heartstrings without even trying. I'd always had a soft spot for Witches, but I couldn't remember feeling so protective over a random girl before. I was struck once more thinking about the way I'd felt when I first saw her. That sense of familiarity was terrifyingly real, and in an instant, I'd felt the need to get her out of that hell hole and to safety whether she agreed to it or not.

"Who did you bribe to be allowed to stay?"

I was already grinning as I looked around to find the owner of that voice. Hazel weaved her way between people, eyes smiling as she stopped in front of us.

I shrugged. "They all want me, what can I say? Even the older ladies want a piece of this."

Hazel rolled her eyes. "Right," she muttered, disbelief dripping from the drawn-out word.

"It's true," I continued. "Trinity had to agree to a kind of custody agreement and everything. Every second day I'm with the Elders, every other day is with Trin except for Sundays. I get those to myself."

Hazel shook her head. "You're not as funny as you think you are."

"At least I'm good looking; you can't teach that," I returned, flexing my muscles.

Hazel raised her eyebrows before giving a pitying laugh that had the ability to cut deep. "Awe, how embarrassing for you."

My ego deflated and Trinity burst into laughter. "Oh, you should see your face!"

I glared at my mate and she doubled over as she laughed harder. Leviah made his way over to us, his curious look swinging between the two giggling women and me.

"What did I miss?"

I shook my head in mock outrage. "Women!"

They laughed harder and I stepped away, pretending to be angry.

"What did you two say to my nephew?" Leviah asked.

I spun back around to face them. "For the hundredth time— *you're not my uncle!*"

The girls laughed even harder and I walked away. A grin curved my lips at their amusement. If being the butt of their jokes made them laugh, then I was more than happy to be of service.

~

TRINITY

"I should have expected this," I whispered as I turned in a slow circle to check out my surroundings.

I was standing in a large, open-plan room. The walls were made of ancient stone, millennia worth of power and history vibrating from them. A massive fireplace was off to my left, a fire crackling inside. It wasn't normal fire, though, every ember glowing with power. The room looked lived in, comfortable. A long lounge was stretched before the fire, a leather high-backed chair beside it. There were real, fire-lit torches hanging from the walls, and a rather extensive library a little further away.

The psychic realm was familiar in feeling, but I had no idea where I was standing. I should have expected to be pulled into one sooner or later though. Memories of our last shared psychic realm assailed me, and liquid heat rushed low. I wanted that again—I needed it. Despite how much I'd enjoyed our last experience, I'd forced myself to put a shield in my head to prevent him from visiting me and from me visiting him in that manner. I knew if I allowed it to continue, I would cave and go to him, and he'd mark me, and then all hell would break loose. But since Dinah had told me we were meant to be together now, I'd removed the shield because I didn't want to be anymore separated from him than I already was.

And now...

"I wanted to show you where I live." Donovan's voice sounded softly, and I turned to see him standing a little behind me, arms crossed over his chest.

"This is your place? Do you live in a castle?" I asked, trying not to dwell on earlier, more heated memories.

Those incredible blue eyes focused on me, a smoldering heat in their depths. Holy hell, he was ridiculously sexy, effortlessly so. And when he looked at me the way he was? It was a wonder I didn't just drop to my knees and call him master.

His lips quirked up slightly, the smirk doing things to me that should be against the laws of nature.

"You are projecting your thoughts," he murmured.

"Oh?" I whispered, throat and mouth suddenly dry.

"I won't object to you calling me master, especially when you're on your knees."

An image of that popped into my head, and I clenched my thighs together. I knew we were in Hell and all, but did the temperature just jump?

I cleared my throat and looked around. "So… you said there was more of your realm?"

He raised an eyebrow. "You want to see it?"

"I mean…" I backed up a few steps, slowly unbuttoning the blouse I was wearing. The way his eyes burned hot caused a pounding to start between my legs. "Do you have a bedroom?" My shirt floated to the ground and my hands dropped to the waistband of my tights. "Maybe a shower?"

Donovan was on me in a second, and I gasped and laughed as he wrapped my legs around his waist and ran with me further into his realm. His mouth was on mine a moment later, and I sighed against his mouth.

Every kiss screamed of sin and sex. I was drowning in it. Without warning, Donovan pushed me backwards onto a huge and stupidly comfortable mattress. I bounced twice before he was on me again, hands roaming, lips tasting, and I was burning up for him. I tore at his shirt and after another moment he waved his hand and was completely naked too. I shivered as his hot skin came in contact with mine, and with a buck of my hips, I rolled us so I was on top.

I kissed him again, deeper, my hands tracing over the hard planes of his chest to his ripped abdomen. I mean, seriously, did he *have* to be so perfectly sculpted? I couldn't find a single flaw, and it would start taking a toll on my self-esteem soon.

His hands slid into my hair and he bunched it, his mouth a sinful weapon slowly stripping away my ability to think. I reached lower until my hand wrapped around the hard length of him and he sucked in a sharp breath. My lips curled up in satisfaction, and I pulled back enough to look at him.

"I want you," I admitted, breath shaky and quiet.

"I'm yours for the taking," he replied with a wicked grin.

Shifting, I ran my hand up and down the length of him a few more times before settling over him properly.

"No warmup?" he asked, voice strained as the tip of him met my heated entrance.

I shook my head, smiling. "No need. I *want* you," I reminded.

"Fuck," he groaned as I slowly sank over him.

His long fingers gripped my hips as I worked my way down his length, and I watched his head tip back and mouth fall open in a wordless moan. The veins and cords in his neck stood out, and I couldn't resist the urge to lean forward and nip at them.

The startled groan he let out filled me with a sense of triumph, and I sighed when he was finally fully seated inside me.

"You are fucking beautiful," he praised, hands sliding up my waist to cup my breasts. I shivered, his words and touch affecting me evenly. I was burning up, I needed more, and so I didn't bother to reply. I lifted up slightly and slid back down, feeling the way he filled me so completely. Donovan's eyes burned up at me, and I did it again, almost lifting entirely off him before slamming back down.

A moan tore from my mouth, echoed by one of his own, and that was enough for me. I watched the rapture on his face as I rode him, loving the sense of empowerment that came with it. I was in control, I was the reason he was in such a state. Me, my body, my very own self could turn this Demon King into the pleasure-drunk being he was. I was hot, desperate, chasing pleasure that seemed *just* out of reach. Before I could do much about it, Donovan sat up and shuffled until he was leaning against the headboard. He adjusted me on his lap and gripped my ass, pulling me tightly to him.

"Ride me, *moya lyubov'*. Get us there," he urged, his rough voice sending a shiver down my body.

Moving my hands to the headboard behind him, I did just that. With this angle, I could take him deeper, hold more control, and I closed my eyes as the feel of him so deep almost sent me over the edge.

I lost myself in him, in the way we moved together. Every murmured praise he made only worked to heighten my pleasure that much more. I could feel him holding on, feel his need to unleash and take over, but he was giving me some kind of control by allowing me to stay on top.

I moaned when his hot mouth latched over my nipple and groaned again when his hands kept their grip on my ass, fucking me down onto him, using my body to bring himself pleasure and drag me along for the ride. I was okay with that, holy *hell* was I okay with that. I continued to move, but he finally took control as he moved me faster and harder, every thrust sending stars bursting behind my eyes.

"Almost there, baby," he groaned and a fluttering started deep inside which quickly built until my inner muscles spasmed and clenched tight around him. I cried out, head thrown back as pleasure took me over and I felt his teeth sink into my shoulder as he came hard. The pain of his bite barely registered as pleasure engulfed me, and I clutched him tighter, nails digging in and body clenched—

I gasped, my body still spasming as I awoke from the psychic realm. My skin was hot, almost burning, and my body hummed and ached for more. Donvan was on me in a second, and I wanted to hold him to me and never let him go. I moaned as his mouth found mine, hungry, desperate, and I melted at his touch. The weight of his body was a craving I'd long had, and the way his big hands roamed over my body made me quiver.

His mouth travelled down my cheek to my jaw, nipping at my neck as his hands slid under my shirt to tease my nipples. I groaned, my back arching as every part of me felt sensitive in the best way.

"So responsive," he groaned against me, rocking his hips.

I wanted more, I needed more. We were burning up, desperate, hungry. I felt a frantic, savage need overtake him, urging him, demanding he take action. It was only the smallest voice in the back of my head that finally registered.

"Donovan, wait," I whispered in his mind, gently pushing on his chest even though all I wanted to do was clutch his shirt and yank him closer to me. But he was gone, too deep in it.

"Donovan, we have to stop."

By some miracle, he stilled, every part of him strung so tight I was afraid the smallest movement would shatter him. I swallowed and kept still, feeling as though we were right on the precipice. One wrong move, and we'd topple over the edge.

"Donovan," I whispered again and he made a sound in the back of his throat, something between a groan and a snarl. "We... we can't. The curse—"

He shot off me like I'd burned him, and I scrambled to sit up as I watched him stalk to the door and yank it open.

He was gone in an instant, leaving nothing but the moonlight spilling in.

Closing my eyes, I reached for him, following the cape of desperation and hunger hanging off him that drew further and further away. He was clinging to control by his fingertips. The burden of carrying his mark was weighing on him. Instincts carved into him were demanding he claim me right now, no more waiting. It rode his body hard, almost eclipsing his will to follow my lead and give us time.

Tears burned my eyes at the wave of helplessness and desperation that crashed over him, and I wanted so badly to shield him from it. How were we meant to keep on like this? The need to complete the binding raged at him like a wild beast scratching and clawing inside his chest, hungry for more, desperate and angry it wasn't being fed. But if we gave in, if *he* gave in, it would spell out doom for his brothers and the entire world as we knew it.

CHAPTER EIGHTEEN
DONOVAN

I'd gone for a long ass walk to cool off after how things went down last night, and after several hours, I found myself checking on Hazel. She'd been fast asleep in her room, and her face looked so much younger as she slept. It was wiped clear of all her stresses, her worries, of all the things she'd had to do to survive so long on her own. I didn't know all that much about her yet, but I'd get answers when she was ready to talk.

I kept my gaze averted from those around me as I made my way back to the cabin Trinity had claimed as hers. It didn't hold much, just a bed and a wooden chest at the base of it. There was a private bathroom for her and a small closet and chair, but otherwise it was unfurnished. She said she didn't need much, and since she was almost never around anyway, it didn't make sense for her to have a large place that would more often than not be empty.

I hated being away from Trinity while here, but I'd barely kept control. I hadn't known the power this urge to mark her could have over me. Honestly, it was terrifying. If I hadn't left last night, I'd have marked her and we'd be in a hell of a predicament.

A gentle brush against my mind pulled my attention, and I realized it was Cole checking to see if I was okay.

"Do you need something?" I asked as I made my way to Trinity's house, avoiding looking at the Oasis's inhabitants. I was disgusted with myself, with my own lack of self-control, and I worried they'd all know my failure if they could look into my eyes. It was probably stupid, but I didn't feel much like I could hold my head up around them, not when I'd almost taken Trinity's free will from her in a place like this.

"Do you? I can feel your self-disgust."

"If you mind your own damn business, you wouldn't," I returned sharply.

"Awe, did you not get laid last night, brother?"

I gritted my teeth. *"What do you want, Cole? I have things to do."*

He deliberated teasing me further, I knew he was considering it, but eventually he just sighed and let it go.

"I told Mika everything."

I halted my walking, my mind a whirl of all the things that could go wrong.

"You held out for a day!"

He groaned. *"I know, but you have no idea how hard it is to hide things from your mate, from someone who is literally in and out of your head so much you don't recognize when they're looking for information."*

I sighed and speared my fingers through my hair. *"How did she take it?"*

Cole scoffed. *"It's the first time I've ever had to sleep on my own*

234

couch."

I winced but couldn't help my grin at envisioning that. *"Does she hate me?"*

"No," Cole answered, and I could have been imagining it, but it almost felt like he was sulking over that fact. *"She says she understands, and that she just wants her sister back. She's glad you have her, that you're with her, it's given her some relief that her sister isn't off being tortured by Angels or held by Rogues."*

I made sure to lock away my reaction to his words. If he knew she'd been taken by Angels and tortured, he'd have to tell Mika and she'd be pissed all over again.

"So... why are you so mad at yourself?"

I hesitated. The less he knew, the better. *"Can't say. You'll get in trouble for withholding information, and it's not something anyone needs to know right now."*

Cole didn't reply for a moment and I resumed walking, catching sight of Trinity's cabin up ahead.

"You'll call us if you need us, right?"

"If I have to, I will, but most of this I have to handle alone."

Cole was silent again before he sighed, and his frustration came through loud and clear. *"When all this is over, I'd better get a fucking explanation."*

"Done," I said without hesitation.

"Don't do something stupid. Mika will probably make me sleep in the Great Hall if you do something to get yourself hurt or killed, and I didn't demand information from you that could have helped."

I grinned at the picture in my head. *"I'll do my best. Thanks, Cole."*

He withdrew as I came to a stop out the front of Trinity's home. We were leaving today to see the Elders, and I'd finally get some answers. I'd known for a long time something didn't add up about the way I remembered things, but it wasn't until Mika came into our lives that it really became apparent. Maybe now

I'd find out why. Trinity stepped onto the porch without me calling for her. Her long dark hair was brushed and carefully braided down her back, and the stunning blue of her eyes were almost a dark gray this morning, stormy and wary.

"Are you okay?" she asked, voice soft.

I moved up the first two stairs so we were closer, and I slowly shook my head, reaching out to touch her braid.

"I'm sorry for leaving. I'm sorry I had such a hard time holding onto my control. I'm better than that—I should be better than that."

Her hands lifted to cup my face and she tipped my head so I was looking her in the eye. "You are exactly who you are meant to be, Donovan. You held on, you fought for restraint against something that is not meant to be contained. And you did it for me. So, thank you."

I leaned down to kiss her, my heart pounding and aching when she kissed me back, not an ounce of reservation to be felt. She truly meant what she said.

She pulled back and kissed my cheek before smiling. "Are you ready for today?"

I dragged in a deep breath and nodded. "Yeah. I need answers. Are *you* ready?"

We'd find out today once and for all if Trinity and Tabitha shared a soul. I was already expecting the answer to be a yes, but I knew Trinity needed it confirmed.

She smiled. "Yeah, I'm ready."

"Shall we go?"

Trinity nodded and took my offered hand, her smile eating away at the shadows of disappointment I felt at myself. She was my light, my life. As long as she was by my side, I would handle anything.

Following Trinity's lead, we made our way to the Elders. Trinity was stopped several times by townspeople who had questions for her, and she made sure to introduce me to them all. I met quite a few, including someone she seemed very excited for me to meet named Wren. I wasn't sure exactly what it was she did around the Oasis, but Trinity said she was like her and went on missions to help Witches. For that alone, she had my respect.

When we finally crested a small hill to a house that sat atop it, my heart began to pound in anticipation.

"Alright, here we go," Trinity said, almost to herself as she let out a long, steadying breath.

We made our way up the three stairs and onto the porch. Before she could knock, the door swung open and Dinah stood there waiting.

"Good, you're on time. Follow me," she said, pushing past us. I exchanged a perplexed look with Trinity before we followed the old Seer down the stairs and around the side of her home.

Around the back, the other two Elders stood waiting on the outside of a circle made of a variety of flowers, twigs, and stones I didn't know the purpose of. A selection of white candles was also placed around the circle in even spaces.

"Welcome, Donovan and Trinity. We did not introduce ourselves yesterday," one of the women said with a warm smile. "I am Mira, and this here is Fleur. Of course, you already know Dinah."

I nodded to each woman in turn and waited.

"Trinity, come here. We'll answer the question most direct to you first," Mira continued, holding out her hands for Trinity. I squeezed her hand in support and let her walk to the Elder. Trinity took the old woman's hands and Mira closed her eyes, her mouth moving as if she were muttering under her breath. I stiffened as Fleur made her way to me, a stick of smoking herbs in her hand that she waved around me, speaking in low tones a language I couldn't quite put my finger on. I guessed it was to cleanse me or something and turned my attention back to Trinity. It only took a few minutes before Mira opened her eyes and smiled softly.

"You do indeed share a soul with your ancestor, Tabitha. I feel her mark on your soul, and it is significant."

I drew in a sharp breath as my suspicions were finally confirmed, and Trinity turned to look at me with eyes shining with unshed tears.

"I knew it," she whispered. "It's why I felt so strongly for you the moment I heard your voice."

I swallowed and nodded, a lump rising in my throat preventing me from speaking. Trinity came back to me, and I wrapped her in my arms, turning my head toward her neck to breathe her in. *Mine.*

"This is good, because it will make the next thing we are to do a lot easier," Fleur told us, winding her way around Trinity now with the burning herbs.

"How so?"

Dinah stepped forward then. "The memories you wish to uncover are of the time you and Tabitha spent together. The spell used to hide or remove your memories was powerful and they cannot be recovered by you alone. But Tabitha was with you during that time, she was the subject of those memories, she witnessed them as you did. With Trinity, we can use the link between your souls to heal the injured parts of your mind."

"It's like a jigsaw puzzle," Mira added. "You hold most of the pieces, but Trinity will be able to fill in the missing ones by helping your mind rewire things that were diverted."

I nodded slowly. I didn't understand the complexities of it, but I didn't need to. "It won't hurt Trinity, will it?"

"No, not physically," Fleur assured, putting the burning herbs into a small metal bowl. "Emotional wounds are different though. You will not only witness your memories, you will experience them—both of you."

I stilled at that, memories of blasting away Angels and everything else within a large radius came to mind.

"Uh, I don't know if that's a good idea. Last time... it didn't end well."

Dinah smiled. "We know. That is why we have drawn a circle. You will both step into it and your memory will be restored. The emotional fallout will be contained within the circle."

"And any reaction I might have won't affect Trinity," I said again, needing her to be safe.

"I'll be fine," she assured, pressing her hands to my chest. I looked back at Dinah for confirmation and she nodded.

Drawing in a deep breath, I nodded before looking down at my mate. "Okay, I'm ready. Are you? I didn't realize this would impact you too."

"I'm ready, and I'm looking forward to feeling what Tabitha felt for you, to understand her better."

I grimaced, wishing she didn't have to relive certain parts.

"Let's get started then," Mira suggested, waving us toward the circle.

We did as she told us, and Dinah picked up a cord of white and gold material. "Put your arms out and clasp forearms," Dinah instructed. "I need to bind you together for the spell to take you both back to the same point in time where you each existed. There are several years' worth of memories that will be filtered into your minds in a matter of minutes, so it is important you do not rush coming back."

I had no idea what that meant, but I was sure it would become clear once we were in there. Trinity nodded again and I watched as the old woman used a blessed cord to bind us. Something inside me burned hot and bright when she finished, and I looked at Trinity, positive she'd felt it too.

Dinah stepped out of the circle and Fleur walked around the circle chanting, closing the binding to keep us safe inside and ensure the Oasis wouldn't suffer any fallout.

"You will not be able to come back until the last memory has been returned. So, prepare yourselves," Mira warned.

"Are you certain, moya lyubov'? This does not end happily, you need to be prepared for that."

Trinity leaned up to kiss me gently, and when she pulled back, I searched her face for any sign that she was having second thoughts.

"This is our history. I just had a different name. I need to know what happened, Donovan. I need to be able to be there for you in the end."

Closing my eyes, I pressed my forehead to hers and drew in a slow, deep breath.

"Ready?" Dinah asked softly.

I swallowed. "Ready."

The last thing I remember before the darkness came was Trinity's beautiful eyes filled with warmth and trust.

CHAPTER NINETEEN

DONOVAN

I blinked and the vision before us came into focus. I immediately pulled Trinity to me so I could shield her from the explosion that went off beside us. When the debris that should have hit us simply fell through, I realized there was no danger here.

"What—" Trinity started, her wide eyes taking in the scene.

I remembered this. The battlefield where Tabitha and I met.

"There, I just saved your life."

I turned at the sound of that familiar voice, my breath catching at the sight of Tabitha. She was kneeling on the ruined ground, her dark hair falling from the tie she'd had it in to curtain around her face. My memories of her were vivid, but seeing her again here and now... I'd forgotten how beautiful she was.

The emotions of the moment sank into me. Amusement, adrenaline, the fire within me at wanting to fight.

A battle cry sounded, and an Angel ran through us, sword raised and aiming right for Tabitha. The man beneath her moved lightning quick, sweeping her beneath his large body and throwing hellfire behind him. The Angel caught fire and screamed, and I turned back to the couple.

I saw a version of myself lying over her, arms caging her in, shit-eating grin on his face as he looked down at Tabitha's stunned expression.

"There, I saved your life too. Now we're even," past-me taunted.

Tabitha grinned and pushed the Demon King's chest until he

moved. *"It is the least you could do,"* she fired back.

I watched the interest that sparked to life in my past self's eyes as he looked at her, and it was no wonder I'd wanted her from the beginning. It was so odd feeling the emotions of that time and still feeling my own now.

"This is so strange," Trinity whispered beside me. I looked down at her to see her eyes on the younger version of me and her past self.

"Tell me about it," I murmured.

"Am... am I allowed to be jealous of... myself? I mean, Tabitha was her own person, and I'm not really her... but we share a soul. And the way she's looking at you and the way you're flirting with her makes me mad."

I chuckled and pulled her tighter against me as we continued to watch until Tabitha left us alone to tend to others.

A carousel of other memories flew by us, a number of other times I'd been injured and Tabitha had come to heal me. Every time we flirted a little, we joked, but standing before them, we could feel what old me and Tabitha felt. I wanted her, but she was reserved, quietly ashamed of her feelings for me. I took no offense to it because I could remember why. Not only did she find herself attracted to a King of Hell, but she had a husband at the time.

Trinity gasped beside me when that news was finally divulged. "You didn't get her to cheat on her husband, did you?" she accused.

I held her closer and frowned down at her. "Didn't I tell you that we never let ourselves admit how deep our feelings went?"

"That doesn't mean you didn't seduce her," Trinity said with suspicion.

I sighed. "I tried in the beginning, I'll admit. But that was after…"

Something was clawing at my mind, at my memory, like a long-ago healed scar being ripped open. There was something important I couldn't remember…

Trinity looked up to me, her smile dying. "After what?"

The scene before us changed to Trinity kneeling beside a bed, holding the lifeless hand of her husband as she sobbed quietly. The sense of mourning in the room was painful, and Trinity's gasp was audible. She pressed a hand to her chest as if it physically pained her, and tears immediately sprung into her eyes.

I held her tighter, wishing she didn't have to feel this. It wasn't her pain to feel.

I saw my younger self standing in the doorway, my every emotion painted across his face. The ache in his chest had been damn near crippling, and his gut soured as he watched his friend mourn the loss of her husband. I'd loved Tabitha, but I would have given anything in the world to bring back her husband at that moment if it could have made her happy. Even if it meant I'd never get to be with her.

I watched Trinity as she took it all in, her gaze landing on me briefly before skirting back to the deceased on the bed.

"How did he die?" she asked.

I heard her question, but I couldn't seem to answer it, not with the sudden sound of static in my mind.

"Donovan?"

My throat was dry, and I was finding it hard to breathe as I stared down at the memory of Tabitha who was carefully getting to her feet.

Trinity gasped, a hand to her mouth. "You didn't tell me she had a baby!"

My world began to tilt on its axis as something in my mind

unlocked. I staggered and fell to my knees when visions flashed before my eyes, memories and feelings too heavy and laden with emotions too intense to handle.

"Donovan!"

Trinity's hands were on me, and I struggled to breathe as I looked up at Tabitha's tear-streaked face and *remembered*.

Marlee.

Baby Marlee.

My little *malishka*.

Emotion choked me, made it hard to breathe, and my eyes burned from tears. *Marlee*.

"Donovan, breathe. What's going on? Talk to me," Trinity coached, her hands soothing as they stroked my back.

Whatever was said between old me and Tabitha was drowned out by the sound of blood rushing in my ears as shock overwhelmed me.

"Marlee," I choked out.

"Marlee?" Trinity asked, confused. "Who is Marlee?"

I shook my head, unable to speak, but I didn't need to. The memory shifted and we were in the same room several weeks later, but it was early morning and a golden beam lit the room within. Tabitha stood by the bed, a bundle wrapped in her arms that she bounced gently while rocking from side to side.

Footsteps drew our attention to the door and when it opened to reveal my younger self, I watched as curiosity and wariness stole across his expression.

"Come hold her," Tabitha offered with a smile.

"Uh, no. I'm good here. I just… I wanted to come check on you and make sure you were okay."

Tabitha's knowing eyes watched his across the room and she started toward him. I watched my younger self stiffen as she got closer and gently laid her daughter in his arms.

"Donovan, meet Marlee. My daughter."

My younger self was scared stiff, frozen in place, not even breathing for fear of hurting the little life in his arms.

Trinity gave a gentle laugh beside me, tears in her eyes, and I swallowed and looked back, pain, loss, and so much love filling me, it was hard to decide which I felt the strongest.

Tabitha laughed gently and leaned in close to my younger self, and I watched how he looked at her, that love and devotion shining brightly for anyone who cared to look. She was busy looking at her daughter, leaning against him and smiling at the baby.

"You really loved her," Trinity whispered beside me, wiping at the tears on her cheek.

I nodded. "I didn't realize how obvious I was about it. Looking at me now, it was clear as day. No wonder my brothers never believed me when I told them we were just friends."

Trinity snickered.

The world shifted around us again, and this time we were outside in the garden. It was a cooler morning, but the sun was up and the world was awake and beautiful.

"Alright, I have to be going," my younger self said. I turned around to find past-me and Tabitha sitting amongst the wildflowers, Marlee on his lap. Her large eyes were so wide and innocent, and she was tugging at the strands of his longer hair.

"She is so cute!" Trinity whispered as if the couple in the memory could hear us. She was cute, I admitted to myself. But the pain that lanced in my chest refused to dislodge, and I knew loss was just around the corner.

"Bye, Miss Marlee. I will see you next time," past-me told the little girl before pressing a kiss to her cheek and handing her to her

mother.

"Have you given any more thought to my request?" Tabitha asked as younger-me got to his feet.

He hesitated. *"Yes. While I don't know how you can possibly make it work, I am happy to help. Just tell me when and where, and I will be there."*

"Really?" Tabitha asked, surprise in her voice as she stood Marlee on her feet and let the baby hold onto her fingers for balance.

Young-me smiled. *"As if I could say no to you."*

A tense silence fell as Tabitha and younger-me stared at each other, the air cracking with chemistry and unspoken words.

"Woah," Trinity whispered again, eyes on the scene before us. I remembered moments like this, moments where one of us would say something that could be taken another way, or something that bordered on that careful line we were oh-so careful to stay behind. It felt like we were playing with fire, a temptation both of us struggled with.

"Thank you, Donovan," Tabitha whispered, the war she waged within herself obvious and painful to watch.

Young me saw it and didn't call her out. *"Anytime."*

Another moment of silence lapsed before past me took a step backwards. He was preparing to leave when he froze, eyes dropping to Marlee. I watched with a growing heart as the little girl looked up at my younger self and took a shaky step forward.

"Tabitha," young-me whispered as if he were scared of frightening the child. She was already watching her daughter with wide eyes as the little girl muttered in her gibberish language and took another shaky step toward my younger self.

Trinity gasped and gripped my upper arm excitedly. "Her first steps were toward *you!*"

My heart broke all over again watching her, and Trinity's

puzzled gaze met mine, no doubt feeling my emotion through the happiness that lived in this memory.

More memories whizzed by us—years where we shared moments of laughter and love, of times where I spent nearly every waking hour with Tabitha and Marlee, or watching over them as they worked in their gardens and playing with the others. Every moment of it, my feelings were clear as day.

"Doni!"

We turned to see a slightly older Marlee fling herself and my younger self, her long brown hair bouncing with curls, her dark blue eyes bright with happiness. I watched myself catch her, the grin on his face one of love, joy, and pride. He spun her around, delighting in her squeals of happiness, and turned in time to see Tabitha start toward them, a hand pressed to her stomach, her bright eyes alight with love and worry.

"Doni?" Trinity whispered, and I knew she was remembering my reaction to Hazel calling me that. My reaction earlier had been swift and ferocious, cutting me to the core, and I couldn't work out why. It was like I could hear Marlee's voice echoing the word from centuries ago.

"Yeah," I rasped out. "She was the only person alive to call me that. And now Hazel..."

Trinity sucked in a sharp breath. "Do you think... could it be possible that Hazel and Marlee..."

I swallowed hard and shook my head. "I don't know, I really don't," I murmured, unable to think too hard on it with the overwhelming emotions pouring over me. I could barely breathe.

We watched the scene change again, and I choked on a laugh as we watched my younger self get ambushed by a group of children who used their magic against me. Tabitha was there, talking and laughing, and Trinity watched as my younger self shouted at the girls as they left him bound on the ground and ran back home laughing.

We both watched as Marlee pressed her hands to either side of my younger self's face and squished his cheeks together. Trinity laughed, wiping a tear from her eye. My heart was simultaneously healing and breaking at the same time, and I wasn't sure how much more of this torture I could take.

"You cannot make promises like that, Donovan. You have your realm to rule and responsibilities outside of us. I will not let you take on that kind of obligation, nor will I let myself rely on it."

Tabitha's words felt like the memory of a story I'd once heard, and deep down, I knew this was the beginning of the end.

"You will not let yourself rely on me, but I insist that you do," my younger self said, edging closer to Tabitha, keeping their eyes locked so she'd understand what he was trying to say.

"Demand it of me, Tabitha. You could ask me for the moon and the stars and I would find a way to get them for you. There is nothing you could ask of me that I would not give my all to make happen. You and Marlee… you are important to me."

Trinity sighed next to me, something wistful and aching. "She really loved you. The strength it took for her not to throw herself at you in that moment is astounding."

I held Trinity closer, appreciating her telling me that.

"Donovan…" Tabitha began, but her sentence faded away.

"You're not asking this of me, Tabitha," younger-me said fiercely. *"I am offering. No, I am demanding you let me do this. Do you think I could stand it if anything happened to you? To Marlee? Do you think I could keep my head up around you if I let anything happen to the others you surround yourself with?"*

We spoke some more, feeling and obligations at war with one another.

"Tabitha?" my young self called out.

She turned back to me, wariness on her face. *"Yes?"*

He hesitated before answering. *"I am here for you, always. All you have to do is call. No matter what else happens or doesn't happen, I am here. In every way that matters, you and Marlee are mine to protect. I will protect you and your family from whatever danger is coming with everything I have, with everything I am. There are no strings attached to that; I promise."*

Trinity pulled in a low, slow breath and swallowed hard. "She loved you a lot, Donovan. As much as you loved her. Just know that."

I pressed a kiss to Trinity's head as the scene changed. We watched Tabitha try to defend keeping me around to her twin sister, Bea, and I smiled, remembering the feisty woman. We'd never been close, and a part of her had always looked at me with wariness, but I'd respected the hell out of her. She'd been a force.

Before long, we were watching my younger self throw Marlee up into the air and catch her again, her giggles plastering a grin across my face. Trinity grinned watching us and sighed.

"That's not fair, my ovaries didn't need to see this," she muttered.

I chuckled but watched Marlee. I was glued to her face, to her grin, to the way she laughed and her eyes sparkled.

Fuck, I'd loved that little girl.

And then a shard of pain stabbed through me as Tabitha and my old self talked. *"Have I ever asked you to stop doing what you do?"* I demanded. *"Have I ever been displeased with you for healing my enemy? Have I ever threatened you or let you down after you healed someone who has previously done me or mine wrong?"*

"No."

"Then why does this have to end? I would never stop you from doing

what you are supposed to do."

"But I would!"

Trinity drew in a shaky breath and wiped at tears on her cheeks. "It killed her to say this."

I cleared my throat. "I know."

We watched—me feeling helpless all over again—as Tabitha told younger-me that we couldn't see each other anymore. The sting of her rejection was as fresh as the day it happened, and I wanted so badly to shake off the helpless feeling that clung to me.

Unblinking, we watched as he took his anger and frustrations out on my brothers, how they gave him constant shit for being in such a pissy mood. Trinity asked question after question about them, and I did my best to clarify what was going on.

We watched Donovan of the past train the Witch children for weeks, but something in him had changed, was wounded and hurting, and seeing it from the outside, I noticed how the girls around me had picked up that something had changed. My heart warmed as Marlee threw herself at him, calling out excitedly, and he caught her little body as she launched at him.

She'd trusted me absolutely, and I'd failed her.

"What's wrong, Marlee?" past-me asked.

"Mama is sad. It feels the same as in here," she said, pressing a hand to his chest.

"Oh, poor baby!" Trinity whispered, eyes wide as she watched.

We watched as he tried to justify why he wasn't around as often and tried to convince Marlee that it was for the best, that it had to be this way, but that he would look out for her always.

Trinity gave a little smile as she watched past-me try to explain that I was a Demon, and that some looked at me like I was the evilest thing to ever exist.

I pressed a hand to my chest as my younger self carried a quietly crying Marlee back to the house, my heart breaking for her all over again. But I knew what was to come was even worse.

Marlee clung to past me tightly. *"If I let you go, you are never going to come back."*

"Never say never, Malishka."

"No!" she cried and stomped her feet. *"I don't want you to go."*

"And I'll never be gone, not really," my younger self tried to soothe, but with the way my chest felt like it was being torn open with rusty nails, it was amazing I'd sounded anywhere near soothing. Marlee threw herself at him again, and he didn't hesitate to hug her back.

"I love you, Doni," she cried.

"I love you too, Malishka. I always will."

A moment later, past-me stood up and left Marlee with her aunt, my heart breaking with every step he took away from her. "Oh, Donovan," Trinity whispered, her voice thick with unshed tears. But no, there was more.

We watched Tabitha call out to past-me as he tried to storm away and he backed her against the house, telling her he was leaving. He couldn't be around her or Marlee anymore, it wasn't right, he was endangering Marlee.

Tabitha and he talked some more, pain ripping through him—through her—and then suddenly it changed to something else, something desperate, something primal.

"Are you still leaving?" Tabitha asked, voice shaky.

"*I have to.*"

"No matter what?"

"Yes." Past me bit the word out, hating it, but meaning it.

"Then kiss me."

We watched as younger-me barely waited to take a breath before he took possession of Tabitha's mouth.

"Umm…" Trinity said, eyes averted and cheeks pink. "This is weird."

"Yeah… I'm not sure how I feel about current-you watching past-me kiss past you," I murmured.

"Yeah, I can *feel* everything," Trinity added, laughing awkwardly. So could I, and neither Tabitha nor my past self were exactly holding back. It wasn't until her sister shouted for her from inside the house that either one of them pulled away.

Trinity covered her face with her hands. "Yeah… her sister and family could feel you two."

I gave a huff of laughter, feeling awkward. It didn't last long, though. The heartbreak of saying goodbye to Marlee and Tabitha came back with a vengeance.

We watched as time blurred past us, pain and regret laced within every line of time we went through.

"Many people pray to experience a love this deep. But the consequence of experiencing such a rare treasure is having to feel the pain of its absence once it's gone," Tabitha was saying to Bea as she worked in the garden, and Trinity nodded, eyes watering.

"She meant that, too. Despite how much pain you were both in, she wanted to hold onto it as a reminder of how strongly you felt about one another."

When we found ourselves standing in a pub, I stiffened at the memory.

"What?" Trinity asked, looking for whatever caused my alarm.

"This is it," I warned. "This is where it all ends… prepare yourself."

Trinity clutched my hand tighter as the vision before us changed and we found ourselves in a field surrounded by Angels and two Witches. Trinity gasped, and I held her tighter as she felt Tabitha's pain. My younger self came whirling into the fray, slashing at Angels.

"Take your hands off her!"

I remembered this, the pain, the fight, the desperation to get to her. We watched as younger-me was eventually overpowered and forced to his knees before Tabitha. I frowned when I didn't remember this next part.

"Malishka?" my younger self asked her, careful not to say Marlee's name incase the Angels made it their mission to find such a Witch.

"Safe," Tabitha assured.

My breath stalled in my lungs and I shook my head. But... how? They all burned in the house with her, I saw it, I remembered it! We watched as Tabitha was tortured and they forced younger-me to watch as they tried to find out how to get to the Oasis. They wanted the Witches, all of them, any of them. Seeing Uriel hurt her all over again reignited my pure and utter hatred of the Archangel.

"How could you stand it?" Trinity whispered, trembling in my arms. I shook my head. "I don't know. It was desperation to save her that kept me going."

I watched as the Angels talked among themselves and Tabitha and my younger self talked quietly.

"You need to use your magic and get out of here. Go somewhere, anywhere. Find my brothers," he ordered.

"And leave you?"

My heart turned over at her words, and I watched as they continued talking.

"They're really safe?"

At Tabitha's nod, I speared my hands through my hair. How? How were they safe? Did they come back for her and get caught? "Was she telling the truth?" I asked Trinity, but before she could answer, Uriel came back. Tabitha wrenched herself free of the

Angel holding her back and she launched herself at younger me, her kiss claiming, desperate... a final goodbye. Her fingers pressed to his temples and I remembered her creating a temporary link between us.

"Say goodbye, Demon King," Uriel said with a smirk, dragging a large blade from his belt.

"Uriel, don't!" But it was too late. He drove it into Tabitha's stomach and Trinity gasped and pressed her hands to her abdomen as if she could feel it.

My past self roared and fought, struggling to break free and get to Tabitha, but we watched as he was once again overpowered. Uriel took Tabitha's limp body into her house and returned a moment later, his expression gleeful.

"Donovan..." Tabitha's voice rang out around us, and I forced myself to keep breathing through the agony as she continued. *"I don't have any more time. I am fading. But I need you to know... I... I was always yours. From the moment we met, you claimed a piece of me, and over time you've taken ownership of my whole heart. You are Marlee's father, her best friend, and I am so grateful you were there in her life... and in mine."*

"Oh my God," Trinty whispered thickly, clutching my hand like a lifeline.

"Don't... moya lyubov', don't give up. Fight." His voice was roughened by unshed tears.

"I have no more fight, Donovan. Marlee is safe, my family is safe and will look after her. They will make sure she knows she was loved fiercely and completely. My time ends here, with the love of my life to help ease my journey to the other side."

I shook my head at the words, desperately wanting to believe them but unable to. The pain of seeing the house go up in flames with them all inside—imagining Marlee in there burning alive—

almost drove me insane. I kept myself in solitude for almost a hundred years in order to protect others against my volatile attitude.

They'd died, but this memory said different...

I watched my past-self fight back, slashing at Angels, tearing into them in a frenzied attempt to get to Tabitha before it was too late. But then Uriel intervened and past-me was down.

I felt the desperation in his call to my brothers once the psychic shield went down, and the way they felt his need and hurried to get to him. But Tabitha was fading, and there was nothing he could do...

"I will take the memory of you into my next life, and every life after that in hopes that you will find me there. I will live on; my soul will remain the same. Come find me, Donovan. Look for me in another life and we can have what we should have had in this one."

I closed my eyes as they burned, and Trinity wrapped her arms around me. I held her tighter to me, breathing in her scent.

"You did it, Donovan. You found her in another life—you found me."

The world swam around us as an almost translucent vision covered the violent one. We were in a field, Tabitha, me and Marlee. It was a memory of better days, and past-me pulled Tabitha into it to stop her feeling pain in her final moments, and to send her off with better memories. Trinity's tears flowed freely as we felt Tabitha's body begin to burn and the way I hid the pain from her, kept her in the fantasy world I'd created to ease her passing.

"Come on, Mama!" dream-Marlee called with a happy giggle.

We watched as past-me kissed Tabitha, the immense emotions washing over us almost enough to drown us.

"Go on, lyubov', your daughter is calling for you," he told her.

"Will you come find me?" Tabitha asked.

"Nothing short of death will stop me from finding you again, moya lyubov'. I will look for you in this life and the next, and all the ones that follow."

Trinity sniffled. "And you did, Donovan. You did."

I clenched my jaw and nodded, wiping at the tear that fell from my eye.

The dream-world faded as Tabitha's spirit passed over, and we were back on the cold battlefield, surrounded by death, pain, and blood.

We watched as my brothers arrived, and with the renewed show of force, Uriel fucked off like the coward he was, and my brothers helped younger me to rid of the Witch and Angels still standing. He slaughtered any who stood in his way, his rage and grief feeding his determination to see every one of them dead and wiped from this planet. And with every passing second, his rage grew into something else.

"Woah," Trinity whispered, pressing a hand to her stomach. "Something else is happening here..."

"We never really had an explanation for what happened," I told her, and we watched as I somehow detonated, the explosion coming from within me. Watching now, I think the only reason I survived it as well was because my brothers were holding onto me.

Then... nothing. We watched my brothers bring in another Witch who healed my younger self's injuries, and after several attempts to talk to him and get him to move, they left.

"What... what happened then?" Trinity asked, watching the last of my brothers disappear. Time sped up, the moon came up, and after a moment, we watched a figure step toward my past self still kneeling on the ground.

"Impossible," I whispered, watching Bea rest on her knees in front of me.

"You did the best you could, Donovan," she began gently.

"I failed her," he whispered, his voice a rasp of sound. *"Why did she stay? When you all left for safety, why did she stay?"*

Bea didn't answer, but she didn't need to. The answer was there on her face and I staggered back even as past me looked stricken. "No."

"Donovan," Trinity tried to console, but I shook my head, watching the scene unfold.

"She stayed because she was worried about me?"

"Tabitha loved you, Donovan," Bea began. *"She loved you so deeply, as much as you loved her. She could never have abandoned you if she thought there was a chance you were in danger."*

"Why didn't anyone make her go? Why didn't you? I'm a Demon King; I would have been fine. But she——" His voice cracked and fell silent.

"The others are safe. Marlee is safe," Bea continued, her voice thick with tears. *"She knows her mama isn't coming back, and she is sad about that. But she has all of us to help get her through it, and she's safe."*

Bea continued to talk, telling him that his training with the girls is what saved them, that they were fast on their feet and confident in their magic. They *all* got out... everyone but Tabitha.

And then Bea told younger me something that suddenly made everything else make sense. *"There is something I can do for you, Donovan. It will help you move on."*

He shook his head. *"I don't want to forget."*

"Not forget," she hurried to say. *"Just... distance you from it. Make the memories a little hazy, the emotions a little less intense."*

Things started to click into place now, but I shook my head. How did I agree to this? To forgetting them, to forgetting Marlee?

"Will you take everything?" he asked hoarsely.

"No. I never want to take her away from you, she lives on in your mind as long as you remember her. But I will lessen your grief slightly and... and alter some of what you know."

He frowned. *"Alter how?"*

She let out a long breath. *"I have a memory prepared, one with another ending to what happened here tonight. You will think that we all died, that you arrived to help Tabitha as you did, but that her family were being held inside the house. They set fire to it, but we were all inside."*

His eyes widened slightly. *"Even Marlee?"*

Her eyes shone with tears and she nodded. *"All of us. We need you to think we're all gone so that you don't one day come looking for us and accidentally put us at risk. We need to know we're safe."*

Fuck.

Of course. Of course the only reason I'd ever agree to what she was suggesting was to protect Marlee. She and Tabitha were it for me, they'd been my greatest loves. If forgetting Marlee would protect her, then of course I'd let Bea take my memories.

"I made her a promise, Bea," past me whispered. *"I told her I would carry her memory with me, that I'd find her again one day. Her soul will be the same, and maybe in another life we'd be together."*

"And you can keep your promise," Bea assured. *"I will not take Tabitha from you. You have my word. I want her in your memories because then this version of her soul lives on forever. But I will lessen the grief, perhaps dull your feelings slightly so that you have a chance of moving on."*

He agreed to her terms but asked her to wait. *"Can you tell Marlee something for me?"*

Bea agreed, her sorrow as deep as mine.

"Please tell her that I love her, that I will always love her. My little

Malishka. Tell her how proud of her I am, how I know she will grow into a beautiful, kind, and powerful Witch who will protect her people and save so many lives. Make sure she knows she was so loved, and that I will love her forever. Will you tell her that, please? I don't want her to feel like I abandoned her."

Bea agreed, and even now I knew she would have passed on my message. My heart clenched as I realized Marlee would have known how much I loved her in the end, that I didn't just disappear on her.

After another moment, Bea began the spell to alter my memory, and the scene around us faded to gray, turned blurry, and then vanished altogether.

I came back to myself, hugging Trinity to me as she trembled in my arms and my cheek was pressed to the top of her head, my cheeks wet. Pain ripped through me at everything I'd gone through, everything I'd lost, everything I'd sacrificed. It was all there in full detail, and I could barely breathe through it.

I knew everything now... but how was I meant to move on knowing what I'd lost?

CHAPTER TWENTY

TRINITY

The silence was loud as we stood together in the circle, holding each other. I was shaking, I could feel it and no matter what I did, I couldn't stop. I wanted to be strong for Donovan, I wanted to be the one he leaned on right now, but coming out of there was like being one big exposed and raw nerve.

I could feel it all, everything. Donovan had tried to shield Tabitha, and he'd tried to shield me in there too out of nothing but pure instinct. I don't even think he knew he was doing it. But I felt it, and it killed me to know what he'd gone through, what he'd lost.

Marlee.

Gods, that beautiful little girl had loved him so much, and he'd loved her even more. He'd been so strong, stronger than I could have ever been in walking away from her and Tabitha in a bid to keep them safe. He'd seen what his influence on Marlee could do to her life and he refused to be the cause of her magic ever potentially backfiring.

And Tabitha...

I felt everything she felt for Donovan. I mean, I already loved the man, although I was yet to say that out loud and dared not in case it completed one of the bonds. But then to have Tabitha's feelings on top of my own? The two had known each other for years, faced death and enemies, and had still fallen in love despite how taboo it had been even back then. Their restraint was a lesson I could do with, because last night had almost taken Donovan and I too far.

I clutched the back of Donovan's shirt now and felt the small tremor in his body and the way he held me as if he were afraid I'd fade away too.

"She lived, Donovan," I whispered softly, gently leaning back to look up at him. The wetness on his cheeks damn near killed me and I wiped away his tears, wishing I could wipe away his pain just as easily. "Marlee was alive, she got out, she survived. The rest of the family did too... you didn't fail like you thought you did."

He shook his head. "Through no help from me," he reminded.

I frowned. "You sacrificed *everything* so they would stay safe. You did the best thing for them at the time, and it was to sacrifice happier memories and the comfort in the knowledge that they'd survived in order to protect them. They survived and remained safe *because of you.*"

His stormy blue eyes searched mine, and I hoped he felt the truth of my words because I meant every one of them. He swallowed and something shattered shone at me from his gaze. "She stayed back to help me, Trin. She could have been safe somewhere, but she stayed for me. Marlee grew up without her mother because of me."

Again, I shook my head. "That was Tabitha's decision and hers alone. You don't get to take away the nobility of her sacrifice by bearing the guilt of her death. She loved you, Donovan, and she would never have gone for safety and left you behind, just as you would have never done that to her."

Pain glittered back at me from his eyes, but the longer I held his gaze, the more acceptance began to seep in. He needed to relieve himself of this guilt he'd been carrying for so long, and accept that Tabitha would have sacrificed herself again and again for him. She was as in love with him, drawn to him, as he had been to her.

Nothing could have stopped her.

I pulled him in for another hug as Fleur walked counterclockwise around the circle, opening it up again now that the potential danger to the Oasis had passed.

"Does remembering help?" Dinah asked softly, and we slowly pulled apart.

Donovan took a moment to calm himself before he looked at the Seer. "Right now, no. But it will in the long run."

She smiled softly and it was then I noticed the book in her hand. It was old, really old, and I recognized it as one of the ones we kept in the history vault.

"We want you to have this," she said, handing it to Donovan.

He frowned and slowly took it. "What is it?"

Dinah hesitated and sighed. "It contains some things about the first family to live here in the Oasis."

Donovan's face paled slightly and his hands trembled. "I..."

"There are letters in there. It's a diary, really."

Donovan looked down at the book and at his swift intake of air I looked at the cover where he was staring. There, in gold embossed print, were five words.

The Diary of Marlee Wardwell.

Donovan swallowed convulsively, and I tightened my hold on his arm.

"Are you sure?" he asked, his voice coming out rough with suppressed emotion.

Dinah nodded, and Mira and Fleur followed suit. "Whenever you get to reading it, you'll understand why. It was never ours to keep; simply to hold onto until you came for it."

Donovan gripped the book tightly and gave a short, sharp nod.

He was overwhelmed, and ripped raw from everything we'd just lived through again. Considering how he felt the first-time losing Tabitha, he was handling this remarkably well. At least this time he'd been somewhat prepared for what he was in for.

"What about…" I trailed off, licking my lips. I wanted to know, but I wasn't sure Donovan could handle the news. "What about Marlee's soul? Since you showed me the vision of Hazel, Dinah, I've felt a pull to her, like she was meant to come with me so I could protect her. Donovan too, felt it. Is it at all possible…"

The Elders looked at one another before Dinah turned back to me with those knowing eyes.

"Souls who are meant to find each other will do so in many lifetimes."

"So, that's a yes?" I asked.

None of them confirmed or denied, they just remained in their neutral silence.

I sighed. They would only tell us so much.

"Let's go," I suggested softly. "Thank you, Elders, for your help," I added.

They nodded and watched us as we left.

Donovan was quiet, a powerful storm brewing beneath the surface, and I wasn't quite sure how to help him. I, myself, was feeling rather battered. I knew it was nothing compared to what he'd been through, but I'd felt Tabitha. For a time there, I'd *been* her again. I'd felt her fear, her love, her desperation to get back to her baby and reunite with Donovan as a family. She'd wanted them to be together after this, to leave her family if they needed it to be that way. She wanted her daughter and the love of her life, and she wanted to be happy.

It had all been taken from her, and in a painful and brutal way. Donovan and I walked and walked, no real destination in mind as we remained trapped in our own heads, reliving parts of that experience together.

We came to a stop on top of a hill, a single tree standing tall atop it. The day was beautiful, showing no indication of the horror we'd just experienced together. Donovan's face was impassive, but his eyes were far away.

"Do… do you want me to give you some space?" I asked, wondering what I could do for him. I'd do anything he asked, I just wanted him to feel better.

He cleared his throat and shook his head. "I don't know what I want. I just… I need some time to sort things out in my head, to put things away."

I sniffled and nodded, feeling a little of the same. "I can come find you in a few hours and make sure you're alright?"

He nodded slowly. "Thank you. I just… that was a lot. More than I was expecting," he answered, his gaze finally resting on me again.

I hesitated, not wanting to leave him alone in this state, but sometimes I needed time and space, and I knew he was the same.

He smiled softly. It was strained, small, but he tried. "I will be okay, *moya lyubov'*."

I nodded, feeling a little better now that he'd called me that endearment again. "Come find me when you're ready; I won't be far."

Donovan nodded and leaned in to brush a kiss over my lips. I kissed him back and rested my forehead against his for a moment when we pulled away. "You'll be okay, Donovan. We'll get through this."

"I know," he assured, kissing my head before straightening.

With another searching look, I squeezed his hand and let go. I started down the hill, wrapping my arms around myself in some form of comfort as tears burned my eyes. Some time apart was probably for the best. I had wounds I needed to tend to before I could help him handle his. The last thing I wanted was for him to feel like he had to put his own feelings on the backburner to help me handle mine. This hadn't been about me; it was about him.

I walked for a long time before I made it to the outskirts of the village, and when I looked up, it was to see Leviah and Hazel. The girl looked at me with a worried expression and started towards me at a fast clip when I turned in their direction.

"Are you okay? You feel... hurt," she asked. I wanted to hug her for her concern, but I still had the feeling she wouldn't appreciate the contact.

"I'm okay. I just... Donovan and I relived a past life together and it was... unpleasant," I answered, clearing my throat.

"A past life?" Lev asked, frowning. After a moment, his expression cleared. "So, you were right? Tabitha?"

I nodded. "Yeah, we share a soul."

"Is Doni okay?" Hazel asked, and the nickname jabbed at me. Her eyes narrowed as if she felt my reaction, and she likely did. She was a Witch, and the more I was around her, the more I realized she was a very powerful young Witch.

"He's okay... sort of. He went through a lot, and reliving it ripped open old wounds. We both need a little time to decompress and compartmentalize."

She nodded slowly, but her worried eyes flicked behind me as if looking for any sign of him.

"Do you want some tea? We can go somewhere quiet and talk?" Lev asked.

I smiled gently and nodded. "I'd like that, thank you."

"Hazel?" Lev offered.

"Uh... no, thank you. I'm going to go for a walk," she said, stepping away from us.

"You know where to find us when you're back," Lev said, his knowing eyes watching her. She nodded, her eyes coming to rest on me for a moment. I felt like she wanted to say something, but she instead gave me a terse smile and turned away.

"She's going to go find him," Lev said.

I sighed. "I know. But she might actually be able to help him right now."

"And you can't?" he asked.

I shook my head. "Not right now, not while I still feel like this."

Leviah's worried gaze rested on me and he sighed. "You and Donvan can't keep this up much longer. I see the strain holding back from the binding is taking on him, and I see what it's doing to you. It is not natural for the two of you to be apart and its consequences are going to be messy, possibly deadly. We need to find the Witch who cursed you and kill her, or you need to find another way around it. This is not sustainable."

I knew all this, I really did, but it was finally sinking in just how on edge both Donovan and I were, and how bad things could go soon if we didn't complete the bond.

"I know," I finally whispered. Lev sighed and pulled me in for a side hug as we made our way back into town.

We'd find a way—we had to.

CHAPTER TWENTY-ONE

DONOVAN

They'd survived.

No matter how many times I thought the words, they seemed impossible. Over two hundred years of thinking they'd died, that I'd failed them all, that they'd all perished in that fire, and one spell to help me remember proved it all wrong. I'd spent centuries agonizing over their deaths, but they hadn't died. Tabitha had, and that was bad enough.

But the other Wardwell Witches... Marlee. They had all lived. I slowly sank to the grassy hillside, closed my eyes, and drew in long, deep breaths.

The book weighed heavily in my hands and I glanced at it again, the gold print at the bottom of the cover jabbing at my heart like a knife. I wanted to read it. I wanted to know what she had to say, what kind of life she'd had... but what if she'd suffered? What if she'd been miserable and lonely? What if she left the Oasis the moment she could and had perished? What if she blamed me for her mother dying?

My little *Malishka*.

As if they had a mind of their own, my shaking hands carefully opened the book to the first page. A small, choked laugh escaped me at the childlike cover page. It was drawn in charcoals and had rudimentary drawings, happily titled, *The Diary of Malishka*. Little hearts, butterflies, and flowers bordered the page, and I traced them gently, almost able to see her drawing them. My heart both broke and healed at the title, and I turned the page, hopeful.

It didn't have any writing, just another drawing. This one was of a child and a woman holding hands, and she'd written her name and "mama" underneath it. I wiped at my eyes again and kept turning. A drawing of me, Marlee, and Tabitha pulled the air form my lungs and I stared at it for a long time.

I kept skimming, feeling connected to her for the first time since losing her. I'd spent the last two-hundred plus years not even remembering her, and here was proof that she hadn't forgotten me.

The first journal entry came up and I read it, smiling at the messy writing and misspelled words. Reading how she missed her mama and her Doni would have taken me to my knees if I weren't already sitting down. I kept reading, wishing I could change every entry that said how much she missed us, how many times she cried, wondering if we would ever see each other again.

I skimmed over the years, reading about how she liked a boy, problems with friends, her first date. I'd never wanted to reach through the pages of a book and punch someone before, but that's exactly what I wanted to do when she wrote about how her first boyfriend broke up with her. She wrote about her Aunt Bea and her cousins and they loved her fiercely. She expressed how she worried she'd lose them too.

I turned the page, and my gaze caught on my name again.

Dear Diary,

I found him.
I promised Bea I'd never approach him if I saw him out in the world,

*that I'd never reveal who I was or what really happened all those years
ago. I wanted to tell him. The moment I saw him, I almost cried. He
looked exactly the same, my Doni. Instead, I just watched him for a bit.
He wasn't doing anything much, just sitting by a river and cleaning his
blades. It's been twenty years since I saw him, and I still remember how
much his heart broke saying goodbye to me. Of course, I hadn't quite
understood why he'd left when I was so young, but Aunt Bea had
explained it all to me.*

He'd been trying to protect me.

Reading those words made me feel dizzy. She'd seen me? She'd
been so close and I hadn't even known? Hungry for more, I read
over the next entries. Freezing when one caught my attention.

Dear Diary,

I spoke to him today.

The words tightened a vice on my lungs so that for a long
moment, I couldn't breathe. The shock of the words kept hitting
me and I sat in disbelief.

*He didn't know me, of course, and I kept my promise to Aunty Bea and
didn't tell him. He was injured, though, and I couldn't just leave him.
So, I offered him my help. At first, he'd been wary, and I kept every
safeguard up that I had to conceal that I am a Wardwell. He let me heal
him, and we talked for a moment. I could feel how he was still in pain,
but not the physical kind. Even so, he was funny. He joked, and I almost
slipped up and called him Doni. Honestly, I almost burst into tears. It's
been four years since I saw him last, and I wanted to tell him about my
life, about my husband, about our girls.*

Something like a sob ripped from my chest and I blinked away
tears as I read on.

I wanted to tell him how I named my oldest Tabitha after my mother,
but how my second born is Donna, after him. I wanted him to know that
I am happy, and so in love, that life is good for me. I wanted to tell him
that I understand why he left, that I knew he tried to save my mother.
But I didn't say any of that.
Instead, I told him that he needed to be more careful, that Witches
aren't just out and about ready to heal as we once were, and that he was
lucky I'd been close by and felt his pain. He'd thanked me, told me he'd
be more careful, and offered to get me back to my home safely. I let him
walk me to a friend's house because it made him feel better to make sure I
wasn't taken by the Angels. Then he thanked me again, smiled, and
shadowed out.
And I went back home to the Oasis.

I searched my memory for what she'd just said, but everything
was so jumbled and raw right now. That time in my life had
been volatile at best. I had stayed in my realm for almost one-
hundred years, only venturing out to engage in battles with
Angels or when I thought I had a lead on Uriel. She must have
seen me during one of those times, in which case I was lucky to
remember anything.
I kept reading, learning about her family, her children. She
ended up having five in total, her eldest and then two sets of
twins. She lost her youngest in childbirth and reading those
passages cut me deeply. But judging from her words, her Aunt
Bea and her husband had been there for her every step of the
way. I wished I could have prevented her from feeling the loss of
a child, but life had not cared much about our plans or wants. I
read about her Aunt Bea's passing, a few cousins, and then her

husband. She wrote about becoming a grandmother and then a great grandmother.

Before I knew it, I was at the last entry and was shocked at what I found.

Dear Doni,

I don't know if these words will ever find you, but I have faith that they will. I have instructed my children to pass along a message to their children and for them to do the same that this diary is to go to you one day. I hope they continue to remember my instructions until this book finds you. Our fates are intertwined, I know that. A Seer Witch who used to live in the Oasis told me as much, and I believe that we met all those years ago for a reason. I don't know how long it will have been since we last saw each other, but I needed to write to you.

I am old now, and tired. If you could see me, you'd laugh. I'm short, my hair is white, my skin is wrinkled, and I don't regret a single thing about it. I have lived a good life, a long life. Things were hard at times, but that's just life, isn't it?

I wanted you to know that Aunt Bea gave me your full message when I was a teenager. She said she wanted to wait until I was old enough to understand to tell me everything. When I was younger, she only told me that you loved me, would miss me, but would be looking out for me from afar. Those words helped ease the pain often and helped me sleep most nights thinking you were out there protecting me and my family.

I love you, Doni. You were the father I never had, and while my memories of you have faded over the years, the love I remember feeling for you has not. I have lived a life I think you would be proud of, and I grew up trying to be everything you wanted. I remembered to be kind and to hone my power, and was protective of my family. I missed my mother often, but like you said, it was okay to miss her. I know you loved me, and I know you would have stayed with me if it was possible. I know you didn't abandon me, and I thank you for having the strength to walk away when you did. I don't know if I could have been as strong as you were if I had been forced to make such a decision.

Maybe one day, in a future life, you'll find me again. Maybe you'll save me and I'll get another chance to be your daughter and this time we'll live it out together. I have faith that day will come. Like I said, your fate and that of the Wardwell Witches are tightly bound, and it would be too cruel for us to not get another chance.

Thank you for protecting me and loving me so fiercely that even though we only got a few years together, the love I felt from you has carried me through all these long years.

I'll love you forever, Doni.

Love, your little malishka.

My vision blurred and my eyes burned. Closing my eyes on the pain, I bowed my head and tried to remember how to breathe. Having her words cut me deeply, but they helped to ease the pain I carried now. She'd lived a long and happy life, full of all the experiences I could have ever wanted for her. Letting her go hadn't been pointless, it had saved her.

Dragging in a deep breath, I let it out slowly and wiped at my face, closing the book because I couldn't look at the words again right now. I'd done the right thing, and she'd had faith that I would find my way to her family again, and that I would need to read her words.

"Thank you, malishka," I whispered aloud, hoping my voice carried to her soul wherever it was.

After several long moments, I moved enough to lean against the trunk of the tree, too exhausted to move anywhere else right now. My thoughts traveled back to Trinity, and I wondered if she was okay. I'd been so overwhelmed with everything I'd just learned, I'd barely taken a moment to talk to her and see how she was really doing.

"Moya lyubov'? Are you okay?"

Her reply was immediate. *"I am, are you? I am worried about you."* I let her words sooth me, the sound of it washing over me and taking away the stabbing pains that now inhabited me.

"I am sorry I let you leave, I should not have let you go without seeing to your needs. Are you sure you are okay?"

"Because you can't tell right now, I'm letting you know I'm glaring at you. Don't you dare apologize for accepting my offer to grieve alone. Your mind was a mess—still is, I guess—and you needed time to process it all."

I frowned. *"Okay, but my first duty is to you. Are you okay? You experienced everything alongside me, felt everything Tabitha felt for me and in her death, her loss. You suffered, Trinity. Are you sure you're okay?"*

"It's not the first time I have suffered, Donovan. I am okay. I was mostly concerned for you, I can handle what I experienced in that memory." I ground my teeth at the reminder of her previous suffering, something I considered another failure of mine. If I had just made the decision to mark her back then, instead of allowing for the ridiculous games we'd been playing, there was no way the Angels could have taken her. I would have been there with her and taken her to safety.

"Are you okay?" she asked, her voice soft, unsure.

"I will be. Thank you for allowing me some time. I'll come back to the village soon."

There was a pause as I waited for her reply, and I breathed deep. The sun would be down in another two hours or so.

"There is a bonfire tonight to welcome Hazel to the Oasis, and they've

*extended the invitation to you as well. If you're up for it, I think it
would be good for you to attend. But if you need more time, then please
take it."*

I thought about it for a moment. *"I'll let you know soon,"* I
answered, knowing I'd likely go. If that's where she was, then of
course I'd be there.

"Take all the time you need," she whispered and I sighed, letting the
conversation go.

"I never took you for the enjoying a sunset type."

I jerked at the sound of a new voice and looked around to see
Hazel making her way up the hill, her cheeks pink and hair
slightly damp.

"Hazel? What are you doing here? Are you okay?"

She grinned and waved me off before sprawling out on the grass
a few feet away, breathing heavily. "I am not as fit as I should be.
That hill was a bitch."

I grinned and she smiled back, waiting.

"What?"

She shook her head. "You're not going to tell me to mind my
language?"

I shrugged. "It'd make me a major fucking hypocrite, wouldn't
it?"

She gave a small laugh and nodded, forcing herself to take in
several deep breaths before she pushed up to a sitting position.

"So... what's up, Doni?"

I raised an eyebrow, pushing aside the stab of emotion that name
conjured. "Up?"

In a way only a teenager could manage, she rolled her eyes as if I
were stupid. "Yeah, you're sitting here in a cloud of misery and
self-loathing, I could feel it three hills away. Trinity didn't look
too happy either, like she was carrying a load that wasn't hers.

What's up?"

I frowned. "Is Trinity okay?"

Hazel shrugged. "I mean, I think so? I didn't stay to find out, but Leviah is with her."

Some of my tension eased, even though I hated the idea of another male soothing her. It was Leviah. I wanted to hate the fucker, but he'd done nothing but prove his loyalty.

"So, you thought you'd come find me and… what? Bond?"

She made a gagging sound. "No, you weirdo. But if you were gonna bail out of here in some kind of tantrum, I wanted to go with you."

She said it as a joke, as if it were nothing, but I saw the underlying fear in her eyes, the worry that I was going to leave her here.

"As if I could leave without taking you with me. You're powerful for your age. I don't want a pissed-off you hunting me down on some vendetta when you're thirty," I replied, shuddering in an exaggerated fashion.

"Well," she said, looking at me as if she were a queen speaking to a peasant. "As long as you are aware of the consequences."

I smiled and glanced out at the horizon, watching the golden sun begin its descent. The temperature had dropped a little in the last hour, but it wasn't unpleasant. I glanced at Hazel from the corner of my eye, but she seemed to be frowning at Marlee's book at my side.

"Something wrong?" I asked.

She shook her head. "Just weird to find you up here reading when you feel so… messy. Are you okay, though? I mean, you're smiling, but you're still all…" she began, struggling to find the words. She waved her hands at me and pulled a strange face. "Cloudy."

I chuckled a little reluctantly, but I couldn't help it. She was a breath of fresh air, and she cared despite how much she tried not to.

"I will be. I just went to see the Elders and they were able to uncover some memories in my head that had been tampered with. Apparently, it was with my full consent... but it hurt nonetheless to live through it all again. Recovering memories forces you to live the moment again, complete with all emotions."

Hazel pulled a face. "Yikes, sounds heavy."

Again, a chuckle worked its way up my throat at her casual assessment. "Yeah, something like that."

"Is Trinity upset that you had to go through all that? She's your girlfriend, and she's a Witch, so she'd feel everything you feel like I can."

That sobered me up, and I made an effort to reel in my emotions again.

"No, I didn't mean for you to hide them. It's kind of nice, actually."

I frowned at her and she sighed.

"Not that you're in pain, but that you weren't hiding. Adults always try to hide the truth when they think it'll make younger people uncomfortable or aware that not everything is bright and shiny in the world. I know it sucks out there, I know it's not all good, so there's no need to hide it when you feel the darkness too."

Her words struck hard, and I wondered just what this girl had been through. I knew she'd suffered, I knew she'd been alone for a long time, but what else.

"How long have you been on your own, Hazel?"

She frowned. "I asked a question first."

I considered her point and decided she was right. She might only be fourteen, but I was looking at a girl who could no longer be considered a regular child, at least not with the experiences she'd been forced to endure.

"Trinity isn't upset that I had to relive the memories, she's upset because she relived them with me. Her soul… it belonged to a Witch I knew several hundred years ago. The memories I needed to recover were of that Witch during that time, and the only way for me to get those memories back was for the Elders to bind us in a way and send us back together. She felt everything her past life felt, and it wasn't all good."

Hazel's eyes widened and her mouth fell open. "Seriously? That's definitely heavy."

I shook my head and looked at her expectantly.

She sighed. "I've been on my own for two years."

I sat up a little straighter. "Since you were twelve?"

She gave me a slow clap. "Well done, Doni! You can count!"

I picked up a twig and threw it at her. "Smart ass."

She grinned and started picking at the blades of grass in front of her, casting another curious look at Marlee's book. "How are you and Trinity together? Isn't it weird for a Demon King and a Witch to hook up?"

I raked my fingers through my hair and tried to temper my smile. "Yeah, it is. But she's not just my girlfriend, that kind of minimizes things. There's a prophecy known to only a few, and it ties us together. We're kind of destined for one another."

Hazel stared in shock again. "For real?"

I nodded. "Yup."

"But like… you're ancient. And she's a Witch. She'll grow old and die—won't that be gross?"

I laughed this time, shaking my head, but I found her lack of filter refreshing. "There is a mark I can place on her that will bind her to me and give her immortality like me."

She perked up. "Can you do that for anyone else?"

I shook my head. "No, just the woman I'm destined for."

Hazel fell silent for a moment, and I looked at her more carefully. "How have you been surviving on your own?"

She was silent so long I didn't think she'd answer, so I tossed another twig at her. "Hey, you asked three questions and got three answers. My turn."

She rolled her eyes, but her lips tugged up in a small smile. "Mostly I stayed low. I barely used my magic unless it was to place a concealment charm on myself. I stayed in abandoned houses or places that were scheduled for demolition and were empty for ages. I used magic to ward off other people who might want to stay there too."

"What about food? School? Did you go looking for other Witches who might help you?"

She sighed. "I stole when I had to, and I worked for money doing odd jobs. I was already several years ahead in school—I'm kind of a genius," she added with a carefree shrug, but a slightly smug smile curled her lips.

"And modest, I see."

She waved a dismissive hand. "Never saw the point of modesty. Anyway, I went looking for some other Witches and one or two might have been genuine and nice, they offered to let me stay, but I didn't trust anyone. There were others who tried to take me in who I felt were less genuine. Mostly, I stayed away from them. Too many are friends with Angels, and so many of my kind are being taken to Heaven and never seen again."

Smart girl.

"What happened to your parents?"

"Isn't it my turn for a question? Your last one was multiple in one."

I sighed but waved her on. "Ask away."

She hesitated, humor dying from her eyes. "What happened in your past and Trinity's past life that causes you so much pain?"

I sucked in a sharp breath and glanced away from her, forcing myself to keep my shield in place. She'd asked me not to hide my emotions, but damn, I couldn't lay all this at her feet. I knew I wasn't doing a good enough job at hiding it all, though.

"I was in love with a Witch all those years ago, felt a draw to her I'd never felt with anyone else, and she loved me too. But she died—was murdered by an Archangel right in front of me—and all this time I thought her entire family died with her. But the fact that Trinity exists tells me someone escaped. It turns out, I'd allowed the sister of the Witch I'd loved to wipe my memories and alter them so I would think they all died. It was to protect them. They were the ones who created this place, and they couldn't have me looking for them and possibly leading danger their way."

Hazel frowned, intelligent eyes narrowed as if she were thinking of something. She stared at her hands picking at the grass when she spoke next. "You're talking about the Wardwell's, right?"

I nodded. "Yeah, Tabitha Wardwell was the one I loved."

She swallowed hard and nodded, and after a moment she blinked and cleared her throat. "Go on."

I sighed and picked up the book beside me. "Tabitha had a daughter, Marlee. I'd been in Marlee's life since day one, and she became the daughter I never had. In altering my memory, she was erased, too, until a few hours ago. And I felt it all over again, loving her, losing her..."

Hazel had gone pale, her eyes swimming in sympathy when spoke softly next. "Is that why I feel pain from you when I call you Doni?"

I tried to smile and nodded. "She was the only person to ever call me that, the only one I ever would have accepted calling me that. It's not exactly badass, is it?"

Hazel's smile was small, unsure, and it took several moments for her to speak again. "Do you want me to stop? I don't want to hurt you."

I shook my head before I could really process what I wanted. "No. It's been... nice, actually. I don't mind it if you call me Doni. But only you."

Her smile was slow, but it lit from within her and she nodded and looked around, a little uncomfortable.

"Alright, out with it," I said. "What happened to your parents?"

Hazel glared at me and leaned back, looking out at the slowly lowering sun. "Dad died when I was little, maybe a year old. I never knew him. And Mom... she died the day before my twelfth birthday when Angels invaded our home and tried to take us. She got me to a safe place in the house protected by concealment magic, but I saw her fight them, saw one of the Angels stab her. I watched her die."

My heart went out to the kid as she tried her hardest not to allow too much emotion to show or be heard as she relayed the events. It had to have been traumatic for her, and my admiration for her rose some more.

"Are you going to leave now?" Hazel asked after a long stretch of silence where we watched the sun sink.

"Leave?"

"Yeah," she said, shrugging. "You know what you needed to know; you're meant to be bound to Trinity and you're a King of Hell which I guess means you have a circle of Hell to run. You have all your answers," she said, gesturing to the book at my side. "What's the point of staying here longer than you have to?"

I shook my head. "There are things Trinity and I need to do, things to sort out before anything else can happen. Until then, I'm not leaving."

Hazel watched me with wide, vulnerable eyes and I leaned forward.

"What's going on?"

"Take me with you," she said in a rush.

My eyes widened and I jerked back. "What?"

"When you go, when you leave the Oasis, take me with you. I don't want to stay here; I don't want to be left alone again. When you go, I want to go with you."

I blinked at her, then turned away, my heart racing a thousand miles an hour. Was it strange that my first instinct was to tell her of course she was coming? That when I pictured leaving here, it was with Trinity *and* Hazel? I hadn't really thought about it, but now that I did, that image had been in my head from the start. There was no idea of ever leaving her here.

"Hazel, the Oasis is a safe place, especially for Witches. Things out in the world are bad right now and—"

"I know how bad they are," she reminded sharply.

"Right," I agreed softly. "I just want to say that… Hell would be safe for you, I know that. And I have sisters-in-law who are Witches and would be happy to welcome you into the fold. But there are fewer freedoms for you there. You can't leave there whenever you want, and the rules are far stricter for your safety."

"So, there are Witches who can help train me, I'd be safe, and I'd be with you and Trinity? I'm failing to see the downside. And what does it matter if I can't leave Hell without you? I can't leave the Oasis on my own either."

She had a point there, I silently agreed.

I considered her request but something was still bugging me. After a moment, I leaned a little closer and made sure she held my gaze when I spoke.

"One more question, and I want it straight and honest."

She hesitated but nodded. "Okay."

Something had bothered me about Hazel since I'd first laid eyes on her, but after everything today, I think I had finally come to terms with what it was, with what some part of me had already guessed but refused to examine. "What is your ancestral Witch lineage?"

I could tell the moment I asked that she wished I hadn't, but I wasn't backing down. I had a feeling I already knew the answer, anyway. She didn't answer right away, and I decided to wait her out.

Finally, she sighed and gave a small shrug. "Wardwell."

CHAPTER TWENTY-TWO

DONOVAN

"Wardwell?"

Hazel nodded and I leaned back, studying her closer. This girl was smart, she was resourceful, and there was more to her than met the eye.

"Why don't you want to stay here, Hazel? Why don't you want to live in the place your ancestors created to keep you safe?"

"I already told you—"

"No, you gave me an excuse, not the real reason. Why don't you want to stay? More to the point, why are you asking to come with me *specifically*? I am a King of Hell, no Witch warms to us as quickly as you have. We're dark, we know that, and you and your kind are generally light. The two don't mesh easily, so tell me the truth."

She shook her head, frustrated. "I feel like I know you guys now. I know you better than everyone here."

"So, give them time and you'll know them too. That's not an answer. Tell me the truth."

She began to look a little desperate and stood up. I stood with her, book in hand, watching her carefully.

"Did someone tell you to stay with me? Did someone tell you to get close to me so you could spy?"

"What?" she gasped. "No! It's not like that."

"But someone *did* tell you to find me. Who? Why?"

"They didn't—"

"You're lying, I can tell. Who told you to find me and why?"

"No, you don't—"

"Who, Hazel?"

"My mom!" she screamed with tears in her eyes.

I frowned at her answer, not understanding. Hazel swore under her breath and paced away from me before she crossed her arms over her stomach and looked out at the setting sun.

"You said your mother died two years ago."

"She did."

I shook my head. "Then I don't understand how—"

"I dreamed about you the night before you found me," she

answered softly. I waited for her to continue, not detecting any lies in her words.

"I didn't see your face or hear your name. I just felt that we would meet soon, and that I needed you to find me. All I saw was your mark, the symbol of the sixth King of Hell. I could feel my mother with me, feel her presence and it was so safe, so… welcoming. And she whispered to go to you, that you'd look after me, that I'd be safe with you."

I swallowed hard at her words, my skin prickling with awareness and a little unease. She was telling the truth, that much was real.

"Yesterday, I didn't realize it was you I was meant to go with until you handed me this," she continued and I watched as she pulled the small knife from her boot that I'd given her, and she handed it back to me. The symbol she spoke of was carved into the hilt of the blade, bright and heavy.

"Why didn't you say anything?" I asked.

She scoffed. "How would that go? You guys ask me to go with you and I say, 'Oh hey, sure, my dead mother told me you'd show up'."

I frowned and thought about her answer for a long moment. She sighed and turned back to look at me, that familiar guard back in her eyes as she forced herself to meet my gaze.

"Are you going to leave me now? Tell Trinity?"

I raised an eyebrow. "Tell her what? That you're her family and a dead ancestor of hers told you to come to us so we could keep you safe? Yes. Will I ask her to kick you out or abandon you here? Have you met my mate? She'd skin me alive."

Hazel shook her head, frowning. "I don't understand. I lied to you; I hid information from you. Why aren't you mad?"

I stepped a little closer and handed the blade back to her, hilt first. "Because you haven't done anything for me to be mad about, Hazel. I was confused and frustrated because I could tell you were hiding something, but I'm not mad. And honestly, it makes sense now."

"What does?" she asked warily, taking the blade back.

"Trinity saw a vision of you being attacked and said she felt a connection to you, a pull, something telling her it was *her* responsibility to find and protect you. And since the moment I saw you, I felt it too. I promised Tabitha I'd protect her kin for as long as I lived, and you are of her blood."

Hazel's eyes shone with unshed tears and her eyes flicked to the book in my hand before she glanced away, pressing her lips together.

"What is it?"

She shook her head and I stepped into her line of sight, waiting until she looked at me.

"Tell me, Hazel."

She studied me, her gaze weighing before her eyes fell once again on the book in my hand. "I'm not an expert and I could be wrong, but I think I'm a little more than just another Witch of the Wardwell bloodline."

My heart skipped a beat, but I forced myself to remain calm. "Oh?"

She sniffled and tightened her arms around herself, nodding.

"Yeah. Since finding you up here, it's been almost impossible for me to keep my eyes off that book. I feel drawn to it. It... it feels like mine."

I sucked in a sharp breath, and instead of surprise, I felt... vindicated. Since the memory restoration earlier today, the idea had been brewing in the back of my head. The pull I felt toward Hazel was strong, but it wasn't just about my oath. She felt *familiar*.

"Tell me your theory," I urged gently, wanting her to be the one to say it, for me to not put words in her mouth. I needed to hear them said and believed by her.

"My name, my *full* name, is Hazel Marlee Wardwell. Marlee, as I was told, is a family name from a long time ago."

My breath left in a rush, and I felt whatever familiarity I'd felt between us grow stronger. She wasn't *my* Marlee; she wasn't the same little girl. This girl had a life and a story of her own, a history I didn't know, and an upbringing I had no part in… but I felt her there, her soul, that part of Marlee that lived on inside her.

My throat felt dry, swollen, and I had to swallow several times to try and make my tongue work so I could form words.

"You think Marlee's soul is… is yours?" I asked, my voice was rough, barely audible.

Hazel wiped quickly at a tear on her cheek and shrugged, her eyes rimmed red. "I don't know, but my mom… in my dream she said that souls who are meant to find each other will do so in many lifetimes. Then she said to go to you and you'd protect me."

Her words forced me back several steps. They were the same words the Seer had said when Trinity asked about Hazel, the exact same words. It was *her*, it had to be her. Somehow, in another lifetime, both Tabitha and Marlee had found their way back to me in the only way they could. In the form of two others that I knew I'd love and protect until the end of my days.

Looking down at Hazel now, at the exhausted, vulnerable, and scared young girl, every instinct I had to protect and shelter her came roaring to the surface. Shifting the book to one hand, I stepped in close and wrapped my arms around her, pulling her close. She froze for a fraction of a second before she wrapped her arms around my waist and held on tight. The small tremor in her body almost broke me, and I closed my eyes when she began to cry.

You're safe. You're here. We found each other, Malishka.

~

TRINITY

"You look beautiful tonight, moya lyobuv'."

Donovan's voice in my head was a welcome sound, and I turned in the direction I felt him coming from. He looked... lighter. He was still hurting, still processing, but he'd had time to decompress and come to terms with things. Hazel was by his side, her smile a little bashful as she waved at me, but she too looked... different. More at ease.

"I see she found you," I noted, watching as Donovan waved her on to speak to some of the other teens that had gathered. The bonfire was yet to be lit, the final rays of sunlight painting the sky brilliant pinks, purples and golds. Everyone had just been waiting for the guest of honor.

"We had a good talk. There's a lot to fill you in on," he said.

I raised an eyebrow. *"Anything I should be worried about?"*

He shook his head. *"Only that souls who are meant to find each other will do so in many lifetimes."*

I remembered Dinah saying those words to us as we left her and the other Elders today, and it took me several seconds to understand what he meant. My eyes widened and my mouth fell open.

"You're sure?"

He nodded. *"Almost definitely. I'd like the Elders to confirm it, of course, but nothing else explains the pull I have felt to her since first seeing her. There's also more to tell you about her but—"*

"Wait," I interrupted as he came to stand in front of me. *"If she and Marlee share a soul, then that would make her a Wardwell Witch."*

He smiled softly and raised a hand to cup my cheek. "Yes."

I sucked in a sharp breath, excitement bursting through me. I knew it—I *knew* it. There was a reason I felt like she was my responsibility from the moment I'd seen her in that vision.

He lowered his mouth to mine, and I didn't hesitate to kiss him back, pressing up on my toes to close the space between us. Kissing him again after even such a short time apart was wonderful, like coming home. I'd hated leaving him on his own to work through his thoughts and emotions, but I'd also known it was the right thing to do. He was used to doing things alone, just as I was. Even being mated, it didn't mean he needed me there watching over him worriedly or making stupid jokes to try and make him laugh.

"I missed you," he whispered against my lips.

I smiled and let my fingers brush the scruff of his cheeks. "I missed you."

Donovan smiled down at me and my smile slipped a little. "Are you okay?"

He drew in a long breath and let it out again, nodding slowly. "I am—or, I will be. I needed answers, I knew it would most likely hurt. I hadn't counted on how much... but I'm still glad we did it. And Marlee——" His voice cracked and he cleared it, holding up the book for me with a soft smile on his lips. "She remembered me. She found me, *twice*, and even healed me once as an adult. She left me a letter."

My heart squeezed at the look in his eyes. It wasn't exactly closure, but it gave him something to hold onto, a connection. There were answers in that book, answers direct from Marlee herself that had obviously done a lot to soothe him.

Dinah greeted everyone and thanked them for coming. I held Donovan's hand as Hazel was welcomed into the Oasis officially. She looked unsure and a little bashful up there in front of everyone, but the moment her gaze found us, something in her relaxed. Seeing how our presence helped her feel safer, I wanted to scream and cry with happiness. She was safe, we'd gotten to her, and we'd protect her always.

"Donovan, Demon King," Dinah greeted, and everyone turned to look at him. Dinah smiled. "Would you mind doing the honors?"

Donovan straightened slightly, and I felt his gratefulness that Dinah had included him. He created a ball of fire in his spare hand and with a flick of his fingers, he flung it into the pile. The wood went up in a whoosh of flames and there were gasps and cheers. Music started playing somewhere, and I watched as serval Witches and their husbands came out laying platters of food out on a long table. And with that, a festive kind of cheer permeated the air.

A few hours passed as everyone talked and danced. Donovan pulled me in for a dance a few times, and he didn't seem to care a single bit that we were being eyed from all sides. His attention was for no one but me.

I love you.

The thought was there in my head, but I couldn't say it, not yet. To say the words would open the door for a bond, and we couldn't afford for that just yet. He was wonderful and so caring. Despite how exhausting the day had been, he kept a smile on his face and danced and made sure we had fun.

Leviah had long ago been accepted by the Oasis and its people, and he talked easily with everyone and seemed to be enjoying himself. My heart just about melted as I watched Donovan dance with Hazel. The girl didn't know how to dance yet, so Donovan spent some time teaching her and they laughed whenever she messed up the steps.

The adoration in her eyes when she looked at him was almost heartbreaking. She'd bonded to him so fast, and if things weren't the way they were, I'd be alarmed. But this was centuries in the making, all of us together. Our souls recognized him, recognized each other, and it paved the way for a quick emotional attachment.

An hour later, Donovan and I were on the outskirts of the group dancing slowly, closely, shadows hiding us from the majority of the group. I closed my eyes as he pressed his forehead to mine and we swayed from side to side, the music gentle now, quieter, allowing for an intimate moment.

Some people had already left or gone to bed, but there were still a good number of people dancing and talking.

Hazel seemed to have hit it off with a bunch of kids around her age, and they were watching her as she showed them how to shoot sparks from her fingertips. It wasn't the most useful of tricks, but it definitely looked cool.

Donovan's hand rested just beneath my shirt, his fingertips pressing into my skin, occasionally brushing back and forth and creating little shivers down my spine. He slid his head to the side, his nose tracing the edge of my jaw before his lips pressed to the pulse in my neck. I sucked in a breath as a zap of pleasure shot from my neck straight to my core. My head tilted of its own accord, giving him better access and I closed my eyes when he kissed his way down, his body swaying with mine, creating a delicious kind of friction.

"Donovan, they are all Witches here. They'll feel this..." I warned, too weak to push him away.

"So... we should go somewhere else then?"

My laugh was breathy and broke off into a quiet moan when his teeth nipped and mouth sucked. Holy hell, that felt amazing.

"Donovan," I warned, feeling his hunger stir and grow. He didn't reply, he just lifted his head enough to kiss me.

I couldn't help but respond, and before I knew it, we were backing up, away from the others and deeper into the shadows. His touch, his kiss, the sure way with which he moved was a seduction, and I found myself almost like putty in his hands. I wanted him, I needed him, and my hunger seemed to be feeding his own.

"We should slow down," I whispered. I knew we should, but the reason why was just out of reach. The sounds of the party were distant now, and it wasn't until my back hit a tree that I pulled back from the kiss, gasping.

"Donovan," I whispered, framing his face. "We need to stop, we have to."

His eyes practically glowed in the faint moonlight, and that need was rising inside him again, clawing, scratching, roaring to be let out like a caged and wounded animal.

"Trinity... we have to do something. We have to figure

something out. This is... not claiming you is turning me into something else," he warned, his voice so low and rough I almost didn't recognize it.

"What do you mean?" I asked, keeping myself open to him.

He clenched his teeth. "I am losing control, and I don't do that. Not since—not for a long time. I am careful, I am controlled, and I can't keep going like this. Something has to change, and I don't want to hear how we'll find a way. I don't know what I'll do if I can't give in to this demand to bind us soon. All I know is that it won't be pretty, and I'd sooner kill myself than harm you. So," he said, dragging in a deep, shuddering breath.

My eyes pricked, and for the first time, his words actually incited fear.

"So what?" I asked quietly.

His eyes searched mine, and even in this low light their color enchanted me. He backed up a step, his expression hard to read and I frowned.

"Donovan?"

Something in him changed. There was a certainty to him now, like a path had been chosen.

"Come with me," he said, taking my hand. Before I could agree or say anything, he was pulling me back to the party. He picked up Marlee's book from where he's stashed it in a tree while the party went on, and he waved to Leviah. Lev excused himself and came over to us, eyes assessing.

"Everything okay?"

Donovan took the ring from his finger and gave it to Leviah.

"We'll be back tomorrow at the latest, take the ring in case you need to talk to us or we need your help."

He frowned but took the ring. "Okay, why?"

"Yeah," I said, just as confused. "Why?"

Donovan clutched my hand tighter, but he was looking at Leviah. "Tell Hazel we'll be back. Make sure you tell her that because I don't want her thinking I left her here. I have an idea to fix this issue," Donovan explained.

Lev looked from me to Donovan and then nodded slowly. "Do you need my help?"

Donovan shook his head. "No. Just keep that on you and come if we call. And look after Hazel while we're gone. Keep her safe."

Leviah looked concerned but he nodded. "Good luck."

Donovan pulled me away again behind a house a good distance away. "Take us out of here."

"What? Why?"

He grimaced. "I have something to do, a plan, and I need to get out of here to do it. You can come right back if you like, in fact, I'd prefer that than you waiting around for me."

"Donovan—"

"Trust me," he cut in. "Please."

Drawing in a steadying breath, I nodded and clutched his hand tighter. Closing my eyes, I whispered the words that would take us out, and when I opened them again, we were standing in an open field covered in wildflowers.

"Wait here and set some wards, or go back to the Oasis where you're safe. I will be a little while, but I'll be back."

"Can you tell me what you're planning?" I asked.

He leaned down to kiss me instead before letting me go. "Be back soon."

And then he vanished.

CHAPTER TWENTY-THREE

DONOVAN

The Great Hall was dark and quiet. It was empty this time of night, which is precisely what I hoped to find.

I'd come up with a solution that would allow Trinity and I to be together... but it wasn't going to be pleasant, not for me or my brothers. I'd already called for a brother to meet me, because there was only one I could see allowing me to go ahead with a plan as crazy as mine. But I had to, I needed to. If I went much longer without claiming Trinity, I worried about the animal I would become. It was too hard not to take her, not to bind us in every way possible. Unfortunately for us, the Witch we needed to kill in order to break the curse rarely left the safety of Heaven, so I had no other options for the time being.

It was this, or I get my brothers to lock me up until the Witch could be found. I'd go crazy locked up, and Trinity would grow old and die or get hurt or kidnapped again. None of those were options I could live with. As it was, the option I'd chosen was hardly any better, but it left everyone alive and safe.

Cassius stepped out of his realm, his eyes quickly appraising me, looking for injuries or any sign of why I had asked to speak to him. He was tall, like all my brothers, and while none of us were anywhere near the porcelain dolls Angels were, he always seemed somehow more... *elegant* than the rest of us.

His perceptive eyes narrowed on me. "You called?"

I took a moment to memorize my brother's presence—the

steady hum of our psychic link, the comfort in it. Because soon, all I'd feel was emptiness.

"We need to talk," I said, gripping the book Trinity had said I could keep in my hands before I stepped past him to my realm. I pushed open the door, and somehow, it all looked different. Nothing had changed, but I was noticing smaller details that were usually shadowed in my memory. Knowing this could be the last time I'd lay eyes upon my realm for some time had me looking at it with new eyes.

"What's going on?" Cassius asked, closing my door behind us. I glanced down at Marlee's book in my hand and drew a deep breath before placing it on the side table by the high back chair. "I'm leaving for a while, and I'm not sure when I'll be back. There are obstacles preventing me from marking Trinity, and I'm barely holding onto my restraint. I fear what I'll do if I wait much longer. I need to mark her, but when I do it, it'll mean cutting off all contact with everyone. No mind links, nothing. I can't reach out to any of you; it's too dangerous."

The idea came to me only minutes ago, but it was the only way out I could see. Trinity's curse couldn't affect my brothers and the legions that we commanded if there was no pathway for it to trickle down into. If I cut myself off from them, the curse only got as far as me, and if I was cut off from Hell, it couldn't get to my Demons.

"What? Why?"

Cassius's outrage was justified. As much as cutting them off was going to hurt me, it would affect all of them too.

We all remembered what it felt like to feel Malik die and lose that connection for a time. I imagined this would be the same, and none of us were eager to feel it again.

"I can't get into it, but this is how it has to be."

Again, Cassius studied me with eyes too intelligent. I took a moment to re-evaluate my brother. Cassius tended to stick to himself, to keep his own company, but not enough to alarm us. He didn't state his opinion often, but now that I thought about it, any time he did, it was usually worth listening to. If any of our brothers called for help, he was there, but more often than not he was off on his own doing—well… I wasn't sure.

"You're sure this is how is has to be?" he asked, jaw tight.

"Yes." My tone left no room for argument. "I'm going to need you to watch my circle of Hell for as long as it takes, but if the others can help, let them."

Cassius considered me carefully before his eyes darkened as he forced his emotions under control. I hated to cause him—or any of them—the kind of distress they were in for, but it had to be this way.

"You know what this means, right?" he asked. "If there's no mind link, there's no emergency button. You can't call out if the sky falls down around you."

I nodded, a sour taste coating my tongue. "I know."

"And you really can't find another way?"

I shook my head. "It's… complicated. Marking her right now can put you all in danger, and I won't risk that. But I can't hold off marking her any longer—it's just not possible."

"So, *you'll* be in danger then, but you're stopping it from reaching us?"

I shook my head. "Yes and no. The important thing is that you'll all be safe, and so will Trinity."

Cassius's jaw flexed. "You're my brother. I know you can handle yourself, but I don't like the thought of you out there, blind and alone."

I smirked faintly, trying to interject some levity into the situation. "You're assuming I won't enjoy the peace."

The look Cassius gave me could have melted stone, he was *not* amused.

"You'll tell the others once I'm gone?" I asked. "They'll be panicked."

Cassius nodded, jaw tight. "I'll call a meeting the moment you're gone."

Again, appreciation for my brother washed over me. I did not envy him the upcoming conversation. For as long as we'd been alive, the links to each other in our mind had existed. It wasn't like the times we lost the ability to *speak* to each other due to the poison on Angel Blades. In those times, we could usually sense that our brother was alive, but nothing more. When I severed these links, it was going to hurt all of us.

Without a word, Cassius reached beneath his shirt and pulled out a gold pendant etched with his sigil and strung on a chain. He pressed it into my palm.

"My Token," Cassius said. "You get into trouble, you call me, and I'll come in swinging. And if you need more than me..." His gaze sharpened. "I'll call the others."

The weight of the Token settled in my hand. I knew that if I held this in my hand and said his name, no matter where I was, he'd be summoned to me whether he wanted to be or not. It was a last resort if I truly needed the help.

"Thank you," I finally said, my voice strained.

For a moment, neither of us moved. Then I pulled him into a hard, brief embrace—warriors, brothers. Kings.

When we stepped apart, Cassius's eyes were grim. "Go to her, then. But don't think I won't bring you back if you get yourself killed and then kick your ass all up and down these halls."

"I smiled for real this time. "I'd expect nothing less."

Refusing to put it off any longer, I nodded to my brother one more time before I shadowed out of Hell. I needed to be quick.

If Cassius succeeded in gathering my brothers together, I had only a few minutes to sever the ties before they found out what I planned to do and came to me in an uproar. Convincing one brother was hard enough, trying to convince seven others was a nightmare waiting to happen.

I chose a place in the mountain, far from civilization, far from Hell... far from *her*.

The air held an icy chill, but it was still, quiet, overlooking an abandoned stretch of black rock resting beneath a velvet sky. It was the perfect place to be alone while I ripped out the roots of my previous life. Trinity was my world now, but I was going to be wrenching out everything I had ever known, and it would hurt.

For as long as I'd existed, my brothers had been there—not just beside me, but inside my head, their presences as constant as my own heartbeat, a subtle hum of thought and emotion. Soon it would all be erased, and I'd have to let it all go.

I stood on the jagged outcrop, closing my eyes, reaching for the braided strand of power that bound each of us together. It thrummed against my mind, warm and familiar, each strand unique and strong.

The bond didn't want to break. It pulsed, resisting, as though it knew this was fundamentally wrong.

"Forgive me," I whispered to my brothers. I felt their reactions; confusion, shock, worry, but I didn't give them any time to reach out or stop me.

Gritting my teeth, I forced myself to sever a core piece of myself. Power surged up my spine, tearing through my skull like white fire. The link strained, it stretched—

And then it snapped.

The silence was instant and absolute.

I staggered, the world tilting under me. The space they'd occupied in my mind was raw and hollow, a permanent injury that throbbed and burned. I could breathe, but every inhale felt shallow, as though something vital had been ripped from my chest and I was left with an open, aching wound that wouldn't stop bleeding.

I felt like I died.

Or worse—like *they* had.

I pressed a hand to my temple, forcing down the nausea that came with the emptiness. This was what I had chosen, it was my path. I did it to protect them, but I also did it for Trinity.

She was worth it.

I told myself that again and again to help take the razor-sharp edges off the screaming wound. My brothers, as pissed as they likely were, would understand when I came back. They'd be furious, yes, but they'd understand why.

After several long minutes, I drew in another painful, deep breath of air and forced my shoulders to relax. My eyes were wet and my stomach felt like it was going to heave again, but the worst of it appeared to be over.

Forcing my spine straight, I prepared myself for what was to come. Glancing down at the token in the palm of my hand, I slipped it over my head, securing it around my neck. The power in it thrummed as a reminder that I wasn't *totally* alone.

And now I could go collect my mate.

Wrapping shadows around myself, I imagined Trinity in the field of wildflowers I'd left her in, and when I opened them again, there she was.

The cold still clung to me, but it wasn't the wind that left me feeling so chilled, rather the emptiness lodged under my ribs, pressing against my lungs with every breath. There was no hum in the back of my mind, no flicker of another's thought brushing

against my own or a presence simply pressing close for a
moment to see if the other was okay.

Her magic brushed against me before I saw her and my pace
quickened as her eyes locked with mine, every stride I took was
full of purpose.

Trinity.

Standing in the clearing, arms crossed, suspicion written in the
set of her shoulders... but I could see the way her breath caught
when she saw me. There was a subtle hesitation, like she didn't
know whether to rage at me for leaving without an explanation
or close the distance and throw herself at me because she was
relieved I was okay.

I didn't give her the choice.

I crossed the space between us in quick, measured strides and
caught her face in my hands before she could speak. My mouth
crashed to hers—fierce, desperate, like kissing her might fill the
hollowness in my head. Her gasp broke against my lips, and then
she was kissing me back just as hard, fingers curling in the front
of my shirt like she was absorbing my pain.

And maybe she was.

Knowing she could very well hate me for my next moves, I slid
my hand up her stomach, her chest, to rest my palm over her
heart. With a feeling of relief and excitement, I dropped the
reins on that part of me I was constantly holding in check. Power
surged through me, flooding me in a rush as my palm burned hot
and bright.

That burning pressed into Trinity and the bond flared bright and
fierce. Sweet relief nearly made me sag against her, but I forced
myself to stay upright. For one shivering second, everything was
right between us, but then came something darker. It slithered
into my head, a sickness, an invasive wrongness that lodged its

claws within me and injected its toxin as it looked for ways out, pathways to invade... brothers to condemn to misery.

Trinity wrenched her mouth from mine, her eyes wide with disbelief. "What—"

"I love you," I cut in, my voice low and fierce.

Her eyes widened—she knew what those words meant, what they could start if she returned them. I didn't give her time to argue.

"I trust you," I said, and opened my mind to her completely. No walls, no shadows, no more holding back. She could feel everything—the emptiness, the loss, the pain I'd just endured... and the solid, unwavering truth that she was worth every piece of it.

"But the curse—"

I didn't let her see my grimace, but I could tell by the protest in her eyes that she saw the curse wind its way through me. "It's done," I murmured. "You're mine, and I'm yours. All you have to do is accept it."

Her lips parted in shock, in protest. "You shouldn't have—"

"I did," I cut in, "I chose you, and I would do it again, every time."

The sickness pulsed through me like an insidious creature, winding its way through my mind, looking for the slightest crack it could push through to infect my brothers, but I held her gaze. Tears clung to her thick lashes, and she gently stroked the back of my neck, fingers tangling in my hair.

"I can feel your pain. Donovan... you didn't have to do that. I never wanted you to do that," she whispered, her voice thick with tears.

"I know," I whispered. "I knew you'd never ask, but it's a sacrifice I'd make for you again and again. I can live without my brothers for a time—I can't continue living without you."

A tear broke free from her eye and tracked down her cheek, and I used my thumb to brush it away.

"Donovan—"

"I don't want to talk about it, not now, not yet."

I saw the struggle on her face to drop the subject, to accept what I'd done and move on. After several long moments, she finally let it go and her lips trembled on a shaky smile.

"I love you, Demon King."

The words were whispered, choked, but the power in them nearly knocked me back. The feel of a second bond clicking into place was both a relief and a powerful force that shook my world.

Closing her eyes, I felt the way she lowered the wards in her mind so that our thoughts and emotions blended together as they were always meant to be. Some of the burning in my mind, still stinging from the loss of my brothers, soothed some.

"I trust you," she murmured against my mind, and the feel of her voice in my head the way it was meant to be after so long nearly took me to my knees. I clutched her to me tighter, breathing her in, letting my breath release shakily.

The emptiness inside me shifted. It wasn't gone, but it no longer felt so hollow.

Opening my eyes, my gaze clashed with hers.

"Mine," I whispered, my blood burning with the sudden need to finish this, to see it through.

"Yours," she agreed before lifting up on her toes and pressing her lips to mine.

~

TRINITY

The mark still burned against my breast as Donovan picked me up, using whatever Demon magic he had to conjure up a bed of blankets and pillows before he lowered me to it.

I could feel the sickness in him, writhing, clawing, infecting him, but it had nowhere to go, nothing else to do. It would circle around looking for a purpose and find none. If it bothered Donovan, he didn't show it.

There was a deep, raw pain in him too, an agony that hadn't been there before, and I wanted to know more about it, but he seemed determined to ignore it for now and to make me ignore it too.

And damn him… it was working.

He kissed me again, slower this time but deeper, as if he meant to memorize the shape of my mind and soul through the touch of our lips.

I moaned and he swallowed it, almost as if he were desperate to catch it and hold it forever. In the next instant, our clothes vanished and I shivered as the cooler air hit my overheated skin. Need was driving him again—driving me—and I was almost as desperate as him to complete this final bond. We'd waited long enough.

"Will you tell me again?" Donovan whispered, his voice a rough whisper against my lips. I lifted my gaze to his as his hands slid down my body and I smiled, feeling the freedom that came with the words he wanted to hear.

"I love you."

As his eyes closed, he pressed his forehead to mine, breathing me in, letting the bond that flared between us at those words burn hot and bright.

"I need you, *moya lyubov'*," he murmured before kissing me again.

"I'm right here, baby. Make me yours."

The growl that rumbled from his chest sent my pulse pounding and blood rushing hot in my ears. How did he do that sound, and why the hell was it so sexy?

Our next kiss was a surrender to the moment, an acceptance of our unity that was *finally here*. His hands explored my body and slipped between my legs, and I arched my back, rocking my hips. I wanted him, wanted this, and our moment had finally arrived. Every touch, every scrape of fingers, was part of something larger—not just desire, but the final step in a binding created just for us.

The sight of him naked and ready above me was more than enough to get me ready for him. This man was the sexiest thing I'd ever seen, and he was all mine. The way he looked at me with such affection, such devotion, such *heat*... It was a wonder we managed to hold out this long.

Donovan settled himself between my thighs and I slid my hand into his hair to pull him to me. His mouth met mine in a hungry moan and I returned it, eager for this to happen, to know what he *really* felt like, not just the psychic dream version of him. Donovan pulled back enough to look at me, and with one sharp thrust of his hips, he drove himself inside me. I cried out, the sound tearing from me without my permission, but if Donovan's praise was anything to go by, he definitely approved.

"Mine," he ground out, surging inside me again.

"Yes," I agreed, lifting my legs further up his torso to take him deeper. Those velvet blue eyes of his met mine, stayed locked there, and I was lost. Our bodies were speaking a language of their own, hard and fast, desperate and beyond any hope of stopping now. Donovan was right, we'd waited too long, put it off far longer than we should have, and we were now careening toward an edge I couldn't see.

My nails dug into his back as he continued to move, every roll of his hips rubbing my clit and driving me insane with a building pressure that promised to explode in fireworks of pleasure. This was not a slow session of love making and exploring, it wasn't meant to be long and torturous. We'd waited so long that it had to be hard and fast, rough and desperate.

"Donovan," I whimpered as he swelled inside me, my body winding tighter and tighter around him. His hands, lips, teeth and tongue were everywhere, his hips rocking forward over and over until I was so hot I could barely breath and my mind was a mess of sensation and need. Words and logic failed to exist as he literally drove me out of my mind with the way his body made me feel.

"Mine forever, *moya lyubov'*, Donovan whispered. They weren't just words, they were a promise, an oath.

"And you're mine, Donovan," I promised as he drove me over the edge. I cried out, back arching as the explosion went off deep inside.

Donovan's cry of release was music to my ears, and the feeling of the last bond snapping into place sent me to a whole other dimension, I swear. Never had I felt anything like this before. It could have been minutes later, hours, days—hell, entire seasons could have passed on by and I wouldn't have known or cared. The weight of Donovan on me as we both struggled to breathe was my version of heaven.

He buried his face against my neck, breathing me in like he could live off the scent of me alone. It was an idea I could understand as I did the same. My hands traced the lines of his back and I wondered if it was possible to anchor myself here to this moment and never lose it. This was years of running and chasing, fear and longing, crashing together until there was no more room for distance or anything else.

Neither of us bothered to try and move, and I knew despite the road ahead of us, that as long as I had him and he had me, we'd find a way to make everything else work.

This was all that mattered now.

CHAPTER TWENTY-FOUR

TRINITY

By the time we finally fell asleep, the sky was beginning to lighten and we collapsed out of sheer exhaustion. It was like once the bonds were made, we were taken over by some kind of frenzy. We were making up for lost time, or maybe the bond required us to seal that last one over and over again. I wasn't exactly complaining.

Although, even though I was a Witch and healed fast, I was beginning to feel raw, so it was good we'd passed out.

I lay beside him now, watching him sleep, and never in my life had I ever experienced such a moment of contentment before. Reliving our past life together yesterday had been extremely traumatic, but it had also helped to explain a few things for both of us. Tabitha had loved him so much back then, as much as I did now, only now we could actually be together. We were bound now, forever and always.

My glee at that was only overshadowed by the sacrifice he'd made. He'd given up his brothers for me, given up their connection and his tie to Hell. What was a Demon King without his throne?

Donovan sighed and groaned. "As long as said Demon King has his mate, he's happy and content."

I smiled, feeling him there in my mind. He was so subtle, so quiet, that I hadn't even realized. It didn't feel intrusive to have him there, but natural and exactly where he was supposed to be. Blue eyes fluttered open to meet mine, and the immediate softening of his expression set loose butterflies in my stomach. I loved him, and it felt so good to finally allow myself to admit it.

"Wanna try something I've heard is really fun?"

I raised an eyebrow at him and couldn't help my small smile. "What?"

He grinned and was on me in a second. I shrieked and laughed as he rolled until I was beneath him, those beautiful eyes smiling down at me. "Morning sex. Apparently, it's all the rage with new couples."

I laughed. "You know what, I've heard something similar."

"Interesting," he pondered, leaning down to press kisses to my cheek, my forehead, the tip of my nose. "Want to see if it's true?"

"I do," I said slowly and he pulled back to look at me.

"What?"

I sighed and gnawed on my lower lip before answering. "Are you okay?"

Donovan didn't answer right away, and I waited to see how he'd respond. In the past twenty-four hours, he'd practically claimed a daughter, relived a painful and traumatic memory from his past, and then severed his ties with his brothers and Hell, all so we could be together the way we were meant to be. He'd given up everything he'd ever known to ensure our union could go ahead. I wasn't convinced in the least that he was okay, especially not after regaining his memory yesterday morning and reliving that trauma.

"I'm okay," he assured.

I raised a disbelieving eyebrow.

Donovan chuckled and brushed my hair back from my face and

sighed. "I'm not completely okay, and I don't think I will be for a little while, but I'm handling it. And knowing I have you takes a huge weight off my mind. Whatever I'm feeling, I can work through it."

I nodded. "I know, and I'm here for you. You don't have to carry it alone. We *will* find a way to get to the Witch who cursed me, and we'll heal the bond between you and your brothers and Hell as soon as that happens."

Donovan leaned forward to kiss me, slow and deep, like we had all the time in the world.

"So... about this morning sex," he murmured against my lips.

I laughed and had just wrapped my arms around him when a presence pricked at my consciousness.

"What was that?" Donovan asked, stiffening above me.

"Get up, someone is here," I said, unease rippling through me. He didn't ask any further questions, and by the time he stood over me, he'd clothed us both and was searching around the perimeter. I got up and tied my hair back hurriedly, looking around us, my heart beginning to pound in fear. Whoever was here, some part of me already knew they weren't friendly.

Not giving our enemy time to attack, I quickly constructed a transparent shield around Donovan and me. It wouldn't protect us against everything, but enough. Until I knew what we were up against, it would have to do.

"Sorry to interrupt," a feminine voice called, and I spun to see a woman step out from the tree line and make her way toward us. The sight of her sent my blood cold, and I backed towards Donovan.

I remembered her from Heaven. She was the Seer who told me and the Angels of the Prophecy of the Brothers' Nine. She'd gleefully told the Angels her plans to bring down Hell and the Demon Kings themselves, and how she would use me to do it.

She'd been the one to curse me.

It was only then that I realized Donovan wasn't looking at her. Casting another wary glance at the Seer, I turned to look at what held Donovan's attention and found Camhael standing not too far away. Flashes of memories blew behind my eyes, the torture he'd forced me to endure, the pleasure he took in hurting me for the sake of it.

It felt like my stomach dropped to my feet and Donovan's hand reached for mine, but he never took his eyes from the Archangel.

"What, you're not even going to say hello, Donovan?" the Seer asked with a fake pout. Surprise rippled through me. *How did she know him?*

Glaring at Camhael, Donovan turned to look at the Witch, and I registered the shock and anger he felt at seeing her.

"You know her?"

"Nera… I was hoping you tripped off a cliff and broke your neck, to be honest," he replied dryly, which only seemed to amuse the Seer.

"How do you know her?" I asked, pouring more of my energy into the shield.

Donovan answered at once. *"Before I finally caught up with you, there was a Witch calling for help on the beach. She was being pursued by Angels and I fought them off, only to have her hit me with a spell that rendered me temporarily paralyzed. They almost got me, and would have had it not been for Amazarak."*

I swallowed hard, goosebumps rippling up my arms. They'd almost taken him using the same tactic they'd used on me and multiple other Witches out there.

"Sorry to disappoint," the Seer replied with a wicked grin.

Donovan shrugged. "I figure you're used to saying that."

ALEXIS MAREE

The smirk disappeared from her face and I waited, watching, wondering if she'd try to attack my shield.

"By the way," Donovan began, sliding a quick look at me. *"You never mentioned you saved a Nephilim baby."*

I gave an internal huff of laughter. *"Now is really not the time."*

"What do you want?" I asked, tired of whatever it was they were trying to do.

"For the kingdom of Hell to fall, of course. What we want to know is why it hasn't happened yet."

I shook my head. "Patience is a virtue," I reminded.

The Witch hissed. "He carries the virus. I feel it writhing within him. It should have been transferred to the others by now and we should be able to feel the strength of Hell waning. Why isn't it?"

"Have you called Leviah yet?" Donovan asked. I mentally kicked myself because no, I hadn't thought to.

"Are you an only child?" Donovan asked her, seeming curious.

"I don't have time for your antics, Demon King," Nera sneered.

Donovan shrugged. "I was just asking because you seem like an only child. Very me, me, me. Not everything is about you."

I tuned them out as Donovan worked to keep them distracted. *"Leviah, I need you."*

There was a second's silence before he responded. *"Words your mate would prefer you never say to another man again…"*

I rolled my eyes. *"This is serious. Camhael is here, as is Nera, the Seer who cursed me. They can feel that Donovan carries the virus but know it has not spread. Things are going to get messy. We need you."*

He didn't joke this time. *"On my way."*

"Enough of this," I heard Camhael snap as I came back to the conversation at hand.

Donovan gave him a pitying look. "I don't know what *your* problem is, but I bet it's hard to pronounce."

311

Camhael opened his mouth to respond, but the Seer beat him to it.

"Just shut up and tell us why the virus has not spread. What did you do?"

"Shh," Donovan told her, holding up a hand and glaring at her. "The adults are talking now."

Her face twisted into a nasty scowl and I shifted beside Donovan, dragging her attention back to me. It worked, her eyes flicking to me and growing dark with hatred.

"Maybe it's time we take you back to Heaven to experiment on some more," the Seer told me.

"Or," a new voice drawled. "We can make this a party."

The Witch spun to see Leviah closing in from the tree line, his huge white wings spread wide, his eyes flashing with warning. He was a warrior appearing from the shadows and relief flooded me at the backup.

"Drop your shield, Trinity. Now!"

I didn't hesitate to do as Donovan ordered, concentrating my energy into a ball in my hand that crackled and hummed.

Donovan created some kind of whip made of hellfire and struck out at Camhael with reflexes so fast I almost missed it.

Camhael's roar of pain yanked the Witch's attention to him and I struck at her with my own power, shielding myself against feeling the oncoming pain.

She staggered, her cloak tangling around her feet and she almost fell. Snarling, she sent a jet of magic my way and I barely constructed a barrier to protect myself against it. Donovan was keeping Camhael distracted and Leviah was helping.

The Witch was mine.

Glaring, Nera dropped her cloak to the ground and raised a hand as she focused on shaping her magic.

A jarring realization slammed into Donovan, and I flicked him a glance before returning my attention to Nera while I prepared to blast her with another wave of power. I didn't want to kill her. Despite what she'd done, I was not eager to kill, and especially not another Witch.

Leviah was fighting Camhael, swords drawn and fury spilling from both of them. Donovan resumed blasting Camhael with fire, but I could tell his attention was divided.

"What is it, Donovan?" I asked again, drawing a ward in the air that would help to deflect whatever magic she threw my way, rebounding it back toward her. It wouldn't work for everything, but it was a precaution.

He didn't reply, but I was in his head, watching as he pieced together old memories he hadn't touched for centuries, information he hadn't had access to due to the memory bind. He seemed interested in the something on the Seer's inner arm, and I followed his train of thought as he put it together.

The second birth in a Wardwell line were often twins.

The second birth? But Mika and I were the twins, which meant... Did I have a *sister*?

And then it all hit me, the shock and revelation that had just slammed into Donovan and brought him up short.

He had been focusing on the mark on her inner arm, and without seeing it, I knew what it would be. I was turning back to Nera when I was suddenly blasted backward off my feet.

Everything seemed to happen in slow motion, or maybe it was just that certain facts I'd ignored now flooded my head at a rapid speed. Her dark hair and her eyes that matched mine. The shape of her face and the curve of her lips... it was true.

My breath stalled painfully in my lungs and I prepared for the pain of landing, but it never came. Strong arms wrapped around me, swinging me around at dizzying speeds before I was shoved back behind a wall of muscle and power. A wave of vertigo washed over me, but I was clear enough to know it was Donovan, that he'd caught me and was protecting me again. He lashed out with a wall of hellfire and I gasped, my mind still a mess from my newest revelation.

"Donovan, don't kill her," I pleaded.

He snarled in my head. *"She cursed you—us—and would see you dead."*

I placed a hand in the middle of his back and took in a shaky breath. *"Please."*

His emotions were at war with one another. His instinct to protect me fought hard against the parts of him that wanted to listen to me, that wanted to do whatever it took to see me happy.

"Trin..."

"She's... she's my sister."

Even thinking the words made me dizzy again. Shit, I had another sister; one I'd never known about. How was that possible? How hadn't I seen her birthmark when she'd cursed me? She had a star on her inner arm, just like Mika and I did. Donovan let up with the hellfire, and I moved to the side of Donovan so I could see. Nera shot us a glare full of rage and venom before she clutched a pendent on her necklace. When an Angel appeared out of nowhere to take her hand and shimmer out, I couldn't do more than stare in numb surprise.

"I forgot she could do that," Donovan muttered under his breath, but I didn't care at this point. Camhael lashed out at Leviah one last time before he shimmered out as well, leaving the three of us alone in the meadow.

"How did I not know? How is it possible I didn't figure it out?" I asked weakly.

Donovan clutched my upper arms in his large hands, those stormy blue eyes of his taking my breath away. It didn't matter what the scenario was, where we were, or what was at stake. Those eyes could leave me breathless.

"How were you meant to figure it out when they purposefully kept it a secret?" Donovan responded gently, leaning forward to brush a kiss over my forehead. I stepped closer and sighed when he wrapped his arms around me, holding me close as the shock of this revelation worked its way through me.

I had another sister... and she wanted me dead.

I stiffened when I felt another presence arrive and Donovan spun around to face our new enemy. Leviah still had his sword drawn, and the three of us prepared for the oncoming fight.

"Woah!"

My eyes widened when Hazel appeared, stumbling. She held her hands up as she caught sight of us, eyes wide with surprise. "I didn't do it."

"What the *hell* are you doing here?" Donovan snarled.

She glared. "You all left, and I wanted to make sure you were alright."

"And you were going to, what? Add your oh-so-considerable power to the fight and save us?" he argued, his words barbed and cutting, but I felt the fear that drove them.

Hazel stiffened, eyes glittering with hurt and defiance. "I have been looking after myself for a long time, I'm not some defenseless kid!"

Donovan growled as he stalked over to her. She held her ground, the heat of embarrassment, hurt, and pure defiance radiating off her. I watched with a small sigh as he took her hand and stomped her back over to us, frustration rolling off of him.

"How did you even get out?"

She raised an eyebrow. "I told you I was a Wardwell, I don't need the Elders to confirm that."

Donovan shoved her shirt sleeve up her arm, and I didn't immediately see a mark that would confirm this. But after a moment, it appeared. It was faint, barely there, but a shadow of the same star-shaped mark was definitely on her arm.

"Why is it so faded?" I asked, frowning.

Donovan's eyes searched Hazel's before he sighed and dropped her hand. "You said your great grandparents were kicked out of the Oasis for misusing magic, correct?" he asked Hazel. She nodded and he shrugged. "Perhaps the connection to the Wardwell bloodline disappeared for a time, ensuring none of you could find the Oasis. Maybe three generations was enough time that it has finally started coming back."

I nodded slowly. That could be a possibility. Still, I wanted the Elders to take a look at her to confirm it anyway. Not that there was really much point. If she could leave the Oasis at will, then she was definitely of my bloodline.

"So, like... what are you all doing here?" she asked.

Donovan's bad mood returned in a rush and he glared at her. "Fighting. And if you'd been sixty seconds earlier, you would have given our enemy the perfect leverage against us. They would have captured you and we would have been forced to do their bidding or they'd have tortured and killed you."

Hazel's wide eyes went wider still. "How was I supposed to know?"

Donovan closed his eyes and I watched him try to force deep breaths. Despite the dangerous situation this had almost turned out to be, I couldn't help but find the humor in it. He was a typical dad of a teenage girl.

"Not fair, all those dads got years to prepare," he grumbled in my head.

My heart turned over at his easy acceptance of his father-like role in Hazel's life, and I'll admit, my uterus clenched a little. Donovan as a dad? Yes, please!

He smirked, a flash of something else lighting in his dark eyes.

"Let's get things squared away with this virus first, then we'll get started on that idea of yours. In the meantime, practice makes perfect."

"Oh, yuck," Hazel exclaimed, her face scrunched and lip curled in extreme disgust.

"What?" I asked, looking her over to make sure she wasn't hurt.

"You two!" she cried in exasperation. "I *am* a Witch, you know? I can sense emotions too, and you two are—"

She shuddered. "Gross."

Leviah's chuckle broke through and my long-time friend made his way closer to us.

"Are you okay?" I asked, sensing a few injuries on him.

He nodded. "Nothing that won't heal on its own. You?"

I started to nod but then shrugged. Physically, I was fine. But emotionally? I'd just been delivered another blow.

"Let's get back to the Oasis. We have things to do, plans to make, and a war to prepare for," Donovan announced.

"War?" Hazel asked, her voice shaky.

"Yes, a war. And this time, you will stay where I tell you to stay so I don't have to worry about you too," Donovan ordered.

Hazel rolled her eyes and sighed as if he were making the most ridiculous request, but I was on Donvan's side. I felt sick thinking of Camhael getting his hands on her and hurting her the way he'd hurt me.

Sighing, I closed my eyes as we made our way back to the Oasis to prepare for war, but I had the feeling that the battle had already begun.

THE KINGS OF HELL
DONOVAN

CHAPTER TWENTY-FIVE
DONOVAN

We arrived back in the Oasis, but I was far from relieved. I was pissed that Hazel had worked out how to leave the Oasis due to her blood-tie, and I was furious that she'd potentially put herself in harm's way because she wanted to help us.

Now, shit was about to hit the fan in a huge way, and I had to get ahead of it. I wanted to take out Camhael and the Seer now, before things went any further, and I didn't want Trinity with me when I did. I saw the way Camhael looked at my mate as if she was the key to my demise—and he wasn't wrong. If he took her again, there was nothing I wouldn't do to get her back safely. I had to make my move before they did.

Letting out a long breath, I pulled Hazel in for another quick hug, thinking of all the things that could have happened had she arrived a minute or two earlier. For a moment, I briefly considered locking both her and Trinity away in one of Hell's cellars, but when Trinity shot me a knowing look, I grunted my displeasure and let Hazel go.

"I need to take a walk and talk to someone. I want you to stay with Trinity."

"Where are you going?" Trinity asked, frowning.

"I'll be back soon," I said, watching Trinity take Hazel's hand.

"And that didn't answer my question," she returned sharply.

I slid my hand into her hair and pulled her forward enough to kiss her. *"I just need some time. Can you stay with her, please?"*

Trinity wanted to refuse, I felt it build within her, but almost at the same time she relented and kissed me back before pulling away. *"Fine, but don't think you're getting out of telling me your plans."*

I smiled and kissed her. I jerked my chin at Leviah in a silent command to follow, and I was relieved when he did so without argument. We walked in silence, and with every foot of distance we put between us and the girls, I gently raised a small wall in my head to keep Trinity from hearing things I didn't want her to hear. The process was tedious and took careful work, but I was determined.

"Where are we going?" Leviah asked as we reached the house Trinity and I had come to yesterday to regain my memories.

"I need to speak to Dinah. I need to know how to break this curse and get them off our backs."

"But you two were able to complete your bond, yes?" he asked as we stepped onto the porch.

"Yes," I said and sighed. "But they won't stop coming after us, and I don't want to be disconnected from my brothers forever. It's not exactly comfortable."

"But it was very telling," a voice added and we turned to see Dinah sitting on a swinging chair to our left.

"Did you know I would do that?" I asked, turning toward her. She shook her head. "Not until you made the decision. I know the strength and sacrifice it took you to do that, and it went a long way to convincing the other Elders that you are willing to do anything for Trinity."

I nodded and came to a stop in front of her. "Anything. But now I need to know how to break the curse."

She sighed. "Unless you can get the Witch who cast it to revoke the curse, you must kill she who cast it."

"She's Trinity's sister," I informed.

"Wait, what?" Leviah asked, startled.

"Right," I said and rubbed my forehead. "You were busy. Yeah, she carries the Wardwell birthmark. Trinity is a twin which is a result of being the second birth of a Wardwell Witch. We just put it together ourselves."

Leviah stared between me and Dinah with shock, but we had no time to linger.

Dinah nodded slowly, gravely. "I know. It's why the curse was so powerful. It is not a curse of words or bound to blood. It is bound to her *soul*. So, even if Trinity were to die and go through the process of reincarnation all over again, the curse would follow her into her next life, and every one that follows until it finally took you and your brothers."

Motherfucker.

"So, killing the Witch will break the curse? There's no other way."

Dinah shook her head and sighed. "No. I know you do not want to kill her because she is Trinty's sister, but there is no other way that this works out well in the long run. You must kill her, but the curse is bound to her soul and Trinity's. When she dies, her soul must be captured and the curse removed from her soul before it can be removed from Trinity's."

I stiffened and Leviah made a pissed off sound behind me before he spoke. "Trinity must die also?"

Dinah hesitated, her face going slack and her gaze glazed. I waited impatiently, and she finally came back to me. "You must reach out to the Reaper and ask for his assistance. Her soul is bound to yours now, Demon King. She will not have to die, but her soul will need to be removed for the Reaper to take the curse."

I frowned. "I don't understand."

She smiled softly. "I know. Find the Reaper and tell him what has happened, and he will assist you from there."

I raised an eyebrow. "You're sure? He's helped us in the past, but he doesn't seem overly happy to do so."

Her smile turned a little knowing, slightly mischievous. "He will help."

The way she said it was so sure, and there was meaning to her words I didn't understand. What else did she know?

"If you wish to keep your plans hidden from Trinity much longer—and I suggest you do for your plan to work—you had best be going. She will not be distracted by the girl for long."

Sighing, I turned away from the Seer when she called me back. "Find Wren—she has information you might find useful before you go. She is leaving soon, so you must hurry."

I grimaced but nodded. "Thank you."

"May Aradia be with you," she farewelled.

Leviah and I walked in silence back to the village center and only then did I realize I had no idea where I was going.

"This way," Lev said, turning left.

I hurried to follow him, careful to keep the barrier in my mind between Trinity and I light and undetectable.

Once she realized it was there, I'd have to put something better up, but I didn't want to do that until it was necessary. She and Hazel were in the hall eating breakfast.

I watched as a dark-haired witch came jogging down a set of porch steps, her attention on a leather strap on her thigh that held a wicked looking blade.

"Wren," Leviah called, and the woman looked up, her gaze sliding from Leviah to me and back again, her smile gentle.

"Hey, guys. I'm about to head out so this will have to be quick. What's up?"

"They want you back?" Lev asked.

"Yeah, something has them in a panic and they want extra hands. Not sure how this one will pan out, but I guess I'll figure it out when I get there. What can I do for you?" she asked as she finished with the strap.

I looked her over and quietly noted that she was a warrior. Everything about her outfit was built for comfort: ease of movement, survival, and everything she had strapped to her body gave her an advantage in a battle.

"We saw Dinah." She said you might have some information for us," Leviah said and explained everything that had happened. Wren looked properly distressed at the idea of what had to happen and she shook her head.

"This is going to be messy, and I'll bet it's why they're calling me back now."

"What do you know about the Witch, Nera?"

Wren grimaced. "She's completely brainwashed. She was taken as a baby and raised with the Angels, so she only knows their way of things. I tried once to gently pry, to see if she could be swayed, but there's no saving her. She believes to her core that she's doing the right thing. She'll die before betraying the Angels or even allowing for doubt."

"Did you know she is Trinity's sister?" I asked.

Wren's expression hardened and she flicked her gaze away for a moment and gave a sharp nod. "Yes."

"And you never said anything?" I asked, curious.

She shook her head. "What would have been the point? As I told you, she is too far gone to save. All telling Trinity the truth would have accomplished is that she would have felt guilt over knowing her sister had to die in order for her to survive. She's too good, Trinity. She is strong and powerful, and she'll take on enemies more powerful than her and win. But at her core...

she'd never be able to kill Nera."

I didn't want to agree, but she was right. Even the slightest hesitation from Trinity when facing that woman could result in her death, and Trinity *would* hesitate because she wasn't a cold-blooded killer.

That was where I came in.

"What do you know of Trinity's family?" I asked, realizing this Witch knew a lot of things she kept close to her chest.

She thought about it for a moment and shrugged. "The oldest—Nera—was kidnapped when she was three years old, and Trinity's mother died trying to get her back. Their father did his best to look after the twins, but they were magical and he was not. He lacked the resources and he didn't know who to trust. He was killed too, but before the girls could be taken, they were placed in foster care by the humans and moved around quite a lot, so it was hard for anyone to track them."

We were silent a moment until Lev spoke. "Do you know when you'll be back this time?"

Wren shook her head, a small, strained smile on her lips. "It's never the same anytime I go up there, and there's always a risk I won't make it back."

Respect for this woman washed over me and I held out my hand to her. "Be safe, Wren. Make sure you come back. Too many people here need someone like you."

She smiled and shook my hand before doing the same with Leviah. "Good luck."

We watched her turn and leave, and I was silently thankful that while Trinity took risks in rescuing Witches, she wasn't behind enemy lines double-crossing the Angels.

"So... what's the plan?" Leviah asked.

I sighed and ran a hand over my head, so tired of my mate being in danger, of feeling as though I was constantly at risk of losing her.

"I don't know. We need a trap, but I'm not using Trinity as bait," I answered, feeling sick at the idea.

"So, use me," Leviah suggested with a heave of his shoulders.

I frowned. "You?"

"Yeah," he said and dropped his hands by his side. "I betrayed them all, they're pissed at me, and if we make it look like I'm an easy target, they'll come."

"Trinity would blast me from one side of the Oasis to the other if I let you use yourself as bait," I reminded.

Leviah smiled and shook his head. "She'd understand. Besides, what other plan is there?"

"Maybe one where you won't die?" I suggested, a bite to my voice.

Lev's smile was a little sad this time. "I have no other purpose, Demon King. Since I betrayed Heaven, I have a constant death sentence hanging over my head. And once the curse is lifted, I cannot keep coming here because Trinity will be with you. At least this way if I do die, it'll be in the service of protecting someone I care about."

Oh, for fuck's—I ground my teeth and sighed heavily. I didn't want to give a shit about a fucking Archangel. But even I had to admit that Leviah was honest and he'd done nothing but protect Trinity.

"I'll find you a home, Lev," I promised.

He raised an eyebrow. "Do I get my own room in Hell?"

I scoffed. "You're not that lucky. No, we'll figure something out."

Again, he laughed. "You know someone wanting to adopt a full-grown Archangel?"

I smirked. "There's always old-age homes for lost, feathered creatures like yourself. We'll find you one."

He smiled, nodding his appreciation of the offer and sighed. He didn't believe there would be a necessity to find him a room when this was done, but I'd do my best to ensure it.

"So, what's the plan now that we have bait figured out?"

~

TRINITY

"So, you seemed to have a good time at the bonfire last night," I said to Hazel as we took our seats.

People were milling about and eating in the hall. With how our morning had started, I was starving.

"Yeah, I guess. Some of the kids are cool," she said with a shrug. We lapsed into a small silence as I tried to wrack my mind for things to talk about. I felt such a connection to this girl, but I didn't know how to talk to her, how to get her to open up to me. I saw the bond she and Donovan had, and I'll admit that a part of me was jealous. I wanted that kind of closeness to her too. It was hard feeling a certain way toward her—so protective, almost territorial, like she was *mine*—and not have anything to actually show for it.

"You know... I had a feeling about you before we met," I confessed, tearing at a piece of the bread in front of me.

She hesitated briefly before she nodded and put down her spoon. "Donovan said something about a vision."

I smiled softly. "I often go to Dinah for visions of Witches who need help and she shares the vision with me. I saw you, and something about you automatically drew me to you. I felt like I knew you somehow."

Hazel's too-old eyes stared at me knowingly. "He said you share Tabitha Wardwell's soul. He and I think I share Marlee Wardwell's soul."

I swallowed hard and nodded. "I know… and so do I. I have suspected it for a while now, actually, and it would make all the sense in the world why both Donovan and I saw you and immediately felt like we needed to protect you."

She sighed and shook her head. "But I'm not Marlee."

I frowned. "We know you're not her."

She shifted awkwardly and shrugged. "I don't want Donovan to leave me here. If he leaves, I want to go with him. But I'm afraid that… that he's going to be disappointed in me."

My hand flexed as I automatically moved to take hers, but I held back, not sure if my attempt to comfort her would be appreciated. "Why would he be disappointed?"

Hazel didn't answer right away, and when she did, she didn't look at me. "Because I'm not Marlee."

"Honey—"

"He misses her so much. It's so engrained in him that he doesn't even realize he's aching, but I can feel the pain in him. I don't think that agony will ever go away. And now here I am, and I feel familiar and I know she and I share a soul, and I just… I don't want him to be disappointed that I'm not the girl he misses."

I didn't hold back this time and quickly reached out to take her hand. "Hazel, look at me."

She paused before slowly doing as I asked. "Donovan knows who you are, and he knows you are *not* Marlee, nor would he want you to try to be. Marlee is in his past, and you're right—a part of him will miss and mourn her forever. But you are the girl he cares for now, the one he laughs with and wants to protect. I promise you... you won't disappoint him."

"How can you be sure?" she whispered, and I saw the very real fear in her soft eyes.

I squeezed her hand. "Because I share Tabitha's soul, and he has never made me feel like I need to pretend to be someone I am not. He has never treated me differently or asked me to be different. I am *me*, and he loves me for that, not for the woman I was in a past life."

After thinking on it for a moment, my words seemed to ease some of the worry from her eyes, but not all of it. I had a feeling we had our work cut out for us making sure this girl knew we cared about her and that we wouldn't abandon her. We'd choose her, and she had nothing to fear with us.

"So... what happened outside the Oasis?" Hazel asked, and I went back to eating my food.

"It's a long story," I said with a sigh.

Hazel shrugged. "I'm not going anywhere."

Smiling at her encouraging look, I explained everything that happened while I was in Heaven—minus the more painful and traumatizing stuff—and then spoke about the prophecy.

"So, you and Donovan are actually *destined* for one another?" she asked, shocked.

I shrugged. "Yeah. I mean, if I wasn't convinced before, now that the bond is complete, I'm absolutely certain."

She seemed to think about that for a moment before shaking her head as if to come back to the matter at hand. "Okay, so what did the other Witch have to do with anything? I could feel some of the emotions left on the field."

I sighed. "I gather you know about my twin, Mika, right?"

She nodded. "I've heard things."

I smiled softly and put down my fork. "It turns out only the second pregnancy from a Wardwell Witch results in twins." Hazel looked at me with confusion for a moment before understanding dawned. Her eyes grew wide and her mouth fell open. "Wait, you're saying you have an older sister you didn't know about, and that the Witch who cursed you and Donovan is *her*?"

I nodded. "Yup."

"Woah," she whispered, shaking her head. "Plot twist."

I laughed and shifted in my seat. "Yeah, you could say that."

"Does she know you're sisters?" she asked, and I frowned.

"Actually... I don't know. I'll have to ask... someone. Maybe Dinah?"

"Let's go see her now," Hazel said, getting up with her tray of food.

"Wait, now?" I asked, standing too.

"Yeah, why not? We can also get her to confirm that my soul is really Marlee's and put that question to bed."

I grimaced. "I already know the answer to that one, but if you want, we can do that."

"I do, and I think it'd be good for you to get some answers about your sister, too."

I frowned at her as we dropped off our plates and trays. "How old are you again?"

"Turning fifteen, why?"

I shook my head. "Sometimes you seem older."

She shrugged. "Old people say that to me all the time."

I laughed and followed her out of the hall and down the stairs. Sometimes she sounded older, and other times she said things that reminded me she was just a kid with her whole life ahead of her.

"I'm not old; Donovan is old," I defended.

"Aren't you like… thirty or something?"

I frowned. "And?"

Hazel gave me a look as if I should be able to piece together her conclusion by myself and I shook my head, grinning. She was a smart ass, and so like Donovan. I frowned and looked around. Actually, it had been a little while since the guys had left, and Donovan never wanted to be away this long.

I reached out gently to see how he was doing, not wanting to interrupt if he was in the middle of something, but I stiffened when I came into contact with some kind of mental barrier. When had he even put that up? I hadn't felt it, and it was strong. I could try to push through it, but if he was doing something important or dangerous, I risked distracting him.

"Trinity?"

I blinked and brought Hazel back into focus, her face creased with concern.

"Are you okay?"

"I—yeah, sorry," I said, shaking my head and forcing a smile. "I must have zoned out."

She gave me a look that screamed *yeah, right*. What was with this girl and her looks that spoke volumes?

"It's not for you to worry about," I assured.

She sighed. "You grownups say that, and the next thing I know, everyone is dead and I'm out running for my life again."

I scoffed. "That is not what is happening here."

"Whatever," she muttered, stepping ahead of me to walk the trail to Dinah's home. I considered biting back, keeping our conversation going, but I was worried about Donovan now. What if he was in trouble? What was he doing that he wanted to

stop me from knowing?
Whatever it was, it couldn't be good.

CHAPTER TWENTY-SIX

DONOVAN

"Well... that escalated quickly," I murmured.

"You think?" Leviah grunted.

I stood back-to-back with the Archangel, swords drawn, and the enemy surrounding us. We'd made our way out to a flat desert area because we wanted to make sure we were alone and that there was nowhere for the enemy to hide from us. As planned, Leviah had been the bait and had been on his own for less than twenty minutes before the first Angel showed up. I took care of that fluffy fucker and a few minutes later, more showed up, and then more... and more again. At least ten of them surrounded us now, and then came several Rogue Demons, and I knew things were about to get interesting. The moment Camhael showed up, my gaze narrowed on him, but then Uriel made an appearance, and my gaze swung between the two, not sure which one I wanted to kill more.

"Told you they wanted me dead," Leviah murmured.

"That's not hard to believe—you're fucking annoying. But how do you know they're not here for me? I'm their life-long enemy, remember? You only just joined their shit-list."

"Is this really a competition to you?" he hissed.

I shrugged. "Just want to remind you that you're not the only one they want to kill."

Leviah gave a shaky chuckle. "Whatever you need to tell yourself."

I opened my mouth to snark back but was cut off.

"If you're both done?"

Uriel stood off to my right, the glower on his face dark and angry. I still wanted to strip him of his skin, pull out every vein, drain him of his blood and stretch his muscles to full capacity before ripping him limb from limb... but since completing the bond with Trinity, I felt differently toward him. I hated him more than any other creature on the planet, but my complete and utter loathing for the fucker wasn't the only thing I was feeling anymore.

On top of rage, I felt rather... smug.

I got my woman, I bound her to me, she was safe, and so was our girl. And he was still left with no way into the Oasis or even how to find it hundreds of years later.

Soon, Camhael and Uriel would both be dead. Everything so far was going according to plan... except for one thing. The Witch—Nera—wasn't here.

She was the one we needed so we could break the curse, but she hadn't shown, and I wasn't sure how to tempt her out of hiding. She did the bidding of the Angels. Whatever they said, she did, so if they told her to stay back in Heaven, she was going to stay back.

"So, what's the plan?" Lev asked.

I shrugged, flexing my fingers around the pommel of my sword. "You go that way, I'll go this way, and whoever gets the highest count is acknowledged as Supreme Warrior."

"Sounds good, Nephew."

"New stakes," I corrected through gritted teeth. "If I win, you don't call me that again."

"And when I win, you admit it?" he asked, amusement laced through every syllable.

I scoffed. "Fat chance."

The moment the last word left my mouth, it was as if a silent signal sounded and our enemy charged forward. I spread the fingers on my other hand and whipped around in a circle, setting the ground around us in a ring of Hellfire. The few Angels unlucky enough to be in its way caught on fire and screamed. Leviah and I used the brief distraction to push away from one another. He went up while I stepped right into the flames, sword raised as I slaughtered whoever stood before me. I was on a mission, determined to rid the universe of as many of these assholes as possible on my way to my real targets: Uriel and Camhael.

I wanted them both dead at my hand, but I'd been hunting Uriel for over two hundred years now, and his death was long overdue. Determined that he be impaled on the end of my sword by the end of this, I surged into the battlefield with renewed energy.

Despite my concentration on the fight, I felt Trinity's feather-like touch on my mind, and I knew she'd discovered the barrier I'd put between our minds. Her curiosity, concern, and annoyance were clear at once, but I couldn't afford to let it distract me now. I needed to get to Uriel and Camhael. Uriel would die today no matter what, but I needed Camhael alive so I could force him to summon the Witch. Of course, Uriel could do this too, but I didn't want him to live another moment longer than necessary. He was an oily bastard and he'd escaped for the last time.

Time slipped by in a mess of blood, screams, and pain. Every Rogue Demon I took down felt like another score for Hell, another insidious poison eradicated from our system. Because of these fuckers, we'd been fighting a war on two sides for hundreds of years and we were fucking sick of it.

Slicing clean through another Rogue, I glanced up long enough to see Leviah battling Uriel several feet off the ground, and I gritted my teeth, desperately wanting to be the one fighting that asshole. Spinning, I raised my blade in time to clash swords with an enemy sneaking up behind me and found myself staring into the hate-filled eyes of Camhael.

At once I was assailed with every memory Trinity had of this asshole. No, she hadn't exactly shared them all with me, but the moment our bond was formed, it was easy to slip into her mind, even when I didn't mean to. She was in my often without realizing it, soaking in information, reliving memories, and the same was true for me.

The moment I blocked his strike, it all hit me at once and the memory of her fears ramped up my anger at him.

"Hey there, fuckface," I greeted cheerily.

Camhael's lips curled up in disgust. "Demon filth!"

I shoved him back and swung my blade, a move he blocked.

"That's Demon *King* filth to you, asshat."

He twisted away from me and swung twice, his moves coming close but not close enough. I blasted his face with hellfire and tried again, the tip of my sword slicing up his torso. It would be painful, but it wouldn't kill him right away.

"Go fuck a dog," he snapped and charged again. I deflected his blow, but the edge of his sword caught my forearm.

"No, thanks. If that's your idea of a good time, that's fucked up," I returned. Neither of us spoke for several long moments before he overstepped and I saw my opening. He realized his mistake and unfurled his wings to fly away from me, but I was already moving. My blade came down on his left wing, and my sword cut through the heavily muscled appendage.

Camhael screamed, and it was a sound I wasn't sure I'd heard an Angel make before. He moved out of the way so that his wing wasn't entirely cut off, but it hung uselessly from his back.

I caught sight of Uriel—he wasn't fighting Leviah anymore but seemed to be looking over the fight with breathless pants as Lev took on several Angels at once. He was injured but still moving. Turning back to Camhael, I watched this Angel's face twist and contort into a kind of savage fury I hadn't been expecting. His movements were slow, sloppy, and I simply stepped to the side as he ran at me with his sword, trying to impale me on its end. This fight was going to go on forever, and I'd had enough. I wanted the Witch, and I wanted Uriel dead. Lashing out at a Rogue Demon who saw his chance to run me through, I cut his arm off turned in time to run an Angel through. Pulling my sword from the dying dipshit, I yanked the Token from around my neck and gripped it in my hand.

"Cassius."

I moved aside as Camhael tried to stab me again, but his wounded wing seemed to keep him off balance and it didn't appear as though he could shrug them back when it was so injured. Instead, my attention was diverted to the other Angels who descended upon me, and a second or two later I felt my brother's presence in the battlefield. Relief surged through me at the added help, and I spared a glance at him to make sure he was okay. Thankfully, he came prepared with his sword already drawn.

"It's rude to send late invitations to parties!" he shouted over the noise.

"I'll remember for next time," I returned, kicking the Angel in front of me to get a better look as to where Uriel had pissed off to. He was still around, but if the tide turned any further, he'd run.

"Sorry we're late," another voice called, and I slashed out at the

Rogue before turning to see Malik beside me, ready for a fight. A wave of emotion tried to take me under at the sight of my brothers appearing on the battlefield, but I had to fight it back. I couldn't afford to be distracted right now.

"Just glad you could make it, brother," I called, sparing him a grateful look that he returned.

Camhael roared and struck out at me, his sword catching the side of my thigh, the steel burning painfully momentarily before I stepped aside and kicked out. My blow knocked Camhael to the ground. One of his wings was still hung half-detached and bleeding profusely.

"Mind if I take it from here?" Tamas's voice pulled my attention to the left, but his furious eyes were on the staggering Angel. I hesitated, but remembered that he had a score to settle with Camhael as well for his torture of Raven. Besides, I had Uriel to track down.

"Have at it, brother," I agreed, stepping back to look for Uriel. The sight of my brother's mates in battle filled me with pride and intense concern. They were each powerful in their own right, but a force not to be reckoned with when they were together. They were making quick work of the Rogue Demons and Angels alike, and I realized more were not showing up. Obviously, they'd been given orders to stay away now that my brother's had arrived.

I turned to look for Leviah, and he was down to two Angels now. Scanning the remaining enemy standing, I looked for Uriel and found him several yards away, furious gaze on me. Gripping my sword tighter, I started toward him, determined to have this out now.

"Time to die," I growled.

As I got closer, a sneer curled his lips, vindictive glee lighting in his eyes. "Not yet, Demon King. I have an appointment elsewhere with someone you might know. I think a trip down memory lane is in order."

I charged at him, fury at the idea that he was going to get away again making me desperate.

Grinning, Uriel shimmered away mere milliseconds before my blade cut through the space he'd been in, and I roared in fury. *Motherfucker!*

Snarling, I looked around for someone to take my anger out on, but they were all dead or dying. Instead, I furiously slashed at the fallen bodies already dead on the ground before forcing myself to take a breath.

"Nephew!"

Leviah's shout jerked my attention to him and I immediately realized the problem. My brothers didn't know he was on my side. I heard Dimitria and Raven call out, trying to tell them that he was not the enemy, and I internally cursed at the poison in my blood preventing me from shadowing to him.

"Stop!" I shouted as I ran and Leviah shimmered away as several of my brothers concentrated jets of Hellfire at him. I staggered and was surprised when a hand caught my arm, and I twisted my head to see Leviah there, but his eyes were on my brothers, waiting, prepared.

"He's not the enemy," Dimitria called out as she ran closer.

"He's Trinity's friend," Raven added as she reached Tamas's side.

I nodded and forced myself to breathe again, trying to ignore the pain in my system. Why was it so hard to ignore when in the past it hadn't been a problem? My knees buckled, and within seconds, I was surrounded by my sisters as they placed their hands on me. Searing heat blasted through my body and I audibly gasped at the feeling. I was used to one Witch healing me, not four at once. The experience was definitely new.

"There. Better?" Raven asked as they gave me room to stand. My usual power coursed through my veins, and I smiled in thanks before getting to my feet.

"Much, thank you. I don't know why I couldn't ignore it like usual," I explained.

"Maybe it has something to do with your fucked up idea to cut yourself off from your brothers and the power of Hell?" Harkyn snapped.

I winced and drew in another breath, preparing for the ass-chewing I knew I deserved. His theory on why I couldn't ignore the pain seemed to fit though.

"Yeah, sorry about that. I... didn't have another choice."

"Obviously," Malik ground out. "But a heads up would have been appreciated. You have no idea what it felt like to wake up to that feeling."

"I tried to explain," Cassius told me. "But you didn't tell me much in the first place, so I couldn't explain properly."

"I kind of want to kick your ass for an hour or so until you get the message," Adrik said. "Calixta wants you to know that she would let me as well."

I realized my second sister wasn't here, but of course she wouldn't be. She was pregnant and taking her to a battle was beyond stupid.

"I'm sorry, okay? There was the very real chance you would have lost me for real if I hadn't done what I did. There was no time to talk, and I knew that if I did tell you all, you'd try to talk me out of it."

"Still fucked up," Tamas murmured, pulling Raven in to kiss the top of her head before his eyes flicked to Leviah.

"Right," I said, stepping back so I stood beside Lev instead of in front of him. "This is Leviah—he's Trinity's friend."

"He's an Archangel," Malik pointed out unhelpfully.

"I know," I said and sighed. "But he saved Trinity's life when she was taken to Heaven around two years ago, and he's been looking out for her ever since."

"Hello again, Leviah," Dimitria greeted softly.

Lev bowed his head slightly. "And you, Dimitria. I am glad to see things worked out well for you."

She beamed and looked up at Harkyn whose expression softened when he looked down at his mate. "It did."

"It's good to see you again," Raven added.

Leviah smiled softly at her. "And you. I am sorry about the last time we met. Camhael had you already, and I could not risk him getting Trinity too. If there had been a way to save you, I would have done so."

"No, I know. And I don't blame you—"

Tamas made a dismissive sound and Raven looked at him with a raised eyebrow. "Need I remind you of *your* contribution to my presence in that Rogue camp that night?"

Tamas's shoulders deflated and I felt the pinch of guilt that pulled at him. "No, you will never need to remind me of that, Blue."

Raven leaned up to brush a kiss across his cheek before turning back to us with a warm smile.

I met Tamas's eyes and raised an eyebrow. "Did you kill him?"

His expression was dark but firm. "Yes. Not as slowly as I would have liked, but Camhael is dead."

I drew in a slow breath and nodded. "Good—the fucker had it coming. Not just for what he did for Raven, but what he did to Trinity, too."

A look of understanding crossed Tamas's face and he pulled Raven a little closer to him, as if protecting her from the memories of her past.

"Then I'm happy to have been the one to deliver justice."

"Umm…" Malik interrupted, his arm around Sawyer who watched Leviah curiously.

"Did the feathered one call you *nephew*?"

I sighed and I knew my expression was one of resignation. Leviah chuckled lightly behind me and I threw him a look of reprimand. "Yes. He likes to remind me that, technically, he and every other Archangel are our uncles because Lucifer was an Archangel once upon a time."

For a moment, each of my brother's faces blanked before crumpling into expressions of utter disgust.

"Fuck off," Adrik spat.

"That's what I said," I replied sympathetically.

"But," I added, turning to look at Leviah. "I won, so no more *nephew* speak."

Leviah raised an eyebrow. "You think you killed more here today than I did? You spent a lot of time dancing with Camhael, and while you were doing that, I was slaughtering enemies left and right. I believe *I* was the victor, *nephew*."

"We're not doing this," I snapped. "We'll have another competition, one where scores can be kept and then we'll see." Leviah shrugged as if it made no matter to him and I turned back to my brothers, letting out a frustrated breath.

"So… where's Trinity?" Sawyer asked eagerly.

"I didn't tell her where I was or what I was doing. It didn't matter, though. We were trying to trap the Witch that cursed her, and she didn't show up. She never leaves Heaven, so I'm not sure when or how we'll get to her."

"Okay, but can we meet her yet?" Sawyer added with a small laugh.

I opened my mouth to reply and stopped. I looked among my

brothers and then frowned. "Where are Mika and Cole?"

As if just realizing they weren't here either, my brothers looked between one another and then at their mates. I waited, my eyebrows raised.

"Mika said her sister needed her, so I think she went looking for Trinity," Cassius volunteered.

I frowned. "But... Trinity is in the Oasis, and Mika hasn't been able to find her before. She always wears a cloaking spell that none of you have been able to break before——" I cut myself off and my blood turned cold as Uriel's words came back to me.

"I have an appointment elsewhere with someone you might know. I think a trip down memory lane is in order."

Without hesitation, I reached for Trinity, desperately hoping to find her in the Oasis where I'd left her. But even before I found her, I knew that wouldn't be the case. She was out in the open, all cloaking spells gone.

"Moya lyubov', what do you think you are doing?" I snapped.

"You are not about to lecture me about doing secret side-missions alone," she argued hotly.

"You can be pissed at me for what I did later. Tell me what you're doing," I replied.

"Putting an end to this once and for all. She's my sister, I can reach her," she replied, and it was then I realized she was talking to Nera.

Fuck.

"Go back to the Oasis, now!"

Defiance crackled back at me. *"Not a chance."*

"Fuck," I hissed.

"Where is she?" Leviah asked, his concern for Trinity loud and clear. He knew my mate as well as I did, and he obviously knew she wasn't in the Oasis.

"Are you wearing the ring?" I asked.

He nodded. "But she isn't."

"Fuck," I snarled, pacing away for a moment.

"Someone wanna fill us in?" Tamas asked with a raised eyebrow.

"I need to get to Trinity; she's in danger. Call the Reaper—we need him."

Adrik frowned. "Mervyn? Why?"

"No time to explain," I snapped and stepped back. "I need to get to Trinity. Uriel is going to take her like he took Tabitha, and I will *not* let that happen again. Get Mervyn and come find us."

"And me?" Leviah asked.

"Go back to the Oasis and make sure Hazel is okay. Talk to Dinah and see if she knows how this will play out or if there's anything we should know."

Leviah nodded and shimmered without another word.

"I'll get Mervyn," Adrik said and shadowed out.

I ground my teeth at the thought of Uriel getting his hands on Trinity. Not again, not *ever*.

CHAPTER TWENTY-SEVEN

TRINITY

I'd been standing uncloaked in the open for fifteen minutes before Donovan reached out to me, and I knew my time was running out to speak to her before my mate appeared and tried to kill her. Yes, I knew she was the reason for my curse, that she had aided in my kidnapping and torture and likely that of several Witches, but I had to do this, I had to try. She'd obviously been brainwashed, maybe there was a chance to save her. If there was, then I was going to take it.

Hazel was safe back in the Oasis, and after Donovan had checked in, I knew he was safe too. All that was left was for me to get a read on Nera. I needed to see if there was a way to save her, to bring her back to our side, to regain a sister I didn't even know I had until this morning.

We couldn't allow for another Witch to die if they didn't need to—especially a Wardwell Witch. If there was a chance to save her, then I had to try.

"This was... unexpected."

I spun around at the sound of the voice and found myself staring at Nera. I'd spent so long thinking of her as "The Seer", as this evil being that had cursed me and tried to bring about the end of the world as we knew it. I had never given myself permission to really *look* at her. Now that I was, I couldn't stop. She was my sister; there was no doubt. That same sense of familiarity I felt with Hazel, I felt with her. Just looking at her made it blindingly obvious. We had the same color eyes, the same shade of dark hair, and even our faces had the same shape.

The feel of her magic was familiar, and not just in the sense that I'd felt it's power before.

"I'm flattered... I managed to do something a Seer didn't see." She didn't look amused. "It happens... rarely."

I smiled awkwardly and nodded. "Did you know... that we're sisters?"

She sighed and rolled her eyes as she stepped closer. "I have known for a long time. No one told me, of course, but there isn't a lot the Angels can hide when I go looking for answers. I saw that we were related about a decade ago."

I frowned and shook my head. "So, you helped them kidnap me, hurt me, even though you knew who I was to you?"

She raised an eyebrow. "And who are you to me?"

"Your sister," I replied, my voice tinged with outrage.

Nera shook her head. "An arbitrary title. The Angels are my family, not you. They raised me, cared for me, and trained me. They have looked out for me my entire life—"

"They killed our parents and kidnapped you," I interrupted. "They stole you from your real family."

"Parents who were robbing us of the chance to reach our full potential. Parents who were going to keep us running and hiding, and who continued to refuse to choose a side in this inevitable war."

I shook my head in disbelief. "Witches aren't meant to choose."

"Oh?" she said, smirking. "What do you call your relationship to the Demon King?"

"That was fate, not my choosing. If you want to talk choices, I am happy with him, but I chose to be friends with Leviah—an Archangel, and I am constantly looking out for my fellow Witch."

"But if push comes to shove, and it will, you'll choose the Demon King. How does your choice make you any better than me?"

I stared at her for a moment, and I could see how deeply she believed that. "How can you trust the very beings who stole you and have manipulated your choices since you were a baby?"

"They haven't manipulated me," she hissed.

"You are not supposed to leave Heaven."

"For my own protection," she snapped. "To stop Witches like you and Demon Kings from killing me."

"It's to keep you isolated so you'll never get to know me or Mika, so you'll be easy to warp into the weapon they need!"

I gasped when her quick-burning anger sent sparks my way, burning my skin wherever they touched. She was glaring at me; her eyes heated with rage. "They are my family—they want me, they love me."

My hands shook as I watched her slowly unravel before me, and I felt a slightly manic emotion pouring from her.

She was sick, her mind warped and poisoned over decades so that I feared there was no saving her.

"So, you're willing to let Mika and I die... so you can jumpstart the apocalypse?"

She sighed as if I were being purposefully ignorant. "The end of the world as we know it is inevitable—the expiration date is up for debate. I would like to see it happen in my lifetime, and I know my family is eager for the same result. Heaven is meant to be on top—everyone knows it, and deep down, so do you."

I stepped back, shaking my head at her cold and detached demeanor. "You're talking about the deaths of millions—billions of humans—about the extinction of Witches and a war that will destroy this planet and most of the population of Angels and

Demons. Who wins in that scenario?" I asked, sickened.

"The Angels, of course." She said as if it were obvious. "Of course, there are going to be casualties in the beginning, a great many losses, but the deaths of humans will provide ample Angelic soldiers that will replenish their numbers. And when order is restored and Angel's rule as they were always meant to, a new order will start on earth."

Any hope I had of saving Nera evaporated as I watched the frenzied light in her eyes while describing the deaths of humans as if it were nothing, a mere blip in the greater plan.

"You're not going to join me, are you?" she asked with a sigh as if she'd expected this answer, but was disappointed in me, nonetheless.

"I didn't realize you wanted me to... but no. I'm not joining you."

A flicker of malice lit her eyes briefly, a smug knowing that made the hairs on the back of my neck stand on end.

"I guess we'll just raise this one ourselves, then," she said with a flippant shrug. I didn't get a chance to ask what she was talking about before someone screamed my name, the sound turning my blood cold.

"Trinity!"

Jerking around, I saw Uriel... and in his arms was Hazel. Her hands were bound behind her back and she had a purpling bruise on the side of her face that turned my vision red.

"Hazel." I whispered her name as my mind took precious seconds to catch up on what was happening. How did he get her? She was in the Oasis, she had been safe!

"I found this one in the bushes, watching. She's a curious one," Uriel answered as if he heard my question. "But you know what curiosity did to the cat."

Hazel's wide eyes pleaded with me for understanding, for

forgiveness, but I wasn't looking at her anymore. My attention was on Uriel as memories of my past life surged forward. Of Tabitha, bound and bleeding, tortured for hours, beaten down as they tried to get her to tell them where the Oasis was. Memories slammed into me of Donovan shouting at them to stop, of his desperate attempts to get to her even as Uriel carried her limp body into the house and set it ablaze. I could feel the flames licking at my skin, and I sucked in a sharp breath.

"Let her go," I whispered, surprised at the venomous hiss that accompanied my words.

Uriel grinned as he brushed back the hair from Hazel's face. "I don't think so. She'll be fun to break in Heaven, and who knows? She's young enough that she might change her alliances with the right kind of ... pressure."

His threat to harm Hazel nearly turned me feral, and I pushed through the need to burn him where he stood. Nera likely knew my next moves, so my only choice was to act in the moment, to not plan it and give her the chance to attack and deflect.

I raised my hand, but Nera delivered a magical blow that knocked me off my feet. I rolled quickly and flipped back to my feet, delivering a magical punch of my own. In a matter of seconds, we entered into a battle. I forced shield up around myself to better protect myself as I sketched wards into the air, sigils that would both protect and harm the one casting curses. Hazel's cries for me only fueled my need to win this battle, but I was suddenly hit with a curse so powerful it sent me flying several feet back. My head slammed into a rock, and for a moment, my vision blurred, the edges tinged with black. Nausea hit me hard and fast, and I rolled over to heave, but nothing came up.

I felt Nera approach, felt the build of her magic as she prepared to hit me again, to end me, and Hazel's scream made my stomach drop as I realized this could be the end.

Just as I was rolling over to try and save myself, I watched a ball of blue magic hit Nera square in the chest. Her body went rigid and began convulsing before a second wave of magic sent her flying backward. She hit the ground hard and I struggled to get to my feet, my head still spinning.

Rough hands gripped my arms and yanked me to my feet. I tried to push them off, their touch nearly burning me, but the world kept spinning.

"Let me go," I snapped, struggling to keep my feet under me.

"I will, but not yet," the owner of that voice said, but it was all wrong. It seemed to be enjoying these moments, and I realized then that it was Uriel who held me. Forcing my eyes to open and sight to steady, I watched as Hazel struggled to her feet even though her ankles were bound and wrists still tied behind her back. Nera approached her, and Hazel's damp eyes moved from me to Nera.

"Leave her alone!" I cried, nausea burning away as my fear for Hazel turned to anger at the Seer.

"In a moment," she replied with a malicious grin, wiggling her fingers to send sparks at Hazel's face, burning her. The girl gasped and tried to turn her face away, but Nera moved closer and fisted her shirt, hauling her closer.

I struggled against Uriel, directing magic backward. He grunted and snarled, wrenching my arms harder so I cried out. He held my hair in a tight fist so that tears burned my eyes, and his grip on my arms was almost crushing. But still, I fought. He could break my bones and tear out my hair, I didn't care. His grip tightened so that I felt bones bruise and I cried out but kept fighting.

Hazel lifted her gaze to Nera again, this time dark with defiance and rage. Rearing back, she then brought her head forward quickly so her forehead slammed into Nera's nose. I heard the crunch from where I was, and stared in surprise as Hazel brought her hands up—now free—and followed her headbutt with a sharp punch, her left hand holding a ball of magic that she shot forward. It hit Nera in the chest and sent her staggering backward.

"Bitch," Uriel snarled.

"Hazel, run! Oasis now!" I screamed.

Nera whipped around to look at Hazel, blood pouring from her nose and fury burning in her eyes. I saw the curse building on Nera's lips and knew Hazel wasn't equipped enough to defend herself. It all seemed to happen in slow motion, and I watched helplessly as Uriel held me back and Nera prepared to throw the curse.

But before she could, Nera was blasted back off her feet again, her body sailing through the air for several feet before slamming into the unforgiving ground. I gasped when Uriel was wrenched away from me and I staggered, almost falling, but new hands steady me. My first reaction was to pull away, but almost immediately a sense of healing invaded and I turned to find myself staring into a familiar pair of dark blue eyes.

"Tomika?"

My sister's blue eyes met mine with relief and warmth, and if it wasn't for the way my wrist was healing and the nausea and dizziness was leaving me, I'd have thought I was imagining her.

"Hey, sis."

Happiness began to well up inside me, but when she raised her hands, gathering more magic to throw at Nera, it halted.

"Wait! Mika... you can't."

"That's where you're wrong," she argued.

"No," I said and touched her arm. "She's our sister. You can't kill her."

Mika hesitated, and I watched her eyes take in our similarities, saw her use another part of herself to sense the connection that existed between us, but she shook her head. "She's a traitor, a liar, but she's not our sister. Blood is all that binds us, and that does not make her family."

Apparently having enough time to recover, Nera let loose a wave or power in our direction, but Mika and I together erected a hasty barrier that allowed the magic to veer off to the sides of us. Several trees shook, and a few began to lift from their roots with the power of Nera's spell.

Mika pushed Nera to the ground with a forceful spell, using her other hand to weave a sigil in the air to enhance the power of her spell and keep her down.

"Don't kill her yet," Leviah said from somewhere to my right. Mika looked at him and frowned, and a new voice spoke up.

"You're Leviah, I assume," a Demon King greeted, stepping up beside Mika. The Demon King was... well, he was sexy as sin, just as I knew them all to be.

His black eyes met mine and he smirked. "Good to meet you at last, Trinity. I'm your new brother, Cole."

I nodded and flicked a glance to Mika who smiled at me and I turned back to look at Nera who glared at us. My mind was having trouble catching up, still a little rattled from the hit it had taken against the rock.

"Donovan?" I whispered, worried now that I didn't know where he was.

"I am here, moya lyubov', just busy." I felt the sudden flash of pain from him before he blocked me, and I suddenly heard the commotion going on behind me. Turning around, I watched a flash of white wings as Donovan and Uriel got into it, a fight that

was fast and fierce, moving so fast it was hard to see every move. Fear for my mate pulled at me, but two other Kings stood by, watching, ready to step in if their brother needed it.

"Help me bind her?" Mika asked, drawing my attention back to her and holding out her hand. I took her hand, and something once broken inside me shivered and seemed to heal at long last. Breathing out a small sigh of relief, I raised my right hand as Mika raised her left and together, we concentrated our magic on binding Nera. She screeched at us as her arms were suddenly forced to her sides, and she stood stiff as if wrapped with an invisible cord. For good measure, I slapped a silencing spell over her mouth to ensure we didn't have to listen to her poisonous words. I held the spell as Mika worked another sigil to hold her there, and I poured what I could into it while keeping some of my attention on Donovan.

The fight behind us was getting louder and harder to ignore, as was the pain being inflicted. I knew Donovan was trying to protect me from feeling it, but it was distracting him. I put up my own barrier and watched as his focus on Uriel became predatory. There was no way he was letting Uriel leave today. I knew this was his end, even as the Archangel fought hard and vicious.

"Trinity."

I turned in time to open my arms for Hazel as she jogged over to me, dried tears on her cheeks. I held her tight and breathed a sigh of relief that she was okay.

"I'm sorry; I just wanted to help. I knew you guys weren't being honest and I thought I could help," she whispered, the small tremor going through her body nearly took me to my knees.

"It's okay, sweetheart. You're okay, that's all that matters," I rasped, wiping at her tears as she pulled away. I wanted to reassure her more, but Donovan was in a hell of a fight, and I began pouring energy into him, wanting to help bring Uriel to his knees at last. But this was Donovan's fight, just his. It was why his brothers weren't stepping in, it was why the number of Witches I now saw standing by them simply waited, watching with concern just like me.

I touched on Donovan's mind, seeing the visions in his head, the way Tabitha had screamed as Uriel stabbed her with a short, sharp blade. I heard her cries, her words of reassurance to Donovan that she could take the pain, she could handle it. I felt Donovan relive the horrifying moment both he and Tabitha had become aware of the moment her body began to burn within the house as he tried to keep her from feeling it. I felt sick with the memories, but they fueled his rage and kept him moving. I saw more recent memories, of when he and Uriel had fought only a few years ago and I bit back a gasp when I saw a Knight of Hell stab Mika through the back as she healed Donovan and Uriel skipped out, escaping his long overdue punishment.

"End this, my love. End this, and come back to me," I whispered gently, knowing that if he stayed in this state too long, it would only hurt him more.

I felt him reach me through the haze of hatred and retribution, a part of him that just wanted this to be over with so he could hold me, so he could check on Hazel and we could move on from this part of our lives. He was tired of it all, and we were both ready for our life to begin together.

I watched as Uriel tried to get a hold of Donovan from behind, and Donovan reached up to grip Uriel at the back of his neck and rip him forward over his head so the Archangel slammed into the ground on his back. He didn't get much of a chance to move before Donovan took up his sword and brought it down, stabbing it through Uriel's chest. The Angel's eyes widened in shock and Donovan circled around to look at him better.

"I told you centuries ago when you killed Tabitha that you had signed your own name upon Death's scroll that day, Uriel. I told you that it didn't matter how long you ran or where you hid away, you'd die by my hand."

I shivered at the cold hatred in Donovan's tone, and watched as Uriel struggled to breathe, struggled to try and dislodge the heavy sword.

"Well, it's retribution day, fuckface, and I keep my word."

With that, Donovan blasted a stream of hellfire at the Archangel, and I whipped Hazel around so she couldn't see and did my best to cover her ears as the Angels shrieked in agony. Donovan's face was a mask of ruthless justification, and after several long minutes, he yanked his sword free of Uriel's chest and brought it swinging down in a powerful arc. I watched with wide eyes as Uriel's head dislodged from his neck. My stomach turned at the sight of all the blood, but another part of me was glad to witness Uriel's death for myself, and somewhere deep down inside me, I felt avenged.

Silence filled the air for several long, tense moments, and I couldn't stop Hazel when she pulled away and turned to look at Uriel's dead form. She'd seen a lot in her years already, and she wasn't a child in the typical sense. She could handle this. Gently, I reached out for Donovan, pushing through the layers of red haze and hatred.

"I'm here, baby. Come back to me."

Red haze turned to yellow, then green and blue until Donovan's rage seeped away and he raised his gaze to mine.

"There you are," I whispered. *"My King, my mate... my love."*

Throwing his sword to the side, Donovan kept his gaze locked on mine as he stalked past his brothers to reach me. I was reminded of that day of our first kiss on the battlefield. The day I'd gone to him at the advice of Dinah, and he'd looked at me the same way he was now.

"Mine," Donovan growled into my mind before his hands framed either side of my face and his mouth was on mine. I didn't hesitate to wrap my arms around him and lift onto my toes to better align our bodies. He kissed me hard and deep, like he was trying to mark me all over again.

"I love you, moya lyubov', you are my world."

I smiled against his lips and pulled away, breathing heavy. *"And you are mine."*

CHAPTER TWENTY-EIGHT

DONOVAN

"Doni!"

I grinned and turned from Trinity to catch Hazel as she launched at me. I wrapped my arms around her and swung her in a circle and let myself fully take in that she was okay, that she was safe. When Leviah had come back and said he couldn't find her, I knew exactly where she was, and I'd just about thrown up on the spot.

"You scared the hell out of me, Hazel," I told her, closing my eyes on the idea of losing her after everything.

"I'm sorry... I was trying to help," she whispered, her voice hitching.

I put her back on her feet and wiped away her tears, relief hitting me again at seeing her alive. The purple bruise on the side of my face dampened my mood and she shook her head.

"It's already healing."

I grunted my displeasure, but let it drop for now. If she was going to keep getting into trouble like this, I needed to teach her to fight with more than her magic. Weapons and hand-to-hand combat were definitely going to become a part of her schooling. Trinity could handle the magic.

"Doni?" someone else said, slightly mocking.

I turned to see Cole looking at me with a shit-eating grin and I glared. Cassius slapped him up the back of the head and Cole cursed.

"What the fuck was that for?"

Cassius met my gaze before it moved to Hazel. "Trust me, you don't want to make fun of that name."

A strange feeling settled in my stomach, and I had the sudden feeling that Cassius knew more than he should.

"What do you know?" I asked, my eyes narrowing.

He shrugged. "I accidentally knocked that book off the table in your realm and saw a letter penned to you."

I ground my teeth. "Accidentally?" I asked, disbelieving.

"Of course," Cassius said with too much innocence.

"And you read it?"

Cassius shrugged easily. "I was curious. And then I flipped back to the start and read it all. It explained a lot... like why you blew up the way you did hundreds of years ago, and why a little girl I spoke to named Marlee told me she hated me and wanted her Doni the day I was meant to take over training the Witches for you."

I stiffened and swallowed hard. "You met Marlee?"

Cassius nodded slowly. "Yeah, just the once. I didn't know what she was referring to, thinking she hated me because of what I was and she wanted her blanket or teddy or something, but it makes sense now."

Cole looked between the two of us with wide eyes. "Makes sense to who? Cause I'm fucking lost."

I pulled Hazel in for a sideways hug and looked to Trinity, my heart warming again. She and Mika were currently hugging as they talked, and for a moment, everything was right. They were reunited at long last.

"Hazel, I'd like you to meet some people," I said as I caught my brothers and mates watching from a small distance away.

"These are my brothers, Adrik, Malik, Harkyn, and Tamas. Those two over there are Cole and Cassius," I began, pointing to everyone as I went. "And these are their mates; Mika—Trinity's twin—Sawyer, Dimitria, and Raven. Cali is back home, but you'll meet her soon enough."

Hazel waved hello to everyone, but they were still looking at me curiously. "This is Hazel, and she and I have a deal. Where I go, so does she. So... you'll be seeing a lot of her."

Hazel grinned up at me and I pressed a kiss to the top of her head. I watched with relief as the women began talking to her, pulling her into their circle.

My gaze fell to Uriel's decapitated form, and I felt something in me settle at long last. His death had been too quick, nowhere near as painful as it should have been. But in the end, it was the fact that he was dead that mattered. He couldn't hurt anyone anymore, and Tabitha had at long last, been avenged.

"So, what are we doing with this one?" Adrik asked, jerking his head in Nera's direction. I sighed and glanced at Mika and Trinity who looked from me to their sister. There wasn't much to discuss here. She was dangerous as the Angels, and she'd have a vendetta now that we'd killed Camhael and Uriel. I couldn't allow a threat to Trinity to stand, and neither would Cole. I met my brother's black eyes, and the answer I had was reflected in his.

"You ladies should go back to the Oasis," I suggested, turning to Trinity. "Take Hazel with you?"

Her blue eyes were filled with emotion, her morals fighting with what she knew had to happen and she pulled away from Mika to come to me.

"I don't know if that's the right move," she said.

"It has to be done, Trinity. I won't allow a direct threat to you to walk around again. I won't risk losing you again, and you can be damn sure Cole won't leave a threat to Mika."

She frowned. "But killing her now would be in cold blood. She's bound, defenseless—" Her words broke off in a gasp and she turned around at the same time as the other women to find Leviah standing over Nera, his sword in her chest.

"Lev," Trinity choked out. He slowly raised his gaze to meet hers before flicking to me and then away.

"It had to be done; there was no other way."

"But—" she tried but Lev shook his head.

"If Donovan had done it, some part of you would have resented him for it, and your new brother having the blood of your sister—estranged or not—on his hands is no way to start a new life with him. I'm okay being the bad guy this time."

My respect for the Archangel rose again, and I made a note to thank him later. He'd taken the choice—the responsibility— from me and my brothers.

Trinity didn't say anything to that, and I knew she needed to take some time to fully process how she felt.

"Looks like I arrived just in time," a new voice drawled. We all turned to see Mervyn step onto the field, his long trench coat billowing around him as he strode toward the dead Witch. Leviah's eyes widened when he saw the Reaper and he stepped back as Mervyn knelt by Nera's dead body.

"What—" Trinity started, but I squeezed her hand and we watched. The Reaper whispered words we couldn't hear under his breath before he plunged his hand into her chest. There was no blood or gore, though, and when he pulled his hand back, he held a pale blue—almost silver—ball in his hand. Small chain-like links seemed to encircle it, and I stared in awe at the Witch's soul.

"It's a rare and rather complicated little curse this Witch placed on you," he said almost conversationally before he slid the soul into a deep inner pocket. Dark eyes met mine and he stood again.

"What are you doing with her soul?" Trinity asked as Mervyn stepped closer. His eyes searched her face and I got the impression he saw more than he let on.

"I'm taking it for safe-keeping. Lately, Witch souls aren't making it through the rebirth cycle, and I intend to see that this one does."

Trinity frowned. "Why aren't they being reborn?"

A corner of Mervyn's lip curved in a small, knowing smirk that quickly disappeared. "I am here to remove a curse placed on your soul. That is a powerful bit of magic, and I don't often have reason to do it when the subject is still alive."

I stiffened and swallowed. "Are you saying Trinity has to die for this to work?"

Mervyn shrugged. "That's one way to do it. I see the two of you are marked, so she would not pass on, but you would likely go through several days of agony when I could simply remove the curse while she lives."

I let out a heavy breath and glared at him. "So, are you going to help us?"

He heaved a small sigh like he was dealing with unruly children. "Yes, Donovan, or I would not be here. Trinity, I need for you to lie down. You are going to stop breathing."

"I thought you said she didn't have to die," Mika reminded, a tinge of panic in her voice.

"And she won't. Not really. The curse Nera placed on her is bound to her soul. So, killing the Seer isn't enough to get rid of the curse. If Trinity dies with this curse still attached, it'll follow her into the next life and everyone after that until she's no longer reborn or the curse is removed. To get rid of it, I'm going to shut down her body as if she is dead, and one of you will need to keep her breathing, another will keep her heart pumping. I have to remove her soul for this to work, and if I do that without these other safeguard in place, she *will* die."

Trinity looked back at me and I pulled her in close.

"Are you ready, moya Lyubov'?"

She hesitated. *"This is the only way you'll get your brothers and your throne back."*

I shrugged. *"If you are not ready, then we wait. I do not think this will hurt, and we will all be here to ensure it goes well. If it goes wrong... you will be lost to me for a while, but your soul will return and we will be okay. I act as your anchor, you will not pass on."*

She frowned. *"But it would hurt you."*

I shrugged. *"It will be worth it to feel whole and to have you in my arms."*

Trinity sighed and nodded, and I gently kissed her.

"Okay, let's do this," Trinity said before turning back to the others. I sat down, and she laid down so her head was resting on my lap and I brushed her hair back. Those dark eyes met mine and I smiled.

"I love you."

"And I love you."

"I'll monitor your heart," Mika said as she knelt by Trinity's side. "And I'll take over your breathing," Sawyer offered.

I nodded my thanks to them both and readied myself. I couldn't imagine this feeling pleasant for either one of us.

I watched as Trinity closed her eyes and tried to even her breathing, and I felt the moment Mervyn reached for her soul. Mika was there, and so was Sawyer, and I felt the moment her soul was lifted.

My breath stuttered and pain ripped at me, but after a moment it settled. Trinity's chest rose and fell with every breath Sawyer took for her, and I could feel her pulse pounding as Mika took control.

I watched Mervyn analyze the silver-blue orb in his hands, dark eyes scanning over each of the tiny links before he paused and smiled.

"There it is," he said softly, and I could see a tiny bead-like ball on one of the links. It barely looked like anything, and it was strange to know such a tiny thing had the potential for such damage. Mervyn concentrated on the bead, and he carefully plucked it from Trinity's soul. Holding it between his thumb and forefinger, he murmured words I didn't understand before crushing it.

"That's it?" I asked, feeling lightheaded and nauseas. I wasn't sure if it was just the idea of Trinity being so vulnerable or if it was that her soul was outside her body.

"That's it, the curse is removed," Mervyn assured before gently placing Trinity's soul back in her body. It took a few long moments, and his every move was careful and exact, underlining just how precious this process actually was.

It took several long moments, but when Trinity gasped, Sawyer and Mika backed up and came back to themselves.

"Moya lyubov'?"

Deep blue eyes fluttered open and she smiled up at me, reaching up to touch my face.

"My love," she said aloud. I grinned and pulled her into my arms and kissed her properly, long and deep, excitement and relief burning through me. She was safe, Uriel and Camhael were dead, the curse was gone, and she was absolutely mine.

Exaggerating gagging ruined the moment and I pulled back with a grin at Hazel who pretended to find it all revolting. A smattering of laughter went around the group and Mervyn stood. We got to our feet as well, and I held out my hand to the Reaper.

"Thank you for coming. I wasn't sure you would, despite our past experiences, but the Seer, Dinah, assured us you would." Mervyn nodded, and I studied him to see if he found that observation odd.

"You don't seem surprised," I said.

He raised an eyebrow. "She is a Seer, and I am here. Obviously, she saw it happen. Why would I be surprised?"

I narrowed my eyes because something felt off. The way Dinah had said it… there was more going on here, and I had no idea how to figure it out.

"It is good to see you all alive and well," Mervyn began, looking around at us all. "By my count, there are only three of you to go. Goodluck."

Before we could say anything more, Mervyn vanished in the blink of an eye and I sighed. I guess I'd know the answers to my questions when the time was right. For now, I had my woman, my girl, and now I could get my brothers back.

"So… I don't suppose any of my wonderful sisters know *how* I can repair the bonds between me and my brothers?" I asked. I hadn't really thought that far ahead.

Malik glared at me but rolled his eyes.

"Cali and Cassius figured it out," Adrik explained.

Relief washed over me, and I shared a grateful look with Cassius. I stiffened when a presence showed up on my radar, followed by another, and another. But my concerns were immediately put to rest when I spotted Wren stepping out of the tree line, followed by Robin and two other Witches.

"Robin?" Raven whispered in surprise before she pulled away from her mate and ran for her sister. We all watched as the two embraced and I pressed a kiss to Trinity's head and let her go to Mika. I might have waited for my mate for a long time, but Mika and Trinity had waited to be together for too long as well.

"Hi, Wren," I greeted, and she looked around at us all.

"We felt the injuries you have all suffered and thought we'd lend a hand in healing. Actually, I felt them, and Robin demanded to come see her sister, and then two others were curious and wanted to offer their help in case it was needed."

I smiled my thanks and made introductions to everyone. Trinity was about to offer to take care of my injuries, but it looked like it physically pained Mika every time her sister pulled away, so I waved her off and let Wren heal me instead. Trinity remained firmly in my mind though, the feel of her fingers in my hair was a constant comfort.

After a moment, Wren left to keep healing and I turned to see Lev sitting a few yards away, eyes searching the forest as if looking for the enemy.

"They're not stupid enough to attack when there are so many of us in one place," I assured.

He shrugged his massive shoulders and looked away again.

"Can't hurt to keep vigilant."

"She'll forgive you, Lev. She just needs some time to let everything that's happened to settle. The last few days have been insanely hectic; we've barely had time to breathe."

He nodded but didn't look at me.

"Thank you," I said after a moment, clearing my throat.

He frowned at me and I sighed. "You took that burden from me, from Cole. Mika didn't seem as concerned about Nera dying, but Trinity was torn. You were right—if I'd done it, some part of her would never have been able to let that go, and eventually, Mika would have likely felt the same if Cole had done it. You took a hit for both of us, and I appreciate it."

Lev nodded slowly, but his eyes were shadowed. "She's my only family."

I hesitated and then tried to look affronted. "So, all that nephew talk was just bullshit to you? Gotcha," I said and pretended to walk away.

Lev's amusement reached me, even if he didn't laugh.

"She'll forgive you, Leviah. You're her family too. She's not even angry at you, just... confused. She doesn't know how to feel about it. Just give her a little time and she'll sort it out."

He nodded again and sighed. "I hope so."

Silence fell between us and he cleared his throat and shifted. "So, I guess you guys will be heading back to Hell soon?"

I nodded. "We haven't talked about it, but yes. I need to be there, and I can't be away from her for too long."

"I'm glad," he said quietly. "I know it drove you nuts, the distance she kept between the two of you. First, she didn't trust how she felt, and then when she found out what she was to you, it all made sense, but it was to keep you safe. As much as you suffered, she suffered at least as much, maybe more."

"I know," I assured and sighed. "And hey, I made you a promise. I said I'd find you a home."

He scoffed. "You don't need to, I'm not a lost puppy."

"No," I agreed. "But I'm going to assume the Oasis isn't going to be an option if Trinity isn't there anymore, and you can't come to Hell—physically or otherwise—and I would suggest staying with Shaye and Hariel, but you're still an Archangel and a giant beacon to all the other Angels, so being with them will only lead danger to their doorstep. You can't be on your own, Trinity would have my head, so, I was thinking..."

He raised an eyebrow. "What?"

I grinned. "How do you feel about Nephilim?"

His expression blanked and he shook his head. "You're joking."

"Not even a little bit."

He scoffed and started walking away from me. "Yeah... I'll

pass."

"I'll talk to Zarak and make arrangements," I called, but he shook his head and started back toward Trinity.

I grinned, and my gaze caught on Cassius who was sitting off to the side as Wren healed him. The two seemed to be in deep conversation, so I slowly made my way closer but stopped when she pulled something from her pocket.

Patting down my chest, I realized I'd lost Cassius's Token, and breathed a sigh of relief when Wren seemed to have found it. Cassius looked at the Witch, and instead of taking it, he took her hand and placed it in her palm.

My internal alarm was going off as she talked to him again, their words too low for me to hear, and with another wary look at him, Wren turned around and walked away before using one of the devices Trinity did to teleport out of the field.

Cassius's gaze followed her and stayed staring at the place she'd disappeared even as I came to stand beside him.

"It's her, isn't it?" I asked as Trinity and Mika stepped up beside me. Their happiness spilled around us, too great to be contained, and I knew for the next few weeks, the two were going to be damn near inseparable. Cole came up behind them, and I could tell he was loving how happy his mate was as much as I loved seeing Trinity shine now that she had her sister.

"Who is what?" Mika asked.

"Huh?" Cole asked, confused.

"Nova just said 'it's her, isn't it?'" Mika explained.

"The Witch Cassius was talking to," I answered.

Trinity smiled. "Wren. She's awesome."

I turned back to Cassius as he stirred and finally looked away from where she'd disappeared.

"Wren," Cassius said her name softly, almost reverently.

"Shit," Cole whispered and I met his gaze in understanding.

"What?" Trinity asked, her eyes bouncing between the three of us.

"She's his mate. Wren is his mate."

CHAPTER TWENTY-NINE

TRINITY

"You're leaving."

I jerked my head up as I reached the top of the hill where the Elders house was situated and smiled when I saw Dinah sitting in a swinging chair on her porch.

After Uriel's death and the removal of the curse, I'd invited my new sisters to the Oasis to see the place I fought so hard to protect. This of course, meant their mates could not come, none except Donovan. He was entrusted with their safety while here, but he assured them all they were safe. Besides Leviah, Donovan was the only other creature who was not a Witch allowed there. Showing them this place had been amazing, and seeing how impressed they were filled me with pride for my ancestors.

Raven and Robin spent most of their time together, and I was glad they'd be able to see each other more often now. Robin was more than content here, and so whenever Raven wanted to come and visit her sister or future niece, I'd be able to bring her through. I knew the rest of the women would want to come back sometimes, and it was good to see how much they wanted to offer their help in any way they could.

They'd all gone home last night, and Donovan and I chose to spend another night here with Hazel to tie up loose ends.

Dinah patted the seat next to her as I stepped onto her porch and I took the offered spot.

"Yes, I'm leaving. My place is with my mate, and he can't be away from his realm so often. But I am going to be making frequent trips here to get vision updates from you, or we can work out some other kind of system for you to deliver them to me as I can keep doing what I'm doing."

Dinah's smile was soft and she nodded. "I know, sweetheart. You've been here since you were fourteen, but you have never truly belonged here. The Oasis will always welcome you. Your ancestors built it, but you belong with your mate."

Tension leeched out of my shoulders at her words, and I was relieved that she was so understanding.

"There's something else," I said, bracing myself for what could potentially be an argument. I knew she'd have good reason to argue with me, but I hoped she'd trust me.

Her smile grew again. "You're taking your daughter with you?"

I jerked back and blinked at her, my heart pounding at calling Hazel my daughter. "Uh... I mean, we haven't asked her yet officially, but yes, we plan on taking Hazel with us if she wants to come. But I don't know if—"

"Okay, so she does not wear the title of *daughter* yet, but that is precisely what she'll become."

I smiled happily, feeling warm from the inside out at her words, but then frowned. "I would think this insight would count as one of those future things you don't share and just allow to happen in case something we do or say changes the outcome."

She grinned then. "I did not see it in a vision; it is just how it will go. Even a blind lady can see it."

I laughed at her joke and she chuckled too.

"Besides," she added, "nothing was stopping that train. From the moment the three of you found one another, it was a rare absolute outcome in the universe that nothing was going to change."

My heart grew at knowing that, and something in me settled,

felt content.

After a moment, I sighed. "I'm going to miss you."

She waved her hand as if waving off the comment. "Hush, sweetheart. You'll be back often enough, and in the meantime, I want you to enjoy the life you have long been denied."

I smiled gently at her words and sighed. "I missed Mika, but it's going to be so strange to be able to see her all the time now."

Dinah nudged my shoulder with her own. "You have a lot of time to make up for."

Yes, I did. Both with Mika and with Donovan.

"Have you spoken to Lev yet?" she asked.

I sighed. "I have. I feel bad that I made him question my loyalty to him or that I could ever cut him out for what he did. He didn't kill Nera out of revenge or spite; he didn't do it just for the sake of it. She was a real threat to me, to Mika, Hazel, and Donovan. Had we let her go, she would have been a risk to all the Kings and anyone else who befriended us. I know there was no other option, it was just so... confronting when it happened."

"And he knows this?"

I smiled. "He does. We're going to take him to see Amazarak, the Nephilim. We're hoping he and his kind will give Leviah a home. And I was wondering if maybe you'd..." I looked at her hopefully, and her knowing eyes were smiling.

After a moment, she closed her eyes and I waited as her face went slack as she went into another vision. After several long moments, she let out a long breath and smiled softly.

"Things will be... rocky. There is potential for things to go wrong, but if Leviah keeps his head down and doesn't annoy too many of the Nephilim, then he should find a happy home there, even some friends."

I raised an eyebrow in surprise. An Archangel friends with

Nephilim? I mean, I guess it wasn't the strangest thing, but I wasn't sure how that would look.

"You should go, sweetheart. You have a big day ahead of you, and someone is waiting to talk to you," Dinah said after another moment. I leaned forward to hug her, appreciation for this woman washing over me. She'd saved me, she'd given me a home, taught me everything I knew, and she'd protected me as well as she could. I owed everything to her.

"I'll see you soon, Dinah."

She turned her head to kiss my cheek and I stepped away, smiling. She waved and I made my way off her porch, feeling lighter and more hopeful than I had in a long time.

~

"I'm coming with you."

Donovan and I stopped talking, and I turned to find Hazel standing behind me, her slight frame stiff, hands clenched at her sides. Her dark hair was pulled back and her backpack was slung over her back as if she were ready to go right this second. One look at her slightly trembling lips and defiant eyes, and I stepped away from Donovan to pull her into a hug.

"You want to come with us?" I asked, excitement bubbling inside me.

"Yes," she said, barely holding onto her courage, her eyes flicking to Donovan as if waiting for him to refuse her.

He just raised an eyebrow. "I bloody well hope you're coming, or I created a whole wing in my realm for you that's just going to go to fucking waste."

"Language," I hissed with a small laugh.

Hazel sucked in a sharp breath, eyes wide. "You mean it?"

Donovan grinned. "Of course, kid. I told you we had a deal. If I leave, you're welcome to come with—*oof!*"

I laughed as Hazel launched herself at Donovan, slamming into him. He grinned and wrapped his arms around her.

"Come on, my *Malishka*, let's go home."

The familiar term of endearment made my heart grow and pound, and the affection I felt coming off him for the girl in his arms had me beaming. Hazel grinned at the nickname, and another part of me just fell even deeper in love with my mate than before. I hadn't been aware that it was possible, but apparently it was.

"Do I get my own key to Hell?" she asked as she pulled away.

Donovan laughed. "No, there are no keys."

"Fine," she sighed. "Is there a way for you to help me come and go from Hell?"

He frowned. "Don't you remember the rest of the conversation we had about you coming with me? There are rules and restrictions."

She waved her hand as if dismissing his words. "Don't worry, I'll find a way on my own."

I grinned at Donovan when he shot me a look of alarm over her head. We needed to be prepared, because if Hazel set her mind to it, she absolutely would find a way to get out of Hell on her own terms.

I held Donovan's hand and took Hazel's in the other, and closed my eyes as Donovan shadowed us out of the Oasis.

When I opened my eyes, it took a moment to orient myself and Hazel staggered back and groaned.

"Oh, that *sucks!*"

I laughed and let Donovan pull me against him for stability as she fought to keep her balance.

"You get used to it," Mika assured as she skipped out of a red door.

I smiled and moved to hug my sister who grinned.

"Welcome home," she whispered.

I smiled wider, hugged her tighter, and then let go to check on Hazel.

"Okay, I'm good," she said, breathing deep before looking around. "Wow it's uh…" she nodded, nose crinkling a little in thought. "It's… hey, I like the red doors."

I laughed at her obvious distaste and Donovan rolled his eyes. "What's wrong with it?" he asked.

"Nothing," she said, eyes wide. "It's just a little… dark. But hey, you're Demon Kings. What did I expect? Can't allow anything lighter I suppose."

Cole barked out a laugh as Hazel wandered down the long hall to check out each of the doors. When she stopped at one, she tipped her head to the side and studied it.

"What is it?" I asked.

She looked back at me, a sliver of vulnerability there, a smidge of awkwardness. "I don't know. It just… feels like home," she said. Without any prompting, she reached for the door and pushed it open, and Mika made a sound of excitement.

"What?" I asked.

"The doors don't open for just anyone," Donovan explained. "Only those who belong here."

Hazel seemed to glow from the inside out, and she ducked her head to hide her smile as she stepped inside. I smiled at Donovan, and he waved me in.

"Oh, awesome fireplace," we heard Hazel call from inside.

"We'll leave you guys to get sorted," Cole said with a chuckle. "Remember to meet out here later tonight so we can get this bond thing sorted. Devlin has managed to get Corvin to agree to come out of hibernation to fix it."

I nodded my thanks and followed Trinity inside, more than ready to welcome my girl's home.

~

We arrived on several acres of empty land beside some bushland and a river. There didn't appear to be anyone around for miles, but these were the coordinates Amazarak had given us. Perhaps he wanted to meet with us this far away from the general public and anyone else that could be harmed.

I let go of Hazel's hand, but I'd already warned her to stay close. If things got bad, I was taking her the hell out of here now that I'd worked out how to shadow on my own. I wasn't risking her getting caught between a Nephilim and an Archangel if things got messy.

"Trinity," a deep voice said calmly.

We all turned to find Amazarak standing behind us, his imposing form appearing even more-so with his giant black wings outspread as they were. If Lev was intimidated, he didn't show it, but I wouldn't have blamed him in the least.

"Hi, Amazarak. Thank you for meeting us here," I replied.

The Nephilim leader shrugged his massive shoulders, and the wings he'd just tucked away vanished as if they had never been. It didn't do anything to lessen the impressiveness of his presence, though. He carried an aura of lethal strength and power everywhere he went.

His black eyes turned to look at Donovan and his lips twitched in some fraction of a smile. "Donovan."

Donovan lifted his chin in greeting before turning to Hazel.

"And who are you?" Amazarak asked, his voice softening slightly.

Hazel looked him up and down, a small frown on her face. "I'm Hazel."

Amazarak cocked an eyebrow. "Something wrong?"

She shrugged. "No... I just thought you Nephilim were supposed to be big."

I choked on a small laugh as I looked at all six-foot-eight-inches of Zarak. "Honey, he *is* big."

She sighed. "No, like giant. I thought I'd get to see a *real* Nephilim."

Donovan started laughing and I slapped a hand over my face. Sometimes the girl had no filter.

"Sorry to disappoint you," Amazarak replied dryly. "Those stories are just that: stories. They're made up by man and Angels to make us out to be some kind of evil product born of Angels and humans."

Hazel nodded as if it were only mildly interesting. "Huh, bummer."

"Okay," I said, cutting in while trying to hold back my laugh. "We had a favor to ask of you."

Amazarak's eyes glinted with humor and he nodded. "Yes, you have an Archangel you'd like us to house," he said, turning his attention to Leviah.

The two males stood looking each other over for a long moment. There was another flutter of movement and Keira appeared beside her mate, another man at her side.

"Hariel," Leviah said with surprise.

Hariel smiled. "Hi, Leviah, glad to see you're still up and about."

Lev nodded once. "The same to you."

Silence fell again and I glanced from Amazarak to Leviah and back. The Nephilim seemed to be studying Leviah, searching him for some kind of answer.

"You can ask whatever it is you are trying to work out," Lev suggested.

"I will give you only one chance to answer each question. At your first lie, we're done and you're on your own. And believe me, I can tell," Amazarak warned, dark eyes narrowing.

Leviah nodded, stiffening slightly.

"Did you break Trinity out of Heaven with the intention of using her to locate the Witches Oasis to then bring the information to whoever you answered to in Heaven?"

I stiffened, eyes growing wide. Wow, he didn't pull any punches.

Leviah shook his head. "No, I did not. I broke her out because it was the right thing to do. I'm only sorry it took me so long to act."

"I'll second that," Donovan muttered. I elbowed him in the ribs and he continued to mutter unintelligible nonsense.

"Since breaking Trinity out of Heaven, have you ever considered handing her back over to ensure your survival?" Amazarak asked, again, not bothering to sugarcoat anything.

"Never," Lev responded.

"Do you harbor any ill-will toward Nephilim or our allies?"

Lev hesitated a moment and I tensed. "No," he finally said, almost thoughtfully. "No, no ill will. In the past, my actions toward your kind were based on following orders, not due to any personal hatred or dislike."

I monitored Amazarak carefully, and he seemed almost impressed with Leviah's honest answer.

"If you were to receive a pardon from Heaven and all who live there, would you go back?"

There was no hesitation this time. "No. Heaven is not the home I remember it to be. We were not following the orders of God, but of those who thought to take his place. I'm not interested in being a part of what it has become."

We waited as Leviah answered several more questions, some of which seemed important, others seemed a little frivolous, but I could understand the need for all of them. Zarak was getting a feel for Leviah, and he had his brethren to answer to. I was already guessing most—if not, all—weren't happy with the idea of Lev being there, and I knew Zarak was doing this for me because he felt like he owed me after I'd rescued the Nephilim baby.

Amazarak sighed. "One last question. If you were granted permission to stay with us, will you consent to a binding charm?"

Lev frowned, and so did I. Amazarak didn't mention anything of a binding charm to me when we talked earlier.

"What kind?" Lev asked.

"My kind don't share my ability to sense lies as easily, or duplicitous intentions. Many of them would feel safer knowing you consented to having certain information about us that you may learn in living with us bound so that you can't report it back to the Angels."

Leviah hesitated, and completely understood his pause. "If I did... Would you let Trinity be one of the Witches involved in working the binding?"

Amazarak thought about it for a moment before nodding. "Yes. You trust her, and so do I. She would work with Penny and they can word the binding charm in a way that will not restrict your freedom unnecessarily."

Leviah looked at me and then to Hariel. I could see he wasn't altogether sure about this situation.

"Please, Lev? You won't be safe out there on your own.

Eventually, they'll find you. I need to know you're safe."
Sighing, he met Donovan's gaze for a moment, then moved to
Hazel and Hariel before finally turning his attention to
Amazarak. "Okay, I'll comply."

Amazarak dipped his head, and I felt a smidge of respect for my
friend that hadn't been there before. "Okay, then I am accepting
you into our home. Keira is going to get Penny, and she and
Trinity can work out the binding, then we'll go home."

Leviah nodded and frowned as Keira left to get Penny. "I'm
not... sharing a room or anything, am I? I'll sleep outside,
honestly."

Amazarak smirked and shook his head. "We have a few smaller
freestanding homes on the property. Penny and her husband—
Keira's father—have one, and we have another ready for you.
It's for everyone's comfort."

I didn't like the sound of that last part. Was he going to be
ostracized there forever? Or would they just need time to warm
up to him?

"Hariel... how have you been acclimating to human life?" I
asked, happy to know the Angel had survived in some form.

He grinned. "I am happier than I have ever been. Eternity no
longer stretches out before me, I have the love of my life in my
arms every night, and my life is good."

His genuine happiness rolled off him in waves and I smiled.

"And now," Hariel continued, eyes shifting to Lev. "I have an old
friend living close by who I can visit. It will be nice to talk to
someone who has seen both sides of life."

Leviah nodded his acceptance, and I felt the twinge of
appreciation he felt at Hariel's offer. It was to show him he
wasn't totally alone, and someone else would understand his
problems acclimating. No, it wasn't the same thing, but it was as

close as Lev was likely to find.

Penny and Keira arrived a moment later, and I talked to them about the baby and how she was growing. The moment I mentioned her, the love everyone had for her was obvious, and I was so glad she'd survived. A moment of sadness washed over me for the loss of her mother, but Donovan was there in an instant, wrapping me in his warmth and comfort.

Penny and I got to work on the binding spell, making sure it wouldn't limit Lev too much. He wouldn't be able to talk to anyone who wasn't a friend about the Nephilim on the property, and the protection charm on the Nephilim grounds would still hold. He wouldn't know how to get there or what it looked like once he left. The moment he had ill-intent toward the Nephilim and wished them harm or death, he would be removed from the property. This did not include minor fights and spats which I foresaw would be an issue without being a Seer. Tempers would rise, and I knew there'd a few clashes. But as long as Leviah didn't wish death on them or start actively planning their deaths and demise, he'd be fine.

After an hour of prepping the spell, Penny and I got to work binding Lev. My friends was tense, uncomfortable, but this was the only place we had. The Oasis needed to go back to being a Witch-only sanctuary.

As the last of the bindings fell over Leviah, he drew in a deep breath and let it out.

"I'll come see you as often as I can," I promised.

He smirked. "I feel like I'm going away to a human prison and you're promising to see me at visiting hours."

I shrugged. "It's up to you how you choose to see this, Lev. You can see it as a prison, or you can see it as a second chance to build a new life for yourself, with new allies and a new purpose. The Nephilim... they are not the enemy. They're wrongly hunted, and you could be a powerful friend for them."

He nodded slowly, and I could tell that he took my words seriously.

"And… we're good, right? I know you said you don't hate me for what I did, but—"

I hurriedly hugged him to shut him up, and I felt the tension in him drain as he hugged me back. "I promise, Lev, we're good. You were protecting me and Donovan, and I appreciate what you did for us."

He hugged me tighter for a moment and I pulled away. Reaching into my pocket, I handed him his ring and he smiled down at it.

"You're sure your boyfriend won't mind?"

"Mate!" Donovan corrected from a few feet away.

I grinned and shook my head. "No, he won't. Keep it on you in case you need to talk or want to catch up. I'll keep mine on."

His silvery eyes met mine and he smiled. "Thanks, Trin. For everything."

"We'll see each other soon, okay? Just give this a real chance, please?"

He nodded. "I promise."

After hugging him again, I watched Hazel hug him and Donovan shake his hand before Keira offered him her hand. After hesitating a moment, he took her smaller hand and we watched as the Nephilim disappeared, Harriel and Penny along with them.

"Come on, family, let's go home," Donovan said, pulling me and Hazel in for a hug.

I smiled, replaying those two words in my head.

Family.

Home.

EPILOGUE

TRINITY

"It's a sword!"

There was gasps all around before the others came scrambling over to the crack in the wall. They peered over my shoulder and crowded close to get a better look. The other Witches had been working at the crack for a while now, and there was a large chunk missing that had revealed an item buried in the black marble. After staring at it for the past two days, I finally figured out what it was.

"How can you tell?" Mika asked, closest to the gap.

"There," I said, pointing to what looked like a long piece of metal. "It's the cross-guard of a sword."

Everyone stared for several long moments.

"Holy shit," Adrik murmured, stepping back.

One by one, everyone took a better look and by the end of it we were all agreed that it was in fact, a sword.

"Okay… so why is there a sword in the wall? And whose sword? And why can we feel *that* much energy coming from it?" Cali asked, resting a hand on her rounded belly.

Raven shook her head. "I don't know, but maybe we'll find out if we're careful and keep digging."

Everyone seemed in agreement to that, and I smiled when I watched Adrik wrap his arms around his mate and press a kiss to her head.

I was so excited for her that she was having a baby, and I couldn't wait to be an aunt. I also couldn't wait to see what a hybrid Demon-Witch would be like. What powers would they have? What abilities? Would this forever change the system of Hell? Would a hybrid baby be reincarnated like regular Witches, or would they be able to die for good like Demons? Whatever happened, though, I was just excited to be apart of this family. No one really seemed to have an answer to the sword in the wall, but I could feel the renewed energy to keep breaking away the wall to see what was in it.

I looked around at the Kings who were sitting around the long table and their mates who stood off to the side talking. I'd met them all now, officially. As promised, Corvin and Devlin had made an appearance to heal the bond between the brothers. Corvin looked like hell... no pun intended. He looked exhausted, worn down, a man beaten down over and over again. I'd gotten the highlights from Donovan of what had happened to him, and my heart bled for him. No one really had answers for most of Corvin's actions, but it seemed as though he'd almost always kept to himself anyway. So, it didn't surprise me that he didn't hang out more than necessary. Cassius had been out and about a lot lately, and according to the others, he was usually off doing his own thing. I think since he'd discovered Wren was his mate, he was looking for her. According to the prophecy, he'd need to take her to keep her safe, which meant she'd be in danger. That wasn't a surprise, and once I explained to Cassius what Wren did on a daily basis, he hadn't looked pleased. I was excited for Wren to join us. I'd adored her for a long time, and I knew she'd fit in among these women.

It had been so much fun getting to know them all. They were all so impressive, and learning each of their stories made me feel a lot closer to them. As expected, hanging out with Mika was my favorite thing. We had years to catch up on, and while I had kept tabs on her over the years, there was still so much I'd missed.

Learning how she and Cole got together filled me with equal parts indignation and humor. It was clear as day that the Demon King was head over heels for her, and I loved seeing their love shine bright. Even when they fought, the two were ridiculously in sync. I was pretty sure Cole said things to piss her off on purpose because he liked getting her riled up and then kissing her into silence. Mika didn't seem to mind it either.

The moment I'd had a moment alone with all the women, they'd been quick to warn me that I could get pregnant, and I could hear Donovan laughing in my head.

I assured them all Donovan had already told me, which resulted in his mated brothers calling him out for being a suck up. Evidently, most of them had either forgotten about the pregnancy fact, or flat out refused to tell them this bit of information.

I watched Hazel as she played Poker with Cole, Harkyn, and Malik. She was a shark, that daughter of mine, and she was constantly surprising her new uncles with her sharp wit. They hadn't been prepared for the kind of sharp sarcasm a teenager could weaponize, and it had been one of my favorite things to witness.

Yes, my daughter. I knew she wasn't Marlee, and I wasn't Tabitha. But our souls were connected on a deep level, and it was why we'd both been free to find Donovan now. The three of us were bound by destiny, and she *felt* like ours, as if she had always meant to be ours.

We'd been here for a month now, and she was settling in great. We went back to the Oasis once a week, and we also used that day to go with the others to heal those who needed it. That's where Hazel had met Skye, and the two became fast friends.

"What are you doing, moya lyubov'?"

I smiled at the feeling of Donovan wrapping his arms around me despite being several feet away, his scent enveloping me and making me want to purr against him like a cat.

"I am just enjoying this moment. I am happy, Donovan, truly content."
His dark eyes met mine from the table, and the warmth In him only doubled the feeling In myself.

"I never dreamed I'd be so lucky."

I imagined kissing his cheek and he went back to his conversation. A few weeks ago, he'd shown me the book Dinah had given him, and it brought me to tears reading the diary of Marlee. Knowing she'd lived a long and happy life seemed to ease some of Donovan's pains, though, and knowing she'd seen him even after he'd forgotten her made him happy. She hadn't lost memories of him at six, she had two other moments as an adult to see him and content herself that he was okay. That final letter left me sobbing, though, and Donovan had to take the book away. No wonder he'd felt so raw after reading it, and yet strangely at peace at the same time.

Hazel was excited to be with us. Donovan wasn't lying when he said he created her an entire wing in his realm. She had a room, a bathroom, a room to practice her magic in, her own library and an entire freaking forest—about three acres in size— complete with waterfall. I loved that he'd made sure she had a connection to nature down here and gave her all the privacy she could want.

She'd gone from being all alone to having eight uncles, five aunts, a bonus uncle in Lev, and a new friend in Skye. Whenever I spoke to her lately, she felt more than content here, and I was glad this had been the right move.

I, too, had gained so much. Running from Donovan had been the right thing to do in the beginning. I hadn't known what he was or what our connection meant, and it had scared me. After my visit to Heaven, it was necessary to keep our distance. But now, I was living the life I had always been meant to live.

And it all started with Donovan.

~

DONOVAN

Hundreds of years of regret and torment had led to this moment.

I had failed Tabitha all those years ago, but I hadn't failed her family. I had promised Tabitha that she and her family would be protected, that I would look after them no matter what happened, and I'd meant it. Now, after having my memory returned, I knew I'd followed through on my promise. At the time, the best thing for Wardwell Witches had been for me to think they'd all died. I'd suffered all those years, but it was worth it to know they'd gotten away and not only survived and thrived, but that they'd been able to help so many other families over the years.

My reward for suffering all those years sat across from me on the couch in Hell, a book in her hand, her feet in my lap. The fire crackled before us, warm and bright, and I couldn't take my eyes off her.

Trinity.

I'd searched for her for hundreds of years, fought to keep her these last five years, and now here she was in our realm, dressed in one of my shirts with her feet in my lap. She was exquisite. She was everything I could ever dream of wanting in a mate, and

I was in awe of being so lucky. I had no idea where the prophecy came from, or what it meant if we failed to find out mates, but I wasn't about to question the very thing that brought me this incredible woman.

A noise drew my attention to the left, and I watched as Hazel came into the room, a book and a small zipped bag in her hands. She smiled warmly at me before taking a seat on the rug in front of the fire, and began sketching. Another grin tugged at my lips, and my heart grew with how much love I felt.

My girls.

Not only had I claimed my mate, but I'd gained a daughter.

A daughter.

I introduced her as my daughter to Skye and her mother the other week, and I politely ignored the way she tried to pretend she hadn't teared up. She was my girl, mine, and I would protect her with my life no matter what. She wasn't Marlee, I knew that. No one would ever replace the little girl I'd lost, and I never wanted Hazel to even attempt to be anyone she wasn't. She was still my girl.

"She loves you too, you know."

I smiled and flicked my eyes to Trinity who watched me with a wealth of love in her eyes. Fuck, that look could sustain me where nothing else ever could. If all I ever got to remember at the end of my days was that look, I'd survive off of it alone.

"I know, I just don't want her to feel obligated."

Trinity's snort rang inside my head. *"I don't know if you've met our daughter, but there's not much of anything anyone can force her to do if she doesn't want to, obligated or not. She connected with you the first moment you met."*

I squeezed her feet in my hands in appreciation and she smiled. My fingers slid down to her ankles and traced along her calf, and her breath stuttered and lids grew heavy.

"Donovan... didn't I satisfy you only an hour or so ago?"

I grinned. She had, in the very best way. Waking up to the feel of her hot pussy sinking over my hard dick was definitely my favorite way to wake up. But I wanted her again.

"I'll never get enough of you, moya lyubov'," I whispered across her mind, letting my fingers trace her legs, pressing my hips up so she couldn't fail to feel how hard I was.

"Did you find that spell you were looking for from the books in our room?" I asked, cocking an eyebrow at her.

She swallowed, eyes flicking to Hazel and back. "No, not yet."

I grinned. "Want help?"

She hesitated a moment and I flashed an image in her head of me on my knees between her legs. Her swift intake of breath and suddenly pounding pulse told me I'd scored a hit.

A book snapped closed and we both turned to see Hazel standing. "You guys are gross. I'm going across the hall to see Mika and learn a new spell."

Trinity's face flushed and I laughed as Hazel marched away. "We love you!" I called after her.

"Yeah, yeah," she muttered, opening the door. "Love you too," she added quickly before slamming it behind her.

"She's too in-tune, even for a Witch. I am guarding our emotions and she *still* picks up on—" I didn't let Trinity finish her sentence and pounced on her. She shrieked and laughed as we rolled to the ground and I used my body to cushion hers.

"We can talk about that later. I need to be inside you right now," I ordered.

Trinity shifted over me, flipping her hair back over her head and smiling down at me.

"Is that an order, Demon King?"

"Yes," I answered, gripping her hips as I rocked up against her, dragging a moan from deep inside her. "It was."

Her smile melted something inside me and I leaned up to grip her hair at the back of her head and drag her mouth to mine. The taste of her exploded within my mouth. It didn't seem to matter how much we kissed, how often we fucked, every time with her was better than the last.

"Good things come to those who wait," she taunted against my mouth. I rolled us until I settled between her thighs and wished away our clothes until we were both naked.

"I've waited long enough; I need you now."

She moaned, quickly losing control of her restraint. "You have me."

"Finally," I agreed before leaning down to capture her mouth with mine once again, our bodies coming together in the very best way.

"Forever, moya lyubov'," I promised.

THANK YOU FOR READING

THE KINGS OF HELL
DONOVAN

DID YOU KNOW…

I HAVE TWO OTHER PEN NAMES?

I know that seems like overkill, but there is a method to my madness.

Books under the name **Alexis Maree** are for paranormal romances. Not everyone likes to read this genre, so I like to keep them separate.

Likewise, not everyone likes contemporary romances, so I have another pen name for those…**T. Maree.**

Then last, but certainly not least, are my sinfully sexy romances, the ones that border on the line of *"should she really put that down in print?"*
Some people don't like those kinds of spicy scenes, and so I decided to keep those separate from the rest under the name **Luna Maree.**

So, if you'd like to check out what else I've written, go onto my website.

Happy reading!

Alexis | Luna | T.

ALEXIS MAREE